Fiery Kisses

"Someday, Miss Brandon," Justin whispered, his breath falling warmly against her lips as he bent close, "you'll learn when to keep silent."

His mouth covered hers before she could utter a word, tell him how detestable he was, that a gentleman would not . . . The thought vanished from her mind when his tongue played upon her lips, then parted them to taste the sweetness of their kiss. Dara felt that all too damning sensation flood through her, making her head spin with a confusion of emotions. Some time ago she had begun to imagine what it would be like to have a man kiss her, hold her in his arms, touch her where he shouldn't, and she had to admit now that it was everything she'd dreamed it would be. Justin made her feel like a woman rather than the little girl her father always called her.

Surrendering to the pleasurable sensations he evoked, she relaxed, savoring the feel of him pressed against her. She longed to free her hands so she might drape her arms around his neck and pull him closer. She moaned softly when his mouth left hers to taste the silken skin beneath her ear and trail burning kisses down her throat. For all of her girlish imaginings, she could never have known how the real woman inside her would react to such forceful passion. . . .

MORE BESTSELLING ROMANCE BY JANELLE TAYLOR

SAVAGE CONQUEST (1533, $3.75)

Having heeded her passionate nature and stolen away to the rugged plains of South Dakota, the Virginia belle Miranda was captured there by a handsome, virile Indian. As her defenses melted with his burning kisses she didn't know what to fear more: her fate at the hands of the masterful brave, or her own traitorous heart!

FIRST LOVE, WILD LOVE (1431, $3.75)

Roused from slumber by the most wonderful sensations, Calinda's pleasure turned to horror when she discovered she was in a stranger's embrace. Handsome cattle baron Lynx Cardone had assumed she was in his room for his enjoyment, and before Calinda could help herself his sensuous kisses held her under the spell of desire!

GOLDEN TORMENT (1323, $3.75)

The instant Kathryn saw Landis Jurrell she didn't know what to fear more: the fierce, aggressive lumberjack or the torrid emotions he ignited in her. She had travelled to the Alaskan wilderness to search for her father, but after one night of sensual pleasure Landis vowed never to let her travel alone!

LOVE ME WITH FURY (1248, $3.75)

The moment Captain Steele saw golden-haired Alexandria swimming in the hidden pool he vowed to have her—but she was outraged he had intruded on her privacy. But against her will his tingling caresses and intoxicating kisses compelled her to give herself to the ruthless pirate, helplessly murmuring, "LOVE ME WITH FURY!"

TENDER ECSTASY (1212, $3.75)

Bright Arrow is committed to kill every white he sees—until he sets his eyes on ravishing Rebecca. And fate demands that he capture her, torment her . . . and soar with her to the dizzying heights of TENDER ECSTASY!

Dara's Desire

Kay McMahon

ZEBRA BOOKS
KENSINGTON PUBLISHING CORP.

ZEBRA BOOKS

are published by

Kensington Publishing Corp.
475 Park Avenue South
New York, NY 10016

First printing: August 1985

Printed in the United States of America

*For two very special people in my life,
Jennifer and Greg McMahon,
my children*

Chapter One

August, 1808
Cambridge, Maryland

Bright, vivid orange interlaced with gold burned against the western sky casting long shadows across the land and heralding the coming of night. A warm summer breeze rustled the tree tops, filling the air with the sweet fragrance of wild flowers. For most, this was a time of rest from the day's toils, but for Dara Brandon it merely signified postponement of the completion of her journey. Standing in the center of the road, she studied the square shafts of light coming through the windows of the only inn the town offered, her plain, light blue bonnet pulled from her head and resting against the back of her neck. Thick auburn hair framed her oval face and long black lashes accentuated her green eyes as she stared worriedly at the building. No boats would be launched this late in the evening so she would have to wait until morning to cross the Chesapeake Bay. She would have preferred going on to taking a room for the night, but she realized it was unlikely that anyone other than drunken sailors would be around the docks. She'd be safer inside. Pulling the drawstrings of her purse open, she withdrew a small bag and recounted her money once more. She longed for a hot bath and wanted to wash her hair, but sadly, she realized she could afford only a room and something to eat. Since she wasn't sure how long she would be away from home, it was best to use her money wisely and forego any luxuries. Squaring her shoulders, she yanked the cloth purse shut again and started for the front entrance of the inn.

Laughter floated out to greet Dara and she paused, hesitating to enter. She truly didn't like to go into a room full of strangers, especially since she might be the only woman present, but she decided she would be a little safer inside rather than on the road in the dark. Nervously, she smoothed the wrinkles from her skirt, took a deep breath, and lifted the latch. The noise from within grew in volume as she opened the door and stepped into the dimly lit room, but Dara relaxed a bit when no one seemed to pay her any heed. A group of men sat around a table near the cold fireplace, drinking ale from their mugs and sharing tales of their journey. In a far corner, a man and woman enjoyed their meal and indulged in a conversation, while next to them a man sat reading a newspaper and leisurely smoking his pipe. Dara remained still a moment, watching a gray haze slowly curl above his head. Forlornly, she remembered how her father had looked when he'd enjoyed the same pastime. Determinedly, she shook off that vision and glanced about for the innkeeper. Spotting a round figure of a man idly drying a glass behind the bar, she straightened, tugged at the bodice of her cotton gown and approached him.

"Excuse me, sir," she said, unaware of the strength her tone implied. "Would you be the keeper of this inn?"

Round blue eyes set in a lined, pudgy face looked back at her. "Yes'm. Thomas Bryant is my name. What can I do for you?"

"I need a room and a meal," she replied more softly.

"Then you're in the right place." He smiled, radiating a friendly warmth. "I got plenty of rooms and my wife just made a fine rabbit stew." Wiping his hands on the white towel wrapped around his thick belly, he glanced at the front door. "Traveling alone?"

Dara nodded.

"Then I'll have my boy see to your carriage," he said, calling out the child's name.

"Oh . . . no . . . I . . ." She frowned, her gaze falling to the purse she held. "I'm traveling on foot."

Thomas' brow wrinkled briefly before he waved off the young man who had responded to his summons, then he settled his gaze on the young woman standing before him. It had been a long while since he had seen anyone so beautiful. Magnificently thick coppery curls fell about her face, and innocence was reflected in her green eyes. He reflected that she should be riding in an expensive landau, the pampered belle of some great plantation. But from her attire, a simple blue cotton gown, and the fact that she had no shawl about her shoulders, he knew that wasn't likely. His cheeks reddened a bit when he realized he was staring, and abruptly he cleared his throat.

"Then you must be tired," he said sympathetically. "Would you like to eat first or rest awhile?"

Dara managed a weak smile. "I'd prefer to eat. I want to go to bed as soon as possible so I can get an early start. I still have a long way to go."

"All right," he said, rounding the end of the bar to take her elbow and guide her to a table set away from the other guests. "Make yourself comfortable and I'll bring the stew. Would you care for some tea or a cool glass of milk?"

"Tea will be fine," Dara answered, untying the strings of her bonnet as she sat down.

"Then tea it is." He nodded, made a slight bow, and moved away to fulfill her needs.

Dara hadn't realized how tired she was or how much her feet hurt until she leaned back in the chair. She longed to remove her shoes but knew she mustn't. That would have to wait until she was alone in her room. Then she could shed all of her clothes. It would be wonderful to lie down on a feather mattress instead of the straw bed she was used to sleeping on at home.

Home. It seemed as if she had been gone for a hundred years instead of only one day. She stretched, rubbing the muscles in her neck and shoulders, and recalling how frightened she had been when she'd started out. Indeed, she was frightened now at not knowing if her effort would reward her with anything more than an empty purse and worn shoes. But she had to try. It might mean saving her father. He would die if she didn't bring Lane home to him. An angry frown crimped her brow. Why must two people who love each other be so stubborn? Why couldn't her father have understood Lane's need to join the Navy and fight the British? Hadn't Taylor Brandon always told his children to be loyal to the United States, to love and protect their country? That was all her brother had wanted to do, but now he was a prisoner of the British, forced to sail on an enemy ship.

Loud laughter from the group of men near the hearth intruded upon Dara's musings and she covertly peered over at them, her curiosity aroused when it appeared they were teasing the youngest among them.

"Go ahead, make fun," he pouted, "but if I ever came across Justin Whitelaw, I'd arrest him."

"Sure, Nathan. That is if ya could get him to surrender," another laughed.

"And I suppose you wouldn't?"

"I don't plan on ever getting that close! A traitor to

his country is probably mean enough to shoot his own mother. He's not gonna think twice about putting a ball in you just for bothering him."

"What I don't understand"—a third broke in—"is why a captain for the U.S. Navy would suddenly switch sides. He was the best officer we had."

"Money, Andrew," another answered. "Tempt a man with enough money and he'll do just about anything. Too bad he got caught, because the way I see it, he tried to help out some of the big landowners. Jefferson's Embargo Act is ruining us. We can't trade with anyone and the British ships aren't allowed in port."

"I agree, Ben," Andrew answered, "but he's not helping anyone anymore except himself. He's a pirate now. He steals from any ship he comes across, then sells the goods in the West Indies to France. And from the way I hear it, he sails under an American flag and comes right up the bay. Why it isn't safe anywhere."

"That's what I mean," Nathan interrupted. "It's bad enough not being able to export without having the goods stolen from us. My father's plantation is in trouble. Whitelaw's men have hit us three times."

Andrew leaned over and jabbed Ben in the ribs. "I think he's more worried about his father not giving him any spending money than the possibility of losing the plantation."

"I am not!" Nathan howled.

The group burst into laughter while the young man fumed, and Dara turned away when Thomas Bryant approached carrying a tray laden with the stew and tea she had ordered. After setting the dishes on the table, he tucked the tray under one arm and smiled down at her.

"If you don't mind my asking, where you headed?"

Dara unfolded her napkin and laid it across her lap,

the smells of cooked rabbit and potatoes making her mouth water. She hadn't eaten since breakfast and she hoped Mr. Bryant would understand if she ate while they talked. "No. I don't mind. I'm going to the capital," she answered, bringing an appreciative whistle from the man.

"That's a long walk. How far have you come?"

"My parents and I live in Drawbridge," she replied, reaching for a spoon.

"Sure must be important to make you travel that far. It's near sixty miles."

"Closer to seventy, and yes, it's very important." She nodded, leaning forward. The delicious aromas coming from the bowl tempted her to taste its contents.

"Look, miss," Thomas Bryant said suddenly, pulling out a chair next to her and sitting down, "I'm not being nosy when I ask all these questions. I'm . . . well, I'm concerned. I have a daughter about your age and I wouldn't want her traveling alone that far, much less on foot."

Dara's face reflected her surprise at the man's concern. Oddly enough, she forgot her hunger and leaned back in her chair to look at him. "But Mr. Bryant, you don't even know me. You'll probably never see me again. Why should you care?"

Bryant smiled lopsidedly and studied the hem of his apron. "Well, whether you know it or not, you're a very lovely-looking young woman. There's word of this Whitelaw fellow being in the area and there's no telling what he might do if he found you traveling alone. I'd never forgive myself if something happened to you because I didn't try to help avoid it."

Dara smiled and touched a slim hand to the one he had rested on the table. "Thank you, Mr. Bryant. That's probably the nicest thing anyone's ever tried to do for me, but I don't know what can be done to resolve my problem. I have very little money and can't afford to hire a rig once I've crossed the bay."

"Oh, but I have an idea," he said enthusiastically. "See that gentleman over there?"

Dara looked in the direction where Bryant pointed and saw the man who had been reading a newspaper when she'd first arrived. "What about him?"

"He told me he's going to Washington just as soon as his boat is ready to sail in the morning."

"And?" she frowned, puzzled.

"Well, I don't see why he wouldn't take you under his protection. He's traveling alone, too."

Dara pulled back, embarrassed. "Oh . . . I don't . . ."

"He seems nice enough. Says his name is Colonel Winslow or something."

"You mean you don't even know him?" she gasped.

Bryant's face flushed and he bowed his head a moment before he glanced up sheepishly. "No, not really. But he told me he's on his way to visit his granddaughter. I've always considered myself a pretty good judge of character so—"

"Thank you, but no," Dara said firmly. "I knew the risks I'd be taking when I started out, and I feel asking a stranger for a ride would be stretching my luck. You're a very kind gentleman to worry about someone whose name you don't even know, but I must insist that I take care of myself."

"Are you sure?" he frowned, apprehensive.

Dara smiled warmly. "Yes. And if you'll extend your kindness one step further and allow me to eat while the food is still hot, I'd be very grateful."

He studied her a moment, then sighed. "All right," he said, rising, "but if you should change your mind—"

"I won't," she said, her green eyes sparkling.

She waited until he had turned to walk away before

13

she grinned and shook her head. People like him were rare, she decided and fleetingly she wished she lived closer to Cambridge. She would have enjoyed getting to know him better.

The warmth and the aroma emanating from her meal again drew her attention and she picked up the spoon, once more intending to sate her hunger. When Lane had lived at home, they'd always had rabbit stew. But a year had passed since he'd left and they had been relying on the fish her father caught for food. The old man's health was failing. His gnarled hands made it difficult to fire a musket, and his eyesight was so poor that he seldom hit his target. Dara had tried repeatedly to master the art of firing a gun, but every time the powder exploded, she shut her eyes and her quarry ran away unharmed. Frustrated, she had set traps but seldom had caught anything. Taking a bite of stew, she wished she had been more persistent in insisting her brother teach her to use a gun, but he had always laughed and said as long as he was around, there was no need for her to learn. How could any of them have known things would turn out as they had?

Before she realized it, Dara had eaten the last tasty mouthful and settled back in her chair to drink her tea, her eyelids heavy. She stretched the tired muscles in her neck and concentrated on finding Mr. Bryant. The sun had barely gone down but she was exhausted enough to fall asleep. She would pay for her meal and room and quickly seek the privacy of her chambers. But the innkeeper was not in sight so she casually watched the other guests in the common room, her pulse quickening nervously when she discovered Colonel Winslow's eyes upon her. Perhaps Thomas Bryant thought him sincere, but for some odd reason Dara got the feeling she shouldn't trust him. She couldn't say why. She just didn't like the way he looked

14

at her. Lane had warned her that men often tried to take advantage of young women . . . especially older men. And Colonel Winslow was certainly old. She judged him to be in his fifties because of his white hair, sideburns, and mustache. He had a gentleness about him, but at the same time he radiated a sense of power. He wasn't the sweet, old grandfatherly type he appeared to be. Dara felt her cheeks redden when she realized she was staring at Winslow. Quickly, she looked down at her lap, busily refolding her napkin and praying Thomas Bryant would return soon.

I've got to get a hold of myself, she scolded silently. I haven't even reached Washington yet, and the dangers for a woman traveling alone will increase as I get closer. How will I manage if I let myself become upset when an old man simply looks at me? Leaning forward, she cradled her head in her hands, her elbows resting on the tabletop. Oh Lane, I wish I knew how to find you. Papa needs you. I need you. Suddenly, even with her eyes closed, Dara could sense someone standing next to her at the table, and she jerked her head up to see who it was. Her heart pounded loudly in her ears when she discovered Colonel Winslow had left his chair, intent on speaking with her.

"Please excuse me." His deep voice was soothing. "I didn't mean to startle you."

Dara straightened in her chair, nervously wondering what she should do. "That's all right. I . . . I was just thinking of something else and didn't hear you approach."

"My name is Colonel Winslow. May I have the honor of knowing yours?" He smiled.

"Dara. Dara Brandon," she said weakly. Now that he stood so near she noticed that his clothes were exquisitely made and fit his slightly rounded physique perfectly. In his younger days, she decided, he must

15

have been very handsome.

"I don't mean to intrude, my dear, but Mister Bryant thought I might be able to assist you in your dilemma," he continued, touching the back of the empty chair opposite her. "May I join you?"

"I really see no need, sir," Dara quickly answered, grabbing her purse and bonnet from the table and rising. "I don't mean to be rude, Colonel Winslow. It's kind of both you and Mister Bryant to care enough to offer, but I must decline. You'll understand, I hope." As she forced a weak smile, she spotted Thomas Bryant coming from another room and started hurriedly toward him as she called out his name.

"I'd like to go to my room now, if you don't mind," she said, peering back at Colonel Winslow to find he had remained where he was. Her heart beat erratically when she noticed his gaze seductively traveling the length of her tiny frame as if he wished to undress her. She gulped and looked away quickly.

"Of course." Thomas Bryant nodded, setting aside a tray stacked with clean mugs. "This way." He extended a hand and led her up the flight of stairs. When they reached the top, he paused outside the first door in a long row. "I hope you'll be comfortable here," he said, swinging the portal open and going inside. He crossed to the window of the room and opened it to let in the cool evening breeze.

Dara studied the interior a moment, thinking how elegant this simple room was compared to her own at home. Her father had always wanted to own a plantation but had never managed to possess anything more than a small farm with one cow, a few chickens, and a field of tobacco, which he sold to feed his family. The house consisted of three rooms, her parents' bedroom and the kitchen on the lower level, and the small room in the loft that she had shared with her

16

brother. A curtain divided the area, providing some privacy, but two straw mattress beds were the only furniture. This room had a feather bed, a dressing table and mirror, and a nightstand. In addition, a high-back chair sat before the stone fireplace. Suddenly Dara frowned, wondering if she could afford the price of such a room.

"How much?" she asked quietly.

"What?" Thomas questioned, turning back to face her.

"How much do I owe you?"

"Oh . . . ah . . ." Thomas stammered, readjusting his apron, "half a dollar will be enough."

Dara surveyed the room again. "For this and the meal?"

"Yes'm." He nodded, and when Dara opened her mouth to question him, he raised a hand to stop her. "This one isn't as nice as the rest so I can't charge the same. And the meal wasn't anything special."

Somehow Dara got the feeling he wasn't telling the truth, but she also sensed it would be useless to argue. She smiled, shook her head, and withdrew the required coins from her purse. "Thank you, Mr. Bryant," she said, handing them to him, "for everything."

"No need to thank me. You're paying for what you get." He moved past her and went to the door, calling back over his shoulder as he caught the latch and started to shut it behind him, "Breakfast is at seven. That's included with the room."

Awestruck, Dara stared at the closed door, then chuckled out loud. "You'll never make any money if you don't stop giving everything away." She laughed, knowing he couldn't hear her. She lingered a moment, wishing everyone in the world were as generous as he; then, with a sigh, she laid her purse and bonnet on the dressing table. If so, there would be no wars and no

17

need for her to be going to Washington. She unfastened the buttons of her gown and stepped from it, carefully laying the garment over the chair. Then, clothed only in her camisole and petticoats, she crossed to the window. Sitting down on the sill, she leaned back to rest her head against the frame and watch the last remaining embers of sunset fade in the distance. The chirping of crickets filled the air, as did the sweet smell of freshly mown hay. Dara longed to be at home. And she would be—just as soon as she found Lane, they would return to their farm outside Drawbridge.

Dreamily, her gaze drifted to the grounds beneath her window. About twenty feet from the inn stood a stable and between the two buildings she could barely discern a garden, a flower bed, a clothesline, and a well. A huge willow tree grew near the inn so she didn't see the man until a flash of white caught her eye. Interested, she leaned out a bit to get a better view just as the figure beneath the tree stepped into the open. Masked as he was by the shadows and the approaching darkness, she couldn't distinguish his identity until flint and steel sparked a flame when the man lit his pipe. Colonel Winslow. He hadn't bothered to leave the commons to smoke his pipe before, so why had he now? Dara shrugged off the question, deciding he probably wanted to enjoy the fresh air. She had started to withdraw into the room when she spotted a second figure moving from the protection of the low-hanging willow branches. Her curiosity mounted when she couldn't recognize him as one of the others from the dining hall. Turning an ear toward them, she strained to hear their conversation. The soft breeze carried their voices up to her, and although she could not distinguish every word, what she heard sent an icy chill coursing through her.

"But he must be eliminated," Colonel Winslow

18

growled. "With Jefferson out of the way, Congress is sure to repeal the Embargo Act. He leads them around like sheep."

"I don't disagree, but Senator Bragg—"

"Senator Bragg is a gutless milksop! He doesn't stand to lose everything."

The other man shifted uncomfortably. "But who can we get to do the job? There are plenty of men who feel as we do, still none of them would have the courage."

"What about this Whitelaw character I've been hearing about? I was told he hates the United States for what they did to him. If he hadn't escaped from prison, they would have hanged him."

"Yes, that's true," his companion replied. "But I rather doubt he'd be interested."

"Why?" the colonel demanded.

"Because this policy plays right into his hands. He's a pirate. He attacks the ships smuggling goods to Canada and they can't do a thing about it. If free trade were established, it would make it that much more difficult for him."

Colonel Winslow grunted irritably. "Well, I think differently. I propose he'd be more than interested."

"Why?"

"Henry, if you had been framed as he claims to have been and no one had lifted a finger to prove your innocence, wouldn't you enjoy getting even by killing the most important man in the United States?"

Henry shrugged. "Maybe. But if he's truly innocent of the crime that put him in that situation, he might still be trying to prove it. Murdering the President of the United States would ruin any chance he might have to clear himself."

"But we won't know until we ask him, will we?" Colonel Winslow sneered. As he bent to tap the ashes from his pipe, he heard the dull thud of a window closing and looked up in time to see the only light on the second story of the inn go out. He straightened immediately.

"Do you think they heard us?" Henry asked nervously.

"I don't know," Winslow hissed, his expression murderous. "But we can't take the chance. Wait for me at the docks as we planned, and I'll find out from Bryant who occupies that room."

"Then what?"

The colonel gave him an evil smile. "I dispose of the poor fool," he said quite matter-of-factly. Then he headed for the inn.

Kneeling on the floor near her window, Dara watched Colonel Winslow through a slit in the curtains until he disappeared from view. She had realized her mistake in closing the window as soon as she'd heard the noise it had created, and extinguished the candle before peeking outside again. Both men were looking up toward her room and from the hasty way in which they parted company, she knew nothing good was in the offing. Sliding to the floor, she leaned her back against the wall, thinking. These men were planning to murder the President of the United States! Dara felt as if every ounce of strength had been drained from her. Who should she tell? Would anyone believe her? She wondered who Colonel Winslow was and whether he was on his way to Washington to visit his grand-daughter or to execute some monstrous plot only she could foil? Suddenly Dara realized the danger she was in. A man who was cold-blooded enough to casually discuss killing another human being would not hesitate to do away with anyone who stood in his way. Even if he had not actually seen who'd been watching them, all he would have to do was ask Thomas Bryant who had rented this room!

20

Frantic, Dara scrambled to her feet and quickly found her clothes. She just couldn't take the chance that Colonel Winslow would forget about her, would figure that a woman so poor she couldn't even afford to hire a rig would do him no harm. She had to leave. She had to get out of Cambridge, sail across the bay, and get to Washington as fast as she could. She might not be able to talk to the president himself but surely she could find someone of importance who would listen.

Fastening the last button of her gown, she grabbed her purse and bonnet from the dressing table, then paused a moment when her eyes caught sight of the feather bed.

"Perhaps another time," she muttered forlornly.

Suddenly, the flesh on the back of Dara's neck tingled when she heard footsteps in the hall outside her room. Dear God, he was already here! Now what was she to do? Glancing around the room for some sort of answer, she smiled briefly when she spotted the water pitcher sitting on the nightstand. Rushing over to it, she seized it by the handle and hurried to hide behind the door. If he managed to get in, she would club him with it and run for her life. Dara cringed inwardly when she realized how true that statement was. Until Colonel Emerson Winslow was caught and imprisoned, she would have to continue to run, for she doubted he would ever give up looking for her.

The doorlatch rattled. Dara's heart pounded in her chest. She shifted her weapon to her left hand and braced herself. The only way he could get in was to use a key, and Mister Bryant hadn't seemed to be the sort who would give any man the opportunity to enter a lady's room uninvited. Then again, Mister Bryant had said he trusted Colonel Winslow, that his instincts told him the colonel was a nice man. Dara could feel a fine veil of perspiration from across her brow and upper lip.

Maybe she should move something in front of the door. Glancing wildly about the room for just such an item, her breath caught in her throat when her gaze fell upon the dressing table. There, as if singled out by the last dying ray of sunset, lay the key to her room. Dear God, the door wasn't even locked! Unshed tears burned her eyes at that discovery, and she knew at that moment the only thing between her and certain death was the water pitcher she clutched so tightly. Drawing in a ragged breath of courage, she straightened and raised it high above her head just as the door slowly creaked open and a yellow glow from the hallway flooded into the room.

Fearfully, Dara watched the shadow centered in the shaft of light advance a step, and her breathing suddenly became quite painful. She wanted to scream. She felt like bursting into tears but she couldn't, not if she wanted to succeed. Only a few steps more. Please, she begged silently, move out of the way of the door. Then, almost as if he had heard her, the figure cleared the wooden barrier separating them, and Dara squeezed her eyes shut as she brought the pitcher down upon Colonel Winslow's head. The finely crafted piece of porcelain shattered into a hundred fragments, and he collapsed to the floor before her, unconscious.

Dara's hands flew to her mouth as she stared, wide-eyed, at the unmoving form. Had she killed him? She hadn't meant to. Her knees shaking, she slowly lowered herself to get a better view. Once she saw the steady rise and fall of his chest, she let out a long sigh. Now all she had to do was find someone who would take her across the bay before the colonel woke up and came after her.

Darkness closed in around Dara as she headed for the pier, but the tall masts of a frigate anchored several hundred yards offshore were silhouetted against the gray black face of night. She swallowed the lump in her throat, knowing the sailors manning the ship were probably getting a bellyful of ale in one of the nearby taverns. Her only comfort came from assuming a few more hours would pass before any seamen would be stumbling about the docks. Hopefully, by then she would have found a gig and someone to take her to the opposite shore.

Dara's pulse quickened, as she passed a long row of darkened storefronts, her footsteps on the wooden sidewalk echoing in the still night air. Rowdy voices from somewhere up ahead indicated the location of one of the town's less savory establishments, and Dara decided to cross the street to avoid passing in front of it. She truly had no idea where she was going, but she hoped to find a fisherman who had slept on his craft and who would be willing to make one last trip across the bay.

Stepping from the sidewalk, she started across the street, glancing back over her shoulder for what seemed the hundredth time to make certain Colonel Winslow wasn't following her. In doing so, she failed to watch where she walked, the toe of her slipper caught the edge of a rut, and she stumbled. Fighting to keep her balance, she trod upon the hem of her skirt, which yanked her sideways, and she promptly fell to her knees, her purse and bonnet flying from her grasp. To avoid further injury, she spread her hands out in front of her to break her fall, a painful moan escaping her when tiny rocks gouged her palms. Tears blurring her eyes, she plopped down to examine the wounds, squinting in the darkness. No real harm had been done. She wondered how such a simple journey could have turned out so badly. It had been her intent to go to Washington and seek aid in freeing her brother. Now she was a witness to an assassination plot, and the man behind it was trying to kill her. Could anything else go wrong?

That question had barely crossed her mind when light spilled onto the street a few dozen feet ahead of her. A trio of men emerged from one of the buildings, the sound of laughter and the odor of rum accompanying them. Dara froze, positive that if she moved they would see her. She hoped they would turn and go the other way.

"I'll tell ya what I need," one of them bellowed. "I need me a wench to warm my bed. I've got an ache in my loins that's near killin' me."

"Yeah, me too," a second agreed. "But where we gonna find one around here? This town locks up its stores and its women when the sun goes down. Look around ya. Do ya see any wenches standin' in line?"

Dara thought her heart would stop when all three glanced left then right, their gazes settling on her almost immediately.

"No, but I see one sittin' there waitin' for us." The first sailor grinned toothlessly and moved toward her. "Since I saw her first, I get to have her first. You two can fight over who's next."

"Oh, no ya don't," the third argued. "We all saw her at the same time." Intending to stress the point, he rushed after his companion, caught the crook of his arm, and spun him around. "I say we choose sticks. Short one wins."

"And I say we don't," the first growled, landing a huge fist on the man's jaw and sending him reeling.

Dara watched fearfully, unable to move, as the man shook off the stunning blow, squared his shoulders, and came at his attacker again. Silhouetted against the yellow light coming from the open doorway of the tavern, they struck out brutally against each other,

24

twisting and turning, landing blows to the stomach, face, and head. The scene enacted before her hypnotized Dara, for she had never seen anything like it in her life. How could two men, possibly even friends, purposely cause each other harm?

"What's the matter, sweet thing? Ya enjoy watchin' men fight over ya?"

The sound of the stranger's voice, so near, startled Dara back to reality. In all the excitement, she had failed to watch the third member of the group, and because of her neglect, he stood only inches from her, spoiling any chance she had to get away.

"I . . . I'm not what you think I am," she said weakly, scooting backward out of reach. "I'm on my way to Washing—"

"You won't be going anywhere, honey, not until we've . . . ah . . . gotten friendly."

Dara's fingers dug into the soft earth beneath them as she tried to pull herself farther away from the man. But each time she moved, he followed her, the evil smile on his face widening as if he enjoyed their game. He didn't have to tell her what he meant about getting friendly. She had heard enough of the sailors' conversation to know. If she was to come out of this untouched, she would have to do something and soon! Her mind desperately sought a solution as she continued inching away. She was sure words or threats would do no good. What would help her? What? Then it hit her. She remembered the story Lane had told her about meeting a bear in the woods. Her brother had gone fishing and was on his way home. It had always been his habit to carry a gun, but on this particular day he hadn't. Unarmed, Lane had thought his life was over. He'd dropped his pole and string of fish, and had slowly backed away from the grizzly, his gaze fixed on the sharp white teeth gleaming in the sunlight. He, too, had stumbled and fallen, only when he'd scrambled to his feet, he'd brought a fistful of dirt with him and had thrown it in the bear's face. Blinded and in pain, the huge animal had roared his anger, wildly clawing at his eyes and Lane had wasted no time in racing for home. It had worked for her brother. Maybe it would work for her. Sinking her fingers into the soil, she scooped up a handful and without hesitation tossed it in the man's face.

Caught off-guard, he inhaled as much as he got in his eyes and came up coughing and gasping for air. But Dara paid him little notice, for she had already leaped to her feet. Spinning around, she ran, using every ounce of strength she could summon.

"Hey! She's gettin' away," one of the men yelled.

But Dara wasn't listening. Skirts held high, she raced for the alleyway and disappeared into the darkness before any of them could catch her. She wasn't sure whether she heard their footsteps or not. Perhaps it was the frantic beating of her heart. No matter. She certainly wasn't going to stop and look around to satisfy her curiosity. Nearly out of breath, she rounded a corner and headed for the next. She had to find a place to hide; she couldn't very well go back to Mr. Bryant's. Her chest hurt and her legs grew weak, but she kept on, finally chancing a look back over her shoulder to find an empty street. A vague smile parted her lips when she realized she had won, and she looked ahead to scrutinize the buildings for a suitable refuge. All of a sudden, a dark figure stepped out of a doorway and they collided head-on, both crashing to the ground.

Dara felt as if she had broken every bone in her body, but she gave that scant attention once she realized she had escaped one bad situation for another. Even in the darkness she could see this was not a gentleman but a somewhat seedy-looking sailor who apparently hadn't bathed or scraped the stubble from his face in weeks. When he pushed himself up on his elbows to look at her, she saw the black patch over his left eye and the dingy, red bandana covering his hair. A knot formed in her throat.

"Well, lass." He grinned. "Don't ya think ya could have found a better way ta be meetin' me?"

"I . . . I'm sorry," she mumbled, awkwardly rising. Brushing the dirt from her skirts, she glanced back down the alleyway, a whimper escaping her lips when she spotted three shadowy figures at the opposite end.

"Somethin' wrong, lass?" the sailor asked in his thick Irish brogue as he came to his feet.

Without looking at him, Dara moved behind him, her gaze fastened on the men who were slowly advancing. But when she started to run again, he caught her wrist and pulled her, struggling, to his hard, wide chest.

"Please," she begged, panic raising the pitch of her voice.

"Do they mean ta do ya harm, lass?" he inquired, his firm words sparking a glimmer of hope in Dara.

"Yes!" she answered quickly.

"Well, now"—he smiled—"we can't be havin' them do that, can we now?" Turning to face the group, he placed her behind him, his hand carefully moving to the butt of the pistol stuck in his waistband. "Might there be somethin' I can do for ya, lads?" he called, his tone almost cheerful, yet Dara sensed an underlying strength.

"Yeah," one of them spat out. "We want the wench."

"This one?" His left thumb pointed over his shoulder at her.

"Yeah. That one. Are ya gonna give her to us or do we have to take her from ya?"

"Sorry," he said with a shake of his head. "I can't be doin' that. I've been lookin' all night for her. She be me little sister and I came ta take her home."

The one who spoke laughed sarcastically. "Yeah, and she's my mother too."

The Irishman straightened as if offended. "And would ya be callin' me a liar?" he challenged.

"Well now, ain't you the smart one?" the other chuckled, his laughter dying instantly when he reached for the knife in his belt.

With lightning speed, he seized the weapon, and hurled it through the air. But before it found its target, the Irishman pulled Dara with him out of the way just as gunpowder exploded. The lead ball hit the man squarely between the eyes. As his lifeless body crumpled to the ground, his companions wasted no time in fleeing the scene.

Wide-eyed, Dara stared at the unmoving form sprawled in the dirt, a wave of nausea washing over her. Her knees were suddenly weak. Unknowingly, she grabbed the sleeve of the Irishman's shirt to steady herself, unaware that the pale blueness of his gaze studied her.

"Are ya all right, lass?" he questioned softly.

Dara managed to shake her head. "I . . . I didn't mean for anyone to get . . . killed."

"They be knowin' the risks when they challenged me," he said flatly as he pulled a small pouch of gunpowder from his belt to reload the pistol. "And they wouldn't have cared if they had killed you with their abuse. The way I be seein' it, they got what they asked for. I be doubtin' anyone will be missin' this one," he added, pointing the muzzle of his weapon at the still body.

"What . . . what are you going to do with him?"

"Do with him?" he repeated.

28

"Yes. You're going to inform the authorities, aren't you?"

His heartfelt laughter rang in Dara's ears, and she looked up at him, a mixture of surprise and anger glowing in her green eyes.

"Did I say something funny?" she asked, annoyed.

"No, lass." He grinned, tucking the pistol in his belt again. "I was just thinkin' how much the constable would enjoy seein' me inside his jail . . . especially if I be comin' there of me own free will. Ya see, lass, he and I don't get along too well."

Dara's face paled, but in the shadows it went unnoticed. "You mean you're wanted for something?"

"A number of things," he admitted with a smile; then he turned to study the deserted alleyway. "I don't think they'll be botherin' ya anymore. But if ya like, I can be walkin' a ways with ya."

Dara knew she should be afraid of the stranger and in the bright rays of sunlight, she probably would have been. But he had saved her life willingly, and right now she felt safer with him than traveling the streets alone . . . even if he was guilty of some crime. From the look of him, she guessed he was a pirate by trade, a man who stole for a living, but at least he wouldn't force himself on an innocent woman as the other three would have done. Besides, he must have a ship, and a ship would be a way for her to cross the bay. She took a deep breath and nodded.

"Yes, I'd like that."

"And where might ya be headed?" he smiled, his nature relaxed and totally at ease.

"The pier," she replied, starting off.

"What?" he rallied, stopping Dara in her tracks. "'Tisn't a place for a lady."

"I'm well aware of that, sir, but it's most urgent I cross the bay tonight," she said firmly. Then, studying

29

her hands, she spoke, almost in a whisper, "You see, those men weren't the only ones after me."

"Oh," he answered, quirking an eyebrow. "An angry husband, perhaps?"

"No, it isn't anything like that." Dara frowned, wondering just how much she dare tell him. "I . . . I overheard something I shouldn't have."

"Snooping, huh?"

"No!" she snapped. "Look, I'm grateful to you for saving me from those . . . those men, but I really don't think I need to explain anything."

"And I don't believe I was askin' ya to." He corrected her playfully. "Just be tellin' me where ya want ta go and we'll be off. The sooner the better. I've got to be gettin' back to me ship." He took a step forward, then stopped abruptly. "And don't go askin' me if I'll take ya on board."

Since the idea had already crossed her mind, now that he'd brought it up, she wasted no time in pressing the issue. "Why not?" she asked excitedly. "It's only about ten miles across."

"Because it isn't me ship exactly. I'm just one of the crew and the cap'n don't like women on board." He squinted his good eye at her. "Says it brings bad luck and I'm inclined ta agree."

"But I wouldn't be any trouble," she swore, dashing after him when he turned and walked away. "I wouldn't be on board long enough. Oh, please? I'll pay you."

"Like I be sayin' before, it isn't me ship or me place ta decide." He glanced back to give her a stern look, his brow crimping when he discovered that she had not only not heard him but had turned around and was walking back down the alleyway. "Where ya goin', lass?"

"I lost my purse back there," she called over her shoulder. "I'm going after it."

"Whoa, there," he warned, rushing to grab her arm and swing her around. "That's the last place ya be needin' ta go. If those two men find ya alone again, they'll finish what they started."

"Let go," Dara snapped, pulling at the strong hand that held her. "All my money is in that purse. I can't go to Washington without it."

"Washington? A little thing like you is goin' all the way to Washington? 'Tis at least thirty miles. Are ya meetin' someone on the other side ta travel with?"

"No, I'm not," Dara barked, still struggling. "Will you let go of me?"

"Then ya be hirin' a rig?"

"Not if I don't have any money, I won't! And what difference is it to you?"

"Ya seem ta forget. I killed a man for ya."

Reminded of the horrifying scene she had witnessed only moments before, she paused in her quest. "And I already told you how grateful I am. But if I don't get to Washington, I may never see my brother again." With that, she brought her foot back and planted her instep squarely on his shin, winning her freedom immediately. "Thank you, Mr.—whatever your name is— but I won't be needing your help any longer," she said stubbornly. For a moment she watched the Irishman hop about on one foot, his injured extremity held in both hands; then her nose lifted haughtily in the air, she squared her shoulders and started off again.

"I'll not be knowin' why, but I think I must warn ya, lass," the stranger called after her. "Once those men have finished with ya, they'll be takin' ya to the authorities and claimin' you're the one who killed their friend. How will ya be findin' your brother if you're sittin' in jail waitin' ta be hanged?" His words brought her to an abrupt halt, and he stood rubbing his leg, waiting for her to turn around.

"Then come with me," she said weakly, not bothering to look at him. His laughter cut through her like an icy winter wind.

"And risk me own life? Not ta mention how ya show your gratitude. Sorry, lass, but your brother isn't worth that much ta me." He straightened, turned, and started down the darkened alley. By the time Dara spun around to plead once more, he had disappeared into the black curtain of night.

Tears boiled up in her. She felt as if she hadn't a friend in the world. She wanted to find her purse. She wanted to go home. Chin quivering, she looked around her, the ebony backdrop of her surroundings closing in on her. She was scared. And, oddly enough, she wanted to find the Irishman again. She didn't even know his name, but she felt safe with him. He was probably right. If the men did find her alone, they would abuse her and then take her to the authorities afterward. Worse yet, they might just kill her for being the cause of their friend's death. Suddenly her purse didn't seem so important and she forced her feet to move in the direction taken by her misguided guardian.

Once she had reached the corner and turned down the next street, she could vaguely make out his shape walking along the pier. He was headed for a longboat tied to the dock with a mooring line. She started to call out to him, but hesitated when he raised a hand as if to summon someone. She paused, stepping behind a stack of boxes so as not to be seen, and watched three men hurriedly join him. Her curiosity aroused, she decided to get a little closer and quietly tiptoed to the end of the alley. Crouching behind the rain barrel there, she peeked out to study the men and to listen to what they had to say, but to her dismay, their words were muffled. She was about to admit defeat and abandon her hiding place, intending to wave at the men to get their attention, when she observed the Irishman reach up and remove his eye patch. Dara's chin sagged. If he had two good eyes, why would he wear such a thing? she wondered; then her mouth snapped shut when the answer came to mind. A disguise! But why would he need one? Had his crimes been so great that this was the only way he could move about freely? And if that was the case, why chance coming here?

Twisting around, she sat down and leaned back against the barrel to consider the puzzle. Of course if he was only a member of the crew, he couldn't very well tell the captain where to dock, but if she were in his place, she would stay on board the ship until it docked in a friendlier port. She shook her head. It was much too confusing. Besides, she had more important things to think about. She must find a fisherman who would take her to the other shore. With a disgusted sigh, she started to push herself up when she suddenly realized the men's voices sounded closer than they had before. Not daring to move lest they discover her, she sat perfectly still, taking in their conversation.

"So where is he?" one of them asked. "I told all of you to meet me at the boat in one hour."

"Don't know, Cap'n. Callahan took off on his own right after you left," a second man answered. "Did you find your contact?"

The captain chuckled. "That wasn't all I found."

"Sir?"

A moment of silence passed while Dara listened to the crunching of pebbles beneath the men's boots as they walked nearer. Knowing they were only a few feet from her, she squeezed her eyes shut, wishing the gesture would make her disappear. Maybe the Irishman was the sort who rescued women in distress, but could the same be said about his captain? What would he do if he found her eavesdropping? Dara's heart

33

throbbed. She didn't have to look at them to know they had moved into the alleyway. She would now be in clear view. All they had to do was turn around. Worriedly, she opened one eye to peer up at them.

"I had the pleasure of bumping into the most beautiful woman I've ever seen," the captain smiled, pausing to reach up and pull the red bandana from his head.

Dara's mouth fell open.

"Aye, Cap'n." One of his companion's laughed. "Leave it to you to find the only one in this entire town. So where is she now?"

The captain shrugged. "I'm not sure, but I imagine she's walking the pier looking for someone to take her across the bay."

"Walking the pier? At this time of night? Is she alone?"

"Yes, to all three of your questions."

"Well, who was she?"

Long, sun-tanned fingers rubbed the stubble of his beard. "I didn't ask her name, but she said she was looking for her brother. She's on her way to Washington."

"And you just let her go?" another asked. "Why, Captain Whitelaw, I think you're slipping."

The muscles across Dara's chest constricted instantly. Whitelaw? The pirate she had heard the men in the inn talking about . . . the one who had escaped from prison . . . a man wanted for treason? And the man Colonel Winslow intended to hire to murder the President of the United States! Suddenly, Dara knew it was vital to get away, but all she could do was pray the men would continue on without looking back. If they discovered her presence, they would know in an instant that she had overheard everything. How could this be happening to her? A seemingly harmless journey to

Washington to seek help for her brother had turned out to be the most dangerous adventure of her young life. Dara swallowed hard, every muscle in her tiny frame trembling. If they would just move ahead a few more feet, she could escape from her hiding place and race for the docks.

"I didn't just let her go, mate," Justin grinned. "Three men were after her and I had to kill one of them." He scanned the darkened alley once more and added, "That's why I want to sail right away. Someone is sure to have heard the shot and the authorities will be looking for the one responsible. I can't risk that just now."

"If ya'd like, sir, I can search for Callahan while you board the ship. If I haven't found him in fifteen minutes, we can sail without him."

Justin's deep-throated laughter echoed in the quiet air. "I have enough enemies already, Maddock. I don't need my first mate hunting me down too. No," he said, turning back slightly, "we'll wait for him. Whatever made him run off like that must have been important."

"Maybe he saw the same woman you did and he's still trying to find her," Maddock teased, slapping another man's shoulder as the group turned toward the pier again. All four came to an abrupt halt when their gazes fell upon the shapely form huddled beside the rain barrel, her eyes wide and a terrified look on her face.

"Well, well, well," Maddock crooned. "What have we here?"

Dara's entire body shook. Her head began to spin and she felt certain she would faint. She took a deep breath and let it out slowly, her attention centered on the man who seemed to tower over his companions. "I . . . I . . ." she stammered, not really sure what she intended to say.

35

"It seems to me, my dear," Justin interrupted, hands resting on his hips, "that this is how you wound up in trouble that last time. I should think you would have learned."

"You know her, Cap'n?" Maddock asked.

"Sort of," Justin replied, his eyes trained on the frightened girl. "She's the one I was telling you about. It seems she overheard something she shouldn't have and someone was after her."

"Like what, Cap'n?"

Justin shrugged. "We never got around to discussing that. But"—he moved a step closer, bent down and took Dara by the wrist, yanking her to her feet—"I think we'll have plenty of time now."

"What . . . what are you going to do?" Dara half whispered as she weakly resisted his grip.

"Up until a few minutes ago, I had decided to forget about you. But that was when you thought I was nothing more than a dirty seaman, and an Irish one at that. However, things are a little different now."

"But—"

"Maddock," Justin said, ignoring the young woman struggling against his grasp, "take Peters with you and find Callahan. We sail within the hour."

"No! Wait," Dara begged. "You can't—"

"Aye, aye, Cap'n," Maddock answered with a brief salute and both men spun around to hurry off down the alley.

"Phillips, you come with me. I need you to take us to the ship. Then you can return to shore and wait for the others."

"Aye, aye, Cap'n," Phillips nodded. "Do you need any help with her?"

Justin smiled down at the beautiful face staring back at him, a look of horror mirrored in her green eyes. "No, I think I can handle her," he said softly. "If she knows what's good for her, she'll behave as properly as a young lady should."

"Very good, sir." Phillips nodded. "I'll see to the boat."

Dara opened her mouth to call out to the man who walked away. She did not want to be left alone with the pirate, Justin Whitelaw, but she discovered she could not force any words from her lips. She breathed deeply, determined to try again, when all of a sudden she felt light-headed and everything around her began to spin. As she lifted her eyes to look at the man beside her, his face grew blurred, and before she knew what had happened, her knees buckled and she slumped in his arms, unconscious.

Chapter Two

A soft, cool breeze gently caressed Dara's face and arms, and she snuggled deeper into the velvet cushion of the quilt, enjoying its comfort and warmth. Her body longed for much-needed rest, but she silently pledged to sleep only a short while before continuing her journey. And no matter what Mr. Bryant had told her, she would pay for her breakfast. A smile played across her face as she thought of her brother and the joy it would bring her father when his son and daughter returned home. She could only pray they would not be too late.

The sound of water being poured into a washbasin penetrated Dara's thoughts and she frowned in her half-conscious state. Had Thomas Bryant sent his wife to her room to awaken her? Had the sun already risen and did he fear her food would get cold? Drowsy, she opened one eye at a time, her puzzlement deepening when her gaze fell upon the dark wood graining of the wall before her. She hadn't remembered the bed being set against a wall. It had stood free on both sides. And the sun hadn't yet risen, for golden streams of lamplight fell across her. Instantly, the events of the day came crashing down on her, her most vivid memory being the last face she had seen before she fainted.

Afraid to move and draw the pirate's attention to her, Dara lay perfectly still, listening to the sounds the man made as he roamed the cabin. It took every ounce of courage she had not to cry, not to explode into a fit of hysteria and beg him not to hurt her. She took several deep breaths and let them out slowly, quietly, having decided the mad ravings of a woman would have little affect on someone as hardened as he. After all, he had been sentenced to hang for treason, had escaped prison, and now he sailed the coastline stealing from the very country that had ordered his death. He wouldn't waste his time listening to her. He'd simply take her out to sea and toss her overboard for the sharks to devour. Dara cringed at the thought and steeled herself for whatever might happen next.

Her teeth chattering from fright, she slowly turned her head to look at him, a plea for mercy on her lips. She froze the instant she saw him. He had stripped himself of his shirt, stockings, and shoes; and he stood beside the washbowl with his back to her, allowing her a moment to appraise him. Dara had lived a secluded life on the farm near Drawbridge, with only her father and mother and Lane. They seldom had any visitors, especially young men, so she had always assumed her brother was a typical example of masculinity. Lane favored their mother. He had her blond hair, blue eyes, slender build, and thin features. But the figure that stood before Dara now most certainly did not compare. Slate black hair curled defiantly against his neck, its ebony depths glistening with moisture from its recent cleansing. Wide shoulders contrasted startlingly with his narrow hips, but it was the thick, hard muscles of his arms and back, flexing with each simple move he made, that caught her attention. Dara had little doubt that this man could easily crush her in his grasp if that was his intent, and the idea of merely asking him to set

40

her free suddenly became laughable. Dara realized any hope of release depended on her. She would have to escape.

Pushing herself up on her elbows, she studied the interior of the cabin. To her left she saw three large, paned portholes with a long wooden bench built beneath them. Opposite her, where the captain stood, eyes fixed on his image in the mirror as he shaved, was a large oak desk filled with maps, books, a spy glass, a lantern, and other paraphernalia she concluded were essential for managing a ship of this size. And to her right . . . Dara's blood pounded through her veins, the anticipation of freedom almost more than she could bear as she stared at the closed cabin door. She took a deep breath. Could she reach it before he saw her? If he did, would she have enough of a head start to get away easily? Sitting up, her attention focused on the sealed portal, she silently estimated the steps it would take to reach it.

"I think I must warn you, the door is locked," the deep baritone voice advised. "And even if it wasn't, my men would never allow you to leave."

Dara jerked her head around, her green eyes wide, to find Captain Whitelaw smiling back at her in the mirror's reflection. The heat of embarrassment scorched her cheeks. He had known simply by watching her what she had planned. Parting from his company would take a little doing.

"When . . . when will you let me go, Captain Whitelaw?" she asked weakly, looking away, for the mocking laughter she saw in his eyes made her uncomfortable.

Laying aside his razor, Justin picked up a towel and blotted his face with it as he turned to look at her. "That depends on you," he said casually, stretching slightly to drape the white piece of cloth on a hook next to the

41

mirror. Pale blue eyes settled on the green ones which stared back at him in surprise.

Dara had been captivated by his muscular physique, but once the warm glow of the lantern's light fell upon his face, she found it impossible to pull her attention away from him. He was, without doubt, the most handsome man she would ever have imagined. Dark brows hooded sky-blue eyes trimmed with thick, black lashes. His gaze seemed to pierce her. He had wide cheekbones and a thin, straight nose, but his most striking feature was his full, almost sensuous mouth, now curved in a gentle smile. Dara's pulse quickened as she watched him move to the edge of the desk and rest one hip upon it. When he leisurely crossed his wrists over one knee and leaned forward slightly, she was sure she would faint again. Each sinewy ripple of his chest and arms, caught by the golden streams of light coming from the lamp, reminded her of a sleek, powerful cougar ready to spring at a moment's notice, and Dara felt as if she had been trapped in his lair with no way out. Her hands trembled and she clasped them together, concentrating on what he'd said.

"What must I do?" she asked, lowering her gaze.

Justin had been aware of the beauty of the young woman who'd come crashing into him in the alleyway but he hadn't realized it was so breathtaking. In the darkness, he couldn't distinguish the color of her eyes or see how her thick locks of hair glowed, almost the shade of fire, in the lamplight. He had seen many a resplendent creature in his travels but none as alluring, as exciting, as the one who occupied his bed at this moment. Her fair complexion seemed to accentuate the innocence reflected in her eyes, and for a brief moment, he almost felt sorry for her. It was quite obvious that she had no idea of the trouble she would be facing by traveling alone to Washington, yet he raised one dark brow, wondering. There was always the possibility that she knew exactly what to expect and planned to use her feminine charms to see her through any situation.

Well, he thought, let's find out. Standing, he rounded the corner of his desk and sat down on the chair behind it, reaching for a cheroot from the tin box sitting on top. "First you can start by telling me your name," he said flatly. Striking flint and steel to spark a flame and light the cigar, he took a long drag and watched the smoke curl upward around him before settling his attention on the young woman again.

For a fleeting moment, Dara wondered if she should tell him the truth, then thought better of it. If he managed to find out she had lied, there was no telling what he might do to her. She opened her mouth to speak, and when nothing came out, she cleared her throat and tried again. "Dara. Dara Brandon, sir."

Justin's eyes narrowed slightly, reflecting disapproval, before he quickly masked the emotion. He took another puff on the cheroot. "Where are you from, Dara Brandon?"

"Drawbridge, sir. It's about fifteen miles inland from here."

"Do you live there with your husband?"

Dara laughed nervously. "I . . . I'm not married."

"Alone then?"

Dara shook her head. "No, sir. With my mother and father."

She noticed that he seemed to relax at her last admission and she frowned, wondering why such knowledge would please him.

"You said you were on your way to Washington to find your brother. Does he live there?"

"No, sir," she said, dismissing her momentary curiosity. "I don't know where he is exactly. That's why

43

I wanted to talk to someone in authority. I was hoping they could help me locate him and bring him home." Dara's gaze dropped to her hands, recalling how their father had spent the last two weeks sitting in a rocker on the front porch staring off into space. Since he hadn't spoken a word since the message about Lane had come, she could only assume he was blaming himself for his son's misfortune. He ate and slept very little, and Dara knew that if Lane was not brought home to him soon, Taylor Brandon would perish from guilt.

"What's his name?"

Caught up in her own unhappiness, Dara did not look at the man who voiced the question. Instead, she crossed her ankles and pulled them to her, tucking her skirts beneath her knees. "Lane," she whispered lovingly. She failed to notice the hardened look that appeared on Justin Whitelaw's face.

"Describe him."

A clear vision of the blond-haired youth came to mind: his smile, his laughter, the moments when he would tease her and she would become angry. But her anger had lasted only a short while, for she could never stay annoyed with Lane. Without him to brighten their dull existence, she had often wondered how she would carry on. Dara's green eyes darkened as she recalled the day he had announced his plans to leave. She had run away and Lane had chased her, grabbing her around the waist and tumbling them both to the ground. She had burst into tears, had kicked and screamed, and declared her hatred of him; but Lane had not said a word. After she had exhausted all of her pent-up emotions he had cradled her in his arms, and softly vowing to return as soon as he could, he had said that America needed him. Whether that was true or not, Dara had realized Lane had to go—for himself—and

44

she could not stand in his way. Now he needed her. With a smile, she glanced up at the man who shared the cabin with her, eager to describe every detail of her brother's appearance, but a chill ran through her when she saw the hate-filled gleam in Justin's eyes.

"Why do you want to know?" she asked worriedly, watching a lopsided grin replace the heated glare.

"The name is unusual, wouldn't you say?" He paused, waiting for a response. She shrugged. "If I told you I had met a man named Lane Brandon a few months ago, you would be reasonably certain he was your brother, would you not?"

"I . . . I might be," she answered hesitantly. For some reason, she didn't trust this man and she was not about to tell him anything else without first knowing his purpose.

"So tell me what he looks like," he urged with a smile, the cheroot clamped between his teeth. When Dara did not respond but merely stared back at him, he suddenly slammed the palm of his hand against the desk top. "Now!" he roared.

Dara started violently and scrambled to the far corner of the wide bed, a knot forming in her throat. "He's . . . he's short, shorter than I, with the same color of hair and brown eyes."

Justin's chair crashed to the floor when he bolted from it and kicked it aside. "You're lying," he growled, both hands pressed against the desk top to support his upper torso. "He's blond with blue eyes and nearly as tall as I!"

"No. He's not. That's . . . that's our uncle. They have the same name."

"And I suppose you're going to tell me he's in his forties?" Justin challenged.

Dara nodded eagerly.

The rage vanished from his face as quickly as it

appeared, and he straightened to cross the cabin and gaze casually out the porthole into the night. "Why are you looking for your brother?"

Since his back was to her, Dara glanced at the door. Then, remembering it was locked, she strained to see the surface of his desk, looking for the key. She had to get away. She had no idea why Lane was so important to him, but from the look on his face when he talked about him, she realized he couldn't wish her brother any good.

"He . . . he ran away from home a couple of days ago," she said, sliding to the edge of the bed. She watched him out of the corner of her eye while she continued to scrutinize the desk top, praying to find the tiny brass key that would free her of his company. "He told Papa that he wanted to marry a woman Papa didn't approve of and he ran away to do it." Quietly, she swung her feet to the floor and slowly stood up. "Papa said he would kill Lane if he caught him, and I'm trying to find him and warn him." She tiptoed noiselessly toward the desk. "The woman lives in Washington. Papa knows that and he sent our uncle after Lane." An irritable frown kinked her lovely brow when the key was nowhere to be seen; then it faded when her gaze fell upon the pistol lying there. She had never been any good at firing a weapon, but Justin Whitelaw didn't know that. All she'd have to do was point it at him, demand the key, and be on her way. "That's probably where you met the other Lane Brandon." She grinned and reached out to pick up the pistol.

"It isn't loaded, Miss Brandon."

Dara jumped at the intrusion of his words, glancing up at him in surprise to find that he hadn't even looked her way. "How? . . ."

"The change in your voice. Besides, I didn't think

46

you'd just sit there," he said, taking a puff on the cheroot. "Now suppose we start again, only this time you can tell me the truth."

"Truth?" she repeated, looking at the pistol again. Was the gun really empty or had he attempted to trick her? She stared at it a moment, trying to decide.

"Sit down, Miss Brandon, before I tie you to the bed," he warned, studying the cigar he held in his fingertips. "In fact, it might not be such a bad idea." Pale blue eyes glanced over at her.

His penetrating glare held her, and Dara suddenly knew he'd meant what he'd said. Her body was trembling so badly she wondered if her knees would support her so she might do as he instructed. Not wanting to risk his anger, she forced her feet to return her to the bunk on which she quickly sat down, too afraid to say anything.

"I met Lane Brandon several months ago," he began, his words tinged with bitterness. "He was a witness at my trial."

Dara's mouth fell open, but she said nothing.

"He testified that I was being paid to look the other way while ships smuggled goods into Canada. He claimed that he was the messenger who gave me the money for the deal, and he said that on several occasions I had even escorted the ships safely to the border. He also told the magistrate that I murdered anyone who stood in my way." He was quiet a moment; then he went to his desk and snuffed out the cheroot before turning to look at her. "The Lane Brandon I knew was a seaman in the United States Navy and a member of my crew. So tell me again what he looked like; then we'll discuss the man you were planning to meet in Washington."

Dara felt sick inside. If everything Justin Whitelaw had said was true, then he wanted Lane out of revenge.

47

Now that she had heard his story, she decided that Lane probably hadn't been captured by the British, that he was hiding somewhere until this treasonous murderer was caught and hanged. Tears came to her eyes. If Justin Whitelaw, a man who knew the area, couldn't find Lane, how could she ever hope to succeed? She looked at her hands, folded in her lap. It would probably be best if she didn't succeed. Lane would only want to come home to comfort his father, and now that Whitelaw knew where they lived, he would have someone watching the farm to tell him when Lane appeared. No, she would have to abandon the whole idea of searching for her brother. She would return home without him.

"Lane is twenty, a year older than I, with blond hair and blue eyes just as you said. He joined the Navy a year ago and we were recently informed that he had been captured by the British. I have no idea where he is, and I was going to Washington to find someone who might," she recited dully, not bothering to look up. "I'm afraid I can't help you, Captain Whitelaw." Green eyes, filled with hatred, found his. "And even if I could . . . I wouldn't."

Justin's blue eyes seemed to devour her, his gaze traveling slowly over her tiny frame, and some of Dara's courage faded.

"I think I can change your mind," he threatened softly, smiling. "I haven't been a pirate long, but I have learned some of their ways of convincing a person to reveal something. Of course, I don't think I'd have to go to that extreme." He grinned almost evilly and started toward the bunk, where Dara sat nervously watching him. "There are certain advantages a man has over a woman."

The muscles in her chest constricted, nearly depriving her of breath, and she instinctively moved farther away from him. "What do you mean? Surely you don't intend to . . . to . . ." Tears filled her eyes. "I don't know where Lane is. I can't help you."

"I think you're lying," he whispered, his massive frame blocking the lamplight as he pressed one knee on the bed.

"No! For God's sake, no!" Dara screamed, jumping to her feet, but Justin easily caught her wrist, yanked her around, and pulled her, struggling, to the bunk with him. Before she had time to draw another breath, he had twisted her beneath him and held both her hands in his. He pressed her into the feathery softness of the bunk. "I'm not lying, Captain Whitelaw. I don't know where to find Lane."

Blue eyes filled with suspicion smiled down at her. "Somehow I don't think a lady would risk traveling to Washington by herself unless she was sure of the results. So why not consider your options. If you tell me where he is, once I have him I'll let you go, or you can deny any knowledge of his whereabouts and pay for his freedom with your maidenhood. Either way, I get the best of the deal."

Dara's face burned a scarlet hue. "You're no better than those men in the alley. In fact, you're worse. You murdered one of them."

Chuckling, he shook his head. "Self-defense, Miss Brandon. If I hadn't, I doubt I would have been able to hold them all off. So you see, I guess you were meant to warm some man's bed tonight. I consider it a pleasure that it will be mine."

"Not if I can help it," she spat through clenched teeth, fighting to push him from her.

Justin brought her into quick submission when he squeezed her wrist and sent a tremor of pain down her arm. "I don't think you have much of a say in the matter, Miss Brandon, unless you tell me what it is I want to know."

"But I can't tell you something I don't know," she whimpered, a tear stealing down her cheek. She gasped when he shifted his weight to one side of her and took both of her wrists in one hand, raising them above her head.

"Then have it your way," he surrendered, his long sun-darkened fingers moving to the first button of her gown and popping it loose. Lazily, he trailed a fingertip along the silky patch of white skin he had uncovered, grinning devilishly when he heard her squeal. "Change your mind?" he mocked.

But before Dara could answer, Justin's fun was interrupted by the knock on the cabin door.

"Who is it?" he called out, not in the least perplexed.

"Callahan, Captain. Can I talk to you a moment?"

Swinging a long leg over Dara's when she wiggled to get free, he answered, "Come on in. The door's not locked."

A low, throaty growl drew Justin's attention back to the shapely form he held trapped beneath him, and he raised questioning brows at the look she gave him.

"And I suppose the pistol is loaded," she hissed.

"Of course. Don't you remember watching me reload it after I shot that man?" he asked, a roguish gleam sparkling in his blue eyes.

Dara opened her mouth, prepared to hurl every vile word she knew at him, only to snap it shut again when she heard the cabin door creak. Wide-eyed, she struggled to lift her head and watch the man who entered, fruitlessly hoping he would have pity on her and demand that his captain turn her loose. But the moment his gaze fell upon the couple lying on the bunk, his face registered surprise for a second then twisted into a smile, and she collapsed back on the bed, disheartened.

"Oh, excuse me, Cap'n," Douglas Callahan apologized, turning to retreat from the cabin. "You should have said something. I can wait."

Justin laughed merrily. "It's all right, Callahan. The lady and I were only talking things over." He smiled down at Dara. "We can finish later."

Callahan glanced back at his captain over a round, muscular shoulder, his stocky frame bouncing with his laughter. "Aye, I suppose you can. But I'm not sure you'll have the time after I tell you what I heard."

Justin nodded, relaxing on one elbow, his other arm draped casually over his hip. "Then I suggest you do just that. I already issued the order to set sail just as soon as you boarded."

Swinging the door shut behind him, Callahan grinned sheepishly and ran his stubby fingers through the few remaining strands of gray hair on his otherwise bald head. "I took the liberty of postponing that order, Cap'n. I figured once you heard my story, you'd be wanting to stay awhile longer."

"Did you now?" Justin chuckled. "Then I propose you make it quick before I charge you with mutiny for counteracting my command."

Callahan's gray eyes twinkled. He was unaffected by Justin's threat. They had sailed together for nearly ten years and whether Justin could make the same claim or not, Douglas Callahan deemed no other friendship quite as worthy. He would give his life for Captain Whitelaw and had nearly done so on several occasions. There had been many times when the two of them had argued bitterly, but despite that, the love they bore for each other never allowed their differences to come between them.

"Mutiny, huh?" Callahan challenged. "And what court did you have in mind to hear the case? Besides, Cap'n, the whole crew thinks you're a little touched anyway."

Justin laughed loudly. "No doubt from listening to you," he accused, agilely pushing himself up from the bed.

He crossed to his desk and reached for another cheroot, but Callahan's attention was not centered on him. Instead, it lingered on the beautiful woman who timidly sat up, her eyes averted as she nervously straightened her attire.

"Quite the prize, isn't she?" Justin teased when he noticed how Callahan stared.

"In more ways than you suspect, Cap'n," Callahan replied with a lift of dark brows. "Where did you find her?"

"I . . . ah . . . 'bumped' into her in an alleyway." He grinned, lighting the cheroot. He studied the tip to make sure it had caught the flame, then crossed his arms over his chest and leaned back against the edge of the desk. "At first I thought it was just an enjoyable accident, but now that I've seen her in full light, I'd say I've been blessed."

"Right, Cap'n . . . on two counts."

Justin cocked his head to one side, studying his first mate, a vague smile parting his lips. "I suppose you're going to tell me you know who she is?"

"Uh-huh," Callahan grunted. "And why she was roaming the streets at night."

Justin nodded. "All right then, tell me."

"She's Dara Brandon, and after I did some checking around, I found out she lives at Drawbridge with her mother and father. About a year ago, her brother, Lane, joined the Navy. The name sound familiar?" Callahan grinned over at him.

"Now tell me something I don't already know," Justin bantered, chuckling at the disappointed look on Callahan's face. "In fact, we were just discussing where

I might find her brother when you came in."

"All right, you cocky know-it-all," Callahan barked, "tell me who she was running from?"

Justin shrugged. "We hadn't gotten around to that."

"Then I will," he replied irritably. "Colonel Emerson Winslow."

Justin took a long puff on the cheroot, studied the smoke circling upward, then settled his gaze on his friend once more. "Sorry, mate, I never heard of the man."

"Now you have," Callahan said sarcastically. "It seems the little lady here overheard something she shouldn't have. Winslow means to kill her if he can get his hands on her."

Both men turned their attention on Dara who was huddled in the corner of the bunk, her green eyes fearfully alert as they shifted from one man to the other. Soft shades of lamplight glistened in her hair and caressed the lovely features of her face. She had drawn her knees to her chest, and yards of skirt flowed out around her in a sea of blue.

"And what might that have been?" Justin asked cautiously.

"I don't know exactly, Cap'n, except that the colonel is offering a nice reward to anyone who brings her to him. And," he added, turning to his companion again, "he wants to see you."

"Me?" Justin echoed.

"Aye."

White teeth flashed in a smile. "And since you're such a waterfall of information, suppose you tell me what it is he wants."

"He wouldn't say. In fact, he doesn't truly know if you'll get the message or not. I never said I knew where to find you, only that I'd heard you were in the area from time to time."

"You mean you talked to him?"

"Of course I did," Callahan answered testily. "How else would I have found out all this?" He shook his head disapprovingly, missing the twinkle that appeared in Justin's eyes. "I was in this tavern having a mug of ale and looking for a woman I know when Colonel Winslow came in. Since I was alone, he comes over to me and asks if I've seen the woman he's looking for. He said she was pretty, but he didn't say just how pretty." Callahan snorted, briefly glancing at Dara. "Anyway, when I asked him what he wanted her for, he mumbled something about her knowing too much. Well, when I said I hadn't seen her, he asked me if I had ever heard of Justin Whitelaw and could I get a message to him that the colonel wanted to talk to him. He told me he'd be staying at Bryant's Inn for a few days until he found the girl or talked to you. Now you know the whole of it, so don't go asking any more stupid questions."

Justin stuck the cheroot in his mouth to mask his grin. "I take it you didn't find your woman."

"No, I didn't," Callahan snapped. "I probably would have if you hadn't sent that fool of a deck hand after me."

"Then I apologize, friend," Justin smiled.

"A lot of good that does my loins," Callahan grumbled, crossing behind the desk to the bottle of whiskey sitting on one corner. "Mind if I have a drink?"

Justin twisted slightly to look at him, his shoulders drooping resignedly when he discovered Callahan had already poured a stout measure into a glass. Shaking his head, he watched the man down the contents in one swallow, wipe a drop from his mouth with the back of his hand, then reach for the bottle once more.

"Well, Cap'n," he said, refilling the glass, "aren't you going to ask the young lady why Colonel Winslow wants to kill her?"

54

"I had thought about it," Justin said ironically.

Callahan shrugged. "Then don't let me stop you," he replied, setting the chair upright before he eased himself into it. "I'd like to hear this too." He swung his feet up to rest on the corner of the desk, ankles crossed, and settled back comfortably to listen.

Justin stared at him a moment, wondering why he tolerated as much as he did from the man; then he said, "You know, Callahan, one of these days you and I are going to have to decide who's captain of this ship."

A wide, devilish grin deepened the lines on Douglas Callahan's face. "There's never been any doubt in my mind," he said, raising his glass in a mock salute and evoking a hearty round of laughter from his captain.

"Then suppose you sit there nice and quiet while I talk with Miss Brandon."

"Aye, aye, Cap'n," Callahan nodded, turning his attention on the frightened face that had witnessed their playful bantering.

A rush of confusing thoughts had raced through Dara's mind as she'd listened to the men, leaving her exhausted and totally frustrated. She had heard a group of strangers talking about a man who had committed treason against his country, a man who had been sentenced to hang, then had escaped from prison and become a pirate. She had concluded the man would be dangerous, maybe even a murderer. Possibly he was dangerous . . . to men. But hadn't he proven to be just the opposite when he'd saved her from being abused by three drunks, and had killed one of them? He had offered his help and protection without knowing who she was, merely the fact that she was a defenseless woman. However, once she had discovered that her savior was Justin Whitelaw in disguise, he had taken her against her will to his ship and proceeded to finish what the three drunks could not. He had become outraged when he'd learned of her brother's identity, seeming to change from a gentle, compassionate man into a demon from hell. Could it be that he was a madman? And would he murder her if she failed to give him the answers he wanted? Oh, God how she wished she was home fixing a dinner her father would refuse to eat!

"Miss Brandon?"

Dara jumped at the sound of his voice and glanced up fearfully at the man who now stood at the edge of the bunk, the expression on his face lost in shadow. Her chin quivered and she bit her lower lip, blinking back the tears which threatened to shatter her brave façade.

"I asked you why Colonel Winslow wants you dead." Justin stated, his tone firm yet gentle.

"If . . . if I tell you, will you let me go?" Her voice came weak despite her effort to sound otherwise, and Dara silently cursed her fading courage, trembling when he simply laughed at her.

"That would be rather foolish, don't you think? You heard what Callahan told me. The colonel has offered money to anyone who finds you and brings you to him. I know very few men who would pass up the cost of a mug of ale and you're worth far more than that. Besides, where would you go?"

Dara hugged her knees tighter to her. "Home," she whispered, unaware that he had lowered his tall frame to sit before her, blocking any chance she had to slip past him.

"And how long do you think it would be before Winslow or one of his men appeared on your doorstep? If Callahan could find out where you lived, don't you suppose the colonel could too?"

Angry green eyes glared up at him. "And what do you suggest I do? Stay here with you?" She laughed sarcastically. "Somehow I don't think I'd be any safer in the company of a pirate . . . and a traitor at that," she blurted out carelessly.

Justin's handsome features hardened. "Tell me what I want to know, Miss Brandon, or I'll force it from you—any way I can."

Dara's breath caught in her throat. Her gaze darted from one man to the other, tears blurring her vision when she saw Callahan grin and raise his dark brows. She looked back at Justin and jumped when he started to reach for her.

"I heard him talking to a man about murdering President Jefferson—he wants you to do it," she admitted in a rush, knotted fists pressed against her mouth as she watched the expression on Justin's face change.

He sat, thoughtfully quiet, for a moment; then he stood, and Dara felt as if she were no longer in the room when he turned from her, dismissing her presence as he would that of a discarded rum bottle. She relaxed a bit, observing both men curiously as they remained silent for several minutes. Finally, Douglas Callahan spoke.

"What are you going to do, Cap'n?"

A soft smile played upon Justin's lips as he tossed the stub of his cheroot in the ashtray and reached for his shirt. "I'm going to pay Colonel Winslow a visit," he stated simply, and Callahan grinned.

"That's what I thought you would say. Mind if I tag along?"

"And who else would I trust at my back?"

Callahan chuckled. "Not another soul, I think. What are you going to wear?"

"My black cape and hat. It's dark enough now, no one will get a good look at me," Justin said, easing the ruffled, white linen shirt over his shoulders. "I want you to go on ahead and tell the colonel to meet me at

57

the bend in the road just outside of town. We can see if he's alone and have the advantage at the same time."

"Aye, aye, Cap'n." Callahan smiled, lifting himself from the chair. "What are you going to do with the girl?"

"She can stay here tonight," he said, crossing to the bench beneath the windows and sitting down to tug on his stockings and shoes. "I'm not through with her yet. So far she's the only lead I've got in finding Brandon, even though she claims she doesn't know where he is."

Reaching up to scratch his chin, Douglas Callahan cast Dara a suggestive grin. "Somehow I don't think you'll have any trouble getting her to cooperate."

"Neither do I." Justin slid off the bench to kneel in front of it. Pulling open one of several drawers built beneath it, he picked up the black cape and hat neatly resting inside and stood. "Ready?"

"After you," Callahan replied, bowing slightly and extending a hand toward the door.

"Then let's go. Tonight should prove to be most interesting." Justin smirked, lifting the pistol from his desk as he passed by. Without a glance in Dara's direction, he opened the door and stepped outside, his first mate close on his heels.

Darkness enveloped the two figures on horseback as they hid among the trees at the edge of town and awaited the carriage that would bring Colonel Winslow to their meeting place. Callahan had rousted the livery stable owner out of bed and paid him double the cost of hiring two horses after the man, irritated by this customer's intrusion on his much-needed rest, had flatly refused to rent them. The livery man's mood had lightened even more when the stranger had informed him that the animals would be returned within the hour although the price paid had covered their use until morning, and Callahan had left the stable with two of the swiftest runners of the lot.

He had taken the steeds to Justin who waited for him behind the building; then he'd traveled on foot to Bryant's Inn where he'd advised the grateful Colonel Winslow that the man he had asked to see would meet him just outside of town in fifteen minutes. When Winslow had objected to the short notice, Callahan had threatened to call the meeting off, telling him that no one could order his friend about, while in truth, Callahan and Justin had agreed that the shorter the amount of time Winslow was given the less of a chance he would have to set a trap should that be his true plan. Being most anxious to speak with Justin Whitelaw, the colonel quickly relented and excused himself from Callahan's presence, stating that he must fetch his cloak and hat before setting out on the journey.

Once Callahan had rejoined Justin, they rode west out of town to wait. It was their plan to follow the colonel and make certain he was alone, but as the minutes ticked away, they feared that Colonel Winslow had changed his mind. When they were about to give up, the rattling of a carriage broke the quiet and they moved deeper into the protection of the trees to await his passage on the road.

"What do ya think, Cap'n?" Callahan whispered, once the colonel's rig had rolled past them. "Is he alone?"

"It appears so," Justin answered after a while when he heard no other sounds than those made by the passage of the carriage. "But just to be safe, we'll let him move on a ways before we follow."

"Aye, Cap'n," Callahan nodded.

They watched the dark shape of the buggy until it was lost in the shadows some distance down the road, then spurred their animals on, glancing back periodically as they listened for the approach of anyone else. When they neared the bend in the road and saw that the colonel waited, Justin nodded to his companion, then reined his horse from the road into the thick undercover. Drawing his pistol, Callahan advanced.

"Good evening, Colonel," he said once he drew up alongside of the carriage.

"Where's Captain Whitelaw?" Winslow demanded, then spotted the gun pointed at his chest. He stiffened in the seat, his eyes wide with worry. "Is this some sort of trick? I assure you that I have no money with me."

"Please step down and move away from the rig," Callahan instructed in a strangely polite tone, ignoring what Winslow had said.

Fearing for his life and never having been courageous when the odds were against him, Winslow did as he was bid, his moves quick and nervous. He stood stock-still in the middle of the road, only his Adam's apple bobbing up and down as he swallowed apprehensively, and watched the man who held the gun walk closer. Certain his life was about to end, he closed his eyes, silently praying his death would be swift, and he jumped when he felt Callahan touch his coat.

"What . . . what do you want? I told you that I don't have any money with me," he said, his voice shaky.

"I'm not after money, Colonel," Callahan assured him. "If I was, I wouldn't bother with formalities. I'd just shoot first and then take whatever I found on you."

"Then?" he asked, raising his hands when the man continued the search of his clothing.

"The captain prefers to speak with an unarmed man, Colonel."

"Oh." He sighed. "Well, I guarantee that I'm not carrying a weapon, sir. I detest guns."

"Did ya hear that, Cap'n?" Callahan called over his shoulder. "The colonel doesn't like violence."

Winslow's green eyes searched the darkness for the man Callahan had addressed, and he swallowed hard when he saw the dark figure of a horse and rider move out from the trees. The hat the captain wore shadowed the expression on his face, and his long black cape shimmered in the moonlight and flowed loosely about his tall frame, giving him a demoniac air. Suddenly Colonel Winslow wondered at the soundness of his plan.

"Y-yes, Captain Whitelaw," he began, glancing first at the man at his side and then back at Justin. "That's true. And that's why I need your help."

He waited, expecting the pirate to comment but when Justin only stared back silently, the colonel shifted nervously.

"I . . . ah . . . I've heard of the trouble you're in, Captain, and I'm here to offer a way to get even." His gaze moved to Callahan and back again. "That is if you're interested."

"And suppose you just tell the cap'n what it is instead of beating around the bush, Colonel," Callahan instructed, his tone low and threatening.

Winslow gave a nervous laugh. "Of course." He gulped and took a deep breath. "Many of us want this Embargo Act of Jefferson's lifted, even some senators and members of his cabinet. But Jefferson won't budge. So we've gotten together, collected money from all the plantation owners up and down the coast, and come up with a plan. We want to hire you to assassinate President Jefferson."

The towering figure before him moved slightly and Winslow quickly added, "It's nearly ten thousand dollars, Captain. I think you'll agree that's a fair price." Winslow could almost feel the intense look the pirate

61

gave him.

"Providing I succeed without getting killed, that is," Justin pointed out.

"Oh, but you will," Winslow quickly promised. "A man who has eluded the authorities for as long as you have would surely find this a simple challenge."

Justin's deep laughter startled the colonel and he fearfully looked from one man to the other.

"Nothing, Colonel, is simple," Justin replied, leaning forward to rest his arm on the pommel of his saddle. "Nor are my requirements."

"Sir?"

"The ten thousand is only a down payment," Justin smiled in the shadow of his hat's brim, and he raised a hand to silence Winslow who had opened his mouth to object. "I don't know you, Colonel, and I'd be very foolish to trust your word since we've just met. The money will guarantee that you're not here as a plot to apprehend me."

"But . . . but I can't raise any more than that, Captain," Winslow pleaded.

"It isn't more money that interests me, Colonel. I want you to have all charges against me dropped."

"What?" he exploded. "But that will take time. And I'm not sure I can do it."

"You said you had friends in government."

"Well, yes, but—"

"Then tell them that their price for my help is seeing my name cleared."

Winslow remained silent for a moment, contemplating Justin's conditions; then he reached up to take off his hat and run his fingers through his hair. "All right. Consider it done."

"And one more thing before I agree. I want the aid of some of your men in the execution of the president."

Colonel Winslow's white hair gleamed in the

moonlight when he shook his head. "If I had men willing to do that, why would I pay for your help when they'd do it for nothing?"

"And do you have such a man, Colonel? One who would raise a pistol against the president knowing that if he's caught he'll be hanged?" Justin studied the man fighting for an answer and he smiled when he realized Winslow had none. "All I want is the guarantee that they will create a diversion once the shot is fired, something that will distract attention from me and allow me time to get away. Now is that too difficult? Because if it is then we have no deal."

Winslow's rounded frame stiffened indignantly. No one had ever dared tell him what to do, and it sorely nettled him that a pirate had done just that. If his need to see President Jefferson dead weren't so great, he would hotly rebuke the man's audacity. However, he knew he needed this scoundrel's help, and for that reason alone, he held his temper in rein.

"I'll see what I can do, Captain," he replied dourly.

"Good," Justin said with a nod of his head. "Have your men in Norfolk in three weeks. President Jefferson is scheduled to be at the christening of a new warship at the end of the month. There will be a crowd big enough for us to go unnoticed. I don't care what tactic they use to aid my escape just so it works. But, Colonel, be warned that if I'm captured, I'll tell them whose idea this was. And if, for any reason, your friends don't come through on their part of the bargain, I'll come looking for you." Straightening, he yanked back on the reins and pulled his horse around. "I'll have one of my men meet you here in one week to collect the money. That will give me a little time to check around."

"For what?" Winslow asked suspiciously.

Justin grinned, his bright smile reflecting the silver streams of light. "To learn if you are who you say you are," Whitelaw replied, then motioned for Callahan to follow him.

Colonel Winslow stood in the road, glaring at the shadows that had covered the pair's departure as easily as their appearance. His green eyes narrowed, his nostrils flared. "Oh, I'll have my men there, Captain. But not to help," he growled softly. "The one who shoots President Jefferson's assassin will be a hero and will be well paid by me." Snarling, he shoved his hat back on his head and awkwardly climbed into his carriage.

"What was that all about, Cap'n?" Callahan asked once they'd put a safe distance between themselves and the colonel. "You're not really intending to shoot the president, are you?"

Justin chuckled. "Of course not. And since when have you questioned anything I do?"

"Well . . . never. But you must admit, you sounded pretty convincing."

"I had to, my friend. If the colonel was willing to pay ten thousand dollars to have the president killed, he'd find someone else to do it if I refused—and the next one wouldn't neglect putting a ball in his pistol."

"Oh," Callahan grinned. "But why all that stuff about using his men to protect you? The crew could manage that and you know you can trust them."

"Agreed. But spoiling the assassination plot wasn't my only motive. I want to see that those responsible are brought to justice, and I rather doubt anyone in authority would believe the word of a traitor. My plan is to catch one of Winslow's men and turn him in. I think with a little persuasion, he might tell them what they need to know."

"You never cease to surprise me, Cap'n," Callahan said, shaking his head as he watched the road.

"Surprise you?" Justin smiled and glanced over at

his companion.

"You don't owe the United States anything. Why are you willing to risk your neck? You know that if something goes wrong and you're captured, you'll be hanged the very same day without a chance to explain."

"That's why I'm counting on you to see that it doesn't," he grinned.

"Oh, thanks, Cap'n," Callahan mocked. "That makes me feel a lot better."

Laughing, Justin leaned over in the saddle and good-naturedly slapped his first mate's shoulder.

"Well, if it's any help, I'm going to stop at the warehouse in Cambridge. I'll have my man there go to Washington to find out what he can about the colonel. Once I'm sure of him, we'll contact George Manning."

"Senator Manning?"

Justin nodded.

"Why?"

"Because George was the only man who never believed I was guilty of treason. I don't imagine he approved of my escaping prison and he'd probably turn me in if he ever spotted me, but it's a chance I have to take. If I can get him to listen, I'll tell him about the deal with Winslow and ask that he accompany the president to Norfolk. With his help, the president will be safe and the colonel's treachery will be unmasked. And who knows? Maybe Colonel Winslow will turn informer to save his own hide and reveal the names of his senator friends."

"Well, I hope you know what you're doing," Callahan added.

"I do," Justin assured him. "I'm just not sure it will work." He waited until his friend glanced worriedly over at him and then flashed him a playful smile before he kicked his horse into a gallop, calling back over his shoulder, "Come on, Callahan. See if you can get that nag of yours to run."

Shoulders sagging, Callahan watched the spirited mount race off, Justin's black cape flying out behind him as if the devil had taken human form. "Someday, Justin Whitelaw," he muttered with a shake of his head as he spurred his horse, "someday I'll learn not to take you seriously."

Chapter Three

For the past hour, Dara had frantically searched Justin's cabin for a second key to unlock the door. She had rummaged through every drawer in his desk and had scattered the contents beneath the bench. She had ripped the covers from his bunk hoping he had hidden an extra key there and had finally resorted to picking the lock with a letter opener. Her efforts awarded her one broken fingernail, a slightly misshapen keyhole and a feeling of hopelessness. Staring at the sealed portal, her frustration boiled up inside her and she kicked the wooden barrier, instantly regretting that move when pain shot up her leg. Limping, tears rolling down her cheeks, she hobbled to the bunk and sat down. She had to get away, not only for *her* safety but for her brother's. If Captain Whitelaw somehow managed to find Lane, he might use her to lure Lane into surrendering, and that would most certainly result in Lane's death.

Sniffling, Dara recalled the reason she was alone in this cabin: Justin Whitelaw was, at this very moment, meeting with Colonel Winslow to plot the murder of President Jefferson. Suddenly the idea of escaping merely to spare herself humiliation at the pirate's hands seemed selfish. Jefferson's life was more important than hers or Lane's. A frown crimped the smooth, flawless line of her brow. But what good did it do to think of a way to warn the president when she couldn't even free herself from her prison?

Disheartened, she curled her legs beneath her and studied the interior of the room again, a pleased smile lifting the corners of her delicate mouth. When Justin Whitelaw had brought her to this cabin, she hadn't given it much thought, but now that the space was in complete disorder, starkly different from the way it had been, she recognized a rare trait in any man. Justin Whitelaw was neat, tidy—everything in its place. This mess was sure to upset him. She snickered, satisfied with her small measure of revenge, and impishly decided to see what other havoc she could create. Glancing around the room, her gaze settled on the three large portholes and her need for further destruction vanished. She knew how to swim. All she had to do was lower herself from the porthole and she'd be free.

New hope rising, Dara jumped from the bed, dragging the sheets with her, and quickly began tearing them into strips. When she had finished, she tied the ends together, producing a long cloth rope. She smiled at the results, certain it would be her means of escape.

"You might think a man has an advantage over a woman, Captain Whitelaw," she said with a haughty lift of her nose, "but you forgot one thing. We aren't as stupid as you assume."

With a snide laugh, she hurried to the desk and secured one end of the sheet rope around a decoratively carved leg. Then she trailed the remainder to the bench and laid it down while she opened one of the three portholes. A flicker of doubt crossed her mind as she peered out and saw the distance to the water. But her determination to succeed surpassed the nervous qualm that tightened the muscles in her stomach, and she straightened courageously. After all, President Jefferson's life depended on her. With a brave lift of her chin, she picked up the rope and tossed it out the window, watching its descent until it stretched full length, swaying gently in semidarkness.

"I hope you know what you're doing," she muttered to herself, glancing up at the shore in the distance. "Swimming in a pond back home is nothing in comparison to this." She took a deep breath, let it out in a rush, and lifted one leg to the sill. "Well, I guess there's only one way to find out."

The journey down proved more difficult than she had assumed it would be. Her skirts kept getting in the way, and after only a short while her arms grew tired. Several times her grip failed to hold and she slid from one knot in the rope to the next, the cloth burning her hands. Still, she knew it was impossible to climb back on board, and since she'd the choice, she decided that whatever minor pain she had to endure would be better than sitting idly by and waiting for Captain Whitelaw to return.

When it seemed she would never reach the end of the rope, Dara carelessly glanced down over her shoulder to see how much farther she had to go. The dizzying height loosened her grip, and she closed her eyes, struggling to hang on. But the weight of her body fought against her and, in the next instant, she found herself falling into the black surface of the bay.

The minute she hit the water, Dara realized the mistake she'd made in not shedding her numerous layers of petticoats. It took every ounce of strength she had just to surface and inhale a much-needed breath of air. She was already very tired and the swim to shore would take more energy than she had. Panic filled her. She thrashed wildly at the water, fighting to stay afloat. Her lungs burned, her arms ached, and she kicked more frantically than before. She opened her mouth to scream for help, but instead swallowed a large gulp of salty water when a sudden swell poured over her, dragging her down. Visions of her home and family came to mind, of her childhood. She saw the huge oak tree standing in the front yard, and strangely enough Dara found that she no longer wanted to fight. Reluctantly giving in to the beckoning pull of the swirling current, she relaxed. Her eyes were drifting shut when, suddenly, a strong hand seized her arm and yanked her from the water.

The cool night air against her wet clothes brought her around instantly. Gasping for air, she was vaguely aware of the rough hands hoisting her into a rowboat, then of someone tossing a cloak over her shoulders and forcing her to sit down on a narrow wooden plank. A huge hand caught the back of her neck, shoved her head to her knees, and a fist beat against her spine.

"Stop . . . please . . ." She coughed and made a feeble attempt to knock away the hand. "You're . . . hurting . . . me."

The small craft rocked slightly when someone moved to sit before her and Dara frantically hung on to the side, fearing she would be toppled overboard. Once the boat settled again and she heard oars cutting into the water, she relaxed somewhat. She was breathing more easily and wanted to thank her rescuer. She pushed the heavy, wet strands of hair from her face, and looked up, but her mouth dropped open when she saw the angry blue eyes staring back at her.

"Just what in hell were you trying to prove, Miss Brandon?" Justin Whitelaw growled.

Dara pulled back, nearly spilling herself from the narrow seat, and tried repeatedly to force some explanation from her lips. "I . . . I . . ."

"You could have drowned and probably would have

70

if we hadn't come along when we did," he hissed, cutting her off. "What good would that have done anyway? It was a very stupid thing to do."

Resenting his words, Dara stiffened. "I know that to you my life isn't worth the mud on your boots, Captain Whitelaw. You couldn't possibly allow me to live knowing what I do. So why should I just sit in your cabin waiting for you to kill me without at least trying to warn President Jefferson?" Dara hugged the cape to her as a chill shook her body, and she missed the surprised look on his face.

"Kill you?" he repeated calmly. "Is that what you think I plan to do with you?"

"Either that or hand me over to Colonel Winslow and let him do it," she answered, rubbing her arms for warmth.

Chuckling, Justin looked past her at the man tugging on the oars. "Did you hear that, Callahan? My reputation has grown a little out of proportion. It seems everyone thinks I'd lower myself to murdering a helpless woman."

"And why wouldn't you?" Dara snapped irritably. "Lord knows how many men you've killed already and it seems to me any man willing to murder the President of the United States isn't above ending the life of a mere woman."

"If that's true, Miss Brandon," he grinned impishly, "would you mind telling me why I bothered pulling you from the water? Or for that matter, why I shot one of the men chasing you?"

Unable to answer, she stared back at him in silence.

"And why not consider this," he continued, amused. "If your life is so unimportant to me, why didn't I take you with me to visit Colonel Winslow? He offered quite a substantial amount of money for you."

Suddenly Dara knew the reason, and she returned

71

his smile. "Because you think I know where my brother is. What good would I be to you dead or in Colonel Winslow's custody?"

Justin nodded. "Very astute, Miss Brandon."

"Thank you," she replied sarcastically. "Now answer this. If I were able to lead you to Lane, what would you do with me then?"

Cradling one elbow in his hand, he scratched his chin thoughtfully. "Hmmm. That's a good question. I guess I hadn't really thought about it."

Dara's chin rose haughtily at her small victory, while she watched him grab the bottom rung of the rope ladder leading to the deck above. After securing their boat to the side of the ship, he looked back at her, a serious expression on his handsome face.

"But I suppose that depends on what transpires between us before then."

Every hair on the back of her neck stood up. She knew exactly what he'd implied, and oddly enough she decided drowning might be more pleasant. She waited until he looked away again, then tossed the cloak from her shoulders and sprang to her feet, ready to jump. But as she lifted a tiny foot onto the side of the rowboat, she heard Callahan shout his captain's name, and in the next instant, a hand clamped onto the many folds of skirt covering her slender backside, yanking her back down. She tumbled to the bottom of the boat.

"If you don't want to be bound and gagged, and hauled onto the ship like a bale of cotton at the end of a rope, Miss Brandon, I'd suggest you get up and start climbing that ladder," Justin snarled. "But one way or another, you will board my ship and you'll do it now!"

"I . . . I can't," she whimpered. "It's too high. I haven't the strength."

Justin glared at her a moment then leaned back to shout up to one of the men watching from above.

"Phillips, toss me down a line."

"Aye, aye, Cap'n," came the reply.

But before the man could fulfill the order, Dara clumsily struggled to her feet. "All right!" she choked out through her tears. "I'll try but I'll probably fall."

Brushing past him, she grabbed hold of the ladder, slipped a toe on the first rung, and started up. One by one, she climbed the steps, pausing each time to jerk the hem of her skirts out of the way and to mutter a few words no one else could hear. After what seemed an eternity, she neared the top and allowed Phillips to take both of her wrists to help her up the rest of the way. But once she stood safely on the deck, she yanked free of him and glared angrily at the tall figure who climbed on board a moment later. She watched him turn to help his first mate aboard.

"Weigh anchor, Callahan," Justin ordered, once the man stood beside him. "I think we've pressed our good fortune far enough for one night."

"Aye, aye, Cap'n." Callahan agreed with a nod and turned to see the order carried through.

"As for you," Justin continued, his gaze falling on the young woman who stood shivering beside him, "I suggest we get you out of those wet clothes before you catch a chill. I may have saved your foolish life twice, but if you get a fever, I can't guarantee I could do it again. I'm not a doctor."

"N-no. J-just a traitor and m-murderer," she mumbled, twisting out of his reach when he started to take her elbow.

"You haven't known me long enough to accuse me of such things, Miss Brandon, and you don't strike me as one who listens to gossip," he replied, his voice low. "Maybe you should wait before you pass judgment."

"The g-gossip I heard came from your own l-lips, Captain Whitelaw." As she rebuked him she noticed his questioning glance. "You're looking for my b-brother, are you not?" She waited for his nod before going on. "You told me he was a witness at your trial. That makes you a traitor. And I m-may be foolish, but I'm not stupid. You w-want to find him and have your revenge. That will make you a m-murderer."

"If you really believe that, then you've also decided that there isn't anything I wouldn't do to have my way, that there are no people I wouldn't hurt to achieve my goal."

"That's right," she said bravely.

"Then before your luck runs out, Miss Brandon, and you find out just how far I'll go, I suggest you turn around and head for my cabin."

A tiny sliver of moonlight spilled out from behind the clouds and fell against the stormy expression on his face, and Dara quickly realized he meant every word he'd said. She would have enjoyed snubbing him, defiantly standing her ground and daring him to make her do as he instructed, but Dara's courage only existed in her imagination when it came to defending her rights, no matter who issued the commands. Besides, she was too cold to argue and, without any money to pay for a room, she had nowhere else to go. She would accept his forced hospitality for now and contemplate her next move in the morning when they dropped anchor in another port. A vague smile touched her lips and disappeared. Hopefully that town would be on the opposite side of the bay. Without looking at him for fear he might read her thoughts, she bowed her head and followed him aft.

By the time they reached the cabin door, Dara's entire body shook uncontrollably and she silently wished the captain would quickly find the key that would let them inside. She would quietly listen to whatever he had to say, agree to any promises he might

74

request that she make, then send him on his way so that she could shed her wet clothes and climb into his bunk for warmth and a much-needed rest. But the instant he lifted the latch and swung the door open to display the shambles she had made of his cabin, she knew she was about to pay a second time for failing in her escape attempt.

Justin's tall frame stiffened the moment his gaze fell upon the disarray. Papers were strewn across the desk top and chair, each drawer hung open. His clothes were scattered over every inch of the cabin, his sea chest had been rummaged through, and his last bottle of whiskey lay broken on the deck. But what seemed to upset him more was the destruction of his bunk. Not only had the coverlet been ripped from it, but the sheets had been torn into shreds and tied together in long strips that dangled out of the porthole. Justin's blue eyes darkened as he took in the sight, his gaze shifting from one mess to another, then back again as if he couldn't believe what he saw.

Dara knew she should turn and run before the full impact of her venture struck home and his wrath descended upon her, but she experienced a calming satisfaction in what she had done even though her heart thumped loudly in her chest. To her way of thinking he deserved a great deal more than having his possessions vandalized. Here was a man who preyed on innocent people for whatever gain he could accomplish. He hadn't the slightest concern for their feelings or the hardships they might endure because of him. Causing a little disorder to an otherwise tidy room hardly compared, and she decided to point that out to him. She took a breath, ready to calmly discuss the issue, when his voice nearly rattled the timbers.

"What the hell have you done, woman?"

Dara stumbled backward, his seething fury canceling her desire to debate his shortcomings, for it seemed at this moment that her very life was in danger. "I . . . I . . ." she began, wondering if there was anything she could say to appease him and trembling violently when he turned his black rage upon her. But before she could voice an explanation of any kind, a huge hand shot out, grabbed a fistful of the soggy fabric covering her shoulders, and yanked her through the door. When he released her to lock them in, she hurried to the opposite side of the cabin, her knees weak and her breath labored, fearing what sort of punishment he would deem fitting for her crime. But once he turned back to face her, she noticed that his anger had lessened as he studied the chaos spread out before him. Several moments passed while she watched him assess the damage with his eyes, foolishly thinking he had excused the ruination of his belongings. Then she heard him sigh disgustedly, and knew she would not be forgiven so easily.

"Take off your clothes," he instructed, his tone flat, as he crossed to the small stove set in one corner of the room. Lowering himself to one knee, he opened the side loading door and proceeded to fill the compartment with kindling, ignoring the young woman who stared fearfully at his back. Once he had finished and a healthy blaze filled the cabin with warmth, he stood and turned to look at her, a frown crimping his brow when he discovered she hadn't moved. "Did you hear me?" he asked irritably. "I said take off your clothes."

"Y-Yes, I heard you," she answered, her voice shaky. "And if you think I'll do it without a fight, you're insane."

"A fight?" he repeated, dark brows drawn together. "Whatever are you talking about?"

"I'm not a whore, Captain Whitelaw. I won't strip for any man just because he wishes it. I've never kissed

76

a man, much less . . ." The words lodged in her throat. "What I did to your cabin is not worth what you want in return."

"What I want in return?" Justin parroted, totally confused. He took a second breath, about to ask her to explain when her meaning suddenly became quite clear, and he threw back his head and laughed loudly, making Dara retreat even farther. "All I want right now, Miss Brandon, is for you to get out of those wet things and warm yourself by the fire. You're too important to me at the moment for me to allow you to be ill."

Dara blushed a scarlet hue. "But I thought—"

"Well, you were wrong," he stated flatly and crossed to the bunk, where he stood a moment shaking his head. With a disapproving grunt, he snatched the rumpled quilt from the floor, turned to face her, and said, "Wrap yourself in this until your clothes are dry." He held the coverlet out for her to take.

Avoiding his eyes, Dara stepped close enough to accept the proffered item then quickly hurried to the stove, its warming affects already dulling her jittery nerves. After sneaking a peek at the captain to find he had gone to his desk and was busily absorbed in straightening the papers scattered on top, she draped the quilt around her shoulders and unfastened the buttons of her gown, letting it fall to her feet. A moment later, petticoats, stockings, and shoes followed, but Dara stubbornly refused to shed her camisole. Maybe he didn't intend to touch her, not now anyway, but she would feel a little safer with more than just a thin blanket protecting her. Glancing at him once more to discover that he was still preoccupied with his task, she quietly moved a chair closer to the stove and draped her garments over it to dry before sitting down on the deck. If she remained quiet, maybe he would forget she was there. And maybe if she wished hard enough, it would snow in August. Her lip curled at the absurdity of such an idea, and she huddled nearer the heat. Her fate was in his hands now. The smooth line of her brow wrinkled. If only she had the courage to demand her release . . . With a sigh, she pulled her long strands of auburn hair over one shoulder and squeezed the water from them.

The slamming of the porthole nearly startled Dara out of her blanket. Clutching it tightly to her, she worriedly looked in the direction of the sound, fearing Captain Whitelaw's temper had flared again. But to her relief, he had only untied the rope of torn sheets, tossed them through the window, and closed out the cool night air. She watched him a moment as he returned to his desk and pulled the bottom drawer open to withdraw two glasses from inside. Her curiosity obliged her to observe further, but when he turned toward her, she looked back at the orange glow of light peeking out between the cracks in the stove and merely listened to him set the glasses down and cross to the door. The key rattled in the lock and Dara looked up in time to see the portal swing shut behind him as he left the cabin. She barely had time to consider the motive for his strange behavior—why did he need the glasses if he meant to leave? . . . did he plan to return before morning?—when the latch clicked a second time and the striking figure of Captain Whitelaw filled the door frame once more. In his left hand, he carried a full bottle of whiskey. Dara's attention shifted back to the fire. Maybe he would get drunk and fall asleep; then while everyone else on board sought rest, she might be able to . . .

What? she thought irritably. *Jump over the side and drown while the ship sails down the bay? You fool. Don't you ever learn?*

A noise behind her drew her attention, and Dara's expression revealed her curiosity as she watched the captain pour a liberal amount of whiskey into the two glasses he had taken from his desk a moment ago. Replacing the stopper in the bottle, he shed his coat, lifted the drinks, and started toward her.

"Here," he said, handing one to her. "It will help."

Dara took the proffered glass only because he forced it into her hand, but the frown on her face showed her disapproval. "I . . . I don't drink whis—"

"Do as you're told." He scowled and walked past her to the bench. When he reached it, he let out an irritable sigh, then stooped to sweep away the contents scattered over the seat. Sitting down, he leaned back against the wall and stretched out his long legs, sending her a murderous glare as he raised the glass to his lips. He drank nearly all of it, closing his eyes as if to savor its effect and relaxing even more as if the weight of the world had been lifted from his shoulders.

Dara watched him, her mouth twisted in a slight snarl. She didn't like him any more than he liked her, and if he said one more thing to her, she was going to tell him so. He had no right to hold her prisoner. She hadn't done anything to him, and she certainly wasn't going to help him find her brother just so he could deal out whatever ghastly punishment he thought Lane deserved. If Lane had testified against this man, then Justin Whitelaw had to be guilty. Lane never lied. He'd always been an obedient son, minded his own business, and done an honest day's work. When he believed in a cause, he fought to defend it. That was why he'd joined the Navy. If he had discovered a traitor among the officers, he would not have been afraid to inform the higher officials even if doing so meant laying down his life. She was proud of her brother, and she would never aid anyone to search for him only to satisfy someone's desire for revenge. Justin Whitelaw would have to kill her before she would do anything he wanted.

"I told you to drink the whiskey."

Bright green eyes widened at the command and without hesitation Dara fearfully raised the glass to her mouth. She swallowed an amount similar to what she had seen the captain drink. Then a frown flitted across her brow when she saw the surprised look on his face and she wondered at the smile that replaced it. She had only done as he'd instructed. Why did he look at her as if she had sprouted two heads? Suddenly her stomach felt as if it were on fire. Not knowing what to expect next, she worriedly clutched her belly just as the inferno exploded, sending waves of scorching heat to engulf her throat and steal her breath away. Tears filled her eyes and she dropped the glass, gasping for air, certain the madman who shared the cabin with her had poisoned the drink he gave her. How could she have been so stupid? Was this what it felt like to die? If she could choke out the words and beg him to help her, would he do something to ease the pain? Oh God, it hurt so much! Gulping several times, she could feel the burning sensation subside a degree and she wondered what torture would follow. Would it be a slow death or would her next breath be her last? Tears streaming down her face, she glanced up at him. He hadn't moved! He just sat there. He was enjoying this! How could he be so cruel?

If God grants me one ounce of strength before I die, Justin Whitelaw, she silently vowed, *I'll . . . I'll . . .*

But her promise was never completed, for as she struggled with the words, the blazing furnace began to cool. Swearing never to miss Sunday worship again if He spared her, Dara's hands moved to her chest in an effort to ease her discomfort as she sucked in long, welcome gulps of air. Only a minute or two had passed but to Dara it felt as if she had just exhausted a year of her life. When she could breathe easily again, she lifted angry eyes to glare at the man who watched her with detached interest.

"You were only supposed to sip it," he pointed out casually, downing the remaining contents in his glass.

"How was I to know?" She coughed. "I . . . I told you that I had never drunk whiskey before."

Justin shook his head in disagreement. "What you said was, 'I don't drink whiskey'."

Dara opened her mouth to inform him that there was little difference as far as she was concerned and then she noticed that his eyes no longer held hers but had lowered to view something else that was obviously more interesting. Frowning, she dropped her gaze to the sight that intrigued him and discovered much to her dismay that during her encounter with the whiskey, she had unknowingly allowed the blanket to fall from her shoulders. The white cotton chemise, still wet from her recent swim in the bay, clung all too revealingly to her breasts and left little to the imagination. Dara's face flamed instantly and she let out a shriek as she frantically jerked the coverlet over her and turned back to the stove.

"If you were a gentleman, Captain Whitelaw . . ."

"You wouldn't be here unchaperoned," he finished in an easy drawl and slowly came to his feet. "But then I have no way of knowing if you're a lady either." He missed the bloodthirsty look she gave him as he crossed to his desk and refilled his glass. "But since neither fact is important, I suggest we get down to business." He turned to look at her, resting a hip along the edge of the desk, his wrists crossed over one knee and the glass dangling from his fingertips.

"And you wouldn't know a lady if she came up and slapped your face," Dara muttered half to herself, for her pride had been sorely injured with his callous remark.

"Is that what you'd like to do, Dara Brandon? Slap my face?"

Hostile green eyes glanced up at him, then concentrated on the narrow shafts of firelight spilling out from around the door of the stove. "Among other things," she mumbled, readjusting the blanket.

"Such as?"

"I'd like to turn you over to the authorities," she answered bravely, though she could not bring herself to look at him. His presence made her nervous and she wasn't sure whether that stemmed from the uncertainty of her future at his hands or whether the mere sight of him sparked a strange feeling in her. Whatever the cause, she planned to keep her distance.

"And if you did that, how would you ever find your brother?"

Long, auburn curls, still heavy with dampness, caught the glow of the fire when she turned her head to look at him. "What has he got to do with my wanting to see you back in prison?"

Straightening, Justin returned to his place on the bench. He sat knees apart, his elbows braced on his thighs as he leaned forward to look at her, his glass cupped in both hands. "What did you plan to do if someone in Washington told you that your brother had last been seen in . . . say . . . Boston? It's an awfully long way to walk, Miss Brandon. And by the time you arrived, he might already have sailed somewhere else." He sat up, took a sip of whiskey, and dropped back to lean against the wall, his eyes locked on hers. "That is of course if you're telling the truth and you don't already know where to find him."

"I *am* telling the truth," she moaned. "I don't *know* where Lane is. And if I have to, I'll walk the entire

United States until I find him."

He shrugged, not doubting the stubborn minx would try. "All right, let's agree you would, but unless you plan to steal, how will you feed yourself? If I'm correct, the only money you had was in the purse you left behind. And how about a bath now and then? Do you propose shedding your clothes along some riverbank? It would make an interesting sight for any man who just might happen by. And I think it's already been proven that you'd be defenseless in stopping him from having his way with you."

"I can take care of myself," she replied obstinately.

"Can you now?" he mocked, setting down his drink. "If my first mate hadn't come when he did, what did you plan to do?"

Dara looked away quickly, feeling the heat rising in her cheeks.

"You would have struggled until all your strength was gone and then I could have done whatever I wanted. And if it hadn't been me, it would have been some other man. You won't last a day by yourself."

"And what do you propose I do," she asked sarcastically, "join this ship?"

"Exactly," he nodded.

"Forget it," she exploded, awkwardly coming to her feet, the blanket slipping from one shoulder. "You're only pretending to be worried about me to scare me. You want me to stay with you because you think I'll lead you to my brother. Well, I won't. And like I already said, I can take care of myself." She turned her back on him and yanked her wet clothes from the chair.

"What do you think you're doing?" he asked, his tone hinting at his impatience.

"I'm getting dressed and going to Washington," she snapped, clumsily trying to keep the blanket draped around her while she stepped into her petticoats.

83

The task proved difficult and she expended more effort in readjusting the blanket than in hiking up the yards of heavy, damp material around her waist. She was just about to succeed when a wide hand shot out, curled its fingers in the waistband of her petticoats and jerked downward. Her own fingers, still numb from her late-night swim, could not hold on and she watched in frustrated silence as the fabric fell to a heap around her ankles. Before she could stoop to retrieve the garment, that same hand clasped her arm and spun her around.

"You're not going anywhere," Captain Whitelaw snarled, his dark brows drawn together in an angry frown. "You'd catch a chill just putting those wet things on and I can't afford to have you get sick."

Dara's own temper flared. "I'm not your property," she spat, twisting free of him. "I'll do what I want and you can't stop me."

"Oh, really?" he challenged, reaching for her again.

But Dara quickly moved out of the way, darting behind his desk, the blanket flying from her shoulders. She made quite a fetching sight, one Justin thoroughly enjoyed, and he relinquished his pursuit of her to feast his eyes on her instead. Long, auburn hair fell in wild disarray about her shoulders, and her pale skin glistened in the lamplight. But his attention was drawn to her full, firm breasts heaving against the thin fabric of her chemise, and to the way the cloth clung damply to her narrow waist and rounded hips. His blood stirred in his veins and his purpose quickly changed from simply teaching her a lesson to more pleasurable goals. With a vague smile on his lips, his fingers moved to the buttons of his shirt.

The color drained from Dara's face as she watched the captain slowly undo the fastening of that garment, exposing the bronzed muscles of his chest and the dark curls that covered it. He didn't have to tell her what he planned; she could see it clearly in the pale blueness of his eyes. She gulped, fighting back the fear that threatened to make her scream and race wildly around the room like a woman possessed. She had to remain calm. She had to think logically. He had already proven that his strength was greater than hers, but he hadn't demonstrated his ability to outguess her. That had always been her one advantage over Lane, and after all, wasn't this a man like her brother?

While the captain pulled his shirttail from the waistband of his breeches and slid the linen fabric from his broad shoulders, Dara frantically surveyed the cabin for a weapon to hurl at him. Only a foot or two to her left she spotted the washbasin he had used earlier while he'd shaved. Mentally, she calculated the steps it would take him to reach her once she lunged for the bowl and decided she could reach it first. But what she hadn't realized was that the captain had seen where her gaze had drifted and had realized her plan long before she moved. She waited, fighting to keep a smile of triumph from parting her lips; then she charged the small table that held the washbowl.

A startled, frightened squeal escaped Dara when her vision was obscured by a massive, thickly muscled chest sprinkled with black curls. How could he have known? And how could he have moved fast enough to cut her off? Suddenly, Dara knew that Justin Whitelaw was not just another man. He had been right in saying she was defenseless, that she wouldn't last a day on her own. In fact, she wouldn't last the night.

Her lower lip quivered and Dara experienced true panic. His huge frame blocked the way to the door, and even if it hadn't, she couldn't very well run around Cambridge dressed in nothing more than her chemise. Tears burned the backs of her lids and she expected to burst into heart-rending sobs at any moment. She had to do something, but she doubted crying would make any difference to Justin Whitelaw, a man who was a traitor, who stole for a living, and who had probably killed dozens of men. What would it matter to him that the young woman before him wanted nothing to do with him? Suddenly, an idea came to her, and she quickly backed away from him, stumbling over the desk chair in her way.

"Wait!" she called out urgently when he followed her moves. In desperation she slid the offending piece of furniture between them. "I . . . I have a bargain to offer."

His pale blue eyes darkened as he watched her, and Dara wondered if he had heard her at all for he stood perfectly still, his gaze slowly, lustfully traveling over every inch of her. Her flesh tingled at the suggestive gleam in his eyes, and she jumped when the long, lean fingers of his right hand captured the back of the chair and effortlessly set it from his path even though Dara clung desperately to it, fighting to keep it between them. A vague smile parted his lips and Dara felt a lump form in her throat when he started to advance. She raced to the other side of the desk.

"Didn't you hear me, you . . . you jackass?" Instantly, Dara regretted her words. Why did she have to call him a name? She swallowed hard and tried again. "Captain Whitelaw, I think you should hear me out." Her heart beat faster as he rounded the corner of the desk, and she hurriedly side-stepped to regain the distance she'd had before. "If you promise to leave me alone, I'll . . . I'll tell you where to find Lane." She smiled brightly at him, certain that was all it would take; then a chill bolted through her when he grinned all the more. Her smile vanished. "Isn't that all you really want, Captain Whitelaw?" she asked in a tiny, trembling voice.

His hair glistened a blue black as he slowly shook his head and took another step.

Only then did Dara realize that nothing would stop Justin Whitelaw from having his way with her. If she were to save herself, she would have to think of something else. Words would not stop him. Tears, she suspected, would merely amuse him. Biting her lower lip to still its quivering, she frantically scanned the surface of his desk, an excited rush of hope shooting through her when she spotted the butt of his pistol peeking out from beneath the debris scattered on top. Lunging for it before he could stop her, Dara scooped up the weapon in both hands, pointed the black bore at his chest, and stumbled away from him.

"Now maybe you'll listen to me," she said, feeling a false sense of security when Justin ceased the chase and straightened, the lust in his eyes fading. The dark scowl that replaced it worried her, however, and she raised the gun higher, its muzzle bobbing up and down. "Don't come any closer, Captain Whitelaw. I know how to use one of these."

"Put it down, Miss Brandon," he warned, his voice low and threatening.

"Or what?" she challenged carelessly. "I hardly think you're in a position to give orders. Move over there." She waved the pistol toward his bunk. When he didn't move, she struggled with the trigger to draw it back and cock the gun. "Now, Captain Whitelaw."

Justin's blue eyes turned cold as he glared at her and reluctantly he did as she bade, keeping his attention focused on her. "If you fire that pistol, my first mate will be here before you have a chance to run. And I guarantee he won't like finding his captain dead."

"Even so, that won't do you any good, will it?" she boasted, drawing courage from the advantage she held. "Now sit down."

She watched him do as she instructed, cautiously glancing to the deck to learn where her clothes had fallen. Hooking a toe in the yards of cloth, she hurriedly slid them in front of her, then bent to rearrange the petticoats so she could step into them while she continued to hold him at bay. That task proved simple enough, but the blue cotton dress posed a greater feat. The gown was still quite damp and heavier than usual. It would take both hands to put it on and that meant laying down the gun. A worried frown knotted the smooth line of her brow as she wondered how she would accomplish such an undertaking, and she glanced up to find the captain smiling crookedly back at her. She straightened indignantly, resenting the cocksure look he gave her as he leaned back to rest casually on one elbow and merely watch. Well, she'd show him that she wasn't as dim-witted as his expression implied.

Collecting the dress from the floor, she moved behind the desk and, with one wide sweep of her arm, cleared the top of its contents. In the center, she placed the gun where she could quickly grab it if he tried anything, its silver muzzle pointed at him. He was too far away to reach her before she could pick it up and aim it, even during the brief moment while her eyes would be covered as she dropped the gown over her head. She returned his stare, a sarcastic curl to her lips, and with remarkable agility, donned the garment before he had a chance to move. After fastening the buttons up the front, her eyes never leaving his, she reclaimed the pistol and stooped to pick up her stockings and shoes. As she headed for the door, her steps slowed when she realized Captain Whitelaw hadn't moved in the slightest. She wondered why he didn't try to stop her exit. Then her hand touched the latch. When it would not budge, she knew the reason.

"Where's the key, Captain?" she asked, aiming the pistol at him and silently praying her voice didn't sound as shaky as she thought it did.

Justin's handsome mouth lifted in a half smile. "In my pocket, Miss Brandon. And if you want it, you'll have to come and get it."

Dara's entire body tingled with apprehension and a nervous qualm sent a tremor down her spine. She swallowed the fear that tightened the muscles in her throat, took a deep breath, and let it out slowly. "Before or after I shoot you?"

Justin shrugged one shoulder. "Either way you'll never get through that door. As I said before, Douglas Callahan is in the cabin next to mine and he'd be standing in the hallway before you could get the key in the lock." Pushing himself up, he slowly rose to his feet and extended his hand. "Now give me the gun before you pay for your foolishness with your life."

Some of Dara's courage faded. "You . . . you won't let him kill me. I'm the only lead you have in finding my brother."

Grinning, he tilted his head back to gaze up at the ceiling. "If I'm dead, how will I stop him?" Light blue eyes found hers again. "Callahan wasn't convicted of treason. I was. He has no need to find your brother, but he is my friend and he wouldn't take kindly to anyone who murdered me. If you give me the gun right now, I won't tell him you tried."

Dara realized her battle was nearing an end, for without the key they could spend the next year staring at each other. By morning, Douglas Callahan would come looking for his captain and with two men to confront, she knew she could never escape. She'd give him the pistol—but only after they'd agreed on one thing. "All right," she said, "you can have the gun, but on one condition."

Justin raised a dark brow, waiting.

"In exchange for my help in finding Lane, you'll promise not to . . . to"—she cleared her throat and looked at the floor—"you know."

Justin's brows lowered. "I thought you said you didn't know where he was."

Dara dared not look at him. If he couldn't see the light coloring that rose in her cheeks, he would surely know the truth by studying her face. She had never been good at hiding a secret. "I lied," she answered quietly, then jumped when she heard the heels of his boots click against the deck as he stepped toward her. She glanced up and reaimed the pistol at him. "Only if you promise," she said in a rush, her voice nearly a whine.

Justin's wide shoulders drooped in disgust. "Woman, right now the thought of bedding a hellcat doesn't interest me. Now give me the damn pistol."

Dara opened her mouth to state her terms a third time only to have him glare heatedly at her before he jerked forward and snatched the weapon from her hand. The wrench of releasing the gun stung her fingers, bringing tears to her eyes, and she looked at the sealed portal, wishing somehow she could pass right through it. If she had suspected the captain's thoughts at the moment, she might have tried, for once he had carefully released the trigger and had locked the pistol in one of the desk drawers, his angry gaze took in the disastrous condition of his cabin.

"I've had a very long, tiring day, Miss Brandon"— his deep voice was impatient—"and although I've never raised a hand against a woman, you sorely tempt me." He turned to look at her. "If you don't care to learn whether or not I'll make an exception in your case, I suggest you get out of those wet things right now before I tear them from you."

Dara's eyes widened, her mouth dropping open at his tirade.

"And then I want you to straighten up this mess." He ranted on. "I want everything back the way it was before you played your little games. Do you understand?"

Dara quickly nodded, not wanting to know if he meant what he'd said, and hastily moved back to the stove, her gaze affixed on the glower he was bestowing upon her. With shaky fingers, she turned her back on him and fumbled with the first button on her gown. She let the bodice fall to her waist, retrieved the blanket from the place where she had dropped it, and twirled it around her shoulders before she untied the strings of her petticoats and allowed both garments to slip to the floor at her feet. Once again, she slid the desk chair nearer the fire and draped her wet clothes over it to dry.

Justin watched her hurried movements from his bunk after he had gotten a fresh drink, electing to retreat to a far corner out of her way. She had a knack for sparking his temper, and although he doubted he would ever strike a woman, he decided not to add to the risk of that possibility. He hadn't slept in two days, not since he had received the message that Lane Brandon had been seen near Cambridge, so his nerves as well as his temper were on edge. He figured it would only be another wild-goose chase. It seemed he'd been on too many during the last three months, but if he wanted to catch the man, he knew he would have to follow every lead, no matter how vague or unreliable the information might be.

Swinging his feet up onto the thick mattress, a knee bent to brace one wrist, he leaned back against the wall behind him and watched Dara submissively refold his clothes and put them back in a drawer. His contact in town had advised him that no one fitting Lane

Brandon's description had been seen anywhere near Cambridge and that just the week before he had gone to the Brandon farm to make certain the young man had not somehow gotten by him. Justin had half expected to hear a disappointing report, for it seemed his luck had been anything but good this past year. Then things had started to look brighter. Not only had he enjoyed the soft, rounded curves that had crashed into him in the alleyway, but the woman had turned out to be the one sure thing that would lead him to Lane Brandon.

Thinking of Dara again, he lifted tired eyes to study her as she fought to keep the blanket around her shoulders while she stacked the papers on his desk. He yawned, finished off his whiskey and set the glass on the deck next to him. He believed that she was going to Washington but he was doubtful as to her reason. At first, she'd claimed she didn't know where her brother was; then when he had backed her into a corner, she'd changed her story. Had that been done out of desperation or was she telling the truth? Folding his arms over his chest, he closed his eyes. Just as soon as she was finished cleaning up the cabin, he would have it out with her once and for all.

Chapter Four

Dara stirred uncomfortably in her bed, every muscle aching. Sunlight streamed into the room and pressed demandingly against her closed lids. Muttering to herself, she pulled the blanket up over her head, hoping to block out the bright rays of morning, but she nearly catapulted herself from the narrow bench when her mind cleared and she recalled the place where she had slept. Eyes wide, she fearfully studied the cabin, the coverlet clutched beneath her chin. The fire in the stove had dwindled to glowing embers that radiated little heat, and she shivered in the cool, crisp air, her attention immediately falling on her clothes hanging from the back of the chair where she had put them the night before. Nervously, she glanced at the bunk on the opposite wall. Captain Whitelaw still slept soundly. If she was quiet and moved about with care so as not to disturb him, she might be able to dress and leave before he awoke.

Her gaze concentrated on his still form, she tiptoed to the chair by the stove, dropped the blanket, and quickly stepped into her petticoats. A moment later she was fastening the buttons on the front of her gown. Then she hurriedly donned her stockings and slippers. Her nose wrinkled disapprovingly as she studied her attire. The blue cotton dress looked as if she had worn it to bed, and she didn't have to see her image in a mirror to know how dreadful her hair must look. Mentally shrugging that off as unimportant since she would be back home again before dusk, she moved to the door but drew back suddenly as if it radiated a burning heat. Until this moment she had forgotten why she had been forced to stay on board the ship. Her previous examination of the cabin had not revealed a second key.

Glancing at the large portholes where she had made her earlier attempt to escape, she quickly abandoned the idea of trying again. With the kind of luck she'd had so far, she would surely drown if she tempted fate a second time. With a disgusted curl of her lip, her gaze fell upon the broad, muscular back Justin Whitelaw presented to her, and a devious smile lifted the corners of her mouth. He had the key. All she would have to do was take it from him. Inhaling deeply, she silently approached the unmoving form.

Obviously, Captain Whitelaw had slept through the night. After he had ordered her to clean his cabin, he had refilled his glass and retired to his bunk, not bothering to remove his boots. Dara noted that he still wore them. She also noticed how tightly the black breeches clung to his muscular hips and thighs, and the sinewy ripples of his arms and shoulders before her gaze timidly traced the curve of his suntanned back. A warmth spread through her. Lane often had worked in the fields of their small farm without a shirt, but the sight of him stripped of that garment had never affected her this way. She was uneasy, confused by her newfound awareness. An angry frown lined her brow, and she set her attention on finding the key.

Dara's heart nearly stopped when Justin suddenly rolled to face her, his eyes still closed in slumber. She waited a moment, holding her breath and closely watching the rise and fall of his chest to make certain he wouldn't wake up at any second. Before she could stop it that strange sensation began to seep through her again. Lane's chest was hairless, but this man's had a thick covering of tiny curls that spread from one shoulder to the other then narrowed to a thin line and disappeared beneath his breeches. Dara could feel a pounding at the base of her throat. She closed her eyes, swallowed hard, and silently scolded herself for letting her mind stray. If she hesitated much longer before obtaining the key from his pocket, she was certain he would awake and show her how strong he truly was.

Collecting her wits once more, she straightened determinedly and leaned forward slightly to examine his attire. She was certain the key wasn't in his pocket, for the fabric lay smoothly across his taut belly and displayed no hidden object beneath. Her shoulders drooped in dismay. Without disturbing his sleep, she would have to get him to roll over again and expose his other hip. Resting one elbow on the wrist of her other arm, she tapped her chin with a fingertip while she contemplated the execution of her feat and absently looked past him to the mattress. Dara's eyes widened, her chin dropped, and she quickly pressed both hands against her mouth to still a shriek of joy. There, shining brightly in the ray of sunshine spilling into the cabin, lay the key.

Hands clasped in prayer, she silently thanked her Maker and grinned excitedly as she started to reach across the sleeping captain. But her smile slowly faded and a worried frown darkened her green eyes. There was no way she could reach it without resting a knee on the bed. In fact, she doubted even that would do it. Tears filled the lower rim of her lashes as she studied the tiny piece of metal. To grasp it she would have to climb over the captain and that most certainly wouldn't work. If she touched him, it would be all over. Still, she had to try. She had to get away and warn the authorities of the plot to kill President Jefferson. Maybe, in exchange, they would help her find Lane and she could tell him of the evil man who hunted him. How their father needed to see him, and how she loved him, and . . .

Stop! she silently cautioned herself. *You can't go to pieces now. You've got to be strong. You can do this. You can get the key and be off the ship before he stirs. You can!*

Blinking away her tears, she drew herself up and studied the situation before her. The captain's bunk, built into one wall, was completely surrounded on three sides. If she wanted that key she would have to climb over him. And right now she wanted that key more than anything. With determination born of a desperate need, she moved to the foot of the bed. Grabbing a fistful of her skirt in one hand and placing the other on the decorative molding carved into the side of the cabin, she raised her hem and gingerly pulled herself up to stand on the mattress at his feet, crouching so that she wouldn't hit her head on the low ceiling. He didn't move, but Dara's heart pounded wildly in anticipation. Holding her breath, she lowered herself to one knee and slowly reached out, her eyes affixed to this sleeping face. Then disaster struck.

Although his eyes remained shut, Justin stretched, then twisted and rolled Dara's way a second time. But before his body covered the key, she quickly snatched it up, and then froze, watching him shift about. However, once he had settled down again, Dara discovered that her skirt was trapped beneath one of his long, lean legs. With her goal so close, it was all she could do to keep from screaming out loud or pounding her fists against his leg, and her panic ran high.

You can do it, she told herself. *Just . . . stay . . . calm.*

For safekeeping, Dara tucked her treasured possession inside the bodice of her gown. She'd come this far and she wasn't about to lose the key again. Resting back on her heels, she grabbed her skirt and slowly started to pull it from beneath the captain, watching him all the while. When the last inch of cloth was freed, she relaxed and let the beating of her heart slow. Now she must climb down from the bed, go to the door, and unlock it. If the captain of the ship still dozed, probably his men did too, so leaving the vessel would be the easy part.

Pushing herself up, she concentrated on stepping over Justin Whitelaw's feet, one hand pressed against the wall at her side for balance. She glanced up at the door for encouragement then back at the captain, a smile on her face, longing to voice her farewell. Then she froze. Pale blue eyes received her message, but obviously they did not share her enthusiasm. Dark brows hooded his intense stare and his mouth was set in a hard line.

"Please, Miss Brandon," he said rising onto one elbow, "correct me if I'm mistaken, but I thought you had no desire to find yourself where you are now."

Dara gave a nervous laugh, hoping to distract him. Her mind raced for some sort of answer that he would believe as she slowly edged her way toward the side of the bed. "I . . . I . . . ah . . ."

"Don't bother lying." He sighed and sat up, his knees bent and his wrists draped over them. "I have a good idea what you were after." He held out a hand. "Now why don't you give it back to me before I'm obliged to take it from you."

"It?" she mocked, forcing a smile. "What 'it'?"

The muscle in his cheek flexed and he looked away.

"Miss Brandon, we've only just met. Until now I've been in an exceptional mood, but I think I should warn you that I am never good natured in the morning."

"Oh, that's all right," she replied as pleasantly as possible, taking another step. "I understand. My father is always that way. I'll just leave you—"

"Don't move another inch!"

Dara halted instantly, her wide, green eyes staring back fearfully at him. Yet she was ready to spring if the moment presented itself.

"I want it, Miss Brandon, and I want it now," he growled through clenched teeth.

She gulped, leaning back against the wall for aid when her knees shook and threatened to buckle beneath her. "I . . . I don't know what you—"

Before she could finish, Justin lunged at her and grabbed the waistline of her dress to pull her down on the bunk with him. She screamed, fighting with every ounce of strength she had, but he seemed to have a thousand hands. Suddenly she feared for her life rather than the loss of the key. The tussle lasted only a moment before he had subdued her. His huge frame straddled her hips, and his powerful hands were clamped around her wrists which he held at her sides. His blue eyes darkened to a violet hue as he glared at her and Dara wondered if she would perish beneath his murderous glower.

"Where is the key, Miss Brandon?" he asked, each word slow and precise.

Without thinking, her gaze went to the bodice of her gown. In the next instant, both her hands were in one of his and raised above her head while his fingers worked the buttons of her dress.

"No!" she wailed, straining to push him from her, but his weight held her down and she could only whimper her disapproval and fear. "Oh, please,

Captain. Stop and I'll give it to you."

Justin's angry eyes glanced up briefly at her, then settled once more on his task, and Dara held her breath as he boldly ran his hands over her breasts in search of the key. Fortunately for Dara, it had fallen between the layers of her dress and chemise, and he found it without much effort. But everywhere his fingers had touched, her flesh burned and she fought the whimper that threatened to escape her lips.

Slipping the key back into his pocket, he lifted himself from her and stood, yanking Dara to her feet to stand before him. "I'll not tolerate your thievery, Miss Brandon," he snarled, still holding tightly onto her wrist.

Dara trembled, not only from fear but from the warm feeling his closeness aroused. The strong fingers clutching her arm branded her and she prayed he would release her. Then his words penetrated her ruffled state.

"I wasn't going to steal anything," she argued, tears choking her. "I only wanted the key so I could leave. You're the pirate, not me. *You're* the one who steals."

Justin's blue eyes narrowed, his gaze intense, but Dara would not be intimidated.

"You're a traitor, a murderer, and a kidnapper. What right have you to label me when all I want is to be free of you? What injustice have I caused you that you should hold me prisoner?" Drawing courage from his silence, she tried to pry his hand loose. His grip tightened and Dara winced with pain.

"I am a traitor because your brother made it so. I've never killed anyone who didn't deserve it. And if you weren't so intent on leaving and would agree to help me find your brother, you would not be a prisoner on this ship but a guest. Not to mention the fact that the moment you step foot on soil again, one of the colonel's men will spot you and your life will end rather cruelly. Grow up, Dara Brandon. You're living in a man's world, and just because you don't like the way things are doesn't mean they're going to change because you want them to."

Dara stiffened, and glared back at him. "Are you married, Captain?"

The anger faded from his face. "No," he replied, one brow lifted curiously.

"It's no wonder," she answered sarcastically. "What woman would want you?"

Dara could feel the sudden rage that engulfed his entire body. It frightened her and at the same time gave her a great satisfaction. Could there possibly have been a woman in his life—one who rejected him? Had she unwittingly spoken the truth and touched a slow healing wound in his heart? She hoped so, for this man intended to kill Lane. If he could be so callous, so could she. At every opportunity she would see to it that her words rekindled his painful memories.

A pleased smile started across her face until she saw the dangerous look in his eyes, the flare of his nostrils, and the way he ground his teeth. Did he plan to strike her? Shrinking back, she pulled at the steel grip holding her, and panic coursed through her veins when he suddenly reached out, caught the hair at the nape of her neck, and yanked her to him. His lips were on hers, hot and demanding, as he pressed her body against his own hard frame and a wild ecstasy exploded within her. The bodice of her gown lay open from their earlier encounter, exposing her thinly clad breasts, and she could feel the rock hard muscles of his chest pressed against her, the contact burning her flesh. Her head began to spin when his mouth moved hungrily over hers, his tongue forcing her lips apart before darting inside, and she moaned fearfully, realizing he would

100

not stop with just a kiss.

When his hand moved to caress the length of her spine and pull her hips to his, Dara twisted her mouth from the searing osculation, but she was unable to draw breath to demand that he stop, nor did she have the strength to push him away. No one had ever touched her in this manner, and she discovered the experience both frightening and pleasurable. For one fleeting instant she had wondered if she truly wanted it to end. Yet when he bent and swooped her into his arms, the romantic splendor of the moment vanished.

"No!" she howled. "Please! Don't do this!"

Arms and legs thrashing wildly, Dara thought he had reconsidered forcing himself on her, had possibly felt pity when he'd seemed to relax and the color of his eyes had softened to a pale shade. Then she felt herself being dropped from his arms, the breath knocked from her as she landed hard on his bunk. She pushed herself up onto her elbows and stared back at him as he stood near the edge of the bed, his face expressionless, his body tense.

"'Twould be more fitting, Dara Brandon," he said, his voice low, "to say there is no woman I would want outside of bed. And if you'd prefer not to become one more of the many before you, I'd suggest you learn to curb your tongue. You wouldn't like what you found out."

The smooth line of her brow wrinkled. "What . . . what do you mean?"

He smiled one-sidedly, though his eyes remained cold. "That you'd enjoy it. You're no different from the rest."

"*I would not!*" she fumed indignantly, sitting up. Then, noticing that his gaze had lowered to the open bodice of her dress, she quickly jerked the fabric shut and began fastening the buttons. "Least of all

101

with you!"

Dara's careless statement in regard to his bachelor-hood had struck a tender spot in Justin's pride, one he was certain she had only guessed at. Yet obviously, she had taken great delight in pressing the point home. He had to admit she was a very beautiful woman and most alluring as she sat there, head bowed over her task and long, coppery curls cascading down her shoulders. She couldn't be more than eighteen and was quite naïve about men or she wouldn't so easily have placed herself in such compromising situations. If things had been different . . . if they had met years ago before his trouble had started, he might have found her innocence refreshing. As it was, her flippant nature only aggravated him. She needed to be taught that a lady didn't say the first thing that came to mind, that she should think before she offered her opinion. Someday, someone would do that for her—someone who had the patience and desire to do so. A lazy smile crept over his mouth. Did he have anything better to do at the moment? He sat down on the edge of the bunk.

Dara's green eyes widened as she watched him tug off his boots. Her chin sagged when he stood up again and faced her, his fingers on the buttons of his breeches.

"W-what are you doing?" she shrieked, scrambling to the far corner of the bed.

Pausing, he glanced up at her with a shrug. "I'm going to prove it to you. That is what you wanted, isn't it?"

"No!" she shouted.

Suddenly Justin wondered if he had rescued a wildcat from the hands of those ruffians the night before instead of a half-grown woman, for Dara had taken off one of her slippers and had braced herself on her knees, waiting for him to advance, ready to club him with the shoe once he came too near. The sight she presented was far removed from any seductive temptress he could imagine, and he couldn't stop the laughter that spilled forth.

"That's all this is to you, isn't it Captain Whitelaw, just a game? You think it's amusing to . . . to force yourself on a woman," she bristled.

Justin cleared his throat and rubbed his fingertips along the corner of his mouth in an effort to resume his composure. "Not at all, Miss Brandon," he replied. "In fact, I have never yet forced a lady."

"Then why not take pride in that and leave me alone!"

"But that's just the point. I won't have to."

"Ohhh!" Dara raged, hurling the slipper at him.

The poorly thrown missile glanced off Justin's arm before he had a chance to duck out of the way, but it failed to cause him any discomfort since the shoe was made of a soft fabric. Smiling at her attempt, he bent a knee to the edge of the bed.

"Stay away," she warned, twisting about in an effort to remove her other shoe.

"Why, Miss Brandon?" he asked. "Are you afraid to find out it's true?"

Slipper in hand, she hesitated, glaring back up at him. "You're the one who should be afraid," she challenged.

"Me?" he countered. "Of what?"

"That you'll be the one proven wrong. What makes you think every woman you meet finds you attractive?"

Easing his huge frame down onto the bed, he argued, "That's not what I said nor meant. There have been many women who have preferred another man's company to mine. But no matter who they share a bed with, the result is always the same. They enjoy being held in his arms. And," he added, moving close enough to reach out and capture the hem of her skirt when the time was right, "you're no exception."

"Oh, yes I am," she rallied hotly.

Justin raised a dark brow. "You mean there has been a man who didn't satisfy you?"

Dara's face flamed. "I've never . . . I mean . . . I haven't . . ."

"Been with a man before," he finished and waited for her to nod. "Then how do you know for certain?"

"Ohhh! This conversation has gone on long enough, Captain Whitelaw," she snapped, scooting toward the edge of the bed. But just as she was about to swing her legs to the floor, she felt an unrelenting tug on her dress and looked back to find it trapped in his long, lean fingers, a devilish gleam in his blue eyes.

"I think we should find out," he murmured, and Dara's pulse beat wildly, her heart pounding in her chest.

"Let go, Captain Whitelaw," she pleaded.

But Justin merely smiled and pulled her closer.

"Please," she tried again, her voice more urgent than before. This time she wouldn't be able to stop him with insults.

Panic raced through Dara when she felt herself slide toward the captain whose handsome face was aglow with mischief. His hands moved higher in the folds of her garment, catching the cloth covering her thigh and it was almost as if she could feel the heat of him radiating through the fabric. Her body went rigid. But when the fingers of his left hand curled around her ankle, ready to draw her beneath him, she let out a scream of terror and kicked frantically at the figure who had raised up on his knees. Then, with one swift jerk, he yanked her down onto the bed and fell between her parted thighs, trapping her wrists in his powerful grip and raising them above her head. Pale blue eyes stared into hers with a hypnotizing effect and Dara fought merely to breathe.

"Someday, Miss Brandon," he whispered, his breath falling warmly against her lips as he bent close, "you'll learn when to keep silent."

His mouth covered hers before she could tell him how detestable he was, that a gentleman would not . . . The thought vanished from her mind when his tongue played upon her lips, then parted them and pushed inside to taste her sweetness, and Dara lay unmoving. That all too damning sensation rose again and flooded through her, making her head spin with confused emotions. Some time ago she had begun to imagine what it would be like to have a man kiss her, hold her in his arms, touch her where he shouldn't; and she had to admit now that it was everything she'd dreamed it would be. He made her feel like a woman rather than the little girl her father always called her. Surrendering to the pleasurable sensations he evoked, she relaxed, savoring the feel of him pressed against her. She longed to free her hands so she might drape her arms around his neck and pull him closer. She moaned softly when his mouth left hers to taste the silken skin beneath her ear and trail burning kisses down her throat, too caught up in the rapture of the moment to feel his agile fingers undo the buttons of her gown. But when his lips moved on to the valley between her breasts, and a warm hand pulled at the cloth of her chemise to free a rose-hued peak, her daydreams were shattered.

"No!" she sobbed. Straining to push him from her, she had a startling experience when her thigh touched the evidence of his desire. "Oh, God, no!"

"I won't hurt you," he breathed, seemingly indifferent to her cries for mercy, his hand entwined in the layers of her skirts as he slowly raised them to her hips.

"Don't! Don't touch me!" she shouted, struggling to

lower her hemline in a futile attempt to regain what modesty she had left.

But he captured her wrists once more and placed both hands above her head as he stared down into her tear-filled green eyes. She was indeed the most beautiful woman he had ever seen, so young, so frightened. She could fill the long, lonely hours that had become his life of late. He hadn't lied when he'd said he had never made love to a lady against her will, and he couldn't understand now what drove him to do so. He wanted her whether she agreed or not, and at the moment, he didn't care if he'd be guilt-ridden every time he looked at her. There was something fresh about her: about her honesty, her spunk, her blind impetuous drive to reach her goals no matter how impossible the odds. Strangely enough she reminded him of himself. After all, wasn't his mission just as challenging, and with a little hope of success? Yet she had set out to accomplish her objective unselfishly, with no thought to the consequences she would encounter along the way. His dark brows came together. Damn the price she would pay. She must have known the chances she was taking in traveling alone. Why should he accept the blame? Well, he wouldn't. He would make love to her, use her, then send her on her way. Freeing her hands, he locked his fingers on the thick mass of auburn hair adorning her face and lowered his mouth to hers, hardly aware of the tiny fists pounding against his shoulders. His passion mounted, lust spurring him on, and he was about to pull her garments from her struggling form when a loud knock sounded on the door of his cabin.

Angrily, he raised his head and shouted, "Who is it?"

"Callahan, Captain," the first mate's voice replied, muffled through the thick oak door. "I brought your breakfast. Figured you and the lady were hungry."

"If you only knew how much," he muttered, feeling his desire die. With a sigh, he looked back at the bright green eyes staring fearfully at him and a smile crept into his voice. "We're not finished, Miss Brandon, I promise you," he whispered and slowly lowered his head to taste their kiss once more, relinquishing the embrace only after his first mate called out to him again.

Pushing up from her, he stood, took the key from his pocket, and went to the door. Unlocking it, he pulled the portal open and extended his arm in a wide sweep of the room to bid the intruder enter.

Douglas Callahan's bright smile fell upon his captain and vanished almost immediately when he saw the irksome scowl on the man's face, his gaze darting instinctively to the bunk. His shoulders drooped and he regretted his decision to bring a tray of food to the captain's quarters rather than have their guest make an appearance in the galley once he saw the young woman's ruffled attire. A scarlet hue stained her cheeks as she frantically tried to button her dress, and what Callahan had interrupted was obvious. But he didn't understand why his untimeliness had upset Justin so. This wasn't the first occasion on which Callahan had appeared at the wrong moment. There had been several. But his captain had never seemed to mind before. What made it different this time? Clearing his throat, he looked back at Justin.

"I . . . ah . . . didn't . . ."

"Mmm," Justin nodded. "You do seem to have a flair for showing up at the most inopportune moment."

"I can leave," Callahan offered in a whisper.

"Only if you go without the tray," Justin replied, leaning his shoulder against the edge of the open door, one hand perched on his hip. "For some strange reason I've lost my appetite for anything other than food."

"I'm sure it will return." Callahan half grinned and

stepped past his friend to place the tray on the desk. "We should reach Norfolk in a few hours. Are you planning on going ashore?"

"Not right away. In fact, I'm rather hoping I won't have to."

"Why's that, Cap'n?" Callahan asked, turning back to look at him.

Straightening, Justin idly walked to the desk, studied the selection of food Callahan had brought, then poured himself some tea and sat down in the chair. Leaning back, he plopped his feet on the corner of the dark oak desk and crossed his ankles as he took a drink, blue eyes gazing out across the rim of the cup at his first mate.

"Because Miss Brandon and I were just discussing whether or not she was intending to help us find her brother when you decided it was time for breakfast."

"Oh," Callahan said, laughter tugging at the corners of his mouth. "Is that what you were doing? I didn't know talking could be so strenuous."

Glancing past him, Justin viewed the delicate creature huddled on his bed. "With Miss Brandon it takes a great amount of energy not to wring her pretty little neck."

"A bit of trouble, is she?" Callahan chuckled.

"That is an understatement," Justin replied dryly. "If I didn't suspect she knew more than she claims, I wouldn't hesitate to toss her overboard. But somehow I don't think the fish would even want her."

"Well, you could always give her to Colonel Winslow," Callahan pointed out. "I'm sure he'd be glad to have her."

A smile gleamed in Justin's eyes. "Yes, he would. And if she doesn't give me the answers I want to hear, I'll do just that." He raised his cup to his lips again, watching an angry frown deepen on Dara's brow and the way her lips moved as she muttered some imprecation. "Was there something you'd like to say, Miss Brandon?"

Unaware that she had been observed, Dara looked up in surprise, her face still glowing from their earlier rencontre, and saw the stern expression he gave her. He seemed to be daring her to argue. His threats and his domineering nature rankled her and sparked a need to prove that she would not be so easily daunted. He could bloody well rot in hell before she'd cower at his feet. She raised her chin.

"I said that would be a quick death compared to the slow agony you've subjected me to." Her green eyes flashed sparks at the first mate when Callahan laughed heartily.

"I say, Cap'n, I do believe you've got yourself a handful with this one." He chuckled, shaking his head as he turned for the door. "Well, I'll leave you two alone to decide who's gonna give the orders around here. I'd like to stay and watch but if I don't get topside pretty soon, the damn crew will run the ship aground." Grabbing the latch as he passed by, Callahan threw back over his shoulder, "Should be interesting to see who wins."

Justin's mouth kinked into a sarcastic grin as he watched the door click shut behind his mate; then he turned to bestow a dour look upon the occupant of his bunk, his expression changing to bewilderment when he witnessed her hurriedly leave the bed and race for the porthole.

"Where's Norfolk?" she demanded, her eyes trained on the vastness of the blue-green plane of water spread out before her.

"Not far from Williamsburg," he answered cautiously.

"Virginia?" she shrieked, spinning around. "But you

were supposed to take me across the bay! I don't want to go to Norfolk."

Dropping his feet to the floor, Justin leaned forward and took one of the plates from the tray, ignoring her outburst. "What you want, Dara Brandon, is unimportant," he said simply, setting aside his cup to reach for a fork. "Now I suggest you eat some of this before it gets cold."

"But you don't understand," she moaned. "I've got to get to the capital."

Popping a fork full of scrambled eggs into his mouth, Justin eyed her wryly. "To meet your brother?" he asked after a while.

Dara instantly opened her mouth to refute the claim, then thought better of it. Maybe if she tricked him into thinking Lane was there, he would take her to Washington in the hope of catching him. Then if she could escape him, she would warn the authorities that the feared pirate Justin Whitelaw was in the area and that he planned to murder the president. She might also find someone who knew where Lane was. She bowed her head in feigned defeat.

"I can't hide anything from you, Captain," she sighed.

Justin nearly choked on the piece of ham he was swallowing. Reaching for his cup of tea, he washed it down and looked up at her. Her ploy was quite obvious. "No you can't, Miss Brandon. Now suppose you tell me the real reason you are so desperate to get to Washington."

Green eyes looked back at him in surprise. How could he have known? What kind of man was this Justin Whitelaw? Anger and frustration tightened the muscles in Dara's throat and she suddenly wanted to cry. She had only been gone from her home for one day, but so much had happened. She wanted to tell him the truth: if she didn't find Lane soon and bring him home, their father would surely die. But Justin Whitelaw wouldn't care. He was looking for her brother too—only he wanted to kill him. Maybe if she told him everything she might strike a sympathetic cord in that toughtened heart of his. After all, what was left for her to do? And maybe with a few tears . . .

"All right, Captain," she began, head down, her hands clasped in front of her, "I'll tell you. My brother and I lived on a small farm outside Drawbridge with our parents. For years my father tried to make something out of that worthless piece of land, but he could only manage enough to keep his family fed. Still, we had a lot of love. He and our mother came here from England because he thought America would make him rich. He became bitter when he failed, but he never blamed this land and its people. He blamed himself . . . for a lot of things." Glancing briefly at the captain to make certain she had his attention, she went to the bunk and sat down on the edge, staring at her hands resting on her knees. "When England and France went to war and blocked trade with America, Lane announced that he was going to join the Navy and help fight for our trade rights. Father didn't want him to go. He said he needed him to help with the farming, but I suspected he had a different reason. He was afraid. He loved his son very much and didn't want Lane killed. He never told Lane the real reason and they fought bitterly. Then, one day, Lane announced that he was leaving, that he had joined the Navy and would sail within the week. That was a year ago."

Tears welled up in Dara's eyes at the memory and she suddenly realized there was no need for trickery. She wept because she felt the hurt her father had tried to hide. Rising, she went to a porthole and stared out across the water.

"Five days ago we received word that Lane had been captured by the British. My father hasn't said a word since. Somehow he blames himself for what happened to his son, and now he just sits in a rocking chair on the front porch and stares off into space. My mother and I had to force him to eat and go to bed at night. He's killing himself, Captain Whitelaw, and if I don't find Lane soon and take him home, he'll succeed." Drawing a ragged breath, she turned to look at him. "I was on my way to the capital in the hope of finding someone who could give me a clue as to where I might start looking for Lane. I don't know where he is or for that matter if he's still alive. Now maybe you'll understand why I refused to help you find him. You want to kill him. And if you do, it will be the same as sentencing my father to death. You will have killed them both."

Justin met her eyes, which glistened brightly with tears, and held them for several moments before he looked away and reached for a cheroot in the box on his desk. Lighting it, he watched the white smoke curl upward as he contemplated her story, wondering how much of it to believe. Callahan had verified most of it. She did, indeed, live near Drawbridge with her parents on a failing farm, and Lane Brandon had joined the Navy to fight against the British. He had been assigned to Justin's ship and had been one of his best crewmen. The boy had constantly talked of his loyalty to the United States and he'd fought with a vigor that confirmed it, sometimes almost carelessly, as if his life was of minor importance compared to freedom for the United States. Justin recalled that he had decided if Lane were to take on the entire British navy alone, he would win. That was what had made Lane's testimony at the trial so strange. He had sworn before God and his country that Justin Whitelaw was a traitor.

Captain Whitelaw made it a practice never to

befriend members of his crew, but Lane Brandon's enthusiasm for the cause was infectious. They had spent a lot of time together, talking of battle plans, politics, and the promise of a bright future as a seaman for Lane. He was constantly at Justin's side, and more than anyone else, he knew that his captain was not guilty of the charges brought against him. So what had happened? What had made the boy lie?

After the trial Justin had been sentenced to prison to await execution. His crew had been disbanded, assigned to other ships, and Lane Brandon had vanished. First Mate Douglas Callahan had also been accused of treasonous acts against the country, but he'd not been as heavily guarded as Justin. He had escaped, hoping to find the boy and beat the truth from him before his captain was hanged. When time ran out and Callahan hadn't a clue to Brandon's whereabouts, he had contacted the members of Justin's crew who had argued on their captain's behalf at the trial. He'd felt some of them would want to right the awful wrong wrought against their captain. Callahan and several of these men got together, and they arranged Justin's escape from prison.

Knowing that it was too dangerous to remain in Washington, Justin and this handful of faithful companions left the capital. The trial had been a mockery of justice, and they soon realized that not only had Lane Brandon lied, but that the magistrate and jurors were equally corrupt. Only one place offered them safety for a while, so they worked their way north to Provincetown, Massachusetts—Justin's home.

Sinclair Whitelaw, Justin's father, had owned one of the largest shipping fleets in the state. He had been a powerful, domineering man who had ruled his family as he did his company, with a strong hand and an unyielding nature. When his eldest son had announced, on the day of his twentieth birthday, that he planned to join the Navy rather than work for his father, Sinclair Whitelaw had disowned Justin. But as the years had gone by and the old man's health had begun to fail, Sinclair had sent for his disobedient offspring. He had hoped to persuade him to reconsider, lest he be forced to place his shipping lines in the hands of his second son, Stewart. But Justin, being of the same mold as his father, had stubbornly refused. He had chosen the life he wanted to live and no threats would change his mind. He'd remained firm even when he'd been summoned to his father's deathbed and told that the old man feared his youngest son's ability to manage such a great empire.

Sinclair Whitelaw had always demanded perfection of himself and he'd demanded it from others. The day his wife had presented him with another son he'd exploded in a violent rage. The birth had been difficult and Stewart had suffered because of it. His left leg had been grossly deformed and his father had shunned him for that reason. To be forced to leave his life's work to a cripple was more than he could bear. But Justin had been firm. He knew that his brother would succeed, for Stewart had a quick mind and good business sense, something that would help Whitelaw Shipping grow. What a shame it was that his father hadn't lived long enough to discover that for himself. Stewart would have made him very proud.

Puffing on his cheroot, he squinted when the smoke drifted into his eyes, and he recalled the look on Stewart's face the day Justin and his crew had appeared on the man's doorstep. Stewart had been surprised. Justin couldn't figure out why. He had docked in Provincetown's harbor many times to visit their mother after Sinclair had died. Of course, it had been over a year since their last meeting and then Justin had

114

stayed only long enough to place flowers on Elizabeth's grave. He had been sailing near Florida the day their mother had died, and from Stewart's unusual attitude toward him, Justin could only attribute the man's bitterness to the possibility that Stewart thought his brother should have stayed closer to home instead of sailing the coast. But what puzzled Justin even more was that Stewart didn't seem at all affected by the news that he had been accused of treason. Stewart only showed emotion when Justin told him that he and his men were taking one of their father's ships. He had become angry, had said that Justin had no right to anything that belonged to their father, had claimed that the ships and the company were his, and had stated that *he* would decide what was done with them.

It had been easy to subdue Stewart. He needed a cane just to stand upright, and when he'd raised that instrument to strike his brother, he had lost his balance and fallen to the ground. Justin remembered how pathetic the man looked trying to lift himself to his feet again. Justin had never seen his brother in that light before, and that scene had burned itself into his memory. They had merely walked away from him, ignoring his cries of outrage, and by the time his brother could summon help, Justin and his men had taken the *Lady Elizabeth,* a frigate named after his mother, and had sailed away.

"You believe me, don't you, Captain?"

Blinking at the sound of Dara's voice, Justin's thoughts of the past vanished and he took another puff on the cheroot before looking at her. "Most of it," he answered quietly.

"Most of it," she repeated irritably. How dare he question her honesty when she had just bared her soul to him! "What part do you doubt?"

Snuffing out the cigar in an ashtray, he stood and

went to the washbasin. "That you don't know where Lane is," he said, pouring water into the bowl.

Dara's slender frame straightened. "And why do you find that so hard to believe?" she asked, watching him dip his hands in the water and splash it over his face and neck.

Silver droplets glistened in his hair and clung to his strong jawline and the tip of his nose as he glanced up at her while he grasped the towel on the hook beside him. His blue eyes raked over her as if he were evaluating a brood mare; then they closed while he vigorously dried his face. When he had finished, he draped the cloth around his neck and motioned for her to come closer.

"I want you to look in the mirror, Dara Brandon," he said, stepping out of the way when she refused to move, his hand extended toward the object.

"Why?" she asked flippantly, folding her arms in front of her.

Dropping his hand to his side in controlled irritation, he retorted, "Must you always test me? Just do it."

Dara felt that his anger was on the verge of exploding and wisely decided not to press too far. Carefully watching him out of the corner of her eye just in case it was some sort of trick, she moved to the small table and the mirror hanging above it. She moaned when she saw her reflection. Her once shiny, silken strands of auburn hair tumbled wildly about her shoulders, tangled and lacking the gleam they usually had. Her blue cotton dress was torn, wrinkled, and smudged with dirt. She had suspected that she looked terrible but until this moment she hadn't guessed just how terrible.

"All right, so I look horrible. What has that to do with it?" She shrugged, turning away.

"Horrible?" Justin echoed, catching her arm and

spinning her back to the mirror. "I'm not referring to your hair or that rag you're wearing. I'm talking about your face. Look at it."

Dara studied the image staring back at her, unable to see any dirt. She frowned. "What's wrong with it?"

"It's probably one of the most beautiful faces I've ever seen, you little fool. What mother in her right mind would allow a daughter who looked like you to wander about the countryside unchaperoned? You were going to meet your brother and she knew it."

Suddenly Dara was aware of his closeness, the scent of him, his strength, and the fact that he had already tried to force himself on her. Worried that he would attempt to do so again, she started to move away, but Justin grabbed her elbow and jerked her around to face him. She shuddered inwardly at his stormy look.

"Maybe, just maybe, you don't know exactly where your brother is, but I'd wager this ship that the message you got really was from Lane, that it told you where to go, and that he intended to meet you. He was seen in this area, Miss Brandon, not more than two weeks ago."

Wriggling free of him, she glared back defiantly. "Then why didn't he just come home if he was so close? He has no reason to hide."

"Oh, but you're wrong," he replied bitterly. "He's hiding from me. He knows I've escaped from prison and that I'm looking for him. Until now he had to keep running."

Apprehension tickled the hairs on the back of Dara's neck. "Up until now?" she asked weakly.

"Yes, Miss Brandon," he snarled, a wicked smile twisting one corner of his mouth. "Now he'll have to come to me. I've got his sister."

He stared at her a moment, his meaning quite clear; then he tossed the towel on the table next to the washbowl and sat on the bunk to put on his boots. Shrugging into his shirt, he crossed to the door of the cabin, opened it, and looked back.

"I'm not going to lock this," he informed her, "because you have no place to go. But I suggest you stay here. My men would enjoy passing you around, and if I thought it would take some of that hellfire out of you, I wouldn't stop them." He nodded at the tray of food. "Now eat something and consider what I've said. You can make this easy on yourself, Miss Brandon, by telling me what you know. Otherwise . . ."

His pale blue eyes seemed to pierce her through and Dara stood, transfixed, long after Justin Whitelaw left her, tears streaming down her face and a sense of doom closing in on her.

Chapter Five

"Problems, Cap'n?" Douglas Callahan smiled, watching Justin stare out at the waters of Chesapeake Bay. An angry frown furrowed Justin's rugged brow.

"Not any more than usual," he answered with a sigh. "Just a new twist to them is all."

"Miss Brandon?"

Turning around, Justin leaned his tall frame back against the ship's railing and folded his arms over his chest. Staring up at the meshwork of rigging that scaled to the crow's nest above him, he replied. "Yes. Things would be a lot simpler if she weren't such a stubborn, strong-willed little minx."

"And it would be less tempting if she was a homely old maid, huh, Cap'n?" Callahan grinned.

Justin's head jerked around toward his first mate. His eyes were hooded by his dark brow, and he was ready to bite out an angry retort until he saw the playful smirk on the man's face. Relaxing, he chuckled and absently turned his attention to the men scrubbing down the decks. "Yes, she is rather beautiful," he murmured.

"*Rather* beautiful?" Callahan objected. "I'd say she's the most beautiful woman I've ever seen. But then, when has an old sea dog like me had a chance to see many beautiful women?" He smiled and glanced over at the men repairing one of the sails. "So did you learn anything from her?"

"Not much more than we already knew," Justin said with a sigh. "Except that she claims her family received word that her brother had been captured by the British."

"If that's true, why was she going to Washington?"

"She said she was going there to find someone who could tell her where she could start looking for him."

"And then what?" Callahan frowned. "Did she plan to swim or walk after him?"

The corner of Justin's mouth crimped. "That's why I don't believe her. I don't think she's stupid enough to just start off without knowing where she's going, especially with no money." A moment of silence passed between them before Justin continued. "I believe the message she got was from Lane telling her where to meet him." He sighed. "But I can't get her to admit it. She thinks I want to kill him."

"Kill him?" Callahan parroted. "But he's the only one who can prove your innocence."

Justin glanced over at his first mate and smiled. "She heard too many stories about us, my friend."

"Then why not tell her the truth? I still think that boy's in trouble. I don't believe he was captured by the British like Miss Brandon was told, but he was too faithful to you, Cap'n, to suddenly turn against you like he did. Someone got to him, and I'd be willing to wager everything I own that was the same person who paid off the magistrate."

Justin idly scratched the stubble on his chin. "She isn't in the mood to hear the truth right now."

"So what do you plan to do?"

"I don't know, but I do need her help . . . especially if she was on her way to meet her brother."

Callahan looked at the deck at his feet a moment,

then straightened to face his captain. "If you don't mind some advice from an old man, I suggest you try talking with her." When Justin looked up at him, he grinned devilishly. "Use some of that charm of yours. It wouldn't take much to convince her that you're telling the truth."

"It's a plausible idea, my friend, but one that won't work."

"Why?"

"She does anything but bring out my 'charming' side."

Callahan grunted. "Didn't look like that to me a little while ago."

Justin's smile gleamed white against his bronze complexion. "Yes. Well, she wasn't exactly willing."

"She might have been if I hadn't interrupted," Callahan argued; then he turned away. "But if you're afraid to find out . . ."

Justin had known Douglas Callahan for the past ten years. They had been friends from the moment Callahan had taken the youthful Whitelaw under his wing to teach him the ways of the Navy and managing a fighting vessel. Callahan was a lieutenant on the warship and was content to be second in command. But Justin never was, and in three short years, when he had risen to the rank of captain, Callahan had requested a transfer to his friend's ship so they might serve together.

Justin didn't know a lot about Callahan's past since the man didn't like talking about himself, but he had told Justin that he'd been married. His young wife and baby had been killed when British soldiers had burned their farm, and to this day the man hated England intensely. Justin felt that was the reason Callahan was such an excellent officer in the struggle with England for trade rights, and he continually thanked God that

121

he was fortunate enough to have Callahan fighting at his side, even more so now that he needed help to disprove the charges brought against them. If it hadn't been for Callahan's friendship, Justin knew he would have been hanged for treason months ago.

When Callahan had learned that Sinclair Whitelaw had disowned his own son, he'd more or less adopted Justin, thinking of him as the son he'd lost, and Justin had been grateful for the sympathetic ear Callahan always gave him. He never lied to Justin, gave advice only when he thought it necessary, and constantly teased his friend about his affairs with women. Justin had always wondered if that might be the reason Callahan never had any of his own. That would have given Justin a little leverage.

"Have you ever known me to be afraid before?" he asked, watching the man out of the corner of his eye.

Callahan thought about it for a minute. "No. But I suspect that's why you always ended your involvement with a lady after a few days. You just wanted to do it before she did."

"You really have a high opinion of me, don't you, Callahan?" Justin laughed.

"Well," he answered with a shrug, "I guess you could change my mind if you went back to your cabin right now and convinced Miss Brandon of your . . . sincerity."

Pushing himself away from the railing, Justin grinned at his friend. "I had planned on going back to my cabin, Lieutenant, but only to shave and change my clothes. So think what you like. Right now I'm not interested in tangling with that she-devil." Touching his brow in a half-hearted salute, Justin turned and walked away.

Callahan smiled as he watched the proud, steady gait of his captain walking back to his quarters, a sadness

122

softening the lines in Callahan's face. He knew the reason Justin Whitelaw never got involved with a woman for very long. Justin did it to protect himself. He had been deeply hurt by a scheming woman several years ago and was not about to let that happen again. He hadn't talked much about Monica Dearborn, only enough to reveal that a week after she'd changed her mind about marrying him she had announced her forthcoming wedding to a rich senator from Maryland. As far as Callahan knew, Justin hadn't seen her since that day, but on rare occasions when Justin had had too much to drink, her name invariably was mentioned with bitterness. Callahan probably knew Justin better than anyone else and he felt the young man would make a perfect husband. But life had played a cruel trick on Justin and he would not so easily forget . . . or forgive. Shaking his head at the shame of it all, Callahan turned his attention on the maintainance of the *Lady Elizabeth*.

When Justin reached the ladder that would take him to the quarter-deck and his cabin, he paused and looked up at the clear blue sky. A warm breeze brushed his face, and he absently gazed out across the water in the bay. Off to port lay the Atlantic Ocean. Justin longed to take the helm and order his men to head for the open sea, to leave behind all their troubles and set sail for distant shores. But he wouldn't . . . not now . . . not until he had found the man who could clear his name. With a sigh, he turned back and descended the ladder, thinking now it wouldn't take too long to accomplish that end. The clue to Lane Brandon's whereabouts was waiting for him in his cabin.

Justin didn't hesitate once his hand touched the doorlatch. It clicked when he lifted it, but when he pushed against the thick oak planks, the door wouldn't budge. His mood darkened.

"Miss Brandon," he grated out, stepping back to glare at the closed entryway. "Open this door."

"Go away," came the frantic reply.

Justin's temper exploded and he raised a fist to slam it against the barrier, but he caught himself and instead slapped both sides of the wood framework with his open hands. Then, leaning his weight against them, head down, he studied the floor and fought to control his anger.

"If you make me force my way in, you're going to be very sorry," he warned, certain the threat would provoke an immediate response.

But when he didn't hear even the slightest sound, he realized Dara Brandon was not easily intimidated—at least not while she had the advantage. He decided on a different tactic. Straightening, he took a deep breath, glanced up and down the passageway to make sure no one witnessed this rather embarrassing situation, and then exhaled slowly before he faced the door again.

"You can't stay in there very long, you know, without opening the door. In a couple of days you're going to get very hungry . . . and thirsty, I might add. I won't leave trays for you in the passage. I'm not going to cater to your whims, Miss Brandon."

"I won't be here that long!" Her reply was muffled, angry.

"Oh?" he mocked. "And what do you plan to do, jump out the window again?"

His patience growing thin, he twisted to lean a shoulder against the edge of the door. Folding his arms over his chest, he decided to wait her out. But as he stood there he suddenly realized what her plan was. She knew the ship was headed for Norfolk, a coastal town with a harbor large enough to accommodate a vessel the size of the *Lady Elizabeth*. All she had to do once they docked was open the porthole and call out to someone on the pier, tell them who captained the ship. There wouldn't be enough time to weigh anchor and sail away before the authorities were summoned. His mouth lifted in a half-smile. Smart little lady; this Dara Brandon, but not smart enough.

"I think you should know, Miss Brandon, that we've decided to change course. As soon as we sail into the mouth of the bay, we're heading for open sea. It's gotten a little dangerous for us so close to land and I think we'd be safer at sea. It might be a week before we dock again. Can you last that long without food and water?"

"You're lying!" she shouted.

Justin grinned. "Are you willing to find out?"

Several minutes passed silently and Justin had just about concluded that his threats hadn't had any effect on her when he heard a noise and sensed she had moved next to the door.

"I'll let you in if you will make an agreement," she said softly.

"No deals, Miss Brandon. I offer you only the chance to spare yourself a sound thrashing by opening the door willingly."

Again he was met with silence. His temper simmered. He'd had enough of this game.

"I'm going to give you until the count of three, Miss Brandon, and then I'm coming in. One . . ."

He hoped she would move whatever blocked the door. He wasn't really sure he could force it out of the way.

"Two . . ."

He reconsidered his position realizing if she had been strong enough to move something in the first place, he most certainly should be able to shove it out of the way. He leaned in, pressed an ear to the door and listened.

When no sound came from within, he heaved a deep, angry sigh and stood up.

"Have it your way, Miss Brandon," he growled. Stepping back, he balanced his weight on his left foot, leaned slightly to one side, and swiftly kicked out against the door with the right as he shouted, "Three!"

Not built for such abuse, the portal moaned and creaked its objection yet it held. Its stubbornness only seemed to spur Justin on and he braced himself for another blow. When the heel of his boot connected with the wooden planks a second time, the door inched open enough for him to see inside, and he silently calculated that one more assault would gain him entry. Without delay, he kicked out again and the door jerked forward, allowing him the needed space to slip between it and the framework. Bracing himself, he seized the edge of the portal and shoved.

Dara had slipped the back of the desk chair beneath the latch and once he could stick his head in far enough to see it, he reached around and knocked it loose, sending it crashing to the floor with a loud bang. With the way now open, Justin straightened, and promising himself that he wouldn't kill the little tigress, he calmly pushed the door wide. He intended to advise his guest that such conduct would not be tolerated in the future, and was about to say so when he suddenly discovered that the cabin was empty. A frown furrowed his dark brow—there was no place for her to hide—and then his gaze fell upon the open porthole on the opposite side of the room.

"Damn," he fumed, rushing toward it. Hadn't she learned her lesson the first time she'd tried to swim for shore? He peered out the porthole to study the water below, hoping he wasn't too late, but only swirling, whitecapped water greeted him. For a brief moment he felt a painful tug on his heart. As usual, Callahan was right. If he had taken the time to explain to the woman, maybe she wouldn't have tried something so foolish. If he dove in to look for her, he might yet save her.

Twisting around to sit down on the bench and yank off his boots, his eyes caught sight of a flash of blue racing for the doorway and he froze, unable to believe that he had been so easily duped. Dara Brandon hadn't jumped overboard. She had merely hidden behind the desk and waited for him to turn his back on her. Now what did she plan to do? Jumping here or over the railing topside would have the same result. And as for hiding on board somewhere until they docked in the hope of slipping off unnoticed, that was ridiculous. There wasn't a corner on the whole ship that someone didn't look into at some time during the day. Collapsing back on the bench, he folded his arms over his chest, a smug look on his handsome face, and waited.

Only a few minutes elapsed before Justin heard the outraged cry of a female voice from somewhere on deck. The equally angry tone of Douglas Callahan followed. Smiling, he settled himself more comfortably on the bench and listened to the screams and protests of the young woman as she and Callahan approached his quarters. A moment later, Dara Brandon was unceremoniously shoved through the doorway, her bright auburn hair flying about her shoulders and her green eyes flashing sparks of hatred at the man who had abused her. Callahan's stocky frame filled the doorway and blocked her retreat.

"We found her trying to lower the longboat, Cap'n," his first mate growled. "If one of the men hadn't spotted her from the crow's nest when he did, she would have dumped the blasted thing in the bay. If ya'd like, I'll toss her in the hold for a while"—his furious glare shifted to Dara—"down there with all them rats."

127

Unaffected by his threat, Dara lifted her nose in the air. Captain Whitelaw wouldn't do that.

"That's not a bad idea, Callahan," Justin agreed when he noticed the way the girl's tiny frame straightened confidently, and he raised questioning brows at her when she whirled to face him, her mouth agape. "Don't you think it's a just punishment, Miss Brandon?"

"Punishment?" she echoed in a shrill voice. "Why should I be punished for anything? You're holding me here against my will. I was simply trying to escape in any way I could."

Justin watched her a moment as if considering her point, then reached up to scratch his chin. "You're right. After all, it was my fault you managed to get that far in the first place."

"But, Cap'n . . ." Callahan objected.

Justin raised a hand to silence the man. "No, Callahan. I don't think putting Miss Brandon in the hold would do any good, except to chase off the rodents." He grinned at her when he heard her rapid intake of breath and he rose leisurely to his feet. "Besides, I've thought of something better."

"Like what?" Callahan questioned him doubtfully. "The only other choice I can see is throwing a net over her and hanging her off the starboard side."

Justin couldn't stop the laughter that tugged at the corners of his mouth as he envisioned the sight that would make. "Well, that's one way of keeping track of her, but it would also bring the authorities down on us in a minute." He crossed the room to stand next to his friend, then looked back at Dara. "No, Callahan, with what I have in mind, I won't even have to lock the door."

"And would ya be willing to tell me what that is?"

Slipping his arm around Callahan's shoulders while

he stared at the young woman awaiting her sentence, he asked, "Well, don't you suppose she'd be less likely to want to leave the protection of my cabin if she didn't have anything to wear?"

Every muscle in Dara's body tightened, and her stomach knotted. When she opened her mouth to object, nothing would come out. Panic flooded through her. She knew there wasn't a single person on board the ship who would object to what Captain Whitelaw had planned. Although she truly didn't want to die, she wished now that she had drowned. At least then she would have been spared what this pirate had in mind for her. She might not have a great deal of experience with men, but she certainly wasn't stupid enough to think he would stop at just taking her clothes. Hadn't he promised to go further when his first mate had interrupted them earlier? Fighting to breathe, she stumbled back, wide-eyed and frantic for some way to protect herself. Her gaze darted from one man to the other before it lingered on the older of the two.

Douglas Callahan, she guessed, was nearly her father's age, even though thick auburn hair still adorned Taylor Brandon's head, and a sudden surge of hope flowed through her. Callahan was angry with her for nearly overturning the longboat when she'd freed the mooring lines. Any good officer would think of his ship before anything else. But now that he'd heard what his captain planned for her, surely his sense of proper conduct where a lady was concerned would take precedence. If she threw herself on his mercy, maybe he would object. With pleading eyes, she looked at him only to have her hopes crumble when she heard his response.

"Aye, Cap'n, I think that should keep her in one spot." He grinned then turned to leave.

"Wait, Mister Callahan," she cried out. "You can't

let him—"

"Sorry, Miss Brandon," he called back over his shoulder without turning around, "but he's the captain on this ship, and whatever he decides is the way it will be."

Dara could only stare disbelievingly as she watched Captain Whitelaw slowly close the door on his mate. As Callahan's footsteps faded into the distance, tears sprang to her eyes. Was there no man who cared what happened to her? Were Lane and her father the only exceptions? Her bright, glistening eyes moved to the man who lounged against the door, his arms folded over his massive chest and a smile of pure delight lifting the corners of his mouth.

"Now, Dara Brandon," he said in a deep, smooth voice, "you can make this easy on yourself or . . ."

"Or you'll show me what kind of a man you really are," she spat out carelessly.

Justin's pale blue eyes twinkled. "Uh-huh." He grinned.

The muscles in her throat constricted and she fought to stop her chin from quivering. "But what if I promise—"

"Promise what? To be a good little girl and do everything I tell you?"

Dara nodded, even though she knew he was only playing with her.

"You mean you'd sit quietly if I told you to, straighten up the cabin, make the bunk, do my laundry, and tell me where to find your brother?"

"I don't know where Lane is!" she shouted, stamping her foot.

"I think you do," he replied calmly. "And since that's the only reason I'm keeping you here and the reason you want so desperately to leave, I fail to see how we'll ever come to terms. So, Miss Brandon, you leave me no choice. Now either you disrobe on your own or I'll do it for you."

They stared at each other for several minutes, each waiting for the other to make the first move. Dara wanted to believe he didn't truly mean what he'd said, that he'd only wanted to scare her into telling him something she didn't know. Suddenly an idea struck her. How would he know if she lied? She could pretend that the message she had received was from Lane and that they were to meet in Washington just as he'd suspected. If she fooled him, he would order the ship to sail back up the bay. They would dock on the western shore and he would take her with him to the "rendezvous." A smile flitted across her mouth and vanished. She would have to make it sound good. Bowing her head, she turned away from him and crossed to the porthole to stare out at the sunlight gleaming on the surface of the water. She mustn't look at him or he'd see through her story.

"All right, Captain Whitelaw," she began with a sigh, "you win. I'll tell you what you want to know about my brother."

Although she still faced the porthole, her mind was centered on the man sharing the cabin and after several long, quiet minutes had ticked by, she inadvertently glanced back at him. He hadn't moved, nor had the smile faded from his handsome face. Her heart pounded in her chest. Gulping, she turned back to look at the swirling current of the bay.

"I was to go to Washington, take a room in one of the inns, and wait until he contacted me. That's all I know."

The silence that followed grated on her nerves, but she steeled herself to wait until he made the next move. She mustn't seem too anxious to have him believe her story. She trembled in spite of herself when the deep timbre of his voice filled the air.

"Didn't you tell me earlier that you had received the message over a week ago?"

Dara frowned, her mind racing to grasp the meaning of his question. When none surfaced, she nodded hesitantly.

"Then why did you wait so long to do as he asked?"

"I . . . ah . . ." she stuttered, frantically searching for a sound answer. "He . . . ah . . ."

She bit her lower lip in frustration. Why couldn't she think of something? Then she remembered telling him how ill her father was.

"Because of Papa," she blurted out, forcing herself not to look at him. "He didn't want me to go. I had to reassure him that I'd be all right." Her lip curled. "And was I wrong," she muttered.

With her back turned to him, Dara missed the way Justin's grin broadened. He didn't believe her, but he was enjoying the game. It had been his intention all along to return to Washington in a few days after his contact in Cambridge had had time to find out what he could about Colonel Winslow. They had only sailed down the bay for safety because of the possibility that his story had been some giant hoax and an army lay hidden somewhere near. Months ago, when his carelessness had nearly gotten his ship seized and the crew captured, Justin had learned never to stay in one place too long. They had sailed up the Hudson River past New York after hearing a report that Lane Brandon had been seen in Manhattan. The *Lady Elizabeth* had docked at one of the piers and Justin had gone ashore. When Lane couldn't be found at the spot where Justin had been told he was, he'd continued his search anyway and had lingered too long. The presence of the strange vessel in the harbor, even though it flew the American flag, had raised suspicions. By sheer luck

Justin had returned to the *Lady Elizabeth* only an hour before a naval commander ordered his men to board the ship. It had taken some quick, skillful maneuvering to outsail the Navy vessesl, and Justin swore then that he would never again allow his passion to find Lane Brandon to interfere with his judgment. Nor, he now concluded, would he ever let himself be fooled by this slip of a girl. Straightening, he took the key from his pocket and locked the door.

"Well, Miss Brandon," he said, going to his desk, "that's all very interesting."

Bright green eyes had followed his every move, and the moment she heard the lock click, she was certain she could guess his next recital. She watched him absently leaf through the papers on his desk, rearrange the brass paperweight and spyglass to the far side, then casually rest a hip on the corner as he slipped the key back into his pocket. And when his pale blue eyes looked up at her, she was sure of her fate.

"I'm afraid I don't believe a word of it." He smiled. "However, I'll give you the benefit of the doubt. Since I have to go to Washington on business anyway, I'll have my men check around to see if anyone has been asking about you. *If* that should be the case and your brother is indeed in the capital, I'll put you up at one of the inns, or I should say, I'll have someone register in your name." He fought the grin that tugged at his mouth when he saw the disappointed, hopeless look on her beautiful face. His gaze drifted slowly down her shapely length, from tousled coppery hair to trim ankles, and he smiled appreciatively. "Of course, it will be a little difficult to find someone who matches your description, but I think I can manage." He shook off the warmth that stirred his blood and stood up. "Now, Miss Brandon," he continued, rounding the desk to sit in the chair behind it, "I'll allow you the modesty of

133

keeping on the . . . underthing, whatever it's called, but the dress and petticoats have to go." Opening a drawer, he withdrew a large book, tossed it on top of the desk, and opened it to skim through the pages until he found what he wanted. Without looking up, he added, "Just toss them out the porthole."

Dara opened and then closed her mouth, unable to get her breath and voice her objection. Hadn't she told him what he wanted to hear? Hadn't they agreed? She continued to struggle for words even after he looked up at her and frowned.

"Was there something else you wanted to say?" he asked, resting his elbows on the edge of the desk.

"But . . ."

"But what, Miss Brandon?"

"I told you . . ."

Leaning back, one hand in his lap, the other cradling his chin as his elbow rested on the arm of the chair, he rasied a brow and said, "A story. You told me a story."

"I told you where you could find my brother. You said that was all you wanted . . . that if I told you, I wouldn't have to . . ."

Justin shook his head and sat forward again to study the ledger. "That's not what I said at all. You're the one who was making promises."

"Yes you did!" she half whined, half cried.

Only his eyes moved to look at her. "All right," he said quietly, "for the sake of argument, I'll pretend I did. Now I've changed my mind." He concentrated on the book again. "Take off the dress and petticoats."

"No!" Dara rallied. "I will not and you can't . . ."

Instantly, both hands flew to her mouth, and she longed to retract the futile challenge she had so carelessly spoken, for she knew quite well that this man could eaisly tear her clothes from her. Biting a knuckle on her left hand, she watched him closely, foolishly praying that God had struck him deaf. But she knew he had heard when she observed the meaningful way he closed the ledger, opened the drawer again, and slipped the volume inside, rising as he slid the compartment shut once more. She stumbled sideways when he rounded the desk and started toward her.

"No . . . please, Captain . . ." she begged, bumping into the sea chest that seemed to have appeared from nowhere.

Having lost her balance, she would have tumbled to the floor if his strong hand hadn't caught her arm when it did and yanked her upright again. Ordinarily she would have been grateful for the assistance, but the gesture hadn't been a kind one and she realized if she hesitated in the slightest, she would be doomed. Her arm still grasped in his steely hold, she quickly lifted her free hand and swung her fist around to land a blow anywhere she could, only to have it imprisoned in a much larger one. Green eyes, glistening with tears, looked up pleadingly into his, and for a moment he only stared at her, his face expressionless. Then slowly, purposefully he drew her arm behind her, pulling her body next to his, and Dara felt the heat of him radiate over her entire length. She thought he intended to kiss her, but when he failed to lower his head, she frowned, wondering what other form of subtle torture he had in mind. Then she knew when he smiled devilishly and twisted her other arm behind her back. He held both her wrists in one hand while the other moved to the buttons of her gown.

"No!" she screamed, straining to break his hold.

But his hand tightened around the delicate bones of her wrists and the pain quickly brought her into submission. She thought of kicking his shins but the agony she was suffering negated physical resistance. Instead she withered and wondered which would break

135

first, the bones he was heartlessly bruising or her spirit. Her answer came when long, lean fingers brushed against her breast as Justin sought to pull the dress from her shoulders, for in that instant she realized that if Justin so desired it, he could do more than strip her of her clothes. Steeling herself against the pain he was causing her, she bent her head and sank her teeth into his hand.

Justin bellowed his distress, letting go of the little firebrand to examine his injured member. His temper soared when he saw small dots of blood appear, for until now he had enjoyed showing her who would make the decisions where she was concerned. But now . . . now she had overstepped her limits and he wasn't about to let her get away with it. Turning on her to scowl his disapproval, he found her frantically trying to refasten the front of her dress.

"Stop right there," he roared, and Dara jumped at the sound of his thundering rage. "Touch one more button and so help me you'll curse the day we met."

"I already do!" Dara rallied.

Justin's tall frame stiffened all the more as she continued to redo the buttons, as if what he'd demanded didn't matter. When she reached for the last button, his temper exploded. Lunging for her, he caught her around the waist, and twirled and tumbled them both onto his bunk. Dara thrashed wildly, raining blows on the side of his head, his shoulders, and chest, her slippered feet connecting with his well-muscled legs. But the tall, leather boots he wore deflected her assault, and although he found himself struggling with a wildcat, the tiny fists that assailed him only aggravated his ill humor but did not win her her freedom. However, when the long nails of her left hand raked across his face in a sudden, unexpected surge of strength, Justin rolled off of her, one hand held to the

136

wounds she'd inflicted, his blue eyes registering surprise and pain. It took him a moment to react, but seeing Dara's thick mane of coppery curls flying out behind her as she fled the bunk, he bolted to his feet, entangled his fingers in her auburn locks, and yanked her back against him. Using one arm to encircle her, he grabbed the bodice of her dress and pulled, easily tearing the seams.

"Damn you!" Dara howled, stomping the heel of her slipper on his toe.

But Justin was determined and barely felt her attack. Shoving her away from him, he yanked down hard on the fabric gathered around her narrow waist. Before Dara could respond, the remnants of her blue cotton gown lay in ruins at her feet. Tears blurred her eyes as she stared down at the shambles he had made of her one good dress even though it was worn and faded, and she looked up at him to hurl every vile word she could summon. She was too numb to realize that he had already untied the strings holding her petticoat in place until the sudden chill of cool air hit her bare legs as the garment glided effortlessly to the deck. When she started to retrieve it, he quickly bent, swept her up in his arms and carried her, kicking and screaming, to the bunk. The next instant found her sprawled on the soft mattress while Justin returned to gather her clothes from the floor and march to the porthole.

"No!" Dara screamed, scrambling from the bed when he waded the dress and petticoats into a ball, ready to hurl them through the porthole and into the bay. "Please! Don't do it!"

But before she could reach him, the yards of blue and white cloth shot through the opening and sailed, uninhibited, into the air, drifting toward the water. Dara's tears turned to rage.

"You bastard!" she shouted, surprised to hear such a

word coming from her own lips. But he deserved it. And he deserved anything else she could rain on him. Bent on revenge and the need to destroy something that belonged to him, her gaze shifted determinedly about the room in search of an item to wreak havoc upon. A vengeful, satisfied smile twisted her mouth when she spotted the spyglass lying on his desk. With hurried steps, she advanced toward it.

"Dara Brandon," Justin hissed, realizing what she intended to do.

But his discovery came too late to stop her, and all he could do was duck out of the way when the projectile was angrily thrown in his direction. Undaunted, she scanned the surface of his desk for something of more value, but in the moments she wasted on a decision, Justin was upon her. His huge hands clamped onto her wrists, twisting her arms behind her as he crushed her to his chest, hoping to calm this she-devil, but he seemed only to infuriate her more. Long auburn hair tumbled wildly about her oval face, her long slender neck, and smooth white shoulders; and green eyes flashed sparks of fire at him. As she strained against him, he could feel the firmness of her breasts through the thin fabric of his shirt and suddenly his anger turned to more pleasurable thoughts.

One hand had moved to the back of her head, the other around her waist, before Justin's mouth swooped down to cover hers in a hot, passionate kiss. Dara's rage vanished instantly. Her experience with men was limited, but instinct told her that this time he would finish what he had started earlier. Panic gripped her very soul, and in a desperate attempt to cool his desires, she clutched his shirt in both hands, hoping to push him away. But she only succeeded in popping the buttons free and exposing the rock hard muscles of his chest. The contact branded her flesh, sending waves of scorching heat through her entire body.

His mouth moved against hers, his tongue parting her lips and stealing her breath away. She fell limp in his embrace, certain at any moment she would swoon. Then he released her and Dara stumbled back, gasping for air. She watched him through a daze as he pulled the white linen shirttail from his breeches, slid the garment from his broad shoulders and tossed it aside before he moved to the bunk and sat down to tug off his boots, his pale blue eyes never leaving hers. Her heart pounded in her chest when his long, lean frame unfolded to full height and he motioned toward her.

"Come here, Dara Brandon."

A whimper caught in her throat and tears flooded the rim of her lower lashes. Dara could only refuse him with a shake of her head. When he took a step forward, she tried to retreat but her feet wouldn't move. It was as if he had hypnotized her and she couldn't understand why. She didn't want this.

"I won't hurt you," he said softly, and Dara wasn't even aware that he continued to advance toward her.

Coppery strands of hair falling over her shoulders shimmered with her denial. She blinked and a tear raced to her chin. This wasn't the way it was supposed to be. She had envisioned the day she would stand before her new husband in the privacy of their bedchamber willing to share everything she had, to offer herself, her love, and her devotion for the rest of her life. They hadn't spoken the vows of wedlock, yet this man didn't seem to care. Maybe if she closed her eyes, she would be whisked away to awake in her small room on the farm near Drawbridge, to discover all of this had only been a bad dream. Yet she knew that wasn't possible. And she also knew that there was nothing she could do to stop Justin Whitelaw—pirate, traitor, and assassin—from doing whatever he pleased with her. Yes, the final victory would be his, but Dara Brandon would not surrender without a fight. Taking a deep breath, she braced herself for battle.

"You know, Captain Whitelaw," she said, her chin held high, "you're about to prove what—"

Suddenly Dara was lifted in his powerful arms as he turned and strode with her to the bunk. She fought frantically to elude his grasp, her slippers flying from her feet as she kicked out, her fists pounding against his chest.

"Put me down!" she wailed, pushing at his broad shoulders.

Bending a knee to the bunk, he chuckled, "As you wish, Miss Brandon."

But instead of gaining her freedom, she fell onto the soft mattress, Justin above her, and she felt quick fingers pull the stockings from her legs, then slide the lacy straps of her chemise from her shoulders. In a desperate attempt to retain her modesty a moment longer, she struggled with the hand trying to strip her, but his weight pressed down on her to still her moves. Her brave façade was fading rapidly and although she wanted to rally a string of hateful words to prove to him that she wouldn't willingly succumb to his desires, tears tightened her throat.

"Lane . . . Lane will kill you for this," she promised with a sob.

Justin ceased his perusal and, as if her threat held merit, raised up to study her face a moment, a vague smile parting his lips. "I don't think so," he murmured.

"Yes, he will," Dara guaranteed in a rush. "After I tell him what you've done . . ."

Justin shook his head, bringing a confused frown to her lovely brow. "You won't tell him."

"Oh, yes, I will," she whimpered.

Dara cringed as his huge hand lifted to brush away a

silken strand of hair from her cheek. "You won't tell him because you won't want to share this with anyone."

Some of the fire returned to her bright green eyes. "I don't want to share this with you!"

One corner of his mouth wrinkled in a half-smile. "You can say that now, but I think I can change your mind."

"What do you mean?" she asked worriedly. Did he intend to kill Lane if she told her brother what he had done to her and Lane sought revenge? Or would he threaten her life as well?

"What I mean . . . Dara Brandon . . . is that I'm going to make love to you . . . slowly . . . tenderly. I'll raise you to heights you haven't imagined existed. And when it's over and we lie in each other's arms, you'll find that what we shared will be most private, something no one else will deserve to know."

A chill and a warmth exploded simultaneously in the pit of Dara's stomach, and rage raced unheeded through every inch of her, paralyzing her thoughts and her body. She could only stare up at him, too numb to deny anything or to stop the hand that easily pulled the chemise from her trembling form. Sunlight streamed in through the portholes at his back, placing his face in shadow, and he suddenly became the figure of her dreams, the man she had envisioned asking her father for her hand in marriage. Magically the moment was transformed into fantasy, and she lay unmoving as he rose to shed his last remaining garment.

He hovered over her, his eyes feasting on the splendor of her nakedness—her exquisite breasts, narrow waist, and shapely rounded hips—the palm of his hand tracing the smooth length of her thigh. This delicate creature was indeed beautiful and his haunting memories of another such woman failed to surface. Long, auburn hair fanned out across the coverlet, accenting her pale, glowing skin, and for a moment he could not take his gaze from her finely chiseled features. Softly arched brows and long, dark lashes framed the sea green shade of her eyes. A pink hue touched her cheeks and her parted ruby-colored lips tempted him to taste the sweetness they promised. Placing one hand on either side of her, he lowered himself to sample their unspoken pledge, his blood stirring in his veins when their lips met.

Blindly, Dara welcomed the embrace, lifting her arms to encircle his neck and draw him closer, and when their bodies touched full length, his naked flesh pressed against her own, she thought she would go mad with the ecstasy of it. His searing kisses moved to her earlobe, her neck, and the hollow in the base of her throat, one arm slipping beneath her waist as his open mouth, hot and moist, then found her breast. His tongue teased its peak while his free hand roamed wickedly over her tingling flesh to linger on the silken skin of her thigh. Dara's heart beat wildly, her pulse throbbing, and she wondered if he, too, experienced the bliss she felt. She wanted this moment to go on forever, to savor the tenderness, *his* tenderness, to long remember the rapturous paradise he was creating for her.

When Justin shifted to place his knee between her thighs, Dara instinctively moved to welcome him, and as his lips found hers again, her breath caught in her throat, for the manly hardness of him hotly touched her. For a fleeting moment she thought to deny him; then he pressed deeply within her and a wave of searing pain overwhelmed her. The pain diminished before she could react, and he remained motionless at first, his tongue playing upon her lips, his mouth moving hungrily over hers. Dara could hear his breathing quicken as if he fought to rein his mounting ardor; then

142

her own passion soared and when she thought he would suspend them for eternity, she arched her hips and moved against him. His long-held-in desires exploded, and they met in a furious clash as though there were no tomorrows and this sensuous interlude would end too soon. She felt the frantic beating of his heart, heard his ragged breath, and matched his fervor with her own until at last they lay, spent and exhausted, in each other's arms.

Curled within his embrace, her head resting on his shoulder, Dara lovingly traced the thick muscles of his chest with her fingertips, smiling in the afterglow of their lovemaking. She was content to remain in his arms forever if he wanted it so, yet she laughed to herself when she realized the impossibility of such a wish. He had a ship to command and a mission to complete. He could spare her his evening hours, but his days belonged to his quest. She wouldn't mind, for she was determined to fill those moments when he came to her with enough memories to haunt his every waking hour.

Rubbing her cheek against the warmth of his flesh, she sighed happily, envisioning what their life together would be like. Then a troubled expression marred her brow and she raised up to look at him.

"After we're married, you will take me with you to find Lane, won't you?" she asked worriedly, frowning all the more when he laughed.

"Married?" he repeated with a grin and rose up to cock his elbow and cradle his head in his hand. His warm gaze took in the blush of her cheeks, then settled on the thick coppery curls falling over her shoulders to hide a most desirable treasure beneath. Tenderly, his fingers touched the smoothness of her neck and slid downward to brush away her reddish brown strands of hair to reveal the fullness of a breast. "My poor innocent Dara," he murmured, his thumb stroking the nipple.

A dreadful fear began to creep through her. "Innocent?" she queried, pushing his hand away.

Not discouraged by her subtle rejection, Justin's fingertips caressed her arm then curled around hers as he lifted them to his lips. "I have no intentions of marrying you," he whispered, kissing the palm of her hand.

Dara jerked free of him and raised herself to her knees, tears coming to her eyes. "But . . . but . . ."

Justin's eyebrows lowered. "But what, Dara?"

"You . . ." She swallowed hard. "You have to."

Sitting up, he glanced around for his breeches. "Because I made love to you?" Lifting the garment from the floor as he sat on the edge of the bed, he quickly slid into it and looked back at her to see her nod. "Dara, just because you lie with a man doesn't mean you have to marry him."

Her chin quivered. Suddenly ashamed of her nakedness, she caught the edge of the coverlet and pulled it up to shield herself. Hugging the quilt to her, she couldn't bear to meet his eyes. "Maybe you don't feel that way, but I do. What decent man would have me . . . now?"

Justin gave a short laugh. "And what man wouldn't want you? You're a very beautiful woman."

"You don't want me," she whispered forlornly.

Had he discussed the subject with any other woman, his temper would have surfaced. But as he stood there studying the tiny creature huddled in his bunk, he felt pity for her. She never should have left her home. Sitting down again, he tried to take her hand, but she pulled back.

"Dara, if it's any comfort to you, I don't want any woman. Mine isn't the kind of life that would allow me to take a wife. I'm wanted for treason, and if I'm caught, I'll be hanged. Would you want a husband like that? I can't even think about settling down until I've cleared my name . . . until I've found your brother."

Dara's green eyes looked up at him in surprise. "Do you mean you're not guilty?"

Justin laughed at the sweet naïveté he saw shining in her face. "That's right. Someone wanted me out of the way. Your brother knows who that was and that's why I must find him."

"You mean you won't kill him when you do?"

"Dara, he's the only proof I have. Why would I kill him?"

"Then I'll help you find him," she smiled brightly. "And after everything is over we can get married."

"Forget about it, Miss Brandon," he said almost angrily as he turned away to put on his boots.

"I *can't* forget about it," she snapped, her own ire erupting. "You *have* to marry me. If you don't acknowledge what you've done, I'll be nothing better than a"—a sob stole her words and she fought not to cry—"a whore."

"You're not a whore, Dara," he replied irritably. Rising, he crossed the room and picked up his shirt from the desk on which he had thrown it.

"Well, that's what they're called . . . women who lie with men without the benefit of wedlock. That's what I am, and it's your fault."

Justin's arms flexed as he pulled on the shirt. "A whore finds herself in bed with a man of her own free will. What happened here was hardly that."

"You mean she doesn't fight him?" Dara asked sarcastically.

"That's right."

"That she doesn't hate every minute of it?"

"Yes," he growled.

145

"I didn't hate it," came her weak reply.

She couldn't have stung him more if she had struck his face with the palm of her hand. Dropping his head, he closed his eyes, fighting with the whirlwind of emotions that assailed him. Finally, he turned to look at her. "If you're trying to make me feel guilty for what I've done, you've succeeded. But that's as far as it goes and I'll tell you why. I was engaged at one time. I was hopelessly in love. My life revolved around the woman. Would you like to know why she didn't marry me?" Before Dara could nod, he rushed on. "Because someone better came along." He stared at her a moment then headed for the door. "I won't ever allow myself to be in that position again, Miss Brandon. So find someone else to marry."

Dara jumped at the slamming of the door when Justin left, her own pain forgotten as she thought of the agony he must have suffered. Twisting around, she sat in the center of his bunk, the coverlet draped about her. Pulling her knees up against her chest, she rested her chin on them, silently contemplating the events of her ill-fated journey.

Chapter Six

"Captain?"

Justin glanced up from the papers on his desk with a frown.

"I was wondering if it would be too much trouble for me to take a bath?" Dara asked timidly.

His gaze swiftly swept the slim figure standing near his bunk clad only in a chemise, the coverlet draped around her and her hands clasped in front of her. Her long, auburn hair hung over one shoulder in a thick braid. She reminded him of an Indian squaw he had seen once, except for her pale skin and the vivid green eyes that could be so bewitching whenever she caught him staring and smiled demurely back at him. Was it his imagination or had this half-grown, wild creature changed into a woman over the past two days? Angry at this thought, he concentrated on his work again.

"I'll see what I can do," he answered gruffly.

"Thank you," she replied in a whisper, certain he hadn't heard. She lingered a moment, watching him sort through the papers spread out before him. He lifted the quill from its well and made an entry before she decided to sit down on his bunk again. Ever since his flat refusal to consider marriage, he had stayed away from the cabin, returning late at night and rising early in the morning. Dara soon realized that her presence greatly disturbed him. She wanted to believe it was because he truly felt guilty for what he had done and in time would change his mind. Crossing her legs and tucking the blanket beneath them, she sighed, knowing it was foolish to hope for such an outcome. She also knew it would be impossible for her to forget Justin Whitelaw.

She had gone over their conversation of that morning repeatedly in her mind and her curiosity about the woman Justin had wanted to marry continued to grow. What had he meant when he'd said someone better came along? He was a captain in the United States Navy. It was quite an honor to have such a title, according to Lane anyway. He was handsome, strong, and aggressive. At times he even had a sense of humor, and if he stayed in America although the authorities were looking for him and he was under the threat of hanging, then he had to be brave. Another man would have taken his ship to foreign shores and lived out the remainder of his life abroad. But not Justin Whitelaw. He had something to prove and nothing would drive him off until he had done so. What kind of woman was she? What did the other man have that Justin didn't? With a sigh, Dara absently looked up at the portholes, knowing these were things she would never learn unless he wanted to tell her.

Bright morning light streamed into the cabin and Dara suddenly felt the need to be warmed by it. Sliding off the bunk, she awkwardly hugged the coverlet to her and crossed the room to look outside at the swirling current. She had no idea where they were sailing since Justin refused to tell her. In fact, he seldom said anything to her and her solitude was slowly eating away at her sanity. She had never been one to remain quiet for very long, but had always drawn her companions into idle chatter whenever the mood struck her. Her brother frequently told her that she talked too much, but she had always shrugged it off, convinced he was only teasing her. What she wouldn't give to have someone with whom to share her secrets now.

Sitting sideways on the bench, Dara opened one of the portholes to let in the fresh, cool breeze. Had they truly sailed to open waters as the captain had threatened or was it possible they had anchored somewhere in the Chesapeake Bay? Crossing her arms over the sill, she leaned forward and rested her chin on them, breathing in the fragrance of salt air. Her father's farm lay five miles from the shoreline, and even though her brother had forbidden her to go near it, saying the current was too dangerous for a young girl, he had taken her there many times just to sit and stare at the bay for hours on end. It had fascinated her. She had wondered what it would be like to board a huge merchant ship and sail up and down the bay, the wind whipping her hair as she stood at the railing. One corner of her mouth crimped. Being trapped inside this cabin wasn't what she had had in mind.

Shifting when her leg started to cramp, Dara's gaze wandered to her right, and she sat up suddenly when she saw the faint outline of trees.

"Captain," she called without turning to look at him, "we're close to the shore. Are we going to dock soon?"

"Possibly," he replied flatly, stacking his papers and sliding them into a drawer. Stretching, he leaned back in his chair and glanced up at her. The coverlet had fallen away from her long, shapely legs, revealing a good amount of white, creamy thigh for him to view. His pulse quickened.

"Where are we?" she continued, still watching the black line on the horizon as it steadily grew larger and more distinct.

149

Blinking, Justin reached for a cheroot, popped it into his mouth, and lit it. But as the smoke drifted upward, his gaze fell on his companion once more and his attempt at distraction failed. Dara Brandon was a fever that was spreading through his entire body. Although he pretended she didn't exist, he was very much aware of her every move, the way she looked, the fragrance of her, her youthfulness, and her fresh innocence. There was nothing artificial about this young girl. She was distinctly different from every woman he had met, including Monica Dearborn. His brow furrowed—especially Monica Dearborn. In the short time he and Dara had spent together, he had quickly observed that she and her brother were a lot alike. If it weren't such a great strain for him to keep from tumbling her in bed every time he got near her, he would try to persuade her to help him find Lane. He took another puff on the cigar. He already knew what her answer would be. If he wanted her help, he would have to marry her first. Angrily, he leaned forward and snuffed out the cheroot in the ashtray. Absolutely not! He could very well do without her assistance.

Rising, he went to the door and opened it. Without a word or glance her way, he left the room, only the sound of the latch marking his exit.

Dara stared at the closed door, a sadness reflected in her eyes, before she turned back to study the shoreline. His reaction had been what she had expected. Justin had very seldom said more than two words to her in the past two days. And when he had spoken he was short with her. She had decided to stay out of his way whenever possible and for that reason had slept on the bench instead of insisting he permit her the use of his bunk. She had the awful feeling that if she pressed him too far he might try to strangle her.

Nearly half an hour passed and in that time Dara

heard the anchor being lowered and the order from above to lower the sails. They had remained a good distance from shore and Dara assumed it was because the bay wasn't deep enough in this area for a ship of this size to drift any closer. Of course this could be Justin's method of guaranteeing that she wouldn't jump overboard and try to swim to freedom. Well, that was a wasted effort. She had already learned her lesson.

Footsteps sounded in the passageway outside the cabin and Dara didn't bother turning around when she heard the door open. Since she and Justin weren't on speaking terms, it wouldn't do any good to ask why they had dropped anchor. But when something heavy thudded against the floor, she jerked her head around to find Callahan and a young boy struggling with a large wooden tub. She opened her mouth to express her delight at their endeavor only to have them turn their backs on her and leave the room again. One finely arched eyebrow lifted. Maybe Justin wouldn't talk to her, but he obviously listened. Scrambling from the bench she hurried to the center of the room and the tub. She'd be sure to thank him when he returned later.

Another ruckus erupted in the hallway before the door was shoved open and two men entered carrying buckets of steaming water. Excitedly, Dara stood aside and watched the hot water pour into the tub, anticipating the pleasure she would enjoy submerged to her neck. When they had finished, Callahan handed the young man his buckets as well, waved him out of the room, and turned to face Dara. He pulled a bar of lye soap from inside his shirt and handed it to her.

"Ain't much," he apologized, staring at what she held. "I mean I know ladies prefer something that smells nice added to the water, but ain't none of us on board who do"—he smiled feebly—"and we didn't expect company who would."

"That's quite all right, Mister Callahan." She grinned. "Besides, a rose-scented bath is something I've never experienced. To be honest, just being allowed a bath of any kind is more than I'd hoped for. Thank you."

Callahan stared at her a moment, his half-smile lingering as he reflected that a beauty such as this deserved more than a simple bath in a wooden tub with lye soap. She should be dressed in fine silks and live in a big house with servants to see to her every wish. She should be escorted to lavish balls and dine with senators and statesmen, not be reduced to begging for a bath on board a pirate vessel. Ashamed for his part in placing her in this situation, yet knowing the necessity of it, he glanced away.

"I hope you can understand why the cap'n keeps you here against your will," he spoke softly.

Dara shrugged one shoulder. "More than I did at first."

Callahan's gray eyes found hers again. "He needs you, Miss Brandon. He needs your help in finding your brother." Dara opened her mouth to respond, but Callahan rushed on before she could say a word. "He doesn't intend to kill Lane. Your brother is the only one who can prove Cap'n Whitelaw's innocence—and he is innocent, Miss Brandon, no matter what rumors you've heard."

"Then why did he escape prison?" She posed the question, knowing it was on everyone's lips. "If he was innocent, someone would have tried to free him and he wouldn't have to be sailing around in a stolen ship. You must admit, his conduct has only strengthened the guilty verdict. I'd like to believe you, Mister Callahan, but my brother never lies and if he said Captain Whitelaw committed treasonous acts then . . ."

Callahan took her hand in his and led her to the

bench to sit down. "Miss Brandon . . . Dara . . . I know you have no reason to believe a word I say, but I'd like to explain what happened. Will you at least listen and then decide? Perhaps if you hear both sides, you'll understand."

Dara studied the lined face staring back hopefully at her. Although she knew nothing about Douglas Callahan, she sensed he would tell the truth . . . as he knew it. She nodded and settled herself comfortably to hear out his story.

"I met Justin Whitelaw close to ten years ago when he was full of dreams about becoming an officer in the Navy. His father owned a huge shipping line based in Massachusetts, and he grew up loving the sea and the adventure it offered. While most young men were content to learn slowly, Justin never was. Within three years he was the captain of his own ship and a damn good captain, I might add. I guess that's why he took an immediate liking to your brother. Lane was of the same mold. Justin doesn't have many close friends other than me—he likes it that way. But he saw himself in that young man from Drawbridge and taught him everything he could about the sea and the ships that sailed her. They were inseparable. I'm only guessing, but I suspect your brother knows more about Justin than I do. There were many times when I would come into the cabin and find them laughing about something, and even though I asked what they found so amusing, they'd never tell me. Your brother sailed with us for nearly a year, Miss Brandon, and not once did we suspect he was unhappy with the way Justin ran his ship and crew. Yet, out of the blue, he turns up as the only witness against his captain, accusing Justin of treason."

Dara had remained quiet during Callahan's recital, but at his final statement she felt compelled to speak.

153

"But he must have known something. He wouldn't just lie for no reason at all."

"We agree, Miss Brandon. We think Lane was in some kind of trouble. I'm willing to bet my life that he was forced to say the things he did."

Dara frowned, not understanding. "But if they were lies and Lane was the only witness when the rest of the crew denied them, why was Captain Whitelaw found guilty? Surely the magistrate—"

"Yes. The magistrate should have thrown out his testimony. The jurors should have found it questionable. But they didn't. They found Justin guilty on the word of one man. You see, no one else was allowed to testify but your brother."

"What?" Dara gasped in shock.

"That's right. The whole trial was a mockery of justice, and the captain and I were found guilty of treason and sentenced to hang. That's why we broke out of prison. We knew there was no other way to disprove the verdict. And that's the reason we must find your brother and have him renounce his claim."

Turning away, tears filling her eyes, Dara thought of Lane, the sweet, honest brother she loved so much. He had to have been in trouble, his life threatened, or he would never have done such a thing. Swallowing hard, she whispered, "But the message we got a few days ago was from the naval department. It said Lane had been captured by the British. Do you think it's a lie too?"

Sensing the pain and anguish the young woman felt, Callahan gently touched her arm. "There's no way of knowing for sure. It's possible, but I rather doubt it."

Green eyes glistening with unshed tears, she looked at him. "Why?"

"I think whoever put him up to this has hidden him away until Justin is caught and hanged. They can't risk our finding him before then."

"But what's their purpose? Why are they so determined to have the captain hanged for something he didn't do? Who would do such a thing?"

"The only answer we've come up with is this. Many plantation owners are suffering because of President Jefferson's Embargo Act. They do anything to sell their wares, including smuggling. Captain Whitelaw was and is the best officer in the United States Navy. Before this whole mess happened, we confiscated a lot of goods being shipped to Canada illegally. He was the single threat to their success and I think they wanted him out of the way."

"But if he and Lane were such good friends, why would Lane turn against him? I know my brother, Mister Callahan. He would give up his life for the United States before he'd let anyone force him into something that went against his beliefs."

"Maybe he had no choice. There is always one thing that can change a man's mind."

Dara frowned questioningly.

"Most men will do just about anything to protect their family. Someone could have threatened to kill you and your mother and father if he didn't do as they instructed. Maybe Lane agreed to help because he thought that once he had testified, he could return home, place his family in hiding, and then go back to someone in authority and reveal the whole plot. I can't help but believe that Lane would have done that if he could have. He liked Captain Whitelaw, and he was one of the most honorable men I have ever met. So you see, Miss Brandon, we're looking for your brother for two reasons: first and foremost to prove Justin's innocence and then to help Lane out of the trouble he's in. To kill him would be stupid. That is not on our minds. All we ask of you is to help us . . . and to help your brother."

Confusion clouded Dara's thoughts and a long while passed before she could speak. "You make it all sound so simple." She sighed, glancing up at him. "Why didn't Captain Whitelaw tell me this in the first place and save us all a lot of trouble?"

A tender smile curled the older man's mouth. "Because you're a woman."

Dara gave a short laugh. "What has that to do with it?"

Glancing at the doorway as if he expected Justin to walk in at any second, he remained silent a moment, contemplating how much he should tell her and whether he should. Justin wouldn't like it if he knew his first mate was talking about him to a woman he'd only met a couple of days ago, but somehow Callahan suspected that if Dara knew a little about Justin Whitelaw, the man, she would understand more clearly what drove him to do the things he did.

"You're never to tell him we talked of this," he warned. "The cap'n can have a mean temper sometimes and I'm the only one who can cool it down. It could be directed at you if he finds out I told you anything about him. So if you want my protection, I advise you keep this to yourself. Understand?"

"He wouldn't hit me, would he?" she gasped.

Callahan shrugged suggestively. Although he knew his friend was incapable of committing such an act against a woman, he wanted her to think Justin was to insure her silence.

Dara was tempted to tell the man to keep his secrets to himself, but curiosity had always been her downfall. After a moment's hesitation, she agreed with a nod of her head.

"The cap'n doesn't trust women. He likes them, but he doesn't trust them. He was engaged once to a beautiful woman he loved very much. I never met her

156

because that happened before he joined the Navy. But from what I gather, she changed her mind about him when he refused to work for his father and his father cut him out of a huge inheritance. She married a rich senator instead."

Dara's chin dropped. "You mean she was going to marry Captain Whitelaw for the money she thought he would have someday?"

Callahan nodded.

"That's terrible. She must not have loved him or she would have known money has nothing to do with happiness."

"It did to Monica Dearborn. In fact, she told the cap'n that once they were married he would have to give up sailing. She wanted him home so that they would be able to go to the theater and other social events."

Rising, Dara shook her head. "I can't imagine anyone thinking those things are more important than love." One dark eyebrow lifted as she turned back to look at him. "And I suppose she told him she didn't want any children." She raised her nose pretentiously, feigning a haughty air. "Good heavens, no. That simply wouldn't do. It's disastrous on one's figure."

Callahan raised a knuckle to his mouth to hide his smile. "I'm not sure about that, but it wouldn't surprise me none."

Heaving a disgusted sigh, she added, "Well, it's no wonder he hates women."

"Oh, I didn't say he hated women, Miss Brandon," Callahan quickly amended. "He just doesn't trust them. In fact," he went on, coming to his feet, "hardly an evening goes by that he isn't in the company of a young lady."

"Oh," Dara replied, a pained expression crimping her brow. "You mean . . ." Suddenly she couldn't bring

157

herself to finish the question. A dull ache throbbed in her chest.

"I mean don't let yourself be foolish enough to fall for his handsome looks and mysterious ways. There's no future in it." Callahan frowned. "Is something wrong?" he asked, noting the troubled look on her lovely face.

Dara shrugged. "I suppose then that he'd never marry a woman he'd . . . he'd . . ."

"Bedded?" Callahan finished with a laugh. "If that were true, he'd have to marry half the women in Washington. No . . ." His thought trailed off, for suddenly Callahan understood why the young girl had asked such a question. He opened his mouth to voice comforting words, but he realized none existed if what he suspected was true. Dara Brandon didn't strike him as the kind of woman who had had any real experience with men before meeting Justin Whitelaw. In fact, he doubted she had even had a young man call on her. Lane had talked a lot about his sister, how innocent and trusting she was, that the first man who paid her any attention whatsoever would find that he could easily have whatever he wanted from her. That had been Lane's biggest regret about leaving home, and he had constantly worried about Dara because she had no one to protect her. Callahan sadly lowered his head. How ironic that the man Lane had feared would capture his sister's affections had been the one man he fully trusted.

"You'd better take your bath before the water gets cold," he said abruptly, his tone flat and tinged with a hint of anger. His eyes trained on the door, he hurriedly crossed the room and made a hasty exit before Dara could question his sudden change in mood.

Standing in the middle of the room, Dara stared at the closed door for a long while, aware that what

Douglas Callahan had said was true. She hadn't wanted to believe Justin when he'd said he would never marry anyone. She'd felt that in time she could persuade him to do otherwise, but now that his friend had reaffirmed the captain's declaration, she felt lost. And all because of one woman—*Monica Dearborn*. The name rang in Dara's head and brought a sarcastic curl to her mouth. Justin Whitelaw didn't seem to be the type that would allow one bad experience to ruin his life. She frowned, biting her lower lip. Could it be that he possibly still cared a great deal for her? Did he try to mask his love by being with other women in an attempt to show the world that she didn't mean anything to him? Disheartened, her gaze drifted downward and a tear pooled in the corner of her eye when she saw how she was dressed and remembered why. Suddenly, she felt dirty . . . not because he had made love to her, but because she hadn't fought him. She was a whore no matter what he'd said to the contrary. Squeezing the bar of soap she held, she shook off the quilt, slipped from her chemise, and quickly climbed into the tub, lowering herself deeply into the tepid water. She would scrub the scent of him from her and hopefully cleanse the memories of their interlude from her thoughts.

Dara spent the half-hour after she'd bathed sitting on the bench looking out at the coastline. The longboat had been lowered from the ship, and two men had gone ashore, perhaps to inspect the area for they returned within minutes. She had no idea where they had anchored and why, but from the looks of the landscape—thick with trees and brush, and no houses or buildings—she could only assume the captain had chosen this spot to insure their safety. That could very well mean they intended to stay in one place for a while. Her brow lifted wonderingly. Could it also mean that the captain planned to leave the ship for a time? Twisting around, she leaned back against a porthole's framework, hugging the blanket to her. Maybe she could talk him into bringing back something for her to wear. She was tired of parading around in only her undergarments. And now that she thought about it, she was tired of being cooped up in this cabin with no one to talk to. In fact, she was sick of being held prisoner!

As if on cue, she heard the sound of the key in the lock, and in the next instant, the door was opened and Justin walked in. Her pulse quickened at the sight of him, for his shirt was open to the breastbone exposing the mass of dark curls covering his wide chest. She forced her attention away from the sight, only to have her gaze fall to the narrow hips and muscular thighs that flexed with each step he took. Little wonder so many women found themselves in his company if the mere sight of him could disturb even her. After all, he meant nothing to her, and once he allowed her to leave, she would go home and forget all about him. A glimmer of doubt darkened her eyes and she silently rebuked herself. Angrily coming to her feet, she yanked the quilt around her, ready to confront him with her demands.

"Captain Whitelaw," she began, chin held high, "we have to talk."

But when his blue eyes glanced over at her and hinted at his irritation, she wished she hadn't sounded so stern. She smiled weakly and watched him turn away without a word as he crossed the room and knelt before the sea chest, one item she had not been able to examine during her earlier quest to find a key. Her brow furrowed as she watched him unlock it and lift the lid.

160

"What about, Miss Brandon?" he asked drily, searching through the contents of the chest. "Wasn't your bath water warm enough?"

Provoked by his sarcastic reply, she opened her mouth to firmly remind him that any inconvenience she might cause him was due solely to his own making, that if she had her way she'd be on that longboat heading toward shore, but the reprimand never reached her lips. Instead it quickly faded from her mind when she witnessed him lift a black leather bag and a red wig from the chest. She continued to stare in muted awe as he went to the desk and, setting the items on top of it, began to unfasten the buttons of his shirt.

"What are you doing?" she questioned, honestly curious.

He glanced briefly at her then pulled his shirttail free and shook the garment from him, tossing it on the desk near the bag. "I'm taking off my shirt," he answered flatly. "Isn't that what it looks like?"

Dara stiffened. "Well, you don't have to be so flippant with me," she snapped. "I was merely wondering why."

"You needn't worry that I might have thoughts of tumbling into bed with you," he scoffed, opening the satchel. "Once was enough."

"Oh, I'm sorry," she jeered. "Didn't I please you? Maybe I'll try harder next time."

Cold blue eyes settled on hers and Dara instantly looked away. God, how could she have said such a thing? There wouldn't be a next time, and even if he forced her, she'd never try to please him! Her face burned and she decided she needed some fresh air. Sitting down on the bench again, she relaxed in the cool breezes floating in through the open porthole.

Justin longed to pull his attention away from the delicate form sitting too near to him, to dismiss her

161

presence as easily as he had any other woman's. But there was something about Dara Brandon that played upon his mind. He frowned, uncertain of what it was. The gentle wind caught the long, coppery strands of her freshly washed hair which shimmered in the sunlight, and he suddenly found himself yearning to feel its silky texture. She had mocked him when she'd said she would try harder to please him, and he'd known she had blurted out the first thing that had come to her mind when he'd seen the horrified look on her face. He smiled to himself, thinking that no matter how hard she might have tried she never could have pleased him more than she had the first time. That was what disturbed him. No other woman had made him feel that way . . . and no other had left him so full of guilt. Frowning angrily, he set his gaze on the task before him.

They had dropped anchor on the western coastline of Maryland, between the towns of Chesapeake Beach and Deale, where the frigate would go unnoticed. One of Justin's ex-seamen lived on a small farm near the bay as a cover while he continually kept his eyes and ears open for the whereabouts of the young man who had accused his captain of treason. He had taken a new name when he'd bought the small piece of land so that the authorities wouldn't think to look for Justin Whitelaw there. Consequently the place offered sanctuary to Justin whenever he was in the area. Maddock and Phillips had rowed ashore to visit Harold Miller, as he was now known, and inform him that their captain would soon arrive. All Justin had to do now was don his disguise.

Searching through the variety of bottles in the black bag until he found the one he needed, Justin withdrew it, selected a soft bristled brush, and then went to the mirror hanging behind him. Setting bottle and brush on the table by the washbowl, he proceeded to splash water on his face, scrub it clean with soap, then towel it dry. Next he opened the bottle, dipped the tip of the brush in the clear liquid it contained, and began to smear the substance down his jaw line, his chin, and beneath his nose. Waiting until the facial glue became sticky, he then went back to the bag and took out a bright red beard. Several minutes passed as he worked it into place, certain it would hold before he lifted the wig from the desk and carefully covered his own dark hair with it. Once more he searched the bag, then added the final touch to his disguise when he slid gold wire-rimmed glasses onto his nose. Going back to the mirror he studied the effect, positive his own brother wouldn't recognize him.

Satisfied with his work, Justin returned the bottle and brush to the satchel, and placed it back in the chest. Then he lifted a plain white broadcloth shirt from inside. Slipping it on, he buttoned up the front all the way to the neck, tucked the tail into his breeches, and took a black coat from the trunk. Rising, he slid the jacket up over his arms, briskly rubbing the wrinkles from its dark cloth. He straightened the collar before he glanced up and discovered a wide-eyed observer.

Dara had sat transfixed all the while the captain had donned his disguise, amazed at the difference it made in his appearance. Nearly lost in thought, she had stared out the porthole to avoid his gaze until she heard him moving about and her fear of his intentions pulled her glance to him. But her worries quickly dissolved into curiosity as she watched him smear the clear liquid over his face, wondering what would ever possess him to do such a thing. Once he had put on the wig and perched the glasses on the bridge of his nose, she realized what his game was. He planned to go ashore dressed and wanted no one to recognize him. The question was why? What was waiting for him once he got there? Her brow wrinkled. And where had he learned to apply a fake beard?

"Captain Whitelaw," she said, shaking her head as her gaze shifted from his head to his toes, "if I hadn't watched you put that on, I never would have guessed who you were. Where did you learn how?"

"An actress friend of mine showed me," he said with a half-smile, oddly pleased by her compliment. "I have several outfits and each one is different. The only thing that might give me away is my height."

Dara continued to appraise the disguise. "Is this how you've managed not to be caught all these months?"

"Well, I'm sure it's part of it," he answered, crossing to his desk. "I try never to wear the same costume twice in the same place, plus I don't stay long. It's not easy for me to change the pitch of my voice. I really worry that it might give me away." He opened one of the drawers, withdrew his pistol, and stuck it into the back of the waistband of his breeches. Then he returned to the sea chest and lifted a Bible from inside.

Dara frowned. "Preachers don't wear guns, Captain."

Grinning, Justin said, "They do when they're wanted for treason." Bowing slightly from the waist, he added, "Reverend Flanagan at your service, lass."

Dara couldn't stop the giggle that escaped her and she raised a hand to her lips when Justin eyed her questioningly. "I'm sorry. I just envisioned you standing at the pulpit preaching hell and damnation, the Bible in one hand and the pistol in the other. I'd wager no one would miss Sunday services for fear you'd shoot them for it."

"Yes, I imagine not." He laughed, studying the delicate lines of her face, but he turned away abruptly when he felt his pulse quicken at the sight of her slim

164

form draped in the thin coverlet. Tossing her clothes overboard had been a good idea at the time, but now he regretted it. She was a very lovely woman and he doubted that even if she were fully dressed he wouldn't feel the urge to take her in his arms. Kneeling, he closed the lid of the trunk and turned the key.

"Where are you going?" he heard her ask.

"To meet a friend of mine," he said flatly. Rising, he went back to the mirror to inspect his attire again to make certain everything was in its place. He frowned disgustedly when he caught her reflection in the glass over his shoulder. He closed his eyes when she stood up and the blanket fell away from the too revealing neckline of her chemise.

"You know, Captain, if you're worried about someone suspecting who you are, I have an idea that would insure your safety."

For some reason, Justin didn't like the sound of her suggestion. "Such as?" he questioned cautiously.

"You can take me with you. They'd never think to look for Captain Whitelaw in the company of a woman." She smiled brightly, then remembered what Callahan had said about the man's numerous affairs and quickly amended her statement, a light blush coloring her cheeks. "I mean . . . traveling with a woman."

A smile lifted the corners of his mouth and he turned slowly to look at her. "Nice try, Miss Brandon, but the answer is no."

"Why not?" she demanded.

Justin's blue eyes traveled the length of her. "Did you truly intend to walk around dressed as you are? I said I have many dsiguises but they don't include one for a woman." He chuckled at the way her face flamed as she jerked the coverlet around her to hide the view she had carelessly given him. "And somehow I don't think it would be as safe taking you with me as it would to leave you here."

He was met with an angry glare. "Are you saying my idea isn't a good one?" she snapped.

"Nay . . . quite the contrary. It's an excellent cover. However, you're not the one I should use."

"And why not?" she asked indignantly. "I *am* a woman, you know."

Justin smiled suggestively. "Oh, there's no question about that, Miss Brandon. You and I both are aware of just how much of a woman you are. But that's also one of the reasons I would never allow you to leave this ship. It's too dangerous for any woman to be with me without the protection of my men."

"I'm not afraid of danger!" she shouted angrily. "If I had been, I never would have left my home."

Justin glared back at her through lowered eyebrows. "I'm reasonably certain you didn't expect to find the kind of trouble you did, Miss Brandon, or you would have stayed at home. But even if I thought no harm would come to you, I still wouldn't take you along."

"Why not?" Her lower lip curled in a pretty pout.

"Because at the moment, you have more interest in seeing me caught than anyone else. You'd love to be standing at my side in the middle of Washington so you could scream your bloody lungs out to tell the world this preacher isn't one at all, but Justin Whitelaw, an escaped traitor." He shook his head. "Sorry, Miss Brandon, the answer is no."

"That's not true," she argued. "Mister Callahan said you were looking for my brother to prove your innocence but also because you think he's in trouble. I want to help you find him. We can work together. With me beside you, who'd ever guess who you were?"

Justin looked at her doubtfully.

166

"You still think I'd turn you in, don't you?" she sighed irritably.

"Wouldn't you?" he asked with a grin.

"No!" she snapped. "How could we ever get married if you were in prison?"

Justin could only stare at her awhile, his chin sagging, before the humor of her insistence that they wed struck him and he laughed. "You're not going to give up, are you? You're bound and determined to have me stand before the altar simply because we made love."

Dara hadn't meant to remind him of her plans. She looked away and shrugged.

"Oh, yes you are," he continued, his smile lingering. With a shake of his head, he rounded the desk and sat down on the corner of it. "Let me ask you something, Miss Brandon. What kind of a man did you hope to marry? Had you envisioned someone your own age with the same dreams and goals in life? Did you plan to buy a small farm and live out the rest of your days there, have a dozen little ones following you around, be content to have nothing more than his love?" When she wouldn't look at him, he sighed, knowing he had guessed correctly. "There's more to picking a husband than just deciding on the one you happen to fall into bed with. If you want to be happy for the rest of your life, you should love the man whose name you carry."

"Oh, I agree," she said without hesitation, and Justin straightened when she moved closer to him, a strange look on her face. "But my chances of having such a life have changed and all because of you. I didn't just fall into bed as you put it. You forced me. Maybe my upbringing wasn't what it should have been, but I was always told that the man with whom I shared a bed would be my husband. As for loving him . . . well, that might come in time, but that is a luxury not all wives enjoy, nor did I count on it." She stopped only inches from him. "Now let me ask you a question, Captain Whitelaw. Let's pretend you had never met me before and you suddenly decided you wanted to marry me. How would you react if I told you that you weren't the first man I had been with? Would your attitude toward me change? Would it make no difference to you? Could you touch me, hold me in your arms and never once think that someone else had done it before you? What would you really think of a woman like that?" She raised a finely arched brow and waited, but when he only looked at her for a brief moment then glanced down at his hands folded over one knee, she laughed sarcastically and turned away. "I thought so. You're no different from any other man. No one would want to marry me knowing that."

"That's not true, Dara," he said softly. "You asked me what I would think. That doesn't mean every man is the same. There's one somewhere—"

Her laughter cut him short. "What? Who would want used goods? I don't agree. I don't want someone's pity," she added, twirling to face him, "I just want a man who accepts his responsibilities." She paused a moment to let her meaning register before continuing. "Let me ask you one final question, Captain. What would you do if I came to you in a few months and told you that I carried your child?"

Justin's complexion paled beneath the red beard.

"Don't bother answering," she laughed bitterly. "I already know. In two months I won't be around. You'll have put me ashore and moved on. That way you'd never have to decide. Am I right?"

Suddenly Justin didn't like the way their conversation was going. "Dara," he warned, coming to his feet,

"I don't even know if I'll be alive in two months. I'm not even sure about tomorrow. And what kind of child would want a father who'd died as a traitor?"

"That's better than no father at all!" she screamed, tears filling her eyes.

"This is ridiculous," he growled, grabbing the Bible from the desk and storming to the door. "You're not going to have a baby and I'm not going to marry you!"

Dara jumped at the loud banging of the door when Justin slammed it shut behind him, and tears streamed down her face. "Oh, yes you are," she whimpered. "You just don't know it yet." As a mixture of anger and hopelessness whirled around in her, she stomped over to the bench and plopped down upon it, arms folded over her chest, knees crossed, one leg swishing back and forth. There was a determined look on her face.

Justin hid among the trees lining the riverbank, absently watching Maddock row the longboat back to the ship. His thoughts should have been on his mission, but anger clouded his mind. After a moment he looked toward the vessel, envisioning the copper-haired beauty waiting in his cabin. How did he always manage to make his life more miserable? After Monica had walked out on him, he had made up his mind never to get involved with a woman again, much less marry one. For that reason he had thrown himself into his work. Commanding a ship always gave him the excuse to end an affair after a few days. What woman would wait for him? But this situation was a little different. He couldn't walk away from her when she lived on board his ship, and if he sent her away now, that would prove everything she'd said about him was true. One corner of his mouth curled beneath the red beard. Besides, he didn't trust her enough to turn her loose . . . especially now. Maybe she wouldn't inform the authorities about him, but he was certain she would hunt for her brother until she found him, tell Lane what had happened between them, and then seek his help in forcing Justin to marry her.

"Women," he muttered beneath his breath. "They're all the same."

Turning away, he clutched the Bible in one hand, readjusted the frock coat, and started off toward Harold Miller's farm. It was nearly thirty miles into Washington, too far to reach on foot before dark. He needed a buggy, one that would add a touch to his disguise and aid in the hasty completion of his journey. He couldn't afford to stay too long.

It was midafternoon by the time the buggy rolled into the busy streets of the capital, and although the man holding the reins appeared to concentrate on the path the mare took, his eyes were ever alert for anyone who paid him undue attention. It was Justin's plan to check the inns for a young man asking about his sister, despite the fact that he doubted Lane was anywhere in the area. Yet he couldn't risk ignoring the possibility that for once Dara Brandon had told him the truth and Lane was, indeed, somewhere close by. If he was lucky, he'd find Mark Wallis, his contact from Cambridge, before too much time had passed and thereby would save himself the effort of visiting every inn and boardinghouse.

Reining the mare to a halt outside Butler's Inn, Justin covertly surveyed the throng of people moving about the walkway, especially seeking military men. He climbed down once he felt certain no one had paid him any notice. He tied the horse to the wooden railing near the steps, lifted the Bible from the buggy seat, held it in his hand so that everyone would see its gold lettering, and then started for the entrance.

The delicate tinkling of a bell overhead announced his presence once Justin opened the door and stepped inside. The air in the lobby was cooler than that in the dusty street, and he silently thanked his good fortune. The wig and beard were uncomfortable enough without having to contend with the heat as well. Glancing about to make sure no one was watching, he reached up to scratch his chin where it tickled; then he settled the glasses more securely on his nose and approached the front desk.

"Good afternoon to ya, lad." He addressed the man standing behind it in the best Irish brogue he could affect. "Me name is Reverend Flanagan and I be needin' your help."

"Of course, Reverend," the desk clerk nodded. "What can I do for you?"

"I am lookin' for a young man and I've come all the way from Ireland to find him."

"What's his name?" the clerk asked, opening the register.

"Oh, I be doubtin' he'd use his real name," Justin continued, leaning forward as if he didn't want anyone else to hear. "Ya see, the young man ran away from the lass he was supposed ta marry and sailed here ta meet another. I've come ta take him home."

"Oh." The clerk smiled.

"He's a crafty one, Michael is," Justin added with a wink. "He'd be nineteen with blond hair and blue eyes, skinny for a lad, and if I'm not mistaken, he'd be askin' if his sister has registered."

"His sister?" the desk clerk asked. "Do you suppose

171

she would use her real name—I mean the woman he's planning to meet?"

"Aye, 'tis possible. Michael would be askin' for Dara Brandon."

"Brandon, Dara Brandon," the man repeated, then shook his head. "We don't have anyone here by that name and as I recall no one has asked for her." He shrugged apologetically. "Maybe you should try another inn."

"Aye, lad, 'tis what I must do," Justin agreed, standing erect as he gently patted the Bible he held. "God bless ya, me son."

"Thank you, Reverend Flanagan," the clerk called out as Justin went to the door.

Stepping back outside into the bright sunlight, Justin paused to allow two ladies to pass before him on the sidewalk. He nodded politely at their cheerful greeting, and said that he hoped they attended church on Sunday. Returning to the buggy, reins in hand, he smiled beneath the cover of his beard. It was probably best if he didn't use this particular disguise anymore. He was beginning to like the undeserved respect he was getting.

The next two hours found him visiting several more inns and always getting the same answer. No one had seen Lane Brandon.

I wonder if you ever tell the truth, he mused, thinking of the red-haired beauty waiting in his cabin. *First you say you don't know where your brother is, then you do, then you don't.* He shook his head. *I'm beginning to think you don't even know who Lane Brandon really is.* Sighing as he pulled the rig around to head toward the edge of town where he intended to get something to eat, he realized his unsuccessful trek through the inns of Washington had gone just as he thought it would. He'd

172

almost wager his ship and crew that the young man was somewhere far away from Washington. The question was where . . . and who was keeping him from coming home?

Sweat beaded his brow, and as Justin reached up to wipe it away with the back of his hand, he spotted a man standing casually in the alleyway a short distance ahead. He recognized him instantly. Mark Wallis nodded in response to Justin's signal, a tug on one earlobe. It had been difficult for Justin to resist scratching his chin where the beard itched, a sign that it was too dangerous to meet. Gritting his teeth, he snapped the reins and hurried the buggy on, thinking that the next time he'd be more selective in choosing a disguise. The facial glue was slowly driving him insane. Calling on every ounce of strength he had, Justin waited until the buggy had passed Wallis so the man could no longer see his face; then he heartily rubbed the irritated area, letting out a long, satisfied sigh as he did. God, how he longed to live a normal life. But a smile brightened his eyes as he clicked his tongue to urge the mare into a canter down the road leading out of town, for he knew, if given the chance, he wouldn't give up the life he had.

Directing the buggy into a stand of oak trees a safe distance from the outskirts of the capital, he welcomed the shade, set the brake, and looped the reins around the handle to await his friend. Only a moment or two passed before he heard the steady gallop of hooves coming toward him. He settled back comfortably into the seat. His search for Lane may have been futile, but somehow he sensed Mark Wallis would make the trip worthwhile.

"Good afternoon . . . ah . . . who is it this time?" the curly-headed man grinned and urged his horse along-

173

side the buggy.

"Reverend Flanagan, laddie," Justin chided. "Have ya come ta have your soul saved?"

Laughing, Mark leaned forward to rest against the pommel of his saddle. "If I had, I certainly wouldn't ask you, Cap'n . . . er . . . Reverend. I swear you get better with those things every time you try."

"Yeah. Well, this one itches," Justin replied, running a thumbnail along his jaw line. "I'll be glad to get out of it. And the sooner the better. So tell me what you found out and let me get back to my ship."

"Sure, Cap'n, but tell me something first. Is it shedding the beard and wig that makes you want to hurry back or the little lady you got stowed away in your cabin?"

Justin's blue eyes narrowed as he gave his friend a good-humored frown. "I assure you, Wallis, if you had to put up with that little minx, you wouldn't be in any hurry to go back."

"Giving you trouble, is she?"

"You could say that. I just spent the last two hours checking every inn I could find because she told me she was to meet her brother at one of them. Of course he wasn't there. And when I get back and tell her as much, she'll think up some other lie to keep me off his trail."

"Maybe you're not using the right method of persuasion," Mark offered with a grin.

"Believe me, if I thought it would work, I'd let you do the persuading."

"Since when?" Mark laughed. "You've always had an eye for the ladies and . . . Oh, I get it. She's an old maid for good reason."

Smiling, Justin propped his booted foot on the framework of the buggy and picked a piece of lint from the knee of his breeches. "No, Mark, that's not it at all.

In fact I think she's one of the most beautiful women I've ever seen."

Wallis straightened with a puzzled frown. "So—"

"Can we just get on with business?" Justin interrupted. "I don't like being so close to Washington. It is where I was sentenced to hang, you know."

Tilting his head to one side, Mark considered his former captain for a minute, then nodded resignedly, knowing that if Justin Whitelaw didn't want to talk about something, he wouldn't. "The colonel's full name is Emerson Edward Winslow. He owns a tobacco plantation near Baltimore and is openly against the Embargo Act. He's been to one meeting since you asked me to watch him. It was held here in town, but the only ones to attend were plantation owners. If he's got a contact in office, I don't know who it is right now, but I can find out if you'll give me a little more time."

"Do you think he likes to hear himself talk, or is there a possibility that he really does have connections?"

"Oh, I think he was telling the truth, Cap'n," Wallis continued. "That man is dangerous. There aren't many around here who aren't afraid of him and the power he carries. And by the way, Cap'n, he's upped the price on finding the young woman. She might be a handful, but for her own safety, you'd better see she stays with you until Colonel Winslow is put away. He means to see her dead."

Justin shrugged. "Then I guess we have to go through with the deal I made with him. And in order to do that I need to talk with George Manning."

"Senator Manning?"

"Is there another George Manning?" Justin grinned.

Frowning, Mark gazed around them, then turned back abruptly to add, "You might as well want to talk with the president, Cap'n. Senator Manning is as well protected as Jefferson."

"He's the only man I would trust for this job."

"All right," Mark relented, hands raised in front of him. "But it isn't going to be easy."

"Has anything we've tried been easy?" Justin smiled.

Wallis stared at his captain for a long while before he sighed and shook his head. "No. And I guess we both like it that way." He chuckled. "Well, while I was snooping around I heard about a masquerade ball Senator Prescott is giving next week. Since you enjoy dressing up like you do"—his outstretched hand indicated Justin's attire—"that part of it will be simple. I'm not positive, but I think Senator Manning will be in attendance. The rest is up to you."

"I suppose it's by invitation only?" Justin asked.

Mark nodded.

"Then do me two more favors." He smiled.

Cocking his head to one side, Mark raised a brow. "One is to get you an invitation. What's the other?"

Justin shifted uncomfortably on the buggy seat, his eyes averted as he studied the deserted road. "Miss Brandon needs a change of clothes. I'd pick them out myself, but it might raise a few questions if the Reverend Flanagan was seen buying a dress and women's accessories. Don't make it anything fancy. I don't want her to get the wrong idea."

Mark watched his captain for several moments, a knowing smile on his lips. Justin Whitelaw didn't have to explain what was going on between him and the young woman. Mark could guess. "All right, Cap'n. I'll see what I can do. The invitation will take a little time, but I can be back with the clothes in an hour or so. Just give me an idea of her size and tell me where you want to meet?"

"Right here. I haven't had anything to eat all day so

176

I'm going back into town," Justin replied, then he roughly described Dara's proportions. Reaching for the reins, he said, "Give me a little head start before you follow."

"Aye, aye, Cap'n," Mark grinned, watching Justin turn the buggy around to direct it toward the buildings in the distance.

Chapter Seven

Ashen streams of moonlight ribboned the blackness of the forest as Justin stood in the shadow of the riverbank and watched the dark shape of the longboat slowly glide toward him. Within a few minutes he would be on board his ship, safe, and would have a chance to calm his nerves. But tonight he was tempted to sleep at Harold Miller's farm. Dara Brandon's presence disturbed him and he couldn't honestly say why. He had had numerous affairs, and although some of the ladies would have preferred their relationship to last longer than it did, none of the beauties he had bedded had ever assumed he would marry them. Even if they had, he was sure their suggestion wouldn't have bothered him as much as Dara's had. Could it be that he thought so much of her brother that he truly felt guilty for what he'd done? Or was it because she was a virgin and he had been the first? That had never been the case before. In fact many of the ladies had lured him to their bedchambers without any prompting on his part. Now that he thought about it, why should he feel guilty about anything? Dara Brandon was a grown woman. She had to have known what she was getting into when she'd left home unchaperoned. A half-smile spread across his face and vanished. If Colonel Winslow had been the one to seduce her, would she have insisted he marry her knowing what she did about him?

"Probably," he muttered to himself as he caught the end of the rope Maddock tossed to him. "The little fool hasn't the sense she was born with."

"You say something, Cap'n?" Maddock frowned as he watched Justin loop the rope around a narrow tree trunk to steady the boat.

"No, just voicing an observation," Justin grumbled, bending to pick up the package near his feet and throw it onto the tiny vessel before he climbed in after it. "And if you want some advice from me, you won't get involved with women."

Maddock's frown deepened. "Aye, aye, Cap'n." He nodded hesitantly, failing to understand what provoked such a comment, but crediting it to one of Justin Whitelaw's odd moods, he shrugged it off as unimportant and asked, "Did everything go all right for you in Washington?"

"As expected," Justin replied, flipping the rope to free it from the tree and set them adrift. "Was anyone snooping around the ship while I was gone?"

"Nay, Cap'n. In fact we haven't even seen another ship since we dropped anchor."

"Good. Maybe if we're lucky, it will stay like that."

"Why's that, Cap'n?" he asked, rowing them toward the *Lady Elizabeth*.

"I sent Wallis on an errand and told him I'd wait here for him. It could take him a few days. We'll be all right if we're not spotted before then."

"Well, don't worry Captain Whitelaw. There're men stationed in the crow's nest day and night. Besides," he added, reaching for the rope ladder on the side of the ship as they neared it, "we could always sail down the bay a ways and come back later."

"Aye," Justin agreed, tying off the longboat and

picking up his package. "It would just be a lot simpler if we didn't have to."

"Aye, Cap'n," Maddock replied, steadying the ladder as Justin climbed aboard. Once they both stood on deck, he added, "Sir? You want me to wake Callahan?"

"No. Let him sleep. I can talk to him in the morning. Good night, Maddock," Justin said, turning for his cabin.

"Good night, Cap'n."

The yellow glow of lantern light flooded the passageway leading to the captain's quarters, and Justin experienced an eerie chill as if he were walking to the gallows.

"This is absurd," he growled beneath his breath as he stopped just outside the entrance. "A man can't even find peace on his own ship." He inhaled deeply then let his breath out in a rush, a determined look on his face. "Well, you're not going to run things around here, Miss Brandon. *I'm* the captain of the *Lady Elizabeth* and you'd better get used to it. What *I* say is the way it is."

Seizing the latch almost angrily, he opened the door and stepped inside, pulling up short when he was met by darkness laced with silver streams of moonlight coming in through the portholes. Had the little minx escaped? How? Surely one of his men would have seen her. Squinting to get a clearer view, he glanced at the empty bench, then remembered that she had hidden behind his desk once and smiled. Satisfied that *this* time *he* would outsmart *her,* he gave the door a gentle nudge. It swung quietly shut as he moved toward the desk and the hurricane lamp sitting there.

"Captain?"

Justin started at the sound of her voice coming from behind him, thankful that he hadn't had the time to light the candle and allow her to see how she had surprised him. He took a breath to calm himself, tossed his bundle on the desk and then fumbled in the darkness for the flint and steel that would spark a flame to the wick. A soft yellow glow filled the room a moment later and he turned to look at her, his heart suddenly thumping in his chest once he saw her. She sat in the middle of his bunk, her thick, shiny mane tossed wildly about her shoulders, and the flickering light played seductively with the alluring curves of her cheeks and throat, exaggerating the valley between the tempting breasts hidden beneath her chemise. No matter how hard he tried, he couldn't pull his gaze from the vision she unwittingly created.

"I didn't think you'd be back tonight," he heard her say. "Did you find your friend?"

Blinking, Justin tugged at the collar of his shirt, thinking how warm the room had suddenly become. "Yes," he answered quietly. He reached up to pull the wig from his head and tossed it onto the desk. Turning away from her, he went to the washbowl and filled it with water. Then he shrugged out of his coat, laid the pistol aside, and stripped to the waist, unaware of the wide eyes that observed his efforts. "Go back to sleep," he added, forcing himself not to look at her reflection in the mirror as he peeled the beard from his jaw.

Dara watched him lather up a small piece of cloth with the bar of soap lying next to the basin and vigorously scrub his face and neck with it. "But you didn't find Lane," she observed calmly, cringing when she heard him laugh.

"You didn't really think I would, did you?" he rallied sarcastically, bending to rinse away the soap and splash water through his hair. Taking the towel from the hook on the wall, he wiped his face dry, rubbed the moisture from his hair, and turned to look at her. "You knew I wouldn't even before I left here, didn't you?"

Dara glanced down at her hands and shrugged. "Yes."

"Then you admit you lied to me."

Timid green eyes looked up at him. "With good reason."

"Oh? Well, suppose you tell me what that was," he ordered, tossing aside the towel as he rounded the desk, then leaned back against the edge, arms folded over his chest. "I'll let you know if I believe it."

Uncomfortable beneath his penetrating stare, Dara glanced away again. "I . . . I wanted a way off this ship. I thought you'd take me with you. Then, if the chance came, I was going to run away from you."

"And tell the authorities where to find my ship and crew," he added matter-of-factly.

Dara nodded. "Until Callahan told me why you were looking for Lane." Her expression softened as she turned back to look at him. "Why didn't you tell me in the beginning why it was so important that you find my brother . . . that you had no intention of killing him? I would have helped rather than sent you searching the streets when I knew he wasn't there."

Justin smiled crookedly. "Would you have believed me?"

"Yes."

He smiled broadly. "You're lying, Miss Brandon."

"Well, maybe not at first, but I would now," she assured him.

"Why?"

Dara opened and closed her mouth repeatedly, trying to find the logical answer, and she frowned angrily when Justin laughed.

"For once," she stormed carelessly, "can't you put the past behind you and realize that I'm one woman who isn't using you?"

Dara's temper cooled instantly when she saw his eyes

darken and his nostrils flare as he fought to control his rage. She bit her lower lip for courage, recalling Callahan's warning about the man's nasty disposition whenever memories of Monica Dearborn were stirred.

"I . . . I'm sorry, Captain Whitelaw. I . . . I didn't think. . . ."

"You never do, Miss Brandon," Justin growled. "And someday you're going to be very sorry you opened your mouth and said the first thing that came to mind."

"But I didn't say it to hurt you," she argued, her throat tight. "I . . . I only wanted . . ." She gasped when he stood up suddenly and started toward her.

"What else did Callahan tell you about me, Miss Brandon? Did he tell you that it's the other way around now? That I use women because of what happened to me? I do, you know. I use them and then leave them behind without a care. I'll do that with you . . . any time I want . . . as often as I want. Would you like me to prove it to you?"

Dara's body trembled and she knew it wasn't from the cool air touching her skin. Grabbing the quilt, she pulled it up beneath her chin, inching away from him when he neared the edge of the bunk. "No," she said in a tiny voice.

"Well, I think I should prove it to you so you'll give up this silly notion that I should marry you." He rested a knee on the bunk. "I'm never going to marry you, Dara Brandon . . . never!" With lightning speed he reached out, caught a handful of her thick mane and yanked her up onto her knees, the coverlet still clutched in her hands as he crushed her body to his.

Dara's slim frame went rigid. Her round, fearful eyes stared back into his, and her thoughts raced, seeking something she could say that would make him stop. "If . . . if you're not going to marry me, Captain

184

Whitelaw," she began, cursing the tears that surfaced in her eyes and belied the strength of her words, "then I can't let you do this."

"And how will you stop me?" he whispered, appraising the creamy whiteness of her skin, the finely boned features of her face, and her ruby-colored lips that begged to be kissed. "Are you hiding a gun somewhere? Maybe I should check." He smiled brightly in the golden light surrounding them and raised his hand to pull the coverlet from her fingers.

Dara fought for possession of the quilt with all the strength she could muster, but when his grip tightened on her long strands of hair and promised to become tighter, the pain he caused loosened her hold and the coverlet was easily torn from her fingers. Overpowered by his physical power to subdue her, Dara made a feeble attempt to lessen the entanglement of her coppery curls, and she gasped when she felt his warm hand boldly fondle her breast then roam downward over her waist and linger on her hip before caressing her opposite side. Frantic to have that torment end, she doubled up a tiny fist and pounded it against his chest.

"You brute," she sobbed. "I don't blame Monica for leaving you!" She squeezed her eyes shut, choking down a scream when he shook her.

"She didn't leave me because I got rough with her, Dara. But if I thought it would work with you, I'd beat you senseless," he snarled.

"And you'd enjoy every minute of it," she cried, unable to stop her tears. "You're a scoundrel, Justin Whitelaw. You take advantage of a helpless woman and then tell her it's her fault. You cad . . . you beast . . . you *traitor!*"

Suddenly Dara found herself sprawled on her back in the middle of the bed, Justin's huge frame towering over her.

"Does this mean you've changed your mind about marrying me?" he jeered.

"No!" she rallied, hoping to greatly disappoint him. "And when I find Lane—"

"You'll what? Blackmail me? You'll tell him not to clear my name unless I right the wrong I've done to his poor, innocent sister? Don't threaten me, Miss Brandon. I don't take kindly to someone who tries to force me to do something against my will."

"Just how do you think I feel?" she shouted. "You're the one who—"

"Who what?" he laughed bitterly. "Made love to you?"

"Rape!" she screamed. "It was rape."

Justin's dark hair shimmered in the lamplight when he shook his head. "No, little one. What those men back in Cambridge intended to do with you was rape. I simply showed you the art of lovemaking"—he smiled one-sidedly—"as I will again."

"No!" she howled, lashing out at him when he lowered himself to the bunk. "Not until you marry me!"

Justin chuckled, ducking a wildly thrown punch intended for his chin, another for his ear, and then easily catching both of her wrists and falling on top of her. "Are you saying that a few words spoken by a minister would make what we're doing perfectly all right?" He grinned down at her, feeling her slender form squirm beneath him.

"Yes!" she exclaimed.

"And you wouldn't fight me?" he continued, his blue eyes flashing mischievously.

Dara ceased her struggles to stare suspiciously up at him. "It would be your right if you were my husband."

"Hmm," he said as if contemplating the idea. "Would Reverend Flanagan suffice?"

Her green eyes darkened to a dangerous shade, rage burning in them. "Of course he wouldn't," she hissed, "and you know it. Now *get off!*" Dara arched her back to push him away and unwittingly pressed her body against his, the thinness of her chemise doing little to veil the contact. She became stiff and stared fearfully up at him.

"It doesn't matter," he said softly, lowering his head. "I rather enjoy the contest. It merely proves who is the stronger. There isn't anything you can say or do to change my mind. You know that, don't you, Dara?"

Her hot denial never reached her lips, for Justin had already pressed his own against them. A wave of heat seared through her body and Dara felt light-headed as if she had been lifted by some magical force to float on love-swept wings. Her desire to fight left her. She wasn't aware that he slid the chemise from her trembling body or that he rose to shed his own garments, only that he came to her with gentleness reflected in his rugged features. Lying down beside her, he tenderly traced the smooth outline of her waist and hip; then his hand moved to the silky flesh of her inner thigh. Dara gasped when his open mouth covered the taut peak of her breast just as his fingers claimed the softness of her, touching her where no other had ever dared. She knew she should hate his gentle probing, demand that he stop, but she couldn't, for in that moment a wild ecstasy exploded within her and she moaned deliriously.

Rising up above her, Justin parted her thighs with his knee and touched his manhood where his fingers had been, his mouth moving to capture hers, his tongue parting her lips and pushing inside. He kissed her softly at first, holding back his desire to take her, and he felt his body tremble when she boldly ran her hands down his back to rest them against his buttocks, urging him on. But he resisted, wanting the sensation to last. As his kiss trailed down the slim column of her throat and across her shoulder, then down to taste her full, ripe breasts once more, he heard her call out his name as he lightly sucked the firm mound of flesh. Then he felt her hands move to cradle his face, hoping to draw his mouth to hers again. But instead he caught a delicate finger and softly kissed it before parting his lips to run his tongue against the tip.

Dara jerked her hand away, shivering deliciously at the sensation he aroused. When he raised his head to look questioningly at her, she smiled alluringly.

"Come to me, Justin Whitelaw," she whispered temptingly and saw passion darken the blueness of his eyes. "Come and know you are mine."

Whether he heard the words she spoke or knew their meaning, Dara could not tell, but without hesitation, Justin shifted his weight and pressed her down into the softness of their bed, his mouth covering hers in a hungry, urgent kiss. A flaming desire to unite their bodies drove him on, and to his surprise she met his first thrust with equal readiness, arching her hips to move in symphonic rhythm.

A long while passed before they lay cradled in each other's arms, the coverlet drawn up to hide their nakedness. Dara snuggled closer, her head resting on his broad shoulder as she ran a fingertip through the dark mass of curls covering his chest. She sighed happily in the warmth of his embrace, knowing that as soon as a preacher could be found, Justin Whitelaw would make her his bride. Together they would look for her brother, who would denounce the charges brought against Justin. Then she would live out her life wherever Justin wanted to take her.

"This doesn't change anything," his deep voice whispered.

Dara lovingly rubbed her cheek against the thick muscle of his breast. "Change what?" she murmured, lost in the afterglow of their passion.

"Between you and I," came the cold answer, but Dara didn't understand immediately.

"I don't want anything to change between us." She laughed softly and pushed herself up to look at his handsome face. Her own paled when she noticed the angry frown that crimped his brow and saw that he wouldn't look at her. Then his meaning became quite clear, and Dara was suddenly filled with a mixture of emotions, the strongest being anger at her stupidity for being tricked into doing what she had done. Her throat tightened. Or had it really been a trick? Hadn't she truly wanted him to touch her, hold her, make love to her? Why? How could she have let it happen? Tears burning her eyes, she sat upright in the bed, yanked the coverlet around her, then slid to the edge and stood up.

"I'm afraid you're wrong, Captain," she said, her voice strained. Choosing not to look at him, she surveyed the deck at her feet to find her chemise and quickly stooped to retrieve it, adding, "because next time I'll fight you to the very end. I'm not Monica Dearborn. I'll take you the way you are, but I'll not again share a bed with you until we can do so as husband and wife." Chin held high, she strode to the desk, cupped one hand around the top of the hurricane lamp and blew out the candle, plummeting the cabin into darkness. In the safety of the shadows, Dara lingered by the desk, one hand touching its surface to steady herself while she closed her eyes and let her tears fall freely. She was so ashamed.

Veiled in the ebony curtain of the room, Justin watched her indistinct silhouette from his bunk, one knee bent and his wrist dangling over the edge. He had meant it when he'd said he could use her, then forget her. He had done that with every woman since Monica. His pale blue eyes clouded with the pain as he recalled the callous way she had announced her forthcoming wedding to Samuel Rutherford—and all because the senator had the money to buy her anything she wanted. Didn't she understand how much he loved her, still loved her? He blinked when the slim figure of another woman moved to stand before the porthole in the cabin, and suddenly his thoughts of the past vanished as he watched the coverlet glide to the floor. Straining to see in the blackness that surrounded him, he had to be content to imagine the shapely curves the chemise now hid from view as he distractedly watched Dara put it on. A lazy smile teased the corners of his mouth as he remembered the flash of fire he had seen in her eyes when he'd mocked her earlier. Resting his head back against the pillow, he closed his eyes and relived the feel of her supple body next to his, the gentle thrusting of her hips as she'd welcomed him, matching his desire with her own. His blood stirred in his veins at the memory of the sweetness of their kiss, of the taste of her silken skin, the fragrance of her hair. Yes, he would forget her in time. He just wasn't sure how long it would take.

Opening his eyes again, his gaze fell upon her slight form now lying on the bench and bathed in muted streams of moonlight. He smiled. She would sleep sitting up if she had to before she'd again allow him to spark the passion hidden deep inside her. He chuckled softly, wondering why she couldn't just admit it was there and enjoy their moments of lovemaking while they lasted. He wasn't going to tell anyone what had happened between them. No one would have to know. Why all this nonsense about getting married? Shaking his head, he pushed himself up on one knee and stepped from the bunk. Well, whether she liked it or not, she would share his bed one way or another.

He crossed the cabin noiselessly, but when he bent to take her in his arms, she bolted upright with a shriek.

"Stay away from me," she warned.

"Or what?" he smiled. "You'll scratch out my eyes?"

"I mean it, Captain Whitelaw," she hissed. "Don't lay a hand on me."

Justin tilted his head to one side. "I repeat, Miss Brandon, or what?"

"Or . . . or you'll be very sorry." Even to her the words sounded empty.

He chuckled. "I've been sorry for a lot of things, and I'm beginning to regret not having left you on the dock to fend for yourself."

"I couldn't have done much worse," she muttered.

"Oh? You mean what happened between us is worse than having one or all of those men rape you and then hand you over to Colonel Winslow? You'd be dead now, Miss Brandon." Her expression was lost in the shadows of the cabin, but Justin didn't truly have to see it to know she was considering that prospect more favorable. He looked down and smiled. "Well, maybe this is not preferable to your way of thinking, but most would say you're better off here. And since there is little you can do about it, I suggest you make the best of the situation. For starters, you can get a comfortable night's rest by sleeping in my bunk."

Coppery strands of auburn hair glimmered in the moonlight when Dara lifted her head to get a better view of his face. "Do you mean that?"

"I wouldn't have said it if I didn't," he assured her, his voice laced with humor. He offered his hand to help her to her feet, and she quickly responded.

"Maybe we could take turns," she said, heading toward the bed.

"Turns?"

"Yes. Tomorrow night you can have the bunk and I'll sleep on the bench."

Justin paused at the edge of the bed, watching her shadowed form climb in and adjust the quilt over her. "No turns, Miss Brandon. What I meant was that we'd share."

The coverlet flashed an obscure white when Dara yanked it back around her and rose to her knees. "No, we won't!" she shouted, awkwardly crawling across the mattress only to halt when Justin blocked her exit.

"I'm tired, Miss Brandon," he said, his voice low, "and all I have in mind right now is to sleep. When I'm tired I get irritable, so don't press your luck. Now lie down, cover yourself up, and go to sleep. *I'm* the captain of this ship and you're going to learn that what I say goes. From now on, you're going to share this bunk with no objections and you'll do whatever I tell you."

"Or what?" she queried sarcastically.

"I'll tie you in it," he said bluntly, leaning forward to look her in the eye. "Would you care to challenge that statement?"

Dara's brave façade crumbled at this threat. She imagined all the horrible things he could do to her if her hands were tied, as she sat frozen, afraid to move.

"Now, Miss Brandon," he ordered through clenched teeth, grinning secretively when she jumped at the command and hurried to the far side of the bunk. "Very good," he added, lowering himself to the mattress. "You learn quickly." After fluffing up his pillow, he grabbed the quilt from her hands, flipped it out to cover them both, and then settled himself comfortably on the bed. "Good night, Dara Brandon."

Huddled in the corner with walls on either side of her, Dara refused to lie down, knowing that the narrowness of the bunk would force her to touch him

192

accidentally should she do so. Although darkness prevented her from seeing clearly, there was no mistaking the fact that he hadn't donned his breeches or any other form of clothing. The thin chemise would be the only hindrance should he change his mind about sleeping. She sat perfectly still, vowing not to move for the remainder of the night, and she silently contemplated various methods of insuring that they didn't make love again. A disappointed pout curled her lower lip when nothing realistic came to mind. Even if she had a pistol to point at him, she doubted it would take much effort on his part to get it away from her. Disheartened, she pulled her knees up to her chest and rested her chin on them, quietly staring at the dark profile of the man who at this moment ruled her life.

Stirring from a comfortable sleep, Dara rolled onto her back and was greeted by bright sunshine streaming into the cabin and across the bunk. Shading her eyes with her hand, she opened one at a time to view the morning and then bolted upright in the bed when she remembered who had shared it with her the night before.

"Good morning, Miss Brandon. Sleep well?" Justin asked with a smile as she quickly surveyed the cabin and finally spotted him sitting behind his desk. Clamping a lighted cheroot between his teeth, he braced his bare feet on the corner of the desk and leaned back in his chair to study her. It never failed to surprise him that this young woman appeared more beautiful each time he looked at her, but this morning she was absolutely radiant . . . especially with that light blush to her cheeks. Brilliant auburn hair tumbled wildly about her shoulders, and her green eyes held a glimmer of fear that added a dimension to her willful, insolent nature. One dark eyebrow rose as he wondered what thoughts might be going through her head when he saw her hug the quilt to her, covering the full swell of her bosom and disallowing any further appraisal on his part.

The rogue doesn't have the decency to clothe himself, she silently observed, for from her place on the bunk opposite him, the desk hid his lower torso from her view. Wide, bronze shoulders, and bare feet and ankles were all that she could see, and she knew she would swoon if he stood up suddenly in the full light of day. Struggling to breathe, she mutely cursed her misfortune for having awakened before he had dressed.

"Are you hungry?"

Blinking, Dara looked at him again, but when he swung his feet to the floor and started to rise, she gasped, dropped the quilt, and buried her face in her hands, too devastated to answer.

"Are you all right?" she heard him ask, and she knew from the sound of his voice that he had rounded the desk and now stood very close to her.

"G-go away," she moaned.

Justin's brow ridged in a confused frown. "What is wrong with you?" he questioned, bending to take her wrist and pull her hand away from her eyes. When she jerked free, his patience evaporated. "Dara, look at me and tell me what's wrong," he demanded.

She shook her head, locks of her colorful hair falling about her face.

"Dara," he growled, irritably grabbing both of her hands and pulling her up to face him. When she still refused to open her eyes, he gave her a bone-rattling shake. "Look at me."

"No," she whimpered. "Not until you dress."

A moment of quiet followed while Dara continued to keep her eyes squeezed tightly shut, vowing there was nothing he could do that would make her look at him. But when she heard his mirth rumble deeply in his chest and then explode into full-fledged laughter, a glimmer of doubt surfaced in her mind.

"And would you walk about all day like this?" he chuckled. When she nodded stubbornly, he added, "'Twill prove most difficult. Maybe I should teach you the methods of a blind man."

Before Dara could object or even question his meaning, he yanked her forward and pulled her from the bed to stumble against him.

"First you must open your hand so that you can feel your way around. Like this," he instructed, slipping his thumb beneath the fingers curled over her palm. When he applied a little pressure to her knuckles, she unwillingly followed his direction as a tremor of pain shot up her arm.

"Justin, don't," she begged, her head turned away and her eyes still closed. She wanted to jerk free of him but knew she couldn't. He held her much too firmly.

"Now, Dara," he crooned, "you don't want to stub your toe, do you? I'm helping. Here, see how it works?" With that, he forcefully drew her fingertips to his bare chest.

"No! Justin!" she shrieked when the contact sent a rampant electrical charge through her whole body. She fought to pull away but his strength forbid it, and she felt a rush of warmth sting her cheeks as he slowly brought her hand down over the firm muscles of his chest and lean belly. Tears burned her eyes when he continued the torment, running her fingers across his ribs on one side then downward once more toward his hip. "Justin! Stop—"

But her demand never was completely expressed, for suddenly the branding heat of his bare flesh against her own ended as he drew her hand over the rough cloth of

195

his breeches. Her eyes flew open in surprise, her smooth brow wrinkled as she stared open-mouthed at the garment. Then she heard him chuckle and knew the game he had played. Exploding in a fit of temper, she twisted free of him, raised her open hand, and gave him a stinging slap across his face.

Justin took the assault gracefully. It had occurred too suddenly for him to prevent it. And after all, didn't he truly deserve it? His smile lingered as he rubbed the back of his hand against his abused cheek, his blue eyes dancing with mischief.

Annoyed that she had failed to destroy the pleasure his prank provided him, she raised her hand once more, ready to hit him again. But this time Justin was too quick for her. He caught her wrist in midair, lowered his chin, and grinned at her.

"I'll not allow it a second time," he warned playfully.

Not the least discouraged, for her pride had been sorely injured, Dara glared back at him, something akin to a snarl curling her lips, and without hesitation she raised the heel of her bare foot to tread heavily on his toe.

Justin grimaced with pain, but somehow he managed to maintain his hold on her. "You little hellcat," he growled, all mirth gone from his eyes. "Someone ought to teach you how to behave."

"Oh?" she mocked carelessly. "And I suppose you think it should be you. What would you do, beat me?"

The words had barely passed her lips before she realized how they sounded. She had given him an open invitation to try, and from the look in his eyes, she knew that he was considering the offer. Her own ire vanished and she gulped, frantically seeking something to say that would change his mind.

"But . . . but, of course, you wouldn't do something

like that," she said, forcing a smile. "You're a gentleman, and a gentleman wouldn't strike a lady." She tried unsuccessfully to pull her hand from his.

"A gentleman," he repeated casually, his blue eyes sparkling roguishly once again. "That was not the title you gave me only last night. Let me see . . ." he said, glancing up at the ceiling as if trying to remember her exact words. "Ah, yes, cad, beast, as well as traitor." He looked back at her. "And now you wish to add gentleman to the list? If I were a gentleman, Dara Brandon, you wouldn't be standing here dressed as you are."

Her cheeks flamed instantly at his reminder that the quilt still lay on the bunk, and a chill touched every inch of her flesh. She forced a laugh. "It was just a misunderstanding. What gentleman wouldn't react the way you did?" She tried again to pull her hand from his, but his grip only tightened.

"Are you saying that if you had been I you would have done the same thing?"

Dara shrugged weakly. "Yes," she replied, hoping to give him the answer he wanted to hear.

"H'm," he said thoughtfully. "Then you do not blame me for making love to you either? I mean, after all, it was a misunderstanding and any gentleman would have acted as I did." He raised one dark eyebrow, waiting.

Suddenly Dara realized the trap he'd set, but she silently vowed not to give him the upper hand. A vague smile lifted the corners of her mouth. "Possibly. But then, had I been you, I would have offered marriage to the woman I had wronged. Don't you agree, Captain?"

Justin's grin danced brightly in his blue eyes. "If you had been I, yes, you probably would have. But herein lies the problem. You're not me, and I would not and

197

will not offer marriage to correct a misunderstanding. 'Tis too great a price for a tumble in bed with a she-wolf."

Dara's temper flared. "A she-wolf? Did you expect me to succumb to your lecherous advances? You're an arrogant fool if you do."

"And no gentleman?" he finished with a smile.

She opened her mouth to affirm the statement, then realized he had only played with her and yanked her hand away. "Why don't you just let me go? Send me back to Drawbridge and forget any of this ever happened."

"I'm sure I could forget it happened, but would you?" he challenged. "Or would I forever have to be looking over my shoulder for an irate father with his musket pointed at me?"

Dara's lip curled in an unflattering snarl. "My father won't have to force you into marrying me, Justin Whitelaw. You'll do it on your own."

"Oh, really?" he laughed, watching her take the coverlet from the bunk and whirl it around her shoulders. "Now who's the arrogant fool?"

Dark green eyes glared up at him.

"Well, you must admit the unlikelihood. After all, what man who lives as I do would seek a woman's hand in marriage because he had bedded her? That would have to be done out of love, Miss Brandon, and I know you'll find this hard to believe, but I don't love you."

"As I've said before, Captain, the union of two people is not always founded on love, but on responsibility." Jerking the quilt tighter around her, she brushed past him and went to a porthole to stare outside at the early morning sunlight. "Given time you'll realize that and seek out a preacher to fulfill your responsibility." She cast an icy glance over her shoulder. "And by the way, I don't love you either, but that shouldn't be too hard to accept. Has any woman you've ever known loved you?"

Dara missed the darkening of Justin's eyes when she turned away to stare out at the bay again. She had meant to hurt him and could only hope she had, although she didn't truly know why doing so was important to her. He didn't mean anything to her. In fact, she honestly detested his cocksure attitude, and if there were some way to undo everything that had happened between them and free herself of his presence, she would do it. Being married to a man like Justin Whitelaw wasn't her idea of the way she wanted to spend the rest of her life. A wave of hopelessness and self-pity washed over her, and her eyes suddenly filled with tears.

Dara had struck a raw nerve in Justin when she'd purposely pointed out that he had never known a woman's love. But instead of experiencing the usual pain that accompanied the thought, he'd become angry and defensive. He didn't need or want a woman's love, much less the companionship of one on a permanent basis. He could very well do without a woman's ever-changing moods, her tirades, her tears. He had learned not to allow himself to open up to a woman, not to let down his guard. He gritted his teeth, his nostrils flaring as he recalled the humiliation he had suffered at the hands of Monica Dearborn when he had begged her to reconsider her decision to wed Senator Rutherford. He would never put himself in that position again, not as long as he lived.

Turning away from the shapely form standing near a porthole, his gaze fell upon the bundle he'd brought back with him from Washington. Scowling, he went to it and picked it up.

"Here," he said, tossing it at her feet. "Put this on. I grow weary of the way you strut about half-naked."

Dara jerked her head around to remind him of who

199

was accountable for her manner of dress, but she spotted the package lying on the floor near her. Her curiosity to see what was inside the brown paper tied with string distracted her, and she bent to retrieve the package, then settled herself on the bench, balancing it on her knees so she might undo the twine and examine its contents. Beneath her nimble fingers, the wrappings fell away quickly to reveal a bright yellow cotton dress with white lace adorning its short sleeves and low neckline. A mixture of surprise and happiness flooded over her, and she lifted her eyes to express her gratitude only to find that he had turned his back on her and was pouring himself a large amount of whiskey from the bottle he had taken from his desk drawer. Deciding he would neither want nor appreciate her thanks at the moment, she concentrated on the present he had given her.

Shrugging out of the coverlet, she took hold of the dress by the sleeves and stood up, intending to unfold the garment so she could examine it. But as she did so, the wrappings slid from her lap and fell to the floor before she noticed something else accompanied the gown. Her mouth dropped open in surprise as she viewed petticoats, chemise, stockings, and yellow slippers lying at her feet. In the midst of them all, she found a pearl-handled brush and a mirror. Tears came to her eyes, and she glanced over at the captain again. However, she bit back her words of joy when she saw him down his entire drink and then pour another. Deciding her thanks could wait until later, she scooped her treasures into her arms and went to the bunk where she lovingly spread them out before her.

Peeking at him once more to make certain he didn't watch, she quickly exchanged her old chemise for the fresh one, pulled on the stockings and petticoats, then shimmied into the yellow dress and fastened the buttons up the front. When she had finished, she let out a long happy sigh, her eyes closed. She felt like a queen dressed in her new clothes, certain she could take on the world with renewed enthusiasm and that nothing Justin Whitelaw might say could spoil any of it. Smiling brightly, she plopped down on the bed and picked up the brush, holding it gently in her hands as if it might break or, worse yet, vanish. She had never owned anything so exquisite and she concluded that if she died at this moment nothing else in her life had made her any happier. Slowly lifting the brush to the long strands of hair draped over her shoulders, she stroked the tangles from her auburn locks.

The whiskey burned his empty stomach yet it eased Justin's distress a little. Imbibing spirits before breakfast was not his usual custom, but then again, discussing marriage wasn't either. If he didn't need Dara's help in finding her brother or if the dangers of her returning home weren't so great, he would turn her loose right now. His life was complicated enough without having to contend with her stubbornness. Finishing off his second drink, he poured another and sat down in the chair behind his desk. Of course, just finding Lane and sending her home wouldn't end his problems. This young woman wouldn't be satisfied until she had a husband to rectify her shame over what they had done. Glass raised to his lips, Justin froze when a thought struck him, and a smile replaced his frown. She had openly admitted that love was never a factor in her consideration of a husband. Therefore, any man who wanted to marry her would do. Yes, that was it! He would find someone willing to wed her; then he would be free to carry on as he had before.

Silently complimenting his cleverness, he tipped the glass higher, smiling into his drink, but he nearly strangled on the whiskey when his gaze fell upon the beauty sitting opposite him. The early morning sunlight that filled the room seemed to radiate in the soft yellow shade of her gown, and it highlighted the golden glow in the coppery curls she was brushing into a shiny brilliance. White lace trimmed the puffy sleeves of her gown and rested intimately along the décolletage of the dress. Caught up in her task, she had unknowingly crossed her knees and had thus revealed trim ankles covered with white stockings and tiny feet adorned with yellow slippers whose hue was similar to that of the gown. At each gentle sway of her shapely calf, white ruffled petticoats peeked out from beneath the hem of her skirts, and Justin suddenly found it difficult to breathe.

Damn you, Wallis, he muttered to himself, taking note of the hairbrush and mirror she held. I told you to make it simple. Now she'll think this was all my idea. I ought to make you marry her just to get even.

Gulping the remainder of his whiskey, Justin slapped the glass down on the desk top. Angrily pushing himself to his feet, he stormed to the door, slamming it noisily behind him as he left the room.

Chapter Eight

The last rays of daylight had faded into a moonlit night veiled by a dense fog that clung heavily to the trees and underbrush. Faint yellow shafts of light emanated from a small farmhouse, illuminating the surrounding blackness, it and the smells of freshly roasted pheasant filled the air. Hidden away in a thick stand of pine, two horsemen sat quietly observing the run-down farm buildings in the hope that one of the occupants would venture to the barn, leaving his companion alone in the house. But nearly an hour had passed since they'd come upon the farm, and they resignedly decided the men who lived inside had settled in for the night. Exchanging glances, they silently agreed to advance on foot and complete the purpose of their journey. Tying their horses to the branch of a pine tree, they withdrew their pistols and started for the house.

"I told you two ta wash up," Emma Thornton barked, her pudgy fists buried in the flab of her waist as she confronted her two sons. "It's time for supper."

"Yeah, Ma," John replied, lifting his mug of ale to his lips again. "We're coming."

"So's winter," she snapped, cuffing him across the

ear. "Now get a move on!" Her stormy glare settled on the youngest of the two, and Willy hurriedly set aside the gun he was cleaning to do as she instructed.

"Ya shouldn't get so excited, Ma," he said, ducking out of the way when she sought to club him as well. "It ain't good for ya. 'Sides, we done told ya we could hire us one of them maids like the Barringston's has so's ya won't have ta do none of the work no more. We can afford it."

"That's right, Ma," John joined in, punctuating his remarks with a chuckle. "Why we could even get us a butler ta answer the door."

"What for?" she asked, her lined face revealing her irritation. "So's he can stand around all day? Nobody comes here, ya blasted fool. Now get up off that lazy arse of your'n and wash up, or ya ain't gonna get a thing ta eat. Ya hear?"

"Yes'm," John muttered, setting down his mug and casting his younger brother a disgruntled look.

He was a full head taller than Willy and twice his weight, yet both men towered over their mother. Nonetheless, for as long as John could remember she had ruled the farm, ever since their father had run out on them years before. Between the three of them, they had barely scratched out enough of a harvest to feed themselves, always longing for a better life and promising themselves someday they would have it. Rising from the chair in front of the fireplace, John now smiled to himself as he recalled how they had come to be ten thousand dollars richer than they were a few short weeks ago.

One night four months ago, John and his brother had gone into town to visit the local pub and drown their sorrows in ale as was their custom every Saturday night. But that time a stranger had approached them, offering money for their services, and at John's insistence, Willy had let the man explain his proposition. He had wanted the brothers to go to Washington and sit in the back of the courtroom during the trial of Captain Justin Whitelaw. They were to stay there until it had ended and the captain had been found guilty. Once it was over, they were to abduct the only witness, a young man by the name of Lane Brandon, take him out into the countryside where no one would see them, and kill him.

Willy had been dead set against it, saying that no amount of money would make him kill a man, but John had quickly agreed. At the time he couldn't explain why, but he'd had a feeling there was more to the story than the stranger cared to reveal, something that promised a greater reward than the mere one hundred dollars he gave them as partial payment, the remainder to be paid once the deed was finished. And John had been right. Only he hadn't figured out the whole story until they'd grabbed Lane Brandon coming out of the courthouse that day. The young sailor had been a member of Whitelaw's crew and had testified against the man, claiming that the captain was a traitor to his country. Since no other crewmen had come forward, John could only assume the boy had lied and whoever was paying to have him killed wanted him dead so he couldn't go to the authorities later and confess. Thus John's plan was born. He would hide Lane Brandon and demand ten thousand dollars from the stranger in exchange for the youth.

Crossing to the washbasin in the tiny three-room house, John remembered with amusement how scared he had been when he and Willy had confronted the stranger two days later. But somehow he had convinced the man that they meant what they said, that they would take the Brandon boy to the magistrate in Washington if they didn't receive the money in one month's time. The waiting had been dreadful, nerve-racking. At any moment, he'd expected someone to break in the front door and shoot them. But as each day had passed, John's courage had grown, and before long he'd decided ten thousand wasn't enough.

He chuckled as he splashed water over his face, recalling how angry the stranger had become when John and Willy had appeared in the man's room at the inn a day earlier than agreed and had announced the new terms of their deal. But, of course, he couldn't argue for John had held a pistol aimed at the man's midsection while Willy had rummaged through his luggage for the money, more than either of them had ever dreamed they would see in a lifetime. It had all gone so easily, and now in little more than two weeks' time, they would have twice that amount.

"Ma," John said, coming to the table, "fix me up a plate ta take to the boy. Then I'll eat."

"He can wait," Emma snorted, plopping down onto a chair that creaked objectingly at the abuse of her huge frame.

"Now, Ma"—John smiled—"ya know he's important. Without him I wouldn'ta been able ta buy ya that purdy dress ya got on."

Dull brown eyes glanced up at him, then back to the table as Emma began heaping her plate full of mashed potatoes and peas. She covered them both with thick brown gravy. "He eats more'n his share," she grumbled, reaching with her fork to stab a piece of meat.

"Ah, Ma, there's plenty," John argued, sitting down beside her as he spooned a small helping of food onto a plate. "Ain't that right, Willy?"

Looking up at his brother, his mouth full of food, Willy nodded then bent over his plate again, devouring as much as he could as fast as he could so he could have seconds before John returned to claim his share.

Noticing how Willy was gorging himself, John leaned forward and slapped Willy's hand. "Save some for me, ya half-wit," he bellowed. Then he stood, glaring down at his brother as he angrily snatched the plate from the table and headed for the door. "If there ain't none left when I get back, you'll be huntin' in the dark for a rabbit ta fix me. Ya hear?" he shouted over his shoulder as he lifted the latch to pull the door open wide. But if Willy gave him an answer of any kind, John didn't hear it, for when the dull lights of the cabin fell out onto the porch, they highlighted the two dark figures standing before it. The plate fell from John's fingers and crashed to the floor.

"Ya clumsy oaf," Emma ranted without turning around to look at her son. "Now the boy can go without and he can blame you! I ain't givin' him no more." A wisp of wind blew into the room and fluttered the flame of the candle sitting on the table in front of her. Twisting around in her chair, she shouted, "And close that—" Emma's face paled instantly when she saw two strangers enter the house, their pistols drawn and pointed at her sons.

"Good evening, Mrs. Thornton," the taller of the two smiled evilly. "I'm sorry to disturb your meal, but we have some unfinished business with the boys here."

"What . . . what do ya want?" she asked hesitantly.

"We've come to collect what's left of the money and see that your guest no longer causes anyone any trouble. Now if you'd be so kind as to tell me where you're keeping Mr. Brandon, we can be on our way."

"H-how did ya find us?" John asked wide-eyed, his gaze affixed to the weapon aimed at his stomach.

"Quite simple, Mr. Thornton," the man replied. "Anyone with any intelligence wouldn't have simply come home to wait. All we had to do was ask a few questions in town. You shouldn't have gotten greedy,

Mr. Thornton. You should have taken what my employer offered the first time and been satisfied. Now you've made him angry and he's sent us here to dissolve the partnership." He raised the gun a degree and, eyes narrowed, asked, "Where are you hiding Lane Brandon?"

"In . . . in the root cellar," Emma quickly offered, thinking the men would leave them in peace once they had what they wanted. Pushing herself to her feet, she hurried to a small cabinet near the fireplace, withdrew a tin box, and turned to face them once more. "And the rest of the money's in here. I told them boys what they done was bad, but they wouldn't listen. Here . . . take it." The metal container clunked loudly when she tossed it on the table and stepped away.

"You're quite right, Mrs. Thornton. What your boys did was wrong, but I'm sorry to say, they must pay for it." A smile crept over his face as he set cold, blue eyes on her. "And so will you, I'm afraid."

Darkness closed in around Lane, the damp chill of the root cellar sending an involuntary shudder through him as he huddled in one corner. Leaning back against the wall behind him, he rested his head against it, eyes closed, knees drawn up, and arms clamped around himself for whatever warmth they might produce. So many days had passed since the morning he had testified at Captain Whitelaw's trial that he had lost track of them, but he was reasonably certain several months had elapsed, most of which he had spent locked in this dark cavity, although sometimes he'd been forced to do the chores the Thornton brothers had demanded of him. Not that he truly minded, for the time spent working in the fields gave him the chance to stretch his legs and feel the warm sunshine on his face.

It also took his mind off his family.

"You tried to tell me, Pa," he whispered, a tear stealing from the corner of his eye to fall unheeded down his cheek. "You said I didn't know what I was in for leaving home. Now I do. And you and Mother and Dara are probably dead because of my foolishness . . . just like Captain Whitelaw." His throat tightened and he fought the flood of tears that threatened to escape him. "There's nothing I can do now to bring him back, but I swear to God I'll clear his name. If—no—when I get away from these men, I'll go straight to the magistrate in Washington and tell him the truth. I'll—"

A volley of gunfire exploded in the quiet of the night, and Lane bolted to his feet. It was too late in the evening for Willy or John to be hunting. Besides, the shots were much too close to the house. What could they mean? Was there trouble? An inner sense of danger charged through his thin frame. He had listened to the Thornton brothers laugh over how they had double-crossed their business partner, and he knew that the only reason he was still alive was because they needed him in the scheme to blackmail the man. Was it possible that he had figured out where the Thorntons lived? Perhaps, at this very moment, John and Willy lay dead on the floor in their run-down house? Racing to the door of the root cellar, Lane struggled to see between the cracks in the wood planking, knowing that if he had guessed right, his life would end very soon as well. Whoever was responsible for the false charges brought against Captain Whitelaw, whoever had forced him to verify them in court, no longer had any need of him. In truth, Lane was a danger to the man.

Shifting to get a better view, he could barely make out the front door of the house, but in the yellow light that fell across the porch he saw two dark figures step outside. The men were the same height and much stockier than either John or Willy, and Lane knew instantly that if he wanted to see the sun rise again, he would have to do something to gain his freedom—fast. He lingered a moment longer, watching the men until one of them motioned toward the root cellar, turned, and started to walk away. The second man headed in Lane's direction. Spinning around, he rushed to one of the fruit bins and frantically tore a board loose, testing its weight in one hand. He'd only have one chance to carry out his plan and he knew he would have to wait until just the right moment. He'd worry about the man's partner once he was free of his prison.

Hearing the man's footsteps just outside the entrance to the cellar, Lane spun around and rushed to hide beside it, praying his heart wasn't beating as loudly as it sounded in his ears. If it were, it would surely give him away the moment the man opened the door and stepped inside. His weapon held high, he heard the heavy bar being lifted. The rusty hinges squeaked as the door was opened, and the dim light of a lantern fell into the tiny space.

"Mr. Brandon," the man's voice called. "You can come out now. We're here to take you home."

Don't listen to him, Lane silently warned himself. It's a trick. He's going to kill you.

"Come now, Mr. Brandon," the deep voice implored. "Surely you want to see your mother and father again. Dara sends her love."

Dara. Visions of his sister exploded in his mind. They had threatened to murder his parents, then use her in a most degrading manner if he didn't cooperate. Those had been his reasons for agreeing to testify against Captain Whitelaw. He gritted his teeth, tears burning his eyes. He would not be fooled. And he must remain quiet. He had to lure the man inside.

"We kept our part of the bargain, Mr. Brandon.

Your family is safe. This was the Thornton boys' idea. We had every intention of taking you home. To be quite honest, son, my employer was outraged when he heard what had happened to you. He even paid the Thorntons money for your freedom."

Lane knew the only way he could get out of the cellar without being shot was to get the man to fire his pistol at something else. Then, before he had time to reload, Lane could storm the entrance and hit him with his club. But he'd have to do something—now. The man wasn't going to be content to carry on a one-sided conversation for much longer. Glancing around, he spotted a discarded burlap bag laying on the floor near him. Nervously, he picked it up, praying against all odds that his scheme would work. Taking a deep breath to ready himself, Lane tossed the bag into the air where the man could see it and flinched when gunpowder exploded an instant later. Without allowing himself time to reconsider the dangers of his plan, Lane jumped from his hiding place and raced through the door, swinging his club in all directions.

The first blow caught the man in the belly, and he dropped the lantern to clutch his stomach, crying out in agony. Undaunted in his quest for freedom, Lane raised the board high above his head and brought it down against the base of the other's skull. The man's knees buckled instantly and he fell unconscious to the ground. Not bothering to look for the man's partner, Lane spun around and ran toward the thick growth of trees surrounding the farm. He had nearly reached their cover when a shot rang out and he was struck in the shoulder by the lead ball. It knocked him to his knees. Although he felt as if his entire body were on fire, Lane forced himself to ignore the pain that coursed through him, knowing that his life depended on reaching the forest and the safety its darkness offered.

211

Stumbling to his feet, he half ran, half staggered onward, hearing the angry shouts of the man behind him. Head spinning, Lane reached out for a tree branch for support, but the narrow limb cracked under his weight and he fell a second time just as another round was fired. The ball whizzed past his ear and he knew if the branch had held him upright, the shot would have caught him squarely in the back.

He longed to lie where he had fallen and ease the pain that bolted through him. He felt as if a hot poker had pierced his flesh and someone sought to drive it deeper, but he realized he couldn't afford to waste a moment in making good his escape. The man had surely already reloaded his gun and was coming after him. With a new surge of strength, Lane clutched his injured arm with his good hand, struggled to his feet, and hobbled farther into the blackness of the forest.

Bright morning sunshine spilled across the land, lighting every corner of the woods and the road that divided it. Two men stood by the side of the heavily traveled thoroughfare studying the trail of blood they had followed since dawn had made its first showing hours before. Not only were these spots dry, after this point there were no more. The duo could only curse their misfortune. Obviously, Lane Brandon had gotten a ride with someone who had come down the road, but with so many tracks in the dirt it was impossible to be sure in which direction he had gone.

"We'll have to split up," the first man growled, pointing to his left. "You go that way. And remember . . . you're not to stop looking. We were sent here to kill that boy and we won't be welcomed back until we do. He couldn't have gotten far, not in his condition. In fact, from the amount of blood he's lost, I wouldn't be

212

surprised if he isn't already dead." Gathering up the reins of his horse, he mounted the steed and added, "I'll meet you in Monterey in one week. One of us should have found him by then or at least have run into someone who has seen him. Good luck, Fletcher."

"Same to you, Reynolds," the second nodded, swinging himself up into the saddle.

With a shout, both men spurred their animals and bolted off down the road in search of their quarry.

The smells of fresh hay and clean bandages filled Lane's senses, yet he was too weak to open his eyes and investigate his surroundings. The occasional honking of geese and the steady clucking of chickens penetrated his half-conscious world, and although no sunshine beat upon his closed eyelids, his body burned from some other form of heat. His mouth was parched, his lips were dry, and he wanted to call out for a drink of water, but he hadn't the energy to do so. He swallowed arduously, wondering if the men who had attacked him had somehow caught up to him, and this was their form of torture. Silently, he prayed it wasn't, for he hadn't the strength to fight them anymore.

As he lay there listening to the slow, steady rhythm of his heartbeat, a new fragrance pleasantly filled his nostrils, a fresh, sweet smell that hinted of cleanliness. He could not identify its source. Then he heard, crystal-clear, the tinkling of water and his agony began again. He longed to moisten his lips. He struggled to open his eyes and instead felt a cool, damp cloth pressed against his brow. He moaned, one eyelid fluttering open, and through a hazy fog he saw an indistinct figure bending over him. He fought to rise.

"Thou must rest. Thy wound is serious," the soft, dulcet voice beseeched, a gentle hand pushing him back

213

onto the bed of straw.

"Where . . . where am I?" he asked, forcing his eyes to focus on the woman at his side.

"On my father's farm," she answered with a smile. Her dark brown hair was pulled back from her pretty face and tied in a knot at the nape of her neck. "Thou are safe now. No one can harm thee."

Although his shoulder throbbed and his body burned with fever, Lane managed a weak smile in return as he took in the simple attire the young girl wore. Her plain gray cotton dress was buttoned all the way to her neck and had no fancy trim. He had only met a few in his lifetime, but he was reasonably certain this young lady was a Quaker.

"My . . . my name is Lane Brandon," he said slowly, trying to hide his pain.

"I am pleased to meet thee, Lane Brandon." She blushed, bowing her head. "I am called Prudence . . . Prudence Mitchell."

Relaxing, he glanced up at the rafters overhead, and sighed. "That's a pretty name, Prudence Mitchell. Were you the one who found me?"

"No. My father did. Thou were lying by the side of road," she answered, dipping her cloth in the bucket of water again. Squeezing out most of the moisture from it, she leaned forward slightly to stroke Lane's brow and cheek in order to ease the fever that glowed hotly in his face. "Thou were unconscious. Who shot thee?"

"I don't know who they were," he said quietly, closing his eyes and savoring the feel of the cool fabric against his heated flesh. "But they won't stop until they find me." Turning his head toward her, he looked up at her. "May I have something to drink? I'm terribly thirsty."

Her dark brown eyes sparkled and Prudence smiled as she moved to fill a dipper with water. Gently lifting his head, she carefully tipped the ladle until he could moisten his lips. "Take only a little," she instructed; then she lowered his head upon the blanket again when he had finished. "It will make thee ill otherwise."

"Thank you," he whispered.

"Thou are welcome," she nodded. "Now rest while I go to the house and get my father. He will want to know thee are better."

It seemed to Lane that he had no sooner closed his eyes than he heard their footsteps coming into the barn again, and when he glanced up at them, he instantly noticed the striking resemblance between the two. The eldest Mitchell wore gray-colored breeches, white shirt and stockings, and black shoes. His hair was just as dark as his daughter's except for a patch of gray at his temples and his brown eyes were as warm and friendly as Prudence's.

"So," the man questioned, "thou are feeling better?"

Lane nodded slowly. "A little. Your daughter tells me I have you to thank for being alive."

He smiled. "I may have helped a little, but thou must thank the Lord for the rest. I am known as Edwin Mitchell, and thou are welcome to all I have to offer, Lane Brandon."

"I am afraid I have no way to pay you for it." Lane frowned.

"Pay?" Mitchell repeated. "I do not expect anything in return, son. I but give aid and comfort to a weary traveler." Touching his daughter's hand, he added, "Tell thy mother that our guest is awake now and to prepare him something to eat."

"Yes, Father," Prudence answered, making a short curtsy. But before she turned to leave, she smiled timidly at Lane, started to blush, and hurriedly made her exit before either man could notice.

Edwin Mitchell watched his daughter's hasty departure with amusement, then he retrieved a bucket from one of the stalls and placed it upside down near Lane. "Thou must forgive my daughter," he smiled, perching himself on the overturned bucket. "We have very few visitors and she is quite taken by thee."

"Her innocence reminds me of my sister," Lane said quietly, his gaze falling on the empty doorway of the barn.

Mitchell watched the young man for a moment, noticing the sadness reflected in his eyes. Bending, he picked up a piece of straw and absently toyed with it. "It's none of my business, Lane, but sometimes talking helps."

Lane glanced up at Mitchell, surprised by the man's ability to guess his thoughts when they were nothing more than strangers.

"I could see it in thy face," Mitchell offered. "Does thy sister have something to do with the reason thou was shot?"

Lane's entire life had been a sheltered one until he'd left that day to join the Navy. Even then he had been fortunate enough to be assigned to a ship with a crew that shared his loyalty to the United States, and he had lived the kind of life he'd wanted. He had never had cause to mistrust anyone until that morning when a message had been delivered to him while the ship was docked in Chesapeake Bay. There had been no signature. It was only a statement of what would happen if he failed to do as instructed. He had wondered if the note had been a lie, if whoever had sent it only hoped to trick him, if his family would be all right; but deep down inside, Lane knew he couldn't take that chance. So he had testified against his captain and had fulfilled his part of the agreement, thinking that once the trial was over he would be free to go home. But as he'd left the courthouse that day, two strangers had approached him with drawn pistols, and he'd been whisked away to live for three long months not knowing what to expect. His faith in honesty and justice had been shattered, and although he wanted to trust someone again, he simply couldn't do it. Edwin Mitchell seemed to be the sort of man he could confide in, but given the whole story and the fact that Lane's mere existence was worth a great deal of money to someone, would this stranger turn against him as well? Closing his eyes, he turned his head away, not willing to answer.

Edwin Mitchell sensed the reason why the boy was reluctant to talk. The lead ball he had dug out of the young man's shoulder had entered from the back, and he knew his wound couldn't have been caused by an accident. Someone had tried to kill him. There could be many reasons why someone thought Lane Brandon's life should be terminated, but to Edwin Mitchell none were good enough. All he wanted to do was help this young stranger, yet he knew he would have to prove it to him before Lane would tell him how he'd come to be lying unconscious on the side of the road two days ago. He truly couldn't blame the young man for not trusting him. Flicking away the piece of straw, he came to his feet and glanced at the doorway.

"We are strangers, Lane Brandon"—he spoke softly without looking at him—"but I am not thy enemy. Rest and after thou has eaten, I will help thee to a room in the attic of my house where no one will think to look for thee." He was silent a moment; then he turned a friendly smile on the troubled face staring back at him. "I will not ask for answers that are not mine to learn, but if thou needs a sympathetic ear, know I will listen." Without another word, Edwin Mitchell quietly left the barn.

"Good morning, Lane." Prudence smiled brightly as

she climbed the last step of the ladder leading to the attic, a tray of food balanced in one hand. "Thou looks much better than thee did a few days ago. Father says thy wound is nearly healed enough for thee to eat with us downstairs."

"I'd like that, Prudence," he answered, pushing himself up to lean back against the headboard of his bed. "I don't mean to sound ungrateful, but I've grown tired of lying in this bed staring at the same four walls." He waited until she had placed the tray on his lap and then added, "And I'd like to thank you and your family for taking care of me these past five days. You didn't have to do it and I know I haven't been a very pleasant guest."

Rubbing her hands on the white apron she wore, Prudence studied its coarse texture as she said, "In our religion every man is our friend. We hold no hatred for anyone. Our way is simple and honest, and we would never ask anything of thee in return. So do not feel the need to apologize, Lane Brandon." Smoothing out her apron again, she looked up at him. "Would thou like me to feed thee?"

Suddenly aware of the sweet innocence of the face staring back at him, Lane wished he had met Prudence under different circumstances. He had never had time to go courting and he realized now that he had no idea of what to do. But what did it matter? Prudence Mitchell was not for him. He was a disgrace to his country and didn't deserve someone like her. Forcing a smile, he looked at the tray of food before him.

"I'd enjoy being waited on, but I think it's time I learned to do this on my own." He grinned. "However, I would like it if you'd stay and talk with me . . . that is if your mother wouldn't mind."

"I think she would understand thy need." Prudence smiled happily, then turned to pull a chair to the side of

218

his bed.

"Your father didn't come to see me yesterday," he said, lifting a forkful of scrambled eggs to his mouth.

"He went to help a neighbor. Their house burned to the ground last week, and whenever father can spare the time, he lends a hand building their new one. He came home very late last night and thou were already asleep, so he didn't want to bother thee," she replied. "He will be up as soon as he finishes his breakfast." She tilted her head to one side when she saw Lane frown. "Is something wrong?"

Lane stared at his plate for a moment then smiled half-heartedly. "He's a very generous man, your father. I hope others are more grateful than I."

"What does thou mean?" Prudence asked, surprised.

Laying down his fork, Lane leaned his head back against the wooden headboard with a sigh, staring off into space. "I've lived through a nightmare these past three months, Prudence, and I no longer trust anyone. I realize that now. I'm ashamed to admit it, but I included your father."

"He understands," she assured him.

His blue eyes moved to look at her. "Do you?"

"Yes," she smiled. "Whoever did this meant to kill thee. I would not trust a stranger either if I were thee."

"That means a lot to me, Prudence," he said. "And I'm thankful that you and your family took me in and cared for me. I would not be alive now if you hadn't."

Prudence bowed her head, a slight blush rising in her cheeks, and Lane suddenly felt a need to touch her hand. But as he lifted his own to do so, the pounding of hooves against the hard earth outside the tiny house tensed every muscle in his body.

"Take the tray," he ordered, shoving it off his lap.

"Thou are not getting up?" Prudence questioned fearfully, but she did as he'd bade, watching him flip

219

the covers from him. But when he swung his feet to the floor, she realized what he intended to do, and she hurriedly set aside the tray and rounded the bed to help him. "Where are thee going?"

"To look outside," he said, leaning his weight against her. "I must see who has come."

The small attic window offered a full view of the yard below and Lane stiffened instantly when he saw the two men on horseback.

"What's wrong?" Prudence asked.

"It's them," he whispered. "The men who want me dead. I've got to get out of here before they find me."

"No, wait!" Prudence begged when he tried to push away from her. "Father will send them away and thou are too ill to travel. Please, just this once, trust us."

Lane could see the pleading in her soft, brown eyes and something inside him melted. The protective cocoon he had spun around him dissolved in that instant, for he knew that if anyone spoke the truth, it would be this young woman who had nothing to gain by lying to him. A smile lifted the corners of his mouth as he turned with Prudence toward the window. In silence they watched Edwin Mitchell approach the men.

Their conversation was indistinguishable through the closed aperture of the attic, and Lane had to be content to wonder what was being said. Not once did Edwin Mitchell glance upward toward the room where his guest was hiding, so Lane's confidence in the man began to grow, especially when he saw Edwin shake his head as if he was unable to help the strangers in their quest to find the young man for whom they searched. After a few minutes had passed, the strangers mounted their horses and rode off, and when Edwin turned back toward the house, Lane could see the mischievous grin on his face. He had lied to them and had obviously enjoyed doing so.

"Now will thee get back into bed?" Prudence scolded.

"Only if you'll tell your father that I'd like to speak with him," Lane replied, turning away from the window. "I think it's time we talked."

"Agreed." She smiled and helped him into bed. "Finish thy breakfast and I will send him up."

It wasn't long before Lane heard Edwin's footsteps on the ladder leading to his room, and he experienced a wave of nervousness. He felt as if he were about to explain to his own father why he had held onto his secret so long, but that feeling vanished the minute he saw the smile on Edwin Mitchell's face.

"Good morning to thee." Edwin was beaming, obviously still delighted with his charade. "How are thee?"

Lane nodded toward the chair beside him in a silent request that Edwin sit down. "I will feel much better once I've told you about those men that were here."

"There is no need, son," he said, settling into the chair, "not if thou does not wish it."

"But I do," Lane sighed, looking at his hands resting in his lap. "It's a long story and the only way you'll understand completely is to hear it from the beginning." He took a deep breath, leaned back against the pillows propped up behind him, and absently stared across the room. "I joined the Navy over a year ago to fight against the British. I was assigned to Captain Justin Whitelaw's ship. Next to my father, I respected Captain Whitelaw more than any other man I have ever known. He taught me everything there was to learn about sailing, and I think I can honestly say we were friends besides."

"Thou speaks of the past. Is he dead?"

Lane closed his eyes, holding back the tears that had

suddenly surfaced. "Yes. And he wouldn't be if it hadn't been for me."

"I do not know the circumstances, but thou must not blame thyself. If Captain Whitelaw died, it was God's will," Mitchell replied softly.

"I wish I could believe that," Lane choked out. "But I can't. I testified at Captain Whitelaw's trial. I said he was a traitor and he was sentenced to hang."

Mitchell straightened with a frown, remembering the gossip of the menfolk in town about just such a trial three months ago. The accused had escaped prison. He opened his mouth to inform the young man that his captain was indeed still alive, but Lane rushed on before he could.

"He wasn't a traitor. I lied." Tears spilled from the corners of his eyes. "They told me they'd kill my parents and abuse my sister if I didn't. They wanted Captain Whitelaw out of the way, and now he's dead because of me."

Mitchell quickly moved to sit on the edge of the bed beside Lane and gently touched his arms. "No, Lane. Captain Whitelaw is not dead."

"Yes, he is," Lane sobbed, looking at Mitchell through tear-filled eyes.

"Calm thyself," Mitchell warned firmly, "and let me tell what I have heard. Have thou been hiding all this time since the trial?"

Lane reached up to wipe his eyes. "I was taken prisoner by strangers and held against my will until I escaped and you found me."

"Then thou do not know what has happened after thee testified?" He waited for Lane to shake his head; then he settled himself more comfortably to relate what he had heard. "I do not listen to idle talk so I cannot give the details, but several weeks ago when I took the wagon to Emmitsburg for supplies, I heard some of the

222

men there talking about the trial. Captain Whitelaw escaped prison and now sails the coast. He has turned pirate."

Lane fell back against the pillow, overcome with joy until he realized the full impact of what Edwin Mitchell had said. Frowning, he looked at him again. "A pirate? Captain Whitelaw? No, that can't be. He is the most honorable man I know. He wouldn't do something like that. It's got to be a mistake."

"I only said it was what I heard," Edwin cautioned. "It was gossip and very well could be wrong. But the point is, Captain Whitelaw is alive and thou have nothing to feel guilty about."

"Oh, but I do. Don't you understand?" he moaned.

"Yes, Lane, I do. His death is not on thy shoulders, but thou feels at fault for thy captain turning against the law . . . *if* that part of the gossip is true."

"I've got to find him," Lane muttered, frowning.

"Why?"

"I've got to clear his name," he hissed. "I've got to right the wrong I've done him. His whole life was devoted to the Navy and serving his country. I can't be the one responsible for taking that away from him."

"Thou will do it, son. But thou must rest and get back thy strength before thee can travel again. Thou will do no one any good if thou are dead." Edwin smiled comfortingly when Lane lowered his eyes and nodded. "Now tell me of these men who shot thee."

"I don't know who they were, only that the man behind this whole thing sent them to kill me, and I don't think they'll go away until they've finished what they started."

Edwin Mitchell smiled devilishly, rubbing the palms of his hands together as if he knew a delightful secret. "Then we shall play hide-and-seek."

"Sir?" Lane questioned.

"I will go to Emmitsburg this afternoon and speak with a friend of mine."

"What for?"

Edwin's brown eyes sparkled impishly. "Thou must promise not to tell my wife or Prudence," he whispered; then he shook his head. "They wouldn't understand."

"Understand what?" Lane chuckled. "I don't even understand."

Grinning lopsidedly, Edwin reached up to tug at his earlobe. "As thee can probably guess from our manner of dress and speech, we are Quakers. We don't believe in raising a hand against our fellow man and because of it"—he paused as if he thought a bolt of lightning would strike him for what he was about to say—"well, my life can be very uneventful at times. What I want to do is lead these men astray while thou heals."

"But there's nothing wrong with that, sir. In fact, it might be the only thing that would save my life."

"H'm," Edwin shrugged. "But I'll have to lie again to do it."

"Oh," Lane said with a smile. "So that's what I'm not to tell your wife and daughter."

Rubbing a finger beneath his nose, Mitchell peeked over at his companion from the corner of his eye, and nodded.

"Then consider it our secret," Lane declared. "And since you'll already be in Emmitsburg, will you do me another favor?"

"Surely," Mitchell agreed.

"See if anyone knows where Captain Whitelaw might be. He's suffered long enough. I'd like to find him as soon as possible."

Smiling brightly, Edwin Mitchell reached over and patted Lane's thigh. "Consider it done, my friend. Now . . . I'd better see what excuse I can find to go to town again, one that will satisfy my wife." Coming to his feet, he started for the ladder, but he paused when he reached it to look back at Lane. "How old are thee?"

A frown flitted across Lane's brow and disappeared. "Nineteen, sir."

"Nineteen," Edwin muttered thoughtfully as he turned away. "That's good . . . very good . . . the same age as Prudence."

Lane watched the lively gait of Edwin Mitchell as he left the room, a confused expression crimping his brow.

"Why, hello, Edwin," Paul Connelly said when he spotted the man coming through the door of the general store. "What brings you back so soon? I usually don't see you but once a month."

Glancing around nervously, Edwin raised a fist to his mouth and cleared his throat. "Ah, well . . . it's been almost three weeks. Grace needs some more flour and a few spices that I forgot the last time I was here."

"Did she send a note with you this time?" Paul chuckled then straightened when he realized what Edwin had said. "Has it been three weeks? I thought you were here just a few days ago."

Edwin smiled crookedly. "Thou know how time can slip by without thee realizing it," he said, wondering if his face glowed hotly at the lie he'd told his friend. "Maybe thou simply missed me."

Connelly laughed heartily. "Yeah, that's probably it, Edwin. I do look forward to seeing your homely old face now and then. Well," he added, grabbing a cloth bag and heading for the bins on the opposite wall, "I can give you the flour, but I don't have too many spices anymore, what with this Embargo Act and all."

Quickly surveying the store to make sure they were alone, Edwin seized his chance to bring up the subject

225

he had so cunningly forced Connelly to introduce. "But I thought I heard someone say the merchants were smuggling."

"Oh, some of them are," Paul replied, dipping his scoop down into the bin. "But the spices come from England and it's harder to get them into the States than it is to get our goods out." He chuckled as he watched the flour pour into the bag he held. "And some of the merchants are finding it even more difficult than before."

"Why's that?"

"Because of Justin Whitelaw and his crew."

"Justin Whitelaw?" Edwin asked nervously as he tugged at his shirt collar. "Oh, I remember. He's the one who escaped from prison, isn't he?"

"Yeah," Connelly answered solemnly, shoving the scoop into the flour again. "The way I hear it he wasn't really guilty of anything. One of his men turned against him and swore under oath that the man had committed treasonous acts against the United States."

"Thou sound as if thou do not believe it."

"Well, I can't rightly be sure, Edwin, but I am entitled to my opinion," he stated, filling the bag to the top.

Waiting until Connelly had tied the sack and was starting back to the counter, Edwin asked, "And what is that?"

"Well, right after the trial, this boy that testified against Whitelaw disappeared, like he had something to hide," he said. Plopping the bag down, he rested one arm across it and stared over at Edwin. "And now I hear Whitelaw is sailing up and down the coastline looking for him. Now why would he do that if the boy didn't lie in the first place and Whitelaw wants him to admit it?"

Glancing down at the floor, Edwin mumbled, "An

226

eye for an eye."

"What?"

Sighing forlornly, Edwin reached into his pocket for the coins needed to pay for the flour. "Maybe he wants to kill the boy for what he did to him. I have heard he is a pirate and therefore capable of such a thing."

Connelly shrugged, accepting the coins Edwin held out to him. "It's possible, I suppose, but I doubt it. Now . . . what kind of spices do ya need? I got some ginger and . . ."

"No thanks," Edwin said, shaking his head and reaching for the sack of flour still supporting Connelly's arm. "We seldom use any."

Paul straightened in surprise and watched his friend head toward the door with the bag tucked under his arm. Edwin Mitchell and he had grown up together, and although Connelly never really understood the Quakers' way of life, he had always liked Edwin and his subtle sense of humor. Could it be that Mitchell was playing some sort of good-natured trick? Or was Edwin's mind failing him? Frowning, he studied his friend as he neared the door, certain that at any moment, he would turn back, smile, and ask what kind of spices he had. But when Edwin stepped outside onto the porch, Connelly's face revealed his disappointment. He could have sworn Edwin Mitchell had been in his store only last week. Shrugging, he rounded the end of the counter and returned to his work.

Edwin's brown eyes darkened as he guided his buggy out of town. While traveling to Emmitsburg earlier, he had decided on a plan that would draw his friend into a conversation on a fabricated subject—an unsolved murder in Fairfield, a small town just over the Maryland border in Pennsylvania. He liked Paul Connelly very much, but if anyone loved to gossip more than he, Edwin didn't know who it was.

227

Therefore if he planted the thought in the man's head that the body they had supposedly found was that of the young man who had testified against Justin Whitelaw, Connelly unknowingly would spread a lie that was sure to mislead Lane's assassins. That was what Edwin had intended to do, but he'd never gotten around to doing it, for once Paul had told him that Captain Whitelaw was looking for Lane, Edwin could think of nothing else. Not only would the young man have to hide from the men who had tried to kill him earlier, but from the very person he wanted to find. Snapping the reins to urge the horse to a faster pace, Edwin wondered what Lane Brandon would do once he learned of the real danger he was in.

"Lane Brandon, sit thee down before thy wound is torn anew," Grace Mitchell scolded when the young man rose from the table intending to clear away the supper dishes.

"But Mrs. Mitchell," he objected, "it's been over a week and I've done nothing but sit. You and your family have been so kind to me that I want to do something to help. Besides, my shoulder is practically as good as new." To prove his point, he lifted his arm from the sling and raised his elbow in the air. "Just a little stiff is all. See?" He smiled at her.

But Grace was not about to relent. With a stern look on her lovely face, she raised a hand and pointed at the chair beside her daughter.

"Thou might as well not argue, son." Edwin grinned as he watched Lane sink back into his chair. "I thought thee knew by now who really runs this house." His smile faded when his gaze fell upon his wife.

"If I did, Edwin Mitchell," she snapped, "thou would not make unnecessary trips to Emmitsburg. Flour,

228

indeed. I have more now than I know what to do with."

"Now, Grace," Edwin said soothingly, reaching out to take his wife's hand, but she quickly twisted away from him and came to her feet. He watched her a moment as she irritably stacked the dirty plates, then he looked at Lane sitting across from him and shrugged. "I only did it to help Lane. Thou would have done the same."

The dishes rattled when Grace angrily set them back on the table and frowned over at her husband. "Yes, I would have, but I wouldn't have lied. I simply would have asked Paul Connelly what I wanted to know."

All evidence of mischief disappeared from Edwin's dark eyes as he said quietly, "Grace, I couldn't. Paul is a friend, but thou know how he cannot keep a secret. If I had told him about Lane, those men who were here a few days ago would know right where to look for him. I think the Lord will forgive me this one time. And I didn't truly lie. We can always use flour."

Grace Mitchell stared at her husband a long while before she cast her gaze from him and returned to her task of clearing the table without a word. A long, uncomfortable moment followed, and oddly enough Grace was the one to ease the tension when she came back to the table, an apple pie held in her hands. She stared at the dessert she had labored over that morning, unable to bring herself to look at their guest.

"I made this for thee, Lane," she said, her voice strained, "because I knew thee would leave today."

"Today?" Prudence echoed in surprise, her gaze turning to the man who sat beside her. "But thou are not well enough. Thou cannot go."

"Prudence," her father warned, "'tis Lane's decision to make, not ours."

Moisture glistened in the young girl's eyes when she glanced back at him, and then she bowed her head. "Yes, father," she answered quietly, choking back her tears. "I just hoped he would stay longer."

"We all do, Prudence. But I think I can speak for him when I say that he will not be at peace until he has found Captain Whitelaw and explained what has happened."

He smiled softly at his daughter when he saw her quickly wipe a stray tear from her face. He had realized from the way Prudence had cared for the wounded boy that she had not done it purely out of compassion for a stranger, but that she had taken a special liking to him almost immediately. And in this short length of time, Edwin, too, realized that Lane Brandon was not just an ordinary man passing through. They would always have fond memories of him, and once he walked out of their lives, his absence would create an emptiness in all of them.

"Please excuse me," Prudence said, abruptly coming to her feet. "I must feed the chickens." Without waiting for permission, she hurried to the door and went outside.

"Prudence," her mother called, starting after her, but Edwin caught her hand.

"Let her go, Grace," he instructed tenderly. "She needs to be alone right now."

His wife opened her mouth to object to her daughter's rudeness, saw Edwin shake his head with a vague smile on his lips, and suddenly understood Prudence's strange behavior. "Yes, Edwin, I guess she does. And if thou will excuse me as well, I will wash up the dishes while thee both sample the pie."

Edwin lovingly watched his wife's slender figure walk away before he turned to look at Lane. A frown settled on his brow when he saw the pained expression on the young man's face. "What troubles thee, son?"

Lane's blond hair glistened in the sunlight streaming

230

into the room as he shook his head slowly. "That it seems no matter where I go, I cause someone to be unhappy."

"Unhappy?" Edwin repeated. "No one in this house is unhappy in the way thou mean. We will miss thee, yes. But we will look forward to the day thou will return to visit."

"Do you mean that?" Lane asked hopefully. "You'll welcome me back if I can come?"

Edwin stiffened painfully as if offended. "If thou doesn't, I will search until I find thee and drag thee back."

A heartfelt smile broke the serious line of Lane's mouth. "I'm going to hold you to that." He chuckled then glanced down at his arm cradled in the sling. "Will you explain to Prudence why I had to go?"

"Yes. But I think she would understand better if thou would tell her thyself," Edwin pointed out. "She will be in the barn."

Lane's blue eyes glanced up at him and he smiled. "Will you excuse me?" he asked, rising.

"Of course." Edwin turned in his chair to watch Lane cross the room and step outside onto the porch.

As he walked toward the barn, Lane experienced a strange flood of emotion. He had never responded to a woman in the way he had to Prudence, and he wondered if what he felt could be love. If it was, he knew it would have to wait. He couldn't let another day go by without trying to undue the shame he had brought down on Justin Whitelaw's head. He only hoped he could make Prudence understand why he must go and that she would allow him to make it up to her later.

Stepping into the cool shade of the barn, he spotted her trim figure standing near one of the stalls. She had her back to him, yet he could see by the way she leaned her head against the post and how her body shook with her ragged sigh that she had not truly intended to feed the chickens, but rather to hide her tears.

"Prudence," he said softly, and watched her straighten nervously at the sound of his voice. Before she turned to look at him, she quickly wiped her eyes with the back of her hand.

"Yes?" she asked, forcing a smile.

"I want to explain," he began, suddenly feeling very awkward. "I'd also like to tell you how I feel. Will you listen?"

Lowering her eyes, she bit her lip and nodded.

"What I did to Captain Whitelaw was unfair, but it was something I had to do at the time. Now because of you and your father, I will be able to correct it. However, the only way I can do that is to find Captain Whitelaw and tell him face to face. I can't trust anyone, not even the magistrate in Washington because I feel that the whole trial was a mockery of justice and I fear for my life should I return there."

He paused a moment to take a deep breath and study the young woman who wouldn't look at him. "I would like to stay, Prudence," he assured her, "but I can't. Those men who tried to kill me are still out there somewhere looking for me, and I won't put you and your parents in that kind of danger any longer." Tilting his head to see her face more clearly, he moved closer to her until they stood only inches apart. With slow deliberation, he took her hand in his. "I care a great deal for you, Prudence, and if you'll allow me, I'll come back as soon as I can and court you the way you should be courted."

"Then take me with thee," she answered in a rush, her brown eyes filled with tears.

"Oh, Prudence, I can't," he moaned, pulling her against him. "It would be too dangerous. Not only

232

must I elude the men who were here a few days ago, but I must avoid Captain Whitelaw's crew as well. It will be easier for me if I travel alone. Besides, if something happened to you because of me, I would never forgive myself." Putting her at arm's length, he added, "Just promise me that you'll wait. I'll be back."

"Only if thou will make it as soon as possible," she said, her lower lip quivering.

Smiling, Lane answered, "Before you have time to miss me."

"I already do," she whispered with a sob.

A shadow fell across the entryway into the barn, and a moment later disappeared, but the couple who shared a passionate kiss wasn't aware they had been watched. A satisfied grin curled Edwin Mitchell's lips as he strolled back to the house.

Chapter Nine

Pale blue eyes openly watched the energetic movements of Dara's young shapely figure as she merrily straightened up the cabin. Once she had flipped the coverlet over the bunk, and fluffed up the pillows, she turned her attention on the stack of dry, freshly cleaned clothes lying on the bench and crossed the room to sit down beside them, unaware that Justin quietly observed her as he sat in the chair behind his desk.

They had spent the past week in strained tolerance of each other, never saying more than was necessary, their eyes seldom meeting. Justin's temper had been short, his nature irritable, while Dara had patiently attempted to discover the reason for his mood. She had tried on several occasions to thank him for the dress, the hairbrush, and mirror, but he had always interrupted her as if he didn't want to hear it. But what had surprised her more than anything was their sleeping arrangements. He had told her that she would share the bunk or he would tie her in it. Yet every night since she wasn't sure where he had slept. After they ate their meal in silence, he would leave the cabin without telling her where he was going, and when it became too difficult to keep her eyes open any longer, she would crawl into the bunk and fall asleep. In the morning he was gone . . . if he ever came back at all during the night. As she sat folding his clothes into a tidy pile, she remembered the only unhostile treatment he'd shown her, the times she'd caught him watching her. Wondering if he did so now, she glanced up and found him staring back at her. She started to smile in return, but when the soft shade of his blue eyes darkened and he frowned, she dropped her gaze and concentrated on her task once more.

Justin knew his mood had been anything but pleasant for the past seven days, and Callahan's constant reminders of that fact only added to his ill humor. He wasn't about to tell the man what was bothering him since he couldn't really pinpoint the cause, except to speculate on the possibility that the presence of his new cabinmate annoyed him. To say that aloud would only bring laughter from his friend, for Dara Brandon hadn't really done anything disagreeable. Truthfully, she had tried to stay out of his way whenever possible. She had cleared away their dishes after they ate, started a fire in the stove when the nights became chilly, made the bunk, washed his clothes and put them away, straightened up his desk, and disposed of the empty whiskey bottles whenever he left them lying around. And if he snapped at her, which he seemed to do constantly, she would simply bow her head and retreat to the bench to read the book he had given her. In all actuality, she treated him as a wife would her husband. He grimaced at the thought and fell forward, his elbows against the desk, trying desperately to focus on the papers spread out before him. If only Wallis would come . . . Surely it didn't take this long to get a simple invitation to a ball. He didn't like staying in one place for more than a few days, and they had already been anchored here for nearly a week.

The sunshine streaming in through the portholes fell across the cabin and seemed to spotlight the brass base of the hurricane lamp sitting on his desk. The reflected glow shone directly into Justin's eyes. Squinting, he straightened in the chair and, glancing up as if to curse its insolence for disturbing him, caught sight of Dara again. He could only guess where she had found the needle and thread, although nothing about her truly surprised him, and he relaxed as he watched her quietly mend one of his shirts. He had to admit that being freed of the menial tasks such as sewing on buttons pleased him, but he would have preferred that Davy, his cabin boy, do them rather than the ravishing beauty who seemed to be the center of his world lately. His dark brows came together as he studied her practiced moves and the way the long auburn hair fell about her shoulders as she bent her head over her work, and his curiosity about her grew.

Any other woman who had been treated as she had would not have accepted her fate so easily. Others would have protested continually, demanding their release and promising him just punishment once they went to the authorities. It was almost as if Dara Brandon didn't know that she had been misused.

One corner of his mouth crimped sarcastically. Oh yes, she did. Otherwise she wouldn't expect him to marry her. Damn. Why couldn't he have returned to his ship earlier that night? Why had he stayed to talk with Wallis those extra minutes? The anger faded from his face. If he had, Dara Brandon would probably be dead. The color of his eyes softened as a half-smile wrinkled his cheek. Maybe that was why she seemed to accept her situation on board his ship. She realized it too. And, of course, she wanted to find her brother and knew she wouldn't succeed on her own. She needed his help. Pushing himself back from the desk, he stood up and went to the cabinet where he kept the whiskey.

"Dara," he said quietly as he lifted the bottle from

inside, "I think we should talk about your brother."

Dara's thoughts had returned to another time when she had been mending a man's shirt, the day before Lane had left their small farm near Drawbridge. She was recalling how sad the occasion had been. She had feared she would never see him again, and now those fears seemed even more real than they had then. Until she had met Captain Whitelaw and his first mate, she had thought her brother was a prisoner of the British and that, with the help of someone in Washington, she would be able to free him. It would be a great feat and probably would require a lot of doing, yet the outcome had looked promising. However, if what Captain Whitelaw told her was true—Lane was in trouble and was hiding out somewhere—her chances of finding him were slim. Tears clouded her eyes, and she paused in her work to blink them away. Startled from her musings when she heard the captain address her by her given name rather than his usual formal address, she glanced up at him, discovering that she was oddly pleased by this familiarity even though his manner was still obviously defensive.

"What about him?" she asked.

Turning back to his desk, Justin poured himself a drink, set aside the bottle and sat down on the chair again. "Lane was on my ship for more than a year. We talked a great deal, but it was mostly about sailing, the war, and what he wanted out of life. He seldom spoke of his family except when I'd ask him questions and, therefore, I don't know much about him before he joined the Navy. I thought if I could learn some of the things he liked to do before then, I might have an idea where to look for him."

"Such as?"

"Well, do you have any relatives living in another part of the state or anywhere in America?"

"No. My father has a brother, but he still lives in England. My mother was an only child."

"Did Lane have a girl . . . someone he thought he could trust?"

Dara's smooth brow wrinkled. "You mean where he could hide?"

Justin nodded.

"But he would have come home to do that," she objected.

"No, he wouldn't," Justin disagreed. "Lane's too smart for that. He'd know that's the first place someone would look for him, and I'm sure he wouldn't do anything that would put his family in danger. Now, did he have a girl or maybe a close friend that would help him?"

Dara's green eyes lowered to look at her lap. "No. No one. He never had time to be sociable. Our father's health was failing and Lane had to do most of the work."

"You mean he never had time for himself?"

"No," she answered solemnly; then she suddenly remembered how much Lane enjoyed fishing. Although he did it to put food on the table, Dara knew that wasn't the only reason he was eager to pick up his pole and head off through the woods. "Well, he liked to fish, but he never went very far from home." She smiled, reminiscing. "There was a stream about half a mile from our house. His favorite spot was near an old abandoned mill. The water was deepest there and he seemed to have the best luck in that particular area. But I really think he chose it because it was so peaceful. Once in a while, he'd take me with him."

"Do you think he could possibly be hiding out there?"

Dara glanced up and gave a shake of her head. "For three months? He loves our father and I really don't feel he would have lived so close to home without at one time or another having come to see us."

Justin shrugged. "It's still worth sending someone to check on."

"You'd be wasting your time, Captain Whitelaw," she sighed. "Whenever I'd get lonely for him, I'd take a fishing pole and go to that very spot. If Lane had been hiding in the mill, he would have seen me, and I'm sure he wouldn't have been content to just watch." She stared at Justin a moment then lowered her head. "What do you really think happened to him?"

"I wish I knew, Dara," he said softly and took a sip of his whiskey. "I really wish I knew."

Looking at him again, she said enthusiastically, "Well, what was the last thing the two of you talked about before you were arrested? Maybe he tried to give you a clue and you didn't recognize it. No one knows my brother better than I, and if you tell me everything that was said, I might be able to help figure it out."

Suddenly Justin saw Dara Brandon differently. She wasn't one of the snobbish women he'd spent time with, not the pampered belle of a great plantation, not a woman who wanted to manipulate him. If he hadn't forced himself on her, she probably wouldn't want anything more than his help in finding her brother, and despite what he had done, she was still willing to offer her aid. Maybe her true motive was selfish, but most women in her situation wouldn't have given him anything except a lot of complaints. Maybe he had misjudged her after all.

Setting down his empty glass, he reached for a cheroot from the box on the desk. "I didn't see Lane the day I was arrested, and I didn't realize what was happening until I saw him in the courtroom two days later. Callahan told me a message had been delivered to him while we were docked at Annapolis. I had gone ashore, and when I came back your brother had already taken his liberty. The next morning I was taken into custody."

"A message?" Dara repeated more to herself. "Didn't Callahan know what was in it?"

"No. But he did say Lane acted rather funny after he read it. He assumed it was bad news from home, but after he was called as a witness at my trial, we were certain it had not been sent by a member of his family."

Laying aside her mending, Dara rose and turned to look out the porthole at the bay. "Well, you were right. We never sent any message. So who did?"

"If I knew that, I'd know who wanted me out of the way." Lighting his cheroot, Lane took a long drag on it, and realizing he was no better off than when they had started this conversation, he frowned. He knew it was foolish to keep looking for Lane. Whoever had exploited the boy had gotten what they were after. Lane was of little use to them anymore. He had probably been killed the moment he'd walked out of that courtroom. Then a thought struck him. "Dara, didn't you tell me that your family received a letter saying that Lane had been taken prisoner by the British?"

"Yes," she answered, glancing over her shoulder at him. "Why? Do you think he really was?"

"No," he grinned, leaning over to snuff out the cigar, "but at least I know he's still alive."

Dara's breath seemed to leave her at this offhand remark. "What do you mean . . . still?" she asked hesitantly. "Do you think someone wants him dead?"

Justin hadn't realized the effect his comment would have on her or he would have chosen his words more carefully. When he looked up at her and saw the pained expression in her eyes, he instantly regretted his thoughtlessness. Quickly coming to his feet, he rounded the edge of the desk and went to her. Yet when he reached her, he found that he was actually afraid to take her hands in his. Instead he touched her arm, nodded at the bench, and waited until she had sat down again before he answered.

"Dara, I shouldn't have said anything, but since I already have, I owe you an explanation," he began, placing one booted foot beside her on the edge of the bench. Leaning his upper torso on the elbow that rested on his knee, he clasped his hands and paused a moment to figure out exactly how he could word his statement. "I want you to set aside your personal feelings for a moment if you can and look at this situation logically. Perhaps you'll understand what I mean." He waited for her nod then continued. "I don't call many men friend, but your brother was one of them. And at the risk of sounding vain, I think Lane considered me his friend. Now if two men felt as strongly about each other as we did, why would one of them suddenly turn against the other unless he was forced into it?"

Dara shrugged. "That seems the obvious reason."

"You believe Lane would tell the truth and I know he would. I also know I'm not guilty of treason. Therefore, he lied because someone made him do it. I don't know who that someone is, nor do I know what was held over him to force him to cooperate, but if you had been Lane, what would you have done after the trial?"

Dara's brow wrinkled as she considered her choices. "It depends on what that someone was threatening me with."

"You know your brother better than any of us. What do you propose it was? What's the one thing in this world Lane Brandon would have protected, even if doing so meant he had to falsely accuse a friend of treason?"

242

Resting her head back against the porthole frame behind her, Dara let out a long, troubled sigh. "His family, I suppose. Lane doesn't have anything else of value."

"All right, then let's say this someone threatened to murder his family. Now, you're Lane and the trial is over. What would you do?"

Green eyes glanced up at him. "After I made sure my family was safe, I'd go to the authorities with the truth."

"Exactly," Justin smiled. "But . . . don't you think that this someone figured that was just what he would do? After Lane had served his purpose, he was a threat to the very person who'd thought up this whole scheme."

Tears constricted the muscles in her throat. "So Lane was to be killed even if he did what he was told?"

"I think so. But," he added with a grin, "I also think Lane didn't give his blackmailer the chance. The letter your family received proves it."

"How?" Dara asked hopefully, for she wanted to be assured that her brother was indeed still alive.

"Everyone up and down the coastline knows I'm looking for Lane. Most think it's because I want to kill him for what he did to me . . . because everyone thinks I'm guilty . . . everyone, that is, except the one who devised this plan. He knows I want Lane so that I can prove my innocence."

Dara frowned. "I don't understand."

"The chances of finding someone taken prisoner by the British are very slim. Being a captain in the Navy, I would realize that. Therefore, if I learned Lane had been captured by the British, been impressed to serve on one of their ships, I would give up my search. That would give this person time to find Lane and finish what he'd started."

"Then"—she fought the tears that threatened to flow freely—"then he's still in danger."

"Yes," he said pointedly, dropping his foot to the floor so he could sit down beside her. "But you mustn't worry about him. Lane is a very smart young man, and the fact that he's still alive after three months should tell you something. I'm certain that at this very moment he's out there somewhere trying to find me."

"But why doesn't he just go to one of your men and send word to you? Obviously you have many contacts," she questioned.

"I said he was smart, Dara, and a smart man would trust no one, including my men. As Lane sees it, my crew knew the charges against me were false and they would seek revenge for what he's done. So, he's got to get to me before anyone else recognizes him." Sighing heavily, he rose. "And that's the difficult part."

"Why?"

"He isn't going to tell anyone who he is, and my contacts aren't about to tell a stranger where I can be found. And I can't very well leave word where I'll be next. I, too, am running."

"But what about me?" Dara suggested excitedly, standing and catching his sleeve as he turned to move away from her.

"What about you?" He frowned, not understanding.

"Couldn't we leave word with your contacts where *I* can be found? I mean, maybe they could spread rumors that Lane's sister is looking for him and that I'll be somewhere where he can find me."

"A novel idea, Dara Brandon, but one that's too dangerous." He smiled, then walked back to his desk and the glass of whiskey he had left there.

"Dangerous?" she echoed. "Why? I'm not running from anyone."

One dark eyebrow lifted questioningly. "Oh?" he

asked. "And what about Colonel Winslow?"

Dara's head began to spin. She felt faint and was certain that at any second she would swoon. Her knees weak, she slowly sank back down upon the bench, her face pale and tears filling the rims of her lashes. It was all so hopeless! Lane was trying to find the captain, but couldn't tell anyone. Captain Whitelaw was looking for Lane, but couldn't leave word of where he could be found. And since Colonel Winslow was looking for her, she couldn't leave the protection of the *Lady Elizabeth*. Closing her eyes, she bit her lower lip to stop the sob that threatened to erupt. Whoever was responsible for this whole mess was out there tracking down her brother. His life depended on her finding him before anyone else did. Swallowing her tears, she straightened her shoulders and opened her eyes to stare bravely at the man who watched her with curious suspicion.

"That's a chance I'll have to take, Captain," she said calmly.

"Oh no, you don't," Justin replied, shaking his head.

"I must," she continued firmly. "Lane won't be free to come home until he's done the right thing, and you won't be able to live a normal life until he has. As for me, I don't intend to spend the rest of my life living here on this ship and hiding from the colonel. It's a small price to pay so that two others will be free of their torment. And besides," she added, lifting her chin in the air, "maybe I'll find Lane before the colonel finds me. Then we can go together to the authorities and expose the culprits."

"And maybe you'll be dead two minutes after you go ashore," he said flatly. "Colonel Winslow is not without influence. He has a lot of men on his side, Miss Brandon, none of whom would hesitate to shoot you the minute they found out who you were. If Winslow

245

wants the president dead, you can wager everything you own that he's not in this alone. Sorry," he said sarcastically, "but you're staying here." Turning his back on her to fill his glass with more whiskey, Justin failed to see the dangerous look she gave him.

Ever since the day he had taken her clothes and thrown them out the porthole, Justin had not bothered to lock the door of the cabin, not even after he had given her new ones to wear. Thus she knew her exit from the room would be unhampered by the lack of a key. Affixing her gaze on her destination, she started for the door.

Justin caught her movement from the corner of his eye and looked up with a frown, failing to understand her intention until she reached out to lift the latch. "Where do you think you're going?" he demanded, setting down his drink with a clunk on the desk top.

"To find my brother," she threw back over her shoulder as she swung open the door. "Maybe you're a coward, Captain Whitelaw, but I'm not."

A strong hand gripped her elbow long before Dara heard the footsteps that hurriedly brought Justin to her side, and in the next instant she was twirled back into the room as he yanked her away from the door and slammed it shut. Turning to confront her, he set a hard look on the stubborn woman glaring back at him.

"Cowardice isn't what keeps me alive, Dara Brandon," he growled through clenched teeth, his blue eyes gleaming with rage. "But stupidity will be your end. It would be to your advantage to practice a little cowardice instead. It just might extend your life by a few years."

"Your insults don't bother me in the least nor do you frighten me," she spat out, tiny fists perched on her hips. "I know what has to be done, and I'm going to do it whether you like it or not!"

246

"Oh, really?" he scoffed. "And how do you plan to get past me and off the ship?"

Dara opened her mouth to hurl back her answer and irritably discovered that there was none . . . not at the moment anyway. Deciding on a different course, she asked, "And why should you stop me? What am I to you? Surely you know by our conversation that here I can't help you find Lane. What good am I? I would think you would prefer your privacy again." She flung out an arm to indicate the bed. "You could have the comfort of your bunk rather than having to surrender it to me."

Even though Dara ranted on about other things denied him because of her presence, Justin wasn't listening. She had made a valid point when she'd said here she was of no use to him in finding her brother, but the idea of recovering his privacy wasn't important to him. Actually, the thought of sleeping alone in that huge bunk wasn't so pleasant. She seemed to think he had slept elsewhere each night while in truth he never had. He had simply waited until he was sure she was asleep before returning to the cabin, shedding his clothes, and slipping quietly beneath the covers. Even now he could feel the warmth of her body next to his, hear the way she murmured in her dreams and curled up close to him, smell the sweet fragrance of her hair. No. He wasn't about to turn her loose, but what worried him was that he couldn't explain why.

"Well?"

Dara's inquiry brought Justin out of his musing. "Well what?" he grumbled, searching his pockets for the key that would lock them in.

"I want to know why you won't let me leave?"

Finding the tiny object he sought, Justin turned around to place it in the keyhole, and was suddenly attacked from the rear by a barrage of fists pounding on his back.

"No!" Dara screamed. "You're not locking me in here. I've got to find Lane before someone kills him."

Justin raised an arm to ward off the blows hurled at his head while he twisted the key in the lock and then returned it to his pocket. But when she clubbed him across the ear, Justin's efforts to be understanding and calm vanished. Whirling on her, he clamped both arms around her, pinning her own to her sides.

"Stop this nonsense right now and listen to me," he ordered, giving her a squeeze when she continued to struggle. "I don't want Lane dead anymore than you do. I need him, and I don't want him to die because of me."

"Then let me go and look for him," she pleaded, tears running down her cheeks. "I'm the only one who can."

"No, you're not. There are just as many men looking for you, as there are for Lane and me. You'd be no safer—in fact, you'd be in greater danger—than either of us if you went scouring the countryside on your own. You must stay here where I can protect you."

"For how long?" she sobbed. "The rest of my life?"

"Only until I get Colonel Winslow out of the way." He gave her a rough shake when she tried to break free of him. "If you'll listen for a minute, I'll tell you what I've got planned."

Round green eyes glistening with tears looked up at him, and Justin felt a twinge of compassion for the girl. Why should she have to suffer for the mistakes and plots of others? It wasn't right that she should be forced to stay on his ship to insure her life. She should be at home mending clothes, fixing meals, and looking for a husband rather than blindly wandering about Maryland in search of her brother. Tenderly, he brushed away the moisture from her face with his thumb, then

248

he guided them both back to the bench to sit down.

"Callahan and I went to meet with the colonel that night to find out for certain what you'd overheard was true. And it was. He offered me a great deal of money to assassinate the president. I agreed only because I know that if I didn't he would find someone else to do it." He gave a short laugh when he saw the surprise registered in her eyes. "I'm not really going to do it, Dara. I'm only going to make it look like I tried."

"Why? What good will that do?"

"It will set a trap in which I will catch one of Winslow's men. Then I will force a confession from him—one that will put the colonel behind bars where he belongs. Punishing him will give the others involved something to think about, and I doubt they will try anything so foolish again. So you see, in two weeks' time, the colonel will no longer be a threat and *maybe* I'll think about letting the word out that you're looking for your brother."

Dara stared at him for a long while reappraising his handsome features, rugged complexion, and muscular physique before she looked away with a smile. "You're going to ruin your image as a traitor, Captain Whitelaw," she said and glanced back up at him when she heard him laugh.

"I'm afraid not. Your brother is the only one who can erase that title." He sighed.

A moment of quiet passed between them while Justin seemed lost in thought of pleasanter times, and Dara suddenly felt sorry for him. He was obviously a man of honor, and that had been stripped from him by someone who'd sought to hurt him for personal gain. Looking down at her hands, she toyed with the nail of one finger, realizing how unfair it had all been.

"Captain, I know I don't have the right to ask

anything of you, but I was wondering if you'd grant me one favor?"

"The right?" he echoed in surprise. "Dara, you have the right to walk off this ship, find the local authorities, and turn me in. *You're* the one being held here against your will, not me. You have the right to ask anything you want." He grinned lopsidedly and shrugged. "Of course, I don't know if I will grant it or not, but you can try."

Instead of the flare of temper that would have been Dara's usual response to his unbending authority, she merely smiled. She suddenly understood that everything he was trying to do was in everyone's best interest.

"It's not much really," she said quietly, "but it might ease my father's stress. I would like to send a letter to him. I want to let him know that I'm all right and that I have the help of a friend who's aiding in my search for Lane."

A vague smile creased his mouth. "A friend, Dara? Is that how you think of me?"

Her own amusement twinkled in her green eyes. "Well, I can't very well tell my father that I'm in the company of a pirate, an accused traitor, much less that the friend is a man. The news would be anything but soothing." She twisted on the seat to look at him. "Will you allow me that much?"

Looking over at her from the corner of his eye, Justin nodded. "Sure. There's paper in the top drawer of the desk. Help yourself."

His appreciative gaze followed the trim figure that crossed in front of him to secure the items necessary to write a note. It felt good to be at peace with her, to have a conversation that wasn't filled with cutting remarks or defensive words. He sighed inwardly. The situation would be a lot easier if Dara Brandon weren't so beautiful and if she were twenty years his senior. Folding his arms over his chest, he watched flowing yards of yellow cotton billow out around her and nearly hide the chair she stood beside while she spread out her skirts to sit down. A curious frown creased his brow when he heard her laugh.

"I'm sorry," she said, looking up to find him watching, "but I was just imagining my father's reaction if I were to tell him in a letter that I was planning on getting married soon. I think that's something better said in person, don't you?" Without waiting for his answer, she pulled open the top drawer and retrieved a piece of paper as she added, "You'll like my father. He and Lane are very much alike. Of course, father is a little more stubborn than Lane, but they think a lot alike." She laughed again as she reached for the quill sitting on the desk top. "My mother is the one who'll truly be surprised. I can't tell you how many times she told me that she doubted I'd ever get married. She said there wasn't a man in the world who would put up with me. I guess we proved her wrong, didn't we?" Bending over the paper to begin her task, Dara suddenly realized Justin hadn't answered her. She looked up to discover that he hadn't moved, and from the blank expression on his face, she wondered if he had even heard a word she had said. "Is something wrong?" she queried.

"Oh, I was just thinking how I agree with your mother," he said matter-of-factly. "I can't imagine any man putting up with you either."

Dara's green eyes darkened at his comment. She hadn't meant her remark to be anything other than idle chatter, not something on which he should agree or disagree. "Well, I guess you'll have to figure out a way

251

to do it, won't you?" she threw back at him; then she settled her attention on the piece of parchment laid out before her.

And you think your father is more stubborn than Lane? he sighed inwardly. *Little one, I doubt they'll ever outdo you.*

Sitting up, he rubbed the back of his neck to ease his tight muscles and he spotted his bunk from the corner of his eye. He hadn't slept well in the past week, and since his companion seemed busy with her letter and the key was in his pocket, he decided to lie down for a while. However, as he stood and started toward the bed, a loud knock sounded against the door.

"Who is it?" he called out, stopping midway across the room.

"Wallis, sir," a muffled voice replied and Justin hurriedly searched his pockets for the key that would allow the man entry.

"I was beginning to think you had forgotten me," Justin said as he closed the door behind his friend. "Did you get the invitation?"

"Yes, sir," Wallis answered, pulling a rolled piece of paper tied with a red ribbon from inside his shirt. "But there's a problem."

"What kind of problem?" Justin frowned.

Wallis shrugged. "Read for yourself."

He watched his captain pull apart the bow and uncurl the parchment before his attention was distracted by the awareness that someone else shared the room. His brown eyes found green ones staring back at him, and without realizing it, his mouth fell open as he saw the beauty sitting in the captain's chair. Bright sunshine illuminated the pale color of the dress she wore, and it glistened in the thick mass of her auburn hair. Mark was momentarily ashamed that he had thought the gown he had chosen for her would mask any flaws she might have. In all his years he had never seen a woman more exquisite than the one Justin Whitelaw had taken under his protection. There was an innocence in the way she smiled politely back at him, and if he hadn't been certain his captain was already bewitched by this young woman, he would have been tempted to flirt. But then again, who had the right to stop him? Justin Whitelaw had no claim on her.

Regaining his composure, he bowed slightly from the waist, and said, "And you must be Dara Brandon, Lane's sister." The light blush that rose in her cheeks made him smile. "I'm Mark Wallis, Miss Brandon. It's an honor to meet you." Before she could respond, he walked the short distance to her and took her hand to place a soft kiss upon her fingers.

Reluctantly, Dara pulled her hand away, blushing all the more. She had never been treated so courteously before and wasn't sure how she should react. "Thank you," she whispered, smiling faintly. Then she caught sight of Justin glaring heatedly at them. The pleasure of the moment vanished and was replaced by a feeling of guilt. She frowned, wondering why Justin's obvious disapproval of this friendly interlude should disturb her. She did not once give a thought to the reason for his annoyance.

"Mark," Justin spoke through clenched teeth, "if you can tear yourself away, we have a matter to discuss."

Mark Wallis had known his captain for more than five years and had the greatest respect for him. He had been serving on Justin's ship the day the constable had come to arrest him, and like all the others who served Captain Whitelaw, Mark didn't think for one minute

253

that he was guilty of treason. Thus when Douglas Callahan came to him for help in breaking Justin out of prison, Mark had quickly agreed. It had been Mark's idea to establish a cover in Cambridge where he could keep an eye out for Lane Brandon should the youth return home, plus listen for any information that might reveal Lane's whereabouts.

Mark and his captain were nearly the same age and had the same zest for life, the same love of women. Whenever Justin had allowed himself the pleasure of going ashore, he, Mark, and Callahan had visited the local pubs together. It had been the first mate's game to entice one of the barmaids into bestowing her affections on his captain, then to see how long it would take for him to steal her away. The game didn't always work, and both men realized it only did when Justin wanted it that way. Mark never truly minded, for he knew his charm and good looks were not equal to Captain Whitelaw's. But he never passed up the chance to outdo his captain, nor did he relinquish the opportunity to needle the man whenever possible. And right now was one of the rare times when Mark could see for himself that Justin didn't want to share.

"Well, it will be difficult, Cap'n, but I'll try." Mark sighed, giving Dara a wink before he turned back to face him. "So what would you like to discuss?"

"This," Justin growled, wagging the invitation in the air. "It's for two. Now unless you're planning to dress up as a woman and be my companion for the evening, I'd say we have a problem."

"Yeah, I kinda thought you'd see it that way," Mark shrugged, spotting the bottle of whiskey on Justin's desk. Without asking, he filled the glass sitting next to it and took a long swallow before he said, "That's what took me so long to get here. I heard Desirée was in

Washington and since I knew what good . . . ah . . . friends you were, I figured maybe she could help. But," he added, shaking his head, "I couldn't find her. Apparently the troupe moved on."

"That's great," Justin hissed, slapping the paper he held against his thigh in disgust. "Any more suggestions? I've got to get to Senator Manning, and soon."

"Well, up until a few minutes ago, I really didn't know what you could do. But now I think I have a solution." Mark's brown eyes sparkled as he turned back to look at Dara who had been listening to their conversation with apparent interest. "I would imagine Miss Brandon would enjoy attending a ball."

"What?" Justin exploded.

"Why not? It wouldn't take much at all to make her look like a woman." He turned back to chide his friend. "Don't tell me you hadn't noticed, Cap'n."

Justin's blue eyes darkened as he glared back at the man from beneath his brows. "The point is, Mr. Wallis, that this particular ball is not meant to be entertaining, and anyone who's in my company is in just as much danger as I will be. She's not going."

"Got somebody else in mind?" Mark challenged, revealing a hint of smile before he hid it behind the glass he had raised to his lips.

Justin's temper was close to exploding before he realized how dark his mood had become, something that seldom happened in the company of Mark Wallis. Having to stay put in one place for so long must have finally taken its toll on him and he was foolishly taking his irritation out on a friend—or so he thought until he witnessed the man rest one hip on the corner of the desk and smile over at Dara. He began to fume all over again.

"Don't you think it's time you got back to

255

Cambridge?" he asked, his tone heavy with sarcasm.

Mark glanced over at him. "Are you throwing me out after I rode all the way here to visit?"

"You had your drink, didn't you?" Justin questioned, his voice low.

Reaching up to scratch his cheek and disguise his smile, Mark nodded. "I guess I did," he said and stood to face the young woman who observed their exchange. "It was a pleasure meeting you, Miss Brandon. I hope there comes a time when we can talk at great length and not be interrupted." He bowed politely, winked at his captain, and left the cabin.

Justin stood in the center of the room, staring at the closed door and wondering why Mark's presence had upset him. Yet he knew it wasn't Mark's being there that had bothered him, but the attention he'd paid Dara. Justin closed his eyes. That couldn't be it. Why should he care if Mark talked with her and made a fool of himself? After all, maybe some man would strike her fancy and his problems would be over. One corner of his mouth rose. Well, Mark certainly wasn't the one for her; he'd toy with her for a while and then move on. Maybe that was what disturbed him about Mark. He knew that no lasting relationship would come of it.

"Captain Whitelaw?"

Dara's soft voice jarred him out of his musings and he opened his eyes to look at her, uncomfortable with the warmth that flooded his face.

"I'd like to help if I can," she continued quietly.

His gaze raked over her, then darkened with his unexplainable anger. "Well, you can't," he growled, turning for the bunk.

"I've told you before that I'm not afraid of danger, and if this has something to do with Lane—"

"It doesn't," he snapped, throwing himself down on

256

the bed. Leaning back against the wall, he unrolled the parchment again and stared disgustedly at it.

"Are you planning to wear a disguise?"

"I was," he sneered.

"Then no one would know who you are. That's the whole idea, isn't it?"

Justin glanced suspiciously over at her. "Yes," he answered cautiously.

"And you obviously need a companion equally unrecognizable?" She waited for him to reply but when he only stared she continued. "I don't think I have to tell you that outside of a few neighbors in Drawbridge, no one knows who I am. And if by some sheer stroke of misfortune one of those neighbors should be attending the ball, they would never expect to see me there. They'd simply think their eyes were playing tricks on them." She smiled sweetly at him but when he remained stone-faced, she shrugged. "As Mr. Wallis pointed out, you don't have another choice. You need someone you can trust."

His blue eyes seemed to devour her and Dara grew uncomfortable under his unwavering regard.

"Perhaps I should tell you why I must attend the ball, Miss Brandon, before you commit yourself to something you would have preferred not to do had you known." Twisting on the bunk, he raised a knee to dangle his wrist over it, one shoulder braced against the wall. "In order to succeed with my plan to trap Colonel Winslow, I will need the aid of someone in authority. There is only one such man. His name is Senator George Manning. He and I were friends before this mess started, and although I believe he doesn't think I'm guilty, he is a man who does his duty. If I sent word that I wanted to speak with him, he would be bound to have the constable waiting for me. Therefore I must

257

seek him out without any forewarning. Even then, I am not certain that he will listen before sounding an alarm. So you see, the possibility that I may never return to my ship after going to the ball is very high, and whoever is with me will also be taken into custody for aiding a traitor. You could go to jail, Miss Brandon, or you could be hanged for being in the wrong place at the wrong time."

Dara's green eyes held his for several minutes before she leaned back in the chair, placed her elbow on the arm, and propped her chin on her fist. "How long have you known me, Captain?"

A smile danced in his eyes but failed to reach his lips as he silently thought the time longer than he had wanted. "A week," he said aloud.

"Do you honestly think you know what goes on inside my head after such a short period of time?" She straightened without giving him a chance to answer. "You don't. You couldn't. So I'll tell you. You don't know anything about me, how I feel, what I believe in or to what lengths I will go. My father and mother gave up everything to come to America because they wanted their freedom. I grew up listening to what a great country this is and how we should honor it, protect it, fight for it. Now someone is planning to murder its president. Do you think I'd be content to sit by and *hope* someone else will foil that plan? I not only want to help you, Captain Whitelaw, I *must* help you. My brother gave up a lot to do his share. Now it's my turn."

Justin studied her for a long while digesting her words and gaining new respect for the troublesome little vixen. Since Monica he had never trusted or believed in a woman, certain that whatever they said or did was for their own benefit. It was true that Dara Brandon was using him, but only to aid in finding her

258

brother; and if he searched his mind for eternity, he realized he would never think of another woman who was willing to put her life on the line to gain her ends. What Dara wanted wasn't sparked by selfish motives. No. She wanted to save the lives of two people she loved very much: her father and Lane. Swinging his feet to the floor, Justin looked at the invitation he held in his hand, contemplating her offer.

"All right," he finally agreed. "But on one condition."

Dara smiled brightly at his consent, oddly exhilarated by her victory. She had, at last, won his confidence and trust. "Anything," she concurred.

A sliver of white teeth were revealed by his grin and he shook his head. "Maybe you should hear what it is before you give in so quickly," he warned.

"I can't think of anything that would change my mind," she assured him, "but tell me anyway."

"Oh, I don't think it will change your mind, but you may find it difficult to do."

"What?" she frowned, worried that there might be something to consider after all.

"You're going to have to do everything I tell you and more importantly you're going to have to keep your mouth shut."

Dara bristled instantly at his bold reminder that her quick tongue had always been her biggest flaw. Lane had many times told her the same thing, and she hadn't liked hearing it even from him. "Don't worry, Captain. I'll manage."

"I'd rather hear you promise, Dara. What we're going to do is very dangerous and truly against my better judgment. Maybe you'll understand why when I tell you there's a strong possibility Colonel Winslow might be in attendance. Mark has told me that the colonel has several friends in Washington."

Dara's face paled. "Oh," she whispered.

"I don't think he'd be foolish enough to try anything with so many witnesses, but I would wager my ship, you wouldn't get far once you left the ball. As long as you avoid him and don't speak to him, I think everything will go all right."

"But what if he sees me? He'll recognize me right away."

"He shouldn't," Justin assured her. "You'll be wearing a mask."

"A mask?" Dara echoed. "Won't that seem a little strange?"

Justin laughed when he realized he hadn't told her what kind of a gathering they would be attending. "It's a masquerade ball, Dara. Everyone will be wearing one," he told her, his smile lingering when he noticed the soft pink hue that stained her cheeks before she looked away. "And that creates another problem," he added, coming to his feet. "I'd better catch Wallis before he leaves. He's going to have to go back to Washington; we're both going to need a change of clothes." Crossing to the door, he paused once before reaching it and looked back over his shoulder at her. "Finish your letter and I'll have someone see that it gets to your father. We'll talk more about the ball when I get back."

Dara accepted her privacy with mixed emotions once the door closed behind him. Any young girl who was about to attend her first ball should be thoroughly excited, and anxious for the moment it would begin. Dara was to some extent, but the fact that she had had to talk her escort into taking her and the thought that Colonel Winslow might be there tarnished the glittering vision she had in her mind. Truthfully, she looked forward to the challenge of eluding the man. So what was it that caused a tear to pool in her eye and her chin to quiver? When Justin had agreed to let her be his companion for the evening, he had silently admitted that he needed her. So why couldn't she be content with that? Why did it bother her that he acted as if she was a nuisance and more so that he seemed not to want her around at all?

Chapter Ten

"Dara, what do you think of Thomas and Elizabeth Wetherell?" Justin asked, his gaze affixed to the scribblings on the paper he had labored over for the past half-hour. "No," he continued with a frown before she had a chance to answer, "it wouldn't fit the character." Leaning back in his chair, he stared thoughtfully up at the ceiling for a moment, the feather tip of the quill stroking his chin. "Myles?" He shook his head. "Grover," he decided, then wrinkled his nose objectingly. Disgusted, he leaned forward against the desk again, the name for which he searched evading him when of a sudden it exploded in his head. "Silas!" he announced loudly and glanced up at his companion for her approval.

The smile faded from his lips once he realized the fragile beauty standing near the porthole was paying him no attention as she gazed out over the waters of the bay. Bathed in the yellow brilliance of early afternoon, she was the epitome of perfection in her soft pastel gown. Golden strands of hair entwined with rich auburn locks as the sunshine played upon her thick mane. She had unwittingly presented her profile to Justin who feasted his eyes upon her exquisite bosom, its curve rising and falling ever so gently with each breath she took. It was easy for him to see why she always sparked the flame of passion in him, for indeed her loveliness could be matched by few others. Yet as he watched her, he could sense a sadness in the downward turn of her red lips and in the tilt of her head as she absently studied the graceful flight of an eagle in the crystal-clear blue sky. She seemed to long to share its freedom, the mobility of its widespread wings. The urge to go to her was strong, and Justin couldn't understand what held him back. All in all, he had enjoyed their short time together, their fights, their laughter, and the blissful moments when they'd made love. But those times spoke of building roots, of learning about the other as one did in a permanent relationship, and that was something Justin didn't want. Thus he resisted the tender emotion he felt whenever it seemed she needed comforting. What they had together would not last, and he knew it would be better if he didn't lead her astray with false hope. No, he would see her married off, then be on his way. Dark eyebrows came together suddenly. Of course, that would take some doing, for he wouldn't let her marry just anyone. She was special.

His blue eyes grew cloudy as he envisioned Dara on her wedding day. Yards of white silk beneath a layer of delicate lace flowed out around her, hiding her slender ankles and shapely legs, while her bodice clung almost possessively to her trim waist. The neckline of the gown was cut low to accent the fullness of her breasts and the smooth creamy skin of her bare shoulders. He imagined her hair piled high upon her head with sprigs of baby's breath adorning its coppery strands, and at each step she took, satin slippers peeked out from beneath her hem as she walked to the altar and the man waiting there. The smile that lifted the corners of her mouth radiated love and happiness, and Justin mentally sighed his approval until the man in his fantasy held out a hand to her. Suddenly he was hit with a wave of jealousy and anger when Mark Wallis turned to envelop Dara in his arms.

"Not you," he growled beneath his breath, slamming a fist against the desk top. His outburst startled Dara out of her musings, something he hadn't intended to do. He snapped back to reality and, in an effort to hide his momentary lack of concentration, feigned irritation with his work. He forced himself not to look up at her.

"Were you talking to me?"

The intoxicating melody of her voice penetrated his brain and set every nerve end aflame. He wondered if words would come to his lips when he opened his mouth to answer. Worse yet, she might notice the flush his careless mutterings had produced. To be safe, he elected to keep his eyes trained on the paper in front of him, and to address the subject of his prior frustration as if that had been his reason for speaking aloud.

"Well, sort of," he said, clearing his throat. "I was curious as to what you thought of the names Silas and Elizabeth Wetherell?"

Although she had heard his question, Dara's thoughts did not linger on her reply; rather she pondered on the happenings of the evening past. As was their custom for the last week, they had shared their final meal of the day in silence, but not by mutual agreement. It had been her choice not to be drawn into conversation. Her confinement in the small cabin was beginning to weigh heavily on her nerves and her aggravation was increased by the feeling that Captain Whitelaw also longed to have things the way they had been before he'd met her. She was sure of that later in the night when sleep would not come and she lay awake staring at the ceiling overhead. The cabin door had opened noiselessly, and in the silvery streams of moonlight coming in through the portholes, she had secretively watched Justin enter the room. The ashen beams played seductively upon his tall, muscular build, creating shadows where her memory revealed what they hid. His movements were sleek and hinted at the strength that lay beneath the outward ease with which he disrobed, and Dara's heart pounded in her chest, thinking that at last he had come to make her his once again. In the translucent shades of platinum and ebony, she watched his lean figure approach, then pause near the bed as if he'd had second thoughts. She was sure her heart stopped in that moment. She yearned to reach out to him and urge him on, but she knew she mustn't, not if she was to know how he felt. He must come to her on his own, not be tempted by her surrender. She held her breath, waiting, and in that fleeting eternity before he pressed a knee to the bed, drew back the coverlet, and gently lowered himself down beside her, Dara's entire body tingled with his nearness. His scent filled her senses, his warmth stirred her blood, and her hands longed to trace the sinewy ripples of his broad shoulders and his wide back before moving to caress his narrow waist and finally rest upon his buttocks as she sampled the sweetness of his kiss. But that moment never came, for within minutes she heard him breathing steadily in slumber. Although tears filled her eyes, her stubborn nature held them back. Perchance he would never again desire to hold her in his arms; nonetheless, he would marry her. Pushing aside her unhappiness, she forced herself to concentrate on what he had said a moment ago.

"Wetherell?" she had repeated quietly. "Am I supposed to know the name?"

"Only while we attend the ball," he'd smiled up at her. "You and I will be introduced as Silas and Elizabeth Wetherell."

"Silas?" she asked with a raised brow. "The title

doesn't quite fit you, Captain."

"Not as you see me now"—he laughed—"but it will."

"What do you mean?"

Sitting up straight in the chair, his elbows resting on its arms, Justin touched the tips of his thumbs and first three fingers together, the remaining two held loftily in the air. Elevating his nose as if offended by his surroundings, he said in a haughty manner, "Shall we say that I will be anything but a devilish rogue?" Looking at her from the corner of his eye, he fluttered dark lashes at her and was rewarded with a bubble of laughter.

"Are you sure you're not supposed to be Elizabeth?" she laughed.

"My dear," he continued playfully, "you insult my good character. Do you not know a true gentleman when you see one?"

Inspired by his tomfoolery, Dara grabbed the fullness of her skirts and presented him with a gracious curtsy. "Your pardon, my lord," she bantered, "but I am a simple milkmaid unaccustomed to such a fine figure of a man. Please forgive my careless tongue."

"All is forgiven," he mimed, coming to his feet and extending his hand toward her. "I believe the music has started. Would you do me the honor of consenting to this dance?"

"Most assuredly," she nodded with a coy lowering of her lashes as she rested her fingertips against the back of his wrist and followed him to the center of the room.

Capturing her delicate hand in his once they faced each other, Justin tucked his other arm behind him, and much to Dara's surprise began to hum a light and airy tune. She was enthralled by his performance, for she had never imagined him to have any knowledge of music, much less possess the rich baritone voice needed to execute such a lovely melody. She was further

267

beguiled by the graceful ease with which he swirled her about the floor and her own ability to master the dance with his gentle guidance. Suddenly, she realized there was much to learn about Justin Whitelaw.

"You dance quite well, my dear," he said in a manner fitting Silas Wetherell. "No doubt I will be hard pressed to have more than one with you the entire evening."

Dara laughed at his silliness, silently praising his talent for creating a most believable character. Then she added her own bit of humor to their game when she replied sweetly, "'Tis true, I fear. But know that while another holds me in his arms, my heart will belong to you."

Expecting to be twirled beneath his arm, Dara found instead that he had caught her around the waist to draw her close, the gaiety of the moment gone. Confused, she lifted a puzzled face to look at him and discovered that all hint of mockery had disappeared from his expression. Recalling the words she had spoken, she could find no cause for his abrupt change in mood, and she was about to question the reason for his silence when he suddenly entrapped the back of her head in his wide hand and brought his mouth down to cover hers. He kissed her hungrily, passionately, and Dara's head began to spin. His sudden desire for her had caught her off guard, enflaming her own wanton needs, and without realizing it, she raised her arms to encircle his neck and meet his kiss with equal ardor.

Justin's long-held-in passion ran rampant at her response, and he clutched her to him as if he feared she would suddenly vanish or have a change of heart and deny him. Her careless statement about being in another's arms had pierced his heart and left it aching. Suddenly, he could not think of allowing another man to claim her as only he had done. Fate had willed her to him, and he would not let her go until the desires she

268

aroused in him had faded. Then and only then would he consider selecting the one who would share her life.

As Justin's mouth moved against hers and his tongue parted her lips, a small seed of logic blossomed in her and began to grow. Although this was what she wanted, to satisfy the yearnings of her body, Dara realized it wasn't enough. Perhaps he wanted her now, but what of the morrow? When the fire of his passion had died, would he look upon her with loving eyes or merely lustful ones? In her heart she wanted him to love her as a woman, but if it was not meant to be, she would have to be content to have him love her as a wife. Until the vows were spoken, she would deny him the pleasures such a union would allow. Only the strength of her conviction enabled her to turn her face from his branding kiss.

"No, Justin, we mustn't," she whispered breathlessly, seeking to push away from him, but he held her tightly in his arms.

"Why, Dara?" he questioned, the pain of her rejection mirrored in his eyes. "It's what we both want."

Afraid that she would reconsider if she looked at him, she kept her eyes averted. "But I want more," she answered weakly, and felt the warmth of his breath against her face when he sighed.

"A promise of marriage."

"Yes," she nodded.

When he released her to return to his desk, there to sit upon the edge and silently stare back at her, Dara felt an emptiness claim her soul. Had her confession erected an impregnable barrier between them, setting them apart? That wasn't what she had meant to do.

"And because I was the first, I must be the one you marry?"

Her silence confirmed his suspicions.

"You would have no other?"

She shook her head.

"Poor Dara," he sighed with a half-smile. "And if I told you nay, and sent you home so that I could live my life the way I want it, would you spend your remaining days turning away every suitor who called just because of your silly pride, therefore denying yourself the pleasures I have taught you in bed?"

"Silly pride?" she rallied, the tenderness of a moment ago evolving into rage. "Pride has nothing to do with it."

"Then what?" he challenged. "Love?"

"Why, you arrogant blackguard," she fumed. "What makes you think that there is anything about you worthy of my love? You're a pirate, a murderer, and a trait—" The words hung in the air when she saw him lift one dark eyebrow. "A trickster," she finished instead, and looked away.

"Aye." He chuckled. "That I am. It's what has kept me from dancing on the end of a rope these past three months." A devilish twinkle appeared in his eyes as he watched Dara move back to the porthole to stare outside. "And I apologize for what I tried to do just now. It was unfair of me to force you into something you'd obviously dislike doing simply because I may never have the chance again." He waited until she turned a questioning frown his way and rose from the desk, eyes averted, to stroll back to his chair.

"What do you mean, you may never have the chance again?"

Justin sighed for effect and lifted the quill from its resting place. "Don't concern yourself, my dear. I spoke out of turn."

"But you spoke nonetheless," she argued, coming to stand near him. "What do you mean?" When he continued to ignore her and set his mind on the doodlings he penned, Dara's patience wore thin, and

270

she irately snatched the feathered item from his hand. "Tell me," she demanded.

Feigning resignation with a droop of his shoulders and a heavy sigh, Justin fell back in the chair to look at her. "It's just that there's a strong possibility someone at the ball will recognize me and I'll be arrested again. I doubt that I'll see the sunrise if they should." As if the thought was more than he could bear, Justin left his place to walk dejectedly toward the bunk. "It's selfish, I know, but I wanted to remember my last moments on earth as pleasant. I wanted to share them with you."

The tormented admission wrenched her heart, and she suddenly wondered how she could have been so blind . . . and cruel. She was the one who was selfish. All she wanted was for him to marry her so that others would not look accusingly at her. Ashamed that she had put her own needs above those of a man whose very life was constantly in danger, she could no longer look at him.

"If you'll excuse me now," she heard him say, "I'm rather tired. I'd like to lie down for a while."

Green eyes filled with tears watched his manly form lower itself to the bunk. He removed his shoes, and she didn't even flinch when he unfastened the buttons of his shirt and pulled the tail from his breeches. Oddly enough, she was drawn to the powerful expanse of his shoulders, the tanned skin that gleamed bronze in the sunlight, and the dark covering of curls that obscured the sinewy ripples of his wide chest then tapered down his lean belly. The mere sight of him stirred her desire, and she closed her eyes suddenly when the image of him dangling, lifeless, at the end of a hangman's noose flashed to mind. She had lied to him when she'd said love had nothing to do with her wants. It was everything. Long ago she had acknowledged the fact that marriage and love didn't always come hand in hand, but it had been her foolish dream that she would find both.

With a disheartened sigh, she opened her eyes and returned the quill to its place then glanced over at the man stretched out on the bunk. He lay on his back, his clasped hands cradling his head, his ankles crossed, and the pale blue shade of his eyes hidden beneath lowered lids. Thick sooty lashes fanned out against his rugged cheeks, and seeing them, Dara's pulse suddenly quickened. She hated the thought that this could possibly be their last time together . . . no, she refused to believe it. Yet as she considered the probabilities, she realized that with each new day, Justin Whitelaw ran the risk of capture. Hesitantly, she started toward him, not knowing what to say, but certain she must have an answer before any decisions were made.

"Justin," she said quietly and felt a delicious warmth spread through her when his gaze fell upon her. "Did you truly mean what you said . . . that you wanted to spend your last moments with me? Or would any woman do?"

Pushing up on one elbow, he smiled tenderly back at her. "Would you believe me if I told you that I have yet to meet another who would interest me more?"

Although she knew she should be honored by his statement because she was certain there had been a lot of women in his life, it wasn't what she wanted to hear. "And if she came along, you'd leave me for her," she replied with downcast eyes.

It had all been a game to him. Justin had wanted to trick her into giving herself to him freely on the pretense that his life could end the next day. But as she posed the truth for him to deny, he realized he couldn't lie to her. Reaching out, he took her delicate hand in his and gently stroked his thumb along her narrow fingers.

"Dara, I'm not the man for you," he said softly, "and

if I could, I'd change things around. You'd still be home in Drawbridge with your parents and Lane would be fishing near the mill. There would be peace between the United States and England, and I'd be sailing the seas as the captain of an American ship. That's all I really want out of life . . . no chains around my neck . . . just to be free to come and go as I please. You'd be unhappy with me because I could never promise I'd be faithful or for that matter even that I'd come home."

Dara studied him a long while before the corners of her mouth lifted in a smile. "You didn't answer my question, Captain. If you had the choice, would I be the one you wanted to spend your last moments with?"

It seemed as if she hadn't heard a word he'd said or rather had chosen to ignore them. His dark eyebrows came together as he considered making his statement again while another part of his mind searched for the answer she had requested. Suddenly, he realized that of all the women he had known, including Monica, the thought of spending a blissful interlude with any other was unsatisfying.

"I can't honestly say why, but yes, Dara, I would want it to be you," he said with a shake of his head.

"And what price would you pay to have your last request?" she asked sweetly, her fingers moving to the buttons of her gown.

"Price?" he repeated, his brow furrowed as he watched her unfasten the first catch. The cloth fell open to reveal the valley between those tempting breasts. His heart lurched in his throat.

"Yes, Captain, price. You see, there is just as much of a chance that you will escape the ball unharmed, and therefore you will have received my gift under false pretenses. I think it only fair that I be guaranteed something in return . . . just in case." Her eyes never left his as her fingers moved to the second button.

"Are you suggesting money?" he questioned disbelievingly.

"No, Captain," Dara smiled, exposing the thin cloth of her chemise beneath the gown's bodice. "A promise."

Dara's meaning hit him with as much force as a gale wind tearing at the sails of his ship in a storm, and he quickly swung his feet off the bunk and stood up to brush past her. "I told you before . . . I am not going to marry *you* or *anyone!*" Crossing to his desk, he leaned forward and braced his hands against its edge.

"Are you sure?"

"Yes!" he shouted back over his shoulder without turning around.

"Well, it seems like such a waste," he heard her sigh.

"What is?" he growled, his angry frown raking over the items on top of his desk without truly seeing them.

"That I'm willing and now you're not. Who would believe it?"

Her gibe burrowed deep into Justin's pride. She had questioned his masculinity. Had she been a man he would have laid a fist to her jaw, but as it was, he could only fume. He straightened but refused to look at her. "I'll have you know, Miss Brandon, that the only reason I'm not willing at the moment is because I won't lie to you. Would you rather I did so that later you could scream about how I wronged you?" Dark brows raised questioningly, Justin spun around to confront her, and he thought his heart had stopped beating when his gaze fell upon her.

She was lying on her side, one long slender leg bent and draped over the other, the pillow propped beneath her for support as she rested against it, and Justin wondered if she had anything on at all until he saw that the lacy straps of her chemise were pulled from her shoulders invitingly. He forced himself to breathe while his gaze wandered freely down the length of her shapely form, his blood pounding in his veins. Then a movement drew his attention and the fire of passion roared through him as he watched a slim hand pat the spot on the mattress next to her. Before he realized it, Justin moved toward the bunk to comply with her wish. But when he reached her, she raised a delicate finger in the air.

"The promise first," she bargained, enjoying the sense of power she had over him. But her pleasure was instantly dashed and her brow knotted worriedly when Justin rested his hands low on his hips, threw back his head, and roared with laughter.

"And what will you do if I don't?" He chuckled. "How will you stop me from taking what you so eagerly offer? You've made a foolish mistake, Dara, one you're going to pay for."

Dara scrambled to her knees, the pillow clutched to her chest, and held out a hand to stop him, her fingers fanned wide. "No, Justin. Wait," she said hastily. "This isn't fair."

"Fair?" he mimicked. "You strip yourself of your clothes, stretch out on the bunk, smile seductively at me, and *then* announce the conditions. In case you hadn't noticed, Dara, I'm a man. And I can't just extinguish my desires as easily as a candle's flame. This time you've gone too far, my little vixen," he warned, bending a knee to the mattress, "and *you're* going to pay the price. I told you before that you should be taught a lesson. You're fortunate that it's I who will do it."

"Fortunate?" she shrieked.

"Yes," he returned sharply. "It could have been Colonel Winslow or one of those river rats in Cambridge. They would have hurt you, possibly even killed you after they were through. And therein lies the

275

difference. I won't." He lifted his other knee to the bunk, and with lightning speed yanked the pillow from her hands.

Trapped like a rabbit in the fox's lair, her only means of protection taken from her, Dara hastily retreated to the far corner of the bunk, arms crossed over her chest, knees drawn up tightly against her, ready to strike when he advanced. Her whole body trembled with fear. She was uncertain as to what kind of lesson he intended to teach her, yet at the same time, her anger at herself for being so stupid set her mind to seek a way to fight back with the only means she had left, her tongue.

"If you don't stop right now, Captain Whitelaw," she said a bit shakily, "I won't accompany you to the ball. Then what will you do?"

Justin's mouth twisted into a wicked grin. "Then Silas will have to go alone and give his excuses for his sick wife," he said, inching his way closer, a determined look in his eye. "Want to try again?"

Her panic rising high, for Dara realized there was nothing she could say or do to stop him, she remained perfectly still, awaiting his first move. Green eyes sparked with the fires of anger glared back at pale blue ones, as she vowed that this time he would not find a willing partner. In fact, he would tangle with a wildcat, and the only thing he'd receive for his efforts would be the scratches and bruises she would bestow upon him.

"What's wrong, Dara?" he questioned with a mocking smile. "Can't you think of anything to say?" He waited for her response, and when she only glowered back at him, he shook his head, feigning sympathy. "Poor Dara. It must be devastating to find yourself speechless. But it's only temporary, I'm sure."

Piqued by his playful sarcasm, tears burned her eyes. "You're cruel, Justin Whitelaw. I can't understand how my brother could ever have found something good about you that would have won his respect." She straightened suddenly at the thought. "In fact, I don't really know that he did. I only have your word for it. Maybe you lied. Maybe everything I've heard about you is true."

Amused by the direction her thoughts had taken, Justin fell on one hip and laid his forearm over a bent knee. "Come now. I thought we'd settled all that."

"Yes, we had . . . but to your satisfaction. I have no way of knowing you spoke the truth."

"And what can I do to prove it to you?" He smiled lazily.

"You can let me off this bed and allow me to dress myself," she replied with a frown.

Chuckling, he reached up to tug on one earlobe. "Somehow I thought that's what you'd say."

"And . . ." she continued.

"Don't tell me," he interrupted with a raised hand, "let me guess. If I do the right thing and marry you, you'll know I've told the truth." He smiled at the firm nod of her head. "That's blackmail, Miss Brandon."

"No it isn't," she argued, hurt that he would think her capable of such a thing.

"Sure it is. You want me to prove my innocence by marrying you."

"That's not what you'd be proving," she snapped.

"Oh? What then?"

"That you're a man of honor and one who will accept his responsibilities," she explained with an irritable frown.

"And if I don't marry you, does that make me a man with no honor?"

"No. It means . . ." Her shoulders drooped in frustration when she realized she couldn't put her thoughts into words. "Oh, you're confusing me," she muttered and started to move off the bed, but Justin

277

quickly came to his knees and blocked her path. "What . . . what are you doing?"

"You still need to be taught not to play with a man's emotions." He grinned, resting back on his heels, his hands braced against his thighs.

"Oh?" she challenged bravely. "Well, what about mine? It's all right for you, but not me. Is that it?" Her lip curled in an unflattering snarl. "You simple-minded lout. Get out of my way!"

Drawing back her hand, she presented him with a stinging slap to the face, and recoiled with a gasp the second she realized what she had done. Maybe if she apologized . . . But the thought had scarcely come to mind before she saw, much to her horror, that Justin was about to return her favor. His open hand caught her squarely on the cheek, and although there wasn't much force behind the blow, the execution of it instantly brought tears and a look of shock to her eyes.

"You . . . you hit me," she gasped, shrinking away from him, her trembling fingers covering the abused spot.

"Uh-huh." He nodded. "And I'll not hesitate to repeat it if you ever raise a hand to me again."

"But . . . but you're not supposed to . . ."

"Why? Because you're a woman? Does that give you the right to hit me?"

"And because you're a man, does that give you the right to take what I don't want to give?" she rallied, her lower lip jutting out prettily as she dropped her gaze and tenderly rubbed her cheek.

Dara's question caught him completely off guard, and Justin found, oddly enough, that he had no answer for her. The more he thought about it, the more he realized she had a very valid point. He didn't have the right to force himself on her. She wasn't here by choice. Every time she'd tried to leave, he'd stopped her. But

278

then again, he shouldn't be here either. He should still be on his ship, the *Lady Liberty,* sailing the coast and serving his country. With a heavy sigh, he slid down on one hip, his upper torso braced on one hand and one arm hooked around a bent knee. And why should *he* be stuck with this little chit? She wasn't his responsibility. Justin cringed when the word seemed to ricochet around in his brain. That was the very reason he hadn't gotten married. He didn't want the obligations that went with it. Now this little twit was claiming just the opposite . . . that it was his responsibility to marry her because of what he had done. Damn. Why couldn't life be simple? Why couldn't he just take what he wanted from it and never feel an ounce of regret? He raised a dark eyebrow slightly as he contemplated that thought. So who said he couldn't? He was a grown man. He was nearly thirty years old, and nobody, including this little spitfire, was going to tell him what to do.

Swinging his feet to the floor, he slipped off his stockings and stood up to unfasten the buttons of his breeches.

Dara's entire body stiffened in surprise as she watched the well-fitted garment slide from Justin's hips, and when he started to turn toward her, she squeezed her eyes shut with a whimper.

"Go away," she begged in a tiny voice when she felt his weight upon the bed. She didn't have to open her eyes to know how close he was; she could feel the heat of his body branding every inch of her. Yet when his hand touched her shoulder and the straps of her chemise, she jumped violently. "No! Justin!" she shrieked, batting away his hand as she scooted toward the edge of the bunk. "I'm not going to let you do—"

Dara gasped when she felt his strong arm encircle her waist and drag her back to the center of the mattress. In frantic desperation, she lashed out wildly at him,

279

praying somehow one blow might connect and startle him into realizing what he was doing. But her strength was quickly diminishing while his grew. Near exhaustion, she gave him one final shove as she tried to twist from his grasp and then she went limp in his arms.

"I really don't understand why you even bother to waste the energy," he murmured, lowering her onto the soft cushion beneath them. "I thought you were smart enough to know that I can do whatever I want with you." A smile touched the corner of his mouth when Dara refused to answer or to open her eyes to look at him. She did not even move, and after a moment, what she had planned was obvious to him. Pressing closer, he placed a warm kiss on her throat and whispered, "Do you really think you can just lie there while I make love to you, Dara?" His lips moved to her ear and he gently traced his tongue along the lobe, failing to get a response of any kind from her.

Dara hoped that if she held her breath whenever he kissed her she would be able to stop her body from experiencing the wave of pleasure he never failed to arouse. She had decided that if she couldn't persuade him to leave her alone he would not find a willing partner. And if her luck was good for once, he wouldn't be so eager the next time he was tempted. Then his fingers slid the strap of her chemise from her shoulder and his branding kiss trailed down the length of her neck, setting her flesh on fire and threatening to shatter her brave façade.

"It isn't going to work, Dara," Justin whispered, pulling the second strap away. "You may want to deny what I can do to you, but your body will betray you."

His breath was warm against her cheek, and for an instant Dara nearly broke her pledge to lie still, for when he lifted her slightly to pull the chemise from her, it took every ounce of determination she had not to cling frantically to it, grasping what little protection it offered. Gritting her teeth, she forced her mind to center on other things and prayed he hadn't noticed the blush on her cheeks after he'd stripped away the garment.

Justin's heart thumped loudly in his chest as his eyes feasted on the beauty of her tantalizing curves. He knew that if he searched the universe he would never find a more magnificent vision than the one he now beheld. Bright coppery curls tumbled about her head, haloing the creamy smoothness of her flawless face with its finely arched brows, dark lashes, and pert little nose. The stubborn set of her chin beguiled him, and her tempting red lips hinted of the passionate woman she was hiding. He had stoked the fires of passion in this slender form and he readily undertook that challenge again. He would awaken in her desires that longed to run free. Lowering himself on hands braced on either side of her, he gently kissed the sweet mouth awaiting his touch, and his own lust ignited, issuing forth in every fiber of his being.

Willing herself not to move, Dara kept her eyes squeezed tightly closed and her teeth clamped shut even when Justin's mouth moved against her and he tried to part her lips with his tongue. It was even more difficult not to look at him when he raised up suddenly. She imagined the angry glare that furrowed his brow because of her tenacious will to defy him. When several moments had passed and he hadn't moved, her mind screamed out for a peek at him, but through sheer determination she remained motionless.

"You're being very stupid, Dara," she heard him say, his irritation clear in his tone. "Pretending I have no effect on you whatsoever will not change my mind. I'm going to have you no matter what, and I would think you'd make the best of it. After all, you enjoy it as much, if not more, than I."

"I'll suffer, thank you," she retorted carelessly. "And so will you."

"Oh, really?" he chuckled, lowering himself down beside her. "Do you think I'll suffer doing this?"

With one fingertip, he lightly traced the nipple of her breast and Dara cringed beneath the searing heat of his caress.

"Or this?" he added, changing the course of his sweet torment as his hand slowly glided downward over her belly to linger against her inner thigh.

"Oh, Dara," he mocked. "Please end my suffering. I will surely perish if you don't."

She gasped when his mouth swooped down to cover her breast and his hand moved to play upon the soft flesh of her womanhood. "No!" she wailed, coming to life in a burst of fury.

Her nails raked his chest then sought to claw at the hand that so brazenly claimed her, and Justin suddenly found himself fighting off the attack of a wildcat. A tiny fist connected with his ear, and he deflected a second assault to his head by raising his arm. Thinking to subdue her merely by capturing her wrists, he pushed himself up on one hip, ducking her wildly thrown punches, and waiting for the moment when Dara would decide she no longer wanted to share the bunk. Launching a second offensive in her quest to be rid of him, she quickly sat up, twisted around, and kicked out with both feet. One blow caught his hip, but the second hit him squarely in the groin, and Justin instantly doubled over in pain.

Dara truly didn't know what she had done, but from the way he groaned and his face twisted in agony, she was certain she had hurt him. She had meant to win her freedom, even score a blow or two, but never at the cost of doing him serious injury. Curling up on her knees, she cautiously reached out to touch his shoulder as he slowly pushed himself up to sit on one hip, an arm folded over his lap.

"Justin? I . . ."

"No!" he barked, one hand raised to stop her. "Don't come near me. Just leave me . . . alone."

"I'm . . . sorry. I didn't—"

"Yes, you did," he growled through clenched teeth as he gingerly inched his way to the edge of the mattress. "God, how I curse the day I met you." Wincing when he bent over to retrieve his breeches from the floor, Justin closed his eyes for a moment to allow a wave of nausea to pass; then he carefully straightened once more. Taking a deep breath, he let it out gradually and added, "I should have let the fish have you when I had the chance."

Dara's sympathy for him vanished at this last remark, and in a huff, she snatched up her chemise from the floor and quickly put it on. "I didn't mean to hurt you, Justin Whitelaw. I don't care if you believe me or not, but to be quite honest, I'm glad I did now. You deserved it."

Only his blue eyes moved to glare up at her before he concentrated on the gentlest method of donning his pants.

"Who do you think you are?" she ranted when she failed to provoke an answer. "How dare you blame me for what happened! I was merely protecting myself and you got in the way."

"Got in the way?" he repeated. "Seems to me you were very deliberate and bent on ruining any future involvements I might have with a lady."

Dara faced him, arms akimbo, but at his last comment, surprise replaced the anger that had gleamed in her eyes. Straightening, she cast her attention away from him and stooped to gather up her dress and petticoats, not able to look at him any longer. "You . . . you mean you'd have affairs even though you're a married man?" she asked quietly.

Justin gave her a stern look before he rolled on his stockings then reached for his shirt. "Madam, if it were my misfortune to be stuck with you for the rest of my life, I would fear for my health when I tried to claim my husbandly rights. And since I do not prefer the ways of a monk, *yes,* I would most certainly seek out the companionship of a lady now and then." Jerking on his shoes, he glanced up at her again and noticed the downward slant of her mouth. "Don't tell me that would upset you, Miss Brandon?" he mocked. "I was under the impression that you only wanted me to right the wrong I've done you. In fact, that's the only way I'd agree to marry you. You can have my name and I can have my freedom. If that is to your liking, Miss Brandon, just say so and I'll send Callahan for the preacher right now."

The flood of emotion that washed over Dara during his recital left her more confused than ever. She was hurt by his rejection, yet she did not understand why it should matter to her. All she really wanted from him was his name, to erase the guilt she felt for being in a man's arms without the benefit of marriage. Might her pain come from the realization that she had been naïve enough to think a man would marry a woman simply because he had lain with her? And was it foolish of her to expect even more?

"Well?"

Dara jumped at the sharp sound of his voice. Clutching her clothes to her, she turned away from him to hide the tears that had filled her eyes. "If it's the only way you'll agree, then yes, I'll settle for that," she answered in hardly more than a whisper.

"Yes, it's the only way I'll agree! You wanted my name; now you'll have it . . . and one thing more. After we find Lane and he clears me, you'll go home with him and make no further demands on me. You'll never once try to find me and claim more than what's agreed upon right here and now. Those are my conditions, Dara. Take them or leave them."

A sob constricted the muscles in her throat and she fought not to let him know how much his callous words had hurt her.

"I won't offer again, Dara. Make up your mind before I change mine," he snarled.

Her chin quivered and all she could manage in response was a feeble nod of her head, and a moment later she cringed at the loud bang of the cabin door when Justin made an angry exit.

Something cold touched Dara's finger and she blinked to break the daze she was in. As he slid the gold band in place, she vaguely heard Justin's deep voice repeating the words the preacher had spoken. Night had encased the countryside and the frigate had anchored near shore before the captain had returned to his cabin with a man he'd introduced as Reverend Hess. From that point on everything became a blur to Dara. She hadn't really expected Justin to go through with his offer to marry her. She'd felt that once he'd stepped outside into the bright sunshine, his anger would disappear and stubbornness would take its place once more. But when the cabin door had opened and the lamplight had fallen upon his tall, muscular build, clearly revealing his irritation in the deep furrowing of his brow, Dara had wondered if by chance he truly wanted to call the whole thing off but his pride wouldn't allow him to do so. She was nearly certain of it when she saw Callahan and Wallis follow their captain into the room, each man fighting to hide a smile. Justin Whitelaw had trapped himself into getting married and now he had no graceful way of backing out. Tears threatened and her throat tightened as she thought about it, for in that moment she had realized the wedding had come about only at her insistence. The smooth line of her brow crimped into a frown. This had been what she'd wanted all along. But now that it had happened, it seemed as if something was missing.

Dara wasn't sure exactly how she had spoken her vows; she only remembered that she hadn't been able to look at Justin or Reverend Hess when the latter had guided her through the words. She had concentrated on the pale yellow cotton of her gown, sadly reflecting on the fact that she hadn't been married in the white dress that had been her mother's. The two Brandon women had many times talked of the day Dara would stand before the altar clothed in her mother's wedding dress, a gown that had been brought from England and lovingly packed away in the hope that someday a daughter would wear it. Studying the gold band on her finger, Dara wondered if her mother would ever forgive her for ruining that dream.

Suddenly, she felt Justin's arms encircle her and in the next instant his lips descended upon hers, a symbol that the ceremony had come to an end. She received the token stiffly, sensing that he performed the duty only because it was expected of him, and a moment later she found herself in another's arms while she watched Justin walk toward the desk and the papers Reverend

Hess wanted him to sign.

"Tradition warrants me to kiss the bride," Mark Wallis grinned down at her. "And I rather doubt that if I don't take advantage of it now, I will never get the chance again, knowing your husband as well as I do. May I?"

Dara smiled weakly back at Mark and nodded her head, but she barely felt the kiss he gave her. His claim that Justin wouldn't allow another man to show any affection toward her confused her, and she decided that Mark obviously didn't know anything about the circumstances of their marriage or he wouldn't have made such a statement. Just as soon as they found Lane and cleared Justin of the charges brought against him, she would be returning to Drawbridge and Justin would carry on his life without her. A tear appeared in the corner of her eye, and she quickly blinked it away before anyone saw it.

"You know, Mrs. Whitelaw," Mark was saying, "I never thought I'd see this day."

Dara frowned in response to his statement.

"That the captain would take a bride," Mark finished with a laugh. "He always told me that he never wanted to be tied down, but I guess when the right woman comes along even the stubbornest man can change his mind." He smiled warmly at her. "Of course, I can't say that I blame him for grabbing you. You're a very beautiful woman, Mrs. Whitelaw."

"Dara," she corrected quietly. "Please call me Dara."

Now it was Mark's turn to be confused. "All right," he concurred; then he glanced quickly at Callahan who stood near them. Something troubled the young woman, and Mark sensed that this whole arrangement had other connotations. He had questioned Justin's abrupt and surprising decision to get married when

Maddock had come searching for him in Washington with the message that Justin wanted Mark to be one of the witnesses. But Maddock couldn't explain Justin's sudden decision nor could Callahan or any of the crew. And there was no talking to Justin. He was angry and silent, and anyone who ventured to draw him into conversation barely escaped with his life. For a man who was about to walk to the altar, Justin Whitelaw didn't seem at all pleased.

"Well," Mark added, uneasy, "I want to wish you and your husband the best. He can be very hard-headed at times, but he's a good man and I know you'll be happy."

"Thank you," Dara whispered, her head bowed as she toyed with the ring on her left hand.

"Excuse me . . . Dara," Callahan interrupted, "but I think the reverend needs you."

Bemused, green eyes looked up at him, and following his directive nod, Dara noticed Reverend Hess smiling over at her, the quill extended in his hand. "Oh . . . yes," she murmured. "I must sign the papers." Frowning, she started to walk away, then paused to turn back toward the men. "Thank you . . . both . . . for . . ."

"Our pleasure, Dara," Callahan answered softly. He smiled and watched her slowly cross the cabin toward the preacher and her new husband as if she were walking to the hangman's gallows.

"Something's going on, Callahan," Mark whispered once they were alone. "When Maddock first told me of this, I suspected that Miss Brandon had somehow blackmailed Justin into marrying her. But I don't think that's the case now . . . not from the way she's acting. It's almost as if neither one of them wanted to do this, and I can't for the life of me figure out why they've gone

288

ahead with it. Can you?"

"No," Callahan replied, his arms folded over his chest as he studied the couple. "They hardly seem like they're in love. I have to admit I was taken aback when Justin announced his plans this afternoon. I've known that young man for nearly ten years, and I don't think a day went by that he didn't tell me he would never get married, even if his life depended on it. And now, all of a sudden, he's doing just what he said he wouldn't . . . and with a woman he's only known for a week."

A smile wrinkled one corner of Mark's mouth. "Oh, I'm not finding fault with the woman he married. Miss Brandon is the most beautiful woman the captain's ever been with. In fact, if he hadn't slid that gold band on her finger, I would have followed through with my plans to court her."

Glancing at his companion from the corner of his eye, Callahan chuckled. "Mark, you'd never pass up the chance to woo any lady . . . beautiful or not. The day *you* settle down will be the day man learns how to fly."

"Oh, I never said anything about settling down." Mark laughed. "I simply meant I'd like to spend some time with her."

"Well, laddie"—Callahan reached over to slap Mark on the back—"you're too late. This one's already taken, and you know how possessive Justin can be. Make a move on Mrs. Whitelaw and he just might shoot you for it."

Mark shrugged a shoulder. "I wouldn't be too sure about that, Cally," Mark corrected, tugging on his earlobe. "Like I said before, neither one of them seem too happy about the situation they've found themselves in. There might be hope for me yet."

Callahan snorted. "Well, if you care to run the risk of

289

facing an angry husband, go right ahead. But I know when to back off. I don't even plan on asking Justin what this is all about. If he wants me to know, he'll tell me in his own sweet time." Straightening when Justin turned to face the pair, Callahan cleared his throat and added in a whisper, "And right now, I suggest we drop the subject."

"What? And pass up a chance to needle the good captain?" Mark rallied with a grin. "Not on your life."

Callahan gave his friend a warning frown, but Mark pointedly ignored him, extending his hand to Justin when the man came to stand before them.

"Congratulations, Captain Whitelaw, and thank you." Mark had a devilish expression on his face as he shook Justin's hand.

"Thanks for what?" Justin scowled.

"For stepping aside and allowing me full rein on all the ladies who will be disappointed to learn you're no longer available. I promise to keep them busy enough not to miss you." He grinned.

"I'm sure they'll appreciate your concern," Justin replied sarcastically. "And I'd appreciate it if you'd take Reverend Hess back to Washington."

"Now?" Mark frowned disappointedly.

"Yes, now," Justin growled. "Do you have some objection?"

Mark shrugged and shook his head. "I was just hoping I might share a drink with the new bride and groom. It isn't everyday Justin Whitelaw gets married."

Justin's blue eyes darkened dangerously. "And it isn't everyday I lose a friend," he warned softly. He waited for the meaning of his words to register; then he asked, "Did you have time to get the clothes I asked you to buy?"

"Yes, sir," Mark replied with a vague smile, knowing when to quit, "I brought them with me."

"What about a horse and buggy?"

"I've made arrangements with Miller. He even volunteered to act as coachman."

"Good. Then everything's set for tomorrow night." Justin nodded. "I just hope it goes as planned."

"It should, Captain," Mark guaranteed. "But in case there's trouble, I want you to know that I've taken the liberty of asking a few of the crew to join me. We'll be stationed outside Prescott's home to create a diversion should you and your wife need help in getting away. I figured Callahan could stay with the ship and have it ready to sail should you need a quick way out of here."

Some of Justin's irritation faded from his face as he studied Mark for a moment. "Thank you. I appreciate your help."

"Oh, I didn't do it for you, Cap'n," Mark grinned. "I simply don't want to see anything happen to that pretty little lady of yours." His smile broadened and before Justin could retort, Mark gave his captain a mocking salute and walked away.

"I'd hate to think how he'd treat me if he didn't like me," Justin muttered, his brow rising as he watched Mark and the preacher leave the cabin.

"You wouldn't like him half as much as you do if he acted any differently," Callahan observed with a smile.

"Yes, well, don't you get any ideas." Justin chuckled. "Having to deal with one such man is about all I can handle."

"Aye, Cap'n," Callahan nodded. "Is there anything I can get you before I go topside?"

"No." Justin sighed. "It's been a long day and I think I'll turn in early."

"All right," Callahan said, turning for the door. "I'll

see you in the morning." But before he made his exit, he paused to glance back at the young woman who was absently rearranging the items on the desk then over at his captain again. "You've always known what you were doing before, Justin, my friend. And I've always stood beside you, right or wrong. But this time, you've confused me. If you need to talk, you know where to find me." He smiled lopsidedly, then left the cabin.

Justin stared at the closed door for a long while, wondering if Callahan could be any more confused about the whole situation than he was. He hadn't any idea what had possessed him to send Maddock for Reverend Hess when Davy, his cabin boy, was nowhere to be found nor what it was that had made him go through with the ceremony once the preacher had arrived. Dara had made him angry, and out of frustration, even bitterness, he had voiced the only conditions he would agree to before consenting to marriage. He'd wanted to hurt her, and now that he'd thought about it, he truly didn't know why . . . unless in some left-handed way he'd intended to get even with Monica.

His dark brows came together in an angry frown, and he crossed to his desk to pour himself a glass of whiskey. Why did it seem that after all these years, her name kept coming to mind? He had put his past behind him, buried himself in his work, and had never allowed himself to get involved with a woman for more than a day or two. Now, here he was married! God, was he going insane? What was it about Dara Brandon that sparked hurtful memories of another woman in his life?

Glass in hand, he turned and rested against the edge of the desk. But when he raised the drink to his lips, his gaze fell upon the woman who was now his wife, and the terms of their agreement rushed to mind. As soon as his life was in order again, he would take her back to Drawbridge and never return. She would have what she wanted, and he would be free. So what was causing the ache in his heart? Downing the whiskey in one gulp, he slammed the glass on the desk top, stormed for the door, and noisily made his departure.

Chapter Eleven

"You know, Cap'n," Callahan said as he approached the man standing at the helm observing the fiery shades of gold the sunset was painting across the sky, "your own mother wouldn't recognize you dressed like that."

Smiling for the first time that day, Justin gave himself a quick examination from lacy, ruffled shirt collar to gold buckled shoes. "And even if she could have, I don't think she'd have wanted to claim this dandy as her oldest son." He gave the delicate lace cuff of his shirt a tug. "Truthfully, Callahan, I wouldn't want anyone to know I'd consider wearing such an outfit. Pink never was my color."

Leaning back against the railing, his arms folded over his chest, Callahan studied the tall figure of his friend while Justin fidgeted with his ascot. Whether the captain agreed or not, he made quite a striking appearance in the mauve velvet coat and silk breeches. The rose-colored stockings and shirt matched the shade of the brocade waistcoat, and although lace cuffs dangled across the back of his hands, Callahan knew the strength that was hidden behind all that finery. He longed to accompany his captain just to watch his flawless performance in convincing anyone who might talk with him that Silas Wetherell was no threat whatsoever. But as Callahan's gaze traveled the full length of the man, his brow furrowed once he saw Justin's face.

"Cap'n," he said, straightening, "are you going to do something about your eyebrows? They're much too dark for that blond wig you're wearing. Somebody is sure to get suspicious."

"Yes, I know. But the mask should hide them and I don't plan on taking it off or staying long enough for anyone to notice. That facial glue is so uncomfortable."

"Yes, I imagine it is." Callahan chuckled. "I'm sure glad you're the one going to this thing tonight. You'd never get me to dress like that."

Falling into character, Justin raised his nose in the air. "My good man, are you finding fault with my attire? After all, it is most fashionable in Paris, you know."

"Oh, whatever you say, Cap'n . . . er . . . Silas," Callahan mocked. "But I really wouldn't know. I've never been to Paris or attended a ball. Somehow brushing elbows with a dozen or so of your kind was never my idea of an enjoyable evening, so I'm afraid I've missed out on the finer things in life."

Justin laughed. "Believe me, Callahan, I'm not too fond of the idea either, and to be quite honest, you haven't missed a thing." Glancing back at the fading sunlight, he sighed. "Well, I'd better see if Dara's ready. It's going to take us a little more than an hour to get to Washington, and although I don't want to be the first to arrive at Prescott's, I don't want to be last either." Turning back to his first mate, he smiled. "Wish me luck, Callahan. I hate the thought of going to all this trouble if Manning doesn't show up or, worse yet, if I'm unable to talk to him."

"He'll be there, Cap'n," Callahan assured him. "Our luck hasn't been too good lately so it's bound to turn around."

Justin nodded his head in agreement; then he stretched, burying his fist in the small of his back to ease the stiffness there.

"Didn't you sleep well last night, Cap'n?" Callahan observed, his vague smile unobserved in the fading light. "I would imagine that bench isn't as soft as your bunk."

Tilting his head to one side, Justin looked over at his friend from beneath lowered brows. "Nothing gets past you, does it, Callahan?" he asked.

"'Twas only a guess," Callahan grinned.

Miffed by his companion's effortless ability to trap him, Justin said the first thing that came to mind. "She had a headache."

Callahan burst into laughter. "Oh, I'm sure she did," he chuckled. "New brides always get a headache on their wedding night. And you, being the gentleman that you are, graciously offered to sleep on the bench." Gray eyes twinkled in the yellow glow of sunlight before Callahan lowered his gaze to the deck. "I hope she feels better tonight, Cap'n," he added, straining to control his mirth, "for your sake. Of course, I could always have a hammock strung up in your cabin. It's more comfortable."

"Very funny, Callahan," Justin hissed. "And quite enough."

"Aye, Cap'n," his first mate concurred, rubbing his knuckles against one corner of his mouth. "If you'll excuse me, I'll see the longboat is made ready while you go get your . . . bride." Stealing one last glance at his captain, Callahan hurriedly walked away, his shoulders bouncing in a futile effort to control his laughter.

Justin watched his friend's easy gait as Callahan walked across the deck and then descended the ladder. He wondered if the whole crew was aware of the odd

297

situation he had gotten himself into. After he had left the cabin the night before, he'd gone topside for a breath of fresh air, intending to get away from the four walls that seemed to close in on him. He had stayed at the helm long after the crew had retired, except for the man in the crow's nest standing watch. He'd enjoyed the solitude of the quiet evening and the still night air. Only the need for sleep had driven him back to his cabin, and even then he had lingered outside the door for several minutes, reluctant to go inside. He wasn't sure what he'd expected to find, but he had been thankful that Dara had already gone to bed and was sleeping soundly. It had been his choice to use the bench for the night, not Dara's, and once the morning sunlight had stolen into the room and awakened him, he'd hurriedly dressed and made his exit before she had opened her eyes. He had spent the day away from her, using the lame excuse of supervising routine work that must be done on his ship. He had eaten his meals in the galley with his men, taken time to tease Davy about the endless letters he'd written to some mysterious sweetheart, and returned to the cabin only when the time drew near to dress and be on their way to Washington. He had managed to exhaust the long hours of one day, but as the second night came upon him, he wondered how he would be able to handle it without being obvious. With a heavy sigh, he raised his chin and stared up at the heavens as if seeking divine guidance.

"Lane," he whispered, "if you have any compassion in your heart for me at all, you'll not waste another minute in finding me."

Dropping his head, he turned and started for his cabin, his steps slow. If he didn't need Dara's presence to gain entry to the Prescott's ball, he'd leave her behind. That would make the events of the evening easier to deal with . . . especially when he had no way

298

of knowing what to expect. She clouded his mind, and right now that wouldn't do at all.

He paused when he reached the cabin door, and raised the back of his hand to rap softly on it. "Dara?" he called out, "are you ready? We really should be going."

A moment of silence followed and he was about to knock again when he heard the key turn in the lock. Lifting the latch, he pushed the door open and froze when his gaze fell upon the shapely woman he now claimed as his wife. She stood in the center of the room, awaiting his approval and clothed in the most elegant satin gown Justin had ever seen. But its beauty paled in comparison to the loveliness she radiated. Her long coppery curls were swept high upon her head, but a stray tendril or two coiled against her ivory neck and before each ear. Pearl-tipped pins adorned her locks and Justin suddenly realized why the cost of their clothes had thinned his purse as much as it had; Mark Wallis had spared no expense in selecting their attire. The full, off-the-shoulder design of the sleeves of Dara's gown exposed her long tapering neck and creamy white shoulders for his enjoyment, while the décolletage of the style partially revealed her full, tempting bosom. The tight bodice accentuated her trim waist, then yards of flowing satin composed the skirt, the same color as the golden sunset he had just experienced. The vision she created nearly took his breath away, and when he forced his eyes to look upon her face, his pulse quickened and the desire to take her in his arms overtook him. Bright emerald eyes held his, her anticipation of his approval clear in them, but his blood stirred at the delicate line of her cheek and at her slightly parted lips that seemed to beg to be kissed. He blinked and forced himself to take a deep breath. Tonight he would be hard pressed to remember their purpose in attending the ball.

Until the moment Justin opened the door and stepped into the room, Dara hadn't realized how much of a change there would be in his appearance. He certainly hadn't resembled Justin Whitelaw dressed as Reverend Flanagan, but clothed in the rich velvet and silk with lace adorning his sleeves and with sandy-colored hair, she was sure no one would suspect his true identity. She would know, of course, and that brought a twinkle to her eye. She probably knew him better than anyone else . . . well more intimately anyway. Her brow wrinkled suddenly when she noticed how perfectly his attire clung to his muscular build, and a spark of jealousy flashed through her. Not a woman in the entire place would fail to notice him, and if one of them openly flirted with him, she wouldn't be able to do a thing about it. That had been part of their agreement . . . a wedding ring for his freedom. A tear pooled in the corner of her eye and she quickly blinked it away, forcing herself to think of other things. With a brave lift of her chin, she waited for his comment on the finished product it had taken her nearly an hour to complete.

"Well?" she questioned when Justin failed to move or say a word. "Do I look all right? I won't be noticed because I look out of place, will I?"

"Oh, you'll be noticed"—he smiled—"but only because you'll be the most beautiful woman there."

Dara could feel heat rise in her cheeks at his compliment and her heart seemed to race a little faster. She glanced down at the floor. "Thank you, Justin," she said quietly. "No one has ever said that to me before."

"Maybe it's because until now every man who looked at you was blind," he murmured. "I wonder how your father could ever have allowed you to go off

300

unchaperoned as he did. He must have known what a temptation . . ." Justin straightened suddenly, realizing the result her trip had brought and his mood darkened instantly. He cleared his throat and glanced around the cabin. "Did Mark have the foresight to purchase a shawl to go with that gown? It could get chilly once the sun goes down."

Sensing Justin's abrupt change in temperament, yet not completely understanding what brought it on, she hurried to the bunk and picked up the wrap Justin thought she needed. Draping it over her arm, she lifted a second object from the mattress and turned to show it to him.

"Do you think anyone will recognize me?" she asked, holding the mask in front of her face.

"No," he smiled softly. "But I'm sure there will be a lot of gentlemen who would like to learn your name."

"And I'll tell them it's Elizabeth Wetherell and that you're my husband, Silas." She laughed softly. "I wonder how they'd treat you if they really knew who you were."

"Not very kindly, I assure you." He nodded toward the door. "Come. It will take us an hour or more to get to Washington."

He stepped aside to allow Dara to exit, but when she reached the door she paused and handed her shawl to him. "Would you mind?"

Without comment or the slightest hesitation, he took the proffered garment and whirled it over her shoulders. But standing so near to her as he was, the fragrance of her freshly washed hair and skin assailed him, dulling his capacity to remain aloof. "Dara," he said quietly, hearing his heart pounding in his chest when she turned soft, green eyes on him, "I want you to stay by me all night. Mark and a few of the crew will be waiting outside Prescott's place, but you and I will be

301

on our own once we enter the house. If something should happen while we're there, I won't have the time to look for you. So I want to know where you are. Understand?"

"I understand." She nodded.

"As much as I'd like to allow you to enjoy the entire evening, I'm afraid your first ball will be brief. As soon as I talk with Senator Manning, we'll be leaving. I can't really push our luck."

"I know, Justin." She smiled warmly. "This isn't meant to be an entertaining evening. You've a job to do and nothing more." Glancing down at the beautiful gown she wore, she lovingly ran a hand over its satiny smoothness. "To be quite honest, just knowing you bought this gown for me would be enough. I've never owned anything like it, and I doubt I ever will again." Smiling back up at him, she turned and walked out into the passageway.

As Justin watched her slender figure move gracefully away from him, he was suddenly hit with a twinge of sadness. He would be sorely pained to simply turn his back on her once he took her home again, even more so to pretend that that part of his life had never happened. With a heavy sigh, he closed the door behind him and followed her to the ladder that led to the main deck.

Every member of the Whitelaw crew paused in their duties to watch the captain and his wife cross the deck toward the longboat that awaited them. Many stood open-mouthed since this was the first time they had seen the woman Justin Whitelaw had taken as his bride. Doubtful opinions on whether the captain had used sound logic in getting married had run through the ship. But now, as they got their first glimpse of Mrs. Whitelaw, they realized that the captain would have been a fool to let her get away. Her beauty was so captivating that several of the men pushed their way closer to get a better view, stumbling over their own feet as they crowded around the couple, hoping to be graced with a smile or a nod of Mrs. Whitelaw's head.

"I think I'd better keep you in the cabin from now on." Justin grinned over at his wife as the longboat glided toward shore. "You caused quite a stir among the men. From the way they eyed you, the entire United States Navy could have surrounded us before they'd have noticed."

"Just curiosity." Dara shrugged and lowered her gaze to idly study the band on her finger. "They only wanted to see who had forced their captain to get married."

Surprised by the sadness reflected in her tone, Justin laughed. "You sound as if you thought they'd expected you to have two heads."

Soft, green eyes looked over at him. "They must have gotten that idea from their captain."

The amusement shining in his eyes faded instantly, and he turned to watch the direction the longboat took. "Don't expect more from me, Dara. I've given you what you wanted."

"Yes," she agreed quietly. "A name, but no future."

Justin's dark frown fell on her. "What is that supposed to mean? That you've changed your mind already?"

"No," she stated. "I didn't simply want a name. I wanted a family as well. With our arrangement, I'll be no better off than a spinster."

Justin laughed derisively. "Unless my seed has already been planted, that's exactly what you'll be . . . all alone for the rest of your life. I have no intention of sharing a bed with you again," he added in a whisper; then he glanced over his shoulder to make sure the mate who rowed the boat hadn't heard. "That was part of the bargain, remember?"

He had meant his declaration to hurt her, but he succeeded only in arousing her defensive nature. "Yes, I remember," she replied coldly. "And I doubt you'll let me forget it. But that doesn't necessarily guarantee I'll be alone once you're gone."

Justin's head snapped around to stare at her, his mouth dropping open in surprise as Dara returned his attention with a haughty lift of her chin. "And what's that supposed to mean?" he demanded.

Cold, penetrating eyes glared back at him, then looked away. "Oh, come now, Captain," she scoffed, readjusting her shawl. "I think you're smart enough to figure it out."

Twisting in his seat, his nostrils flared, Justin set a hard look on her, intending to discuss the matter further, but the bow of the boat roughly glided into the muddy bank and the craft jerked to a stop. Angry at the intrusion, he glowered over at the men awaiting their departure from the skiff. He realized the conversation would have to be postponed awhile, but he had no intention of letting it pass. If he'd understood her correctly, he would most certainly have to set her straight on how his wife should conduct herself in his absence.

Rising, he held out his hand to her, intending to help her from the longboat when he heard a splash of water and Mark Wallis called out to him.

"I'd be honored, Cap'n, if you'd allow me to help Mrs. Whitelaw to shore." The young man smiled.

Fighting to hold back an angry retort, Justin turned a dark scowl on his friend, ready to decline the offer, only to find that Mark had waded nearly knee-deep into the water and now stood beside the boat. To refuse would certainly attract attention and would most assuredly add fuel to Mark's obvious delight in provoking him. With a reluctant nod, Justin stood aside to watch the man agilely sweep Dara into his arms and effortlessly carry her to shore.

"If you'd like, Cap'n," Wallis threw back over his shoulder, "I'd be more than willing to carry you as well. We wouldn't want you to get your stockings wet."

Choked laughter filtered through the crowd of men observing his departure from the boat but it quickly died out when their captain sent them an ominous glower before he moved to the bow of the vessel. With skillful ease, he placed a foot on the tip of the boat and deftly leaped onto dry ground.

"Now that you've all had your fun," he snarled, "I suggest you straddle those horses and ride into Washington ahead of the carriage. Even you must admit it would look a little strange for us to be escorted by such an ungainly group."

"Yes, Cap'n," they concurred and swiftly moved away.

Justin watched them until the last man had mounted and ridden off; then he turned to question Mark on the location of the buggy and its driver, his temper flaring again when he found his wife still held in the younger man's arms.

"You may put her down now, Mark," Justin growled, noting that the smile on Dara's face proclaimed that she enjoyed the attention of her protector.

"I would, Cap'n," Mark replied, his gaze centered on the slight burden he carried, "but it's still a little muddy here and I wouldn't want her to soil this beautiful gown."

"Your consideration is touching, Mr. Wallis," Justin scoffed, moving toward the couple. "But since Dara is *my* wife, she is my responsibility." Before Mark could object, Justin slipped his arms beneath her and easily lifted her into them. "Now I suggest you catch up with the others. We've wasted enough time already."

"Aye, Cap'n." Mark grinned then presented Dara with a gallant bow. "Mrs. Whitelaw, it has been my pleasure to serve you, and I offer my help in the future whenever you might need it."

"Thank you," Dara replied sweetly, feeling Justin tense at their exchange.

"Cap'n." Mark nodded, then turned and strode away under the dark scrutiny of the other.

"I don't know why it upsets you to have someone pay a little attention to me." With an innocent tilt of her head, Dara baited Justin once Mark had moved far enough away.

"I'm not upset," Justin snapped as he started through the small stand of trees on the hillside that led to the road a few yards away.

"Then why were you so short with Mark?"

Justin's dark blue eyes looked at her. "Mark, is it? Since when do you consider yourselves on a first-name basis?"

"You are upset," Dara sighed, fighting down a giggle.

"I am not!" he roared. "I simply don't want my wife flirting with one of my crew."

"Flirting?" Dara laughed. "If I was flirting with the man, I'd still be in his arms, not yours."

"Oh, really?" Justin rallied. "And I suppose when my back is turned, you'll take up where you left off."

Dara bit the inside of her lip to still the laughter that threatened to give away the game she played. "I'd be most discreet, Justin."

He stopped suddenly a good distance from the buggy and let her feet glide to the ground. "You could never be discreet with Mark Wallis. The entire ship would know everything the two of you did, and I'd be laughed at behind my back. You're to stay away from him, do you understand?"

306

"Why, Justin," Dara teased, "you're jealous."

"I am not jealous," he howled; then he glanced toward the buggy and the man who waited to drive him into Washington. Miller's expression was lost in the shadows of early evening, but Justin was sure he had heard the outburst. Gritting his teeth, he turned back to Dara and whispered, "I simply will not have my wife involved with other men."

She smiled up at him, then lifted her skirts and started toward the carriage. "I do not plan to spend the rest of my life alone, Justin Whitelaw, and there isn't anything you can do to change that," she stated matter-of-factly.

"You're my wife!" he roared, angrily catching her arm as she walked away.

Glancing down at the fingers securely holding her, she casually lifted her eyes to look at him and said, "And you're my husband. If you plan to be unfaithful, then so do I." Jerking free of him, she started off again, only to pause at the side of the buggy to await his assistance.

Justin's chest heaved with anger even though he couldn't justify the reason. He had no more right than she to seek out the companionship of others, yet it seemed only natural for him. What bothered him was the thoughts of her in *anyone's* arms other than his. Was he jealous? Or just appalled to think that she would consider doing such a thing? Unable to find the answer and frustrated that he should even be forced to try, he bit back a reply and closed the distance between them. Without a word or a look her way, he took her hand and helped her into the carriage, calling out for Miller to hurry as he climbed in beside her. Settling himself in the corner of the landau, one arm resting on its edge, the other draped across the back of the seat behind Dara, he set his gaze on the road ahead, an angry expression on his face.

Dara took pleasure in his obvious annoyance at the subject they had elected to debate, knowing she would never brazenly seek out the affection of another man no matter how lonely she became. Still, it delighted her to see how angry the idea made Justin, and if she'd known him better, she would have placed the blame for his distress on the possibility that he truly was jealous. As it was, she could only sit in amused silence and ponder over the cause of his anger.

The trip to Washington passed hurriedly for the couple that sat quietly in the landau, neither of them looking at the other nor attempting to make conversation. To all appearances, each was not outwardly aware of the other's presence, but in truth, Dara sensed every move Justin made, each breath he took. She was very aware of the warmth of his body next to hers. Justin, too, experienced the same feelings, many times stealing a glance her way when she had turned to view the countryside. Her soft fragrance constantly assailed him and he forced himself not to run the back of his fingertips along the soft, smooth curve of her cheek, not to press a kiss to the slender column of her throat. That he refused to allow himself such a pleasure irritated him even more. With a disgusted curl of his upper lip, he turned his attention to the horizon that was filled with the tiny glittering lights of the nation's capital, thankful for the distraction.

While most towns slowly withdrew from the hustle and bustle of daylight at the coming of night, Washington's streets seemed to come alive after dark. Not only were the thoroughfares jammed with carriages, but the wooden walkways teemed with people. The warm yellow glow of the carriage lanterns mingled with the glow of street lamps to create a friendly atmosphere, and anyone who noticed the arrival of the

Whitelaw carriage did so only because of the handsome couple riding in it. However, as they passed a lone figure standing at the end of an alley, the man's eyes never left the beautiful woman with coppery hair. And when the open-topped carriage rounded the corner to head toward the elite part of town, that darkly clothed figure left his retreat, half running, half walking in an effort to keep up with the quickened pace of the landau. He followed for nearly three blocks before the rig pulled into a long drive that led to the front steps of an elegant mansion. Ducking into the cover of the trees lining the pathway, he covertly approached the main entrance in the hope of catching a closer glimpse of the woman, but he had to fall back when it seemed that practically everyone in Washington had gathered outside the main doors of the mansion. Carefully staying hidden behind a huge oak tree, he frantically prayed for a brief moment when he might step out into the open and see the woman face to face, perhaps when her blond-haired companion descended from the landau. But when the tall, well-dressed man stepped down and turned to assist the lady, the stranger's hopes plummeted. The man was wearing a mask. Certainly she had now donned hers as well. Cursing his luck, he decided to stay where he was until everyone had gone inside. Then he would sneak around to the back of the house where he might glimpse her through a window. If she stepped into the gardens for a breath of fresh air, then he would confront her and settle the question of her identity.

"I don't mind telling you how nervous I am," Dara whispered as Justin offered his arm to guide her into the Prescott house.

"Think of it as a challenge," he smiled, casually but purposely studying those who milled about the main entrance as they waited to go inside. "A game, if you will. No one knows who you are and it's their goal to find out."

"That's the part that makes me nervous," she replied, forcing a smile when it seemed everyone around them stared. "What if they should? The colonel probably has men looking everywhere for me."

"Put your mind at ease," Justin replied, nodding his head in silent greeting to one of the couples who passed by. "I've taken care of that. Mark and several of the crew are stationed close by and I've given them orders to get you away from here as quickly as possible should there be any trouble. If there is, and we become separated, I want you to go outside and get away from the house. Someone will find you and take you back to the ship."

"But what about you?" She frowned.

Justin's blue eyes twinkled beneath the mask. "Don't worry. I can move faster on my own. In fact, I'll probably be in my cabin long before you arrive. So relax and enjoy yourself. You won't be here long if I can find Manning right away." Straightening, he readjusted the silk tie at his throat, adopted the foppish air of Silas Wetherell, and extended his hand toward the steps leading to the veranda. "Shall we go, my dear?"

Dara's apprehension quickly left her once she and Justin moved across the wide porch and entered the front door. On either side of the entryway two elegantly dressed butlers awaited each new arrival, one taking the ladies' wraps while the other checked the invitations of their companions. Dozens of finely clothed men and women filled the spacious foyer, and Dara was suddenly caught up in the thrill of it all. In the center of the large area, a wide staircase graciously stretched upward toward the second floor. Its thick mahogany balustrades, like huge arms, beckoned her into its embrace. Overhead hung a magnificent teardrop chandelier, its numerous candles reflecting a rainbow of color all about the room. Many oil paintings decorated the walls, and each piece of furniture in the room was trimmed with gold-leaf paint.

The people who preceded Justin and Dara slowly began to move toward the tall archway to their left, and a tremor of excitement pulsed through Dara when the tinkling melody of a waltz floated out to greet them. When they finally stepped into clear view of the ballroom, she could almost feel her chin sag, so awed was she by the spectacle before her. Scores of lavishly dressed couples, their faces hidden behind their masks, gathered around the perimeter of the dance floor while others swirled in perfect rhythm to the refrain provided by a harpsichord, a cello, and several violins.

"Impressive, isn't it?" Justin bent to whisper in her ear.

"Oh, yes." Dara sighed. "It's grand."

"Not too long ago, hardly one of these affairs was given that I didn't attend." He chuckled as he guided her farther into the room. "Isn't it strange how one's life can change over a matter of months?"

"And speaking of that"—Dara glanced around to make sure no one would hear—"how will you ever recognize Senator Manning or even find him in this crowd?"

A servant carrying a tray of goblets filled with dark red wine paused before the couple, then moved on after Justin lifted two of the drinks from the sterling silver receptacle and handed one to his lovely companion.

"It shouldn't be too hard," he replied, the glass raised to his lips as he surveyed the room. "George Manning's appearance is quite striking. It would be difficult for him to disguise it behind a simple mask."

311

"How do you mean?"

"He has very dark brown hair with noticeable gray patches at the temples, and his cleft chin will give him away. He's a very handsome man, and I rather doubt you'll find him standing with a group of men. In fact, I truly expect you'll see him in the company of several beautiful women, all of them bidding for a chance to dance with him."

He winked over at her, then raised the glass to his lips again. But as he took a sip, his gaze fell upon a couple dancing near him. Every muscle in his body tightened, for although their faces were hidden beneath their masks, Justin instantly knew them.

It had been more than ten years since he had seen Monica, and while most women lose their shapely figures once they're married, Monica Dearborn hadn't. In fact, she was more beautiful than he remembered. Her flaxen-colored hair was swept high upon her head, diamond-studded pins adorning its soft curls, and equally sparkling gems dangled from her earlobes and around her long, slender neck. She had chosen to wear a teal blue silk gown cut low over her ample bosom, an asset she had always been well aware of and had used to her advantage. The muscle in Justin's jaw flexed as he decided she had probably used her womanly curves as well as her charm to entice Senator Rutherford, a man twenty years her senior, into marrying her. After all, hadn't she done the very same thing to him?

Monica Dearborn was one of twelve children, and her father was nothing more than a poor fisherman who worked the coastline near the Whitelaw Shipping Line. He could barely earn enough to feed his family. At the age of ten Monica had made up her mind that she would marry a man who could give her everything she wanted and she'd vowed that love would never play a part in her choice. She had heard of the Whitelaw brothers from her father when he'd tried to get a job working for Sinclair Whitelaw and had been turned away. Knowing that someday the shipping line would belong to the brothers, she had determined to marry one of them. On her sixteenth birthday she'd figured out a way to meet the brothers, but Justin had sailed off on one of his father's ships the week before so she'd had to be content with Stewart, the youngest of the pair. It hadn't taken long for her to find out that Stewart was not the favored son—in truth, he was rejected by his father—and that Justin, in time, would inherit everything. Thus, while she awaited Justin's return from England, she allowed the smitten Stewart to court her, eagerly accepting the lavish gifts he bestowed upon her.

Almost three months had passed before Justin sailed into port again, and by that time Stewart had asked Monica to marry him. Although she had never actually refused Stewart, she had cunningly postponed giving him an answer of any kind. She intended to use him to meet his older brother, and she did. In three weeks' time, she had charmed Justin into proposing and her future seemed secure. Then, one cold November morning, Justin announced that he was joining the United States Navy, despite his father's wish that he manage the shipping line. She had been furious with him and had told him that being married to a naval officer was no marriage at all. Then she had flatly stated that if he didn't reconsider, she would leave him. Justin had countered her argument by declaring that it wouldn't matter how much money he had if she truly loved him. Monica had left the next morning.

Only Justin's pride had kept him from going after her. He'd wanted her to come back to him of her own free will, thereby proving that his wealth, or lack of it, had nothing to do with how she felt. But the hours turned into days, the days into weeks, and a month later news of her marriage to Senator Samuel Rutherford reached him. From that moment on, Justin Whitelaw swore he would never allow himself to be manipulated by a woman again.

Justin hadn't realized how he'd been staring until the senator swirled his wife's lovely face from view and presented his own dark glare in silent warning. A half-smile replaced the bitter frown that had settled on Justin's brow, and he nodded his acknowledgment of the man's wishes before he lifted the glass to his lips again. He had thought that with the passing of years he had gotten over Monica, but now he wasn't so sure. The sharp thorn of jealousy still pierced his heart. When he had first learned of Monica's marriage, Justin couldn't understand how anyone could fall in love with someone else so quickly. Now as he studied the man Monica had chosen to spend the rest of her life with, he knew love had nothing to do with it. Samuel Rutherford was several inches shorter than she, slightly bald, and had such a protruding belly that it was difficult for him to pull her close. Obviously, money had been the only thing that had ever meant anything to Monica. That was all she wanted from Rutherford, and Justin realized that had been all she'd wanted from him as well. When he had taken that away from her, she had gone in search of a man who had it. Yet in spite of everything, Justin could still feel the old longing stir in him as he watched her, so caught up in memories that he failed to notice that the woman who stood at his side was silently observing him.

"She's very beautiful," Dara said quietly. "Do you know her?"

For some unexplainable reason, Justin found that her innocent question struck a nerve. Gulping the rest of his wine in one swallow, he exchanged the empty glass for a fresh one as a servant passed by. "I know a

314

lot of people," he growled, forcing himself not to look at the couple again. "And right now the only one I'm interested in is George Manning." Placing his hand against the middle of her back, he gently guided her through the group of people standing near them. "And we won't find him standing in one spot all night."

Dara could only guess what Justin's thoughts had been while he'd watched the beautiful stranger, but from the various expressions she'd observed on his face Dara knew that this woman had been a vivid part of Justin's past. He'd been surprised when he'd first seen her, but that reaction had quickly changed to one of approval as he'd openly studied the woman's beauty. Then her partner had noticed the undue attention Justin paid her and had quite possessively whirled the woman away. Did Justin know that man as well? Had the stranger recognized Justin? Apparently not or Justin wouldn't have decided to mingle further with the group of faceless people. Allowing him to lead her toward a table filled with a wide assortment of foods at one end of the room, Dara covertly glanced over her shoulder at the couple, noticing again the richness of the woman's teal blue gown and her precious gems that sparkled in the candlelight. Justin had claimed that none of his affairs had ever lasted longer than a few days, that those brief encounters never lingered in his thoughts. So what woman from his past could be the exception? With startling clarity it came to her, and she glanced up at her companion.

"Was that Monica?" she asked a bit too loudly.

Frowning angrily, Justin quickly took the goblet from her hand and set it on the table alongside his own before he roughly seized her arm and drew her to the dance floor. Falling into step with the gentle rhythm of the waltz, he masterfully glided her across the floor and away from the crowd standing near the spot they'd vacated. Forcing a smile for the sake of those who might be watching, he spoke through clenched teeth.

"I don't relish the thought of going back to prison, Dara. So would you mind watching what you say and how loudly you say it?"

Following his lead, she, too, pretended to be thoroughly enjoying herself. Smiling up at him and fluttering dark lashes, she half whispered, "Well, is it?"

"Yes," he snapped, and whirled her once more.

"Who is she with?"

Justin sent his partner a murderous glare. "It doesn't matter. Now drop it."

"But I want to know," Dara said sweetly as she nodded to a couple dancing near them.

"Why?" he hissed; then he smiled again.

"Because I'm curious about the woman in my husband's past. Any wife would be."

Justin gave her a doubtful glance. "Under normal circumstances I would agree. But we are hardly a loving couple."

"Yes, that's true. But you are my husband and she could pose a threat to my marriage."

"Ha!" Justin exploded, his hand tightening around the slim one he held. "I haven't enough money to suit her way of life. The gentleman she's with is a senator and her husband, and I'm reasonably certain he purchased the diamonds she wears. I couldn't afford the tiniest stone. Unlike you, she finds that type of thing more important than just loving a man."

Although the smile lingered on his handsome face, the pain in his voice reflected the hurt he still suffered from that woman's rejection of him years ago, and Dara felt a twinge of regret that she had pressed the issue and stirred up old memories.

"Do you still love her?"

Dark blue eyes glared down at her as the song came

316

to an end, and without a word, he turned, guiding her away from the dance floor. "We're here to find Manning—remember?—not discuss my personal life," he snarled.

Dara's sorrow deepened, but in a different vein, for she suddenly and sadly realized that the man she had married still cared a great deal for another woman. And now that he had found her again, Dara doubted that Justin would hesitate to seek her out. Hadn't he already told her that he intended to continue seeing other women even though he was married?

The John Prescott mansion was known for its exquisite beauty throughout all of Washington, for its priceless paintings, rare vases, and imported custom-designed furniture. Yet all of these were overshadowed by the unique architecture of the home. Although it was located in the center of a cluster of equally fashionable residences, the Prescott mansion was set on several acres of land, most of which was heavily wooded although a narrow stream ran through the far edge of the property. John had selected this particular spot as the location of his home, because he'd wanted a place where he could escape from the pressures of the day to go fishing without leaving his own grounds, yet he'd also wanted to capture the beauty of the landscaping he had seen created on the estates of one of his distant cousins in England. Knowing that the bitterly cold winter months in Maryland would force him inside, away from his retreat, he'd ordered the carpenters to build French doors into one entire wall of the ballroom so he could overlook his grounds and enjoy viewing the serenity of the gardens at any time he wanted.

But John Prescott didn't stop there. He wanted a place where he could entertain guests on a warm August evening, much like the night of the masquerade ball, with all of these doors open so anyone could step out onto the terrace and the ballroom would never be crowded. Once outside, his guests could rest from their exhausting evening of dancing on the many wicker settees and chairs arranged artfully on the terrace. Those who wanted privacy could stroll down one of the many flagstone walkways lined with tall hedges that circled out for several hundred feet before each path joined once more at the gazebo in the center of Prescott's property. Many confidential conversations had been held in that summerhouse, and because of the layout, none could be overheard unless the parties wished it so. With any kind of luck, Justin planned to lure Senator Manning to that very spot.

As Justin and Dara stepped onto the terrace, the other couples were too caught up in their varied conversations to notice how the tall, handsome stranger covertly studied them. And when a new waltz began, many left the quiet solitude outdoors to return to the merriment and the dancing of the ballroom. Discovering that Manning wasn't one of those who remained, Justin positioned himself just outside one of the many open doorway so he could get a clear view of the interior. He hoped to spy the senator's tall, lanky frame. Dara, meanwhile, ventured to an empty settee set away from the others and a good distance from her husband.

She had never expected to see anything quite as awe-inspiring as the grounds surrounding the Prescott mansion. Huge willow trees shaded the terrace, and on either side of her, pathways disappeared into the shadows. The sweet smell of jasmine filled the air, and she closed her eyes to breathe in its scent as she enjoyed the harmonious sound of stringed instruments drifting out from the ballroom. She did not, at first, notice the couple that had decided to enjoy the cool night air

318

because they came onto the terrace through the French doors at the far end.

"Darling, would you be a precious and get me a glass of wine?" Dara heard the woman request.

"Of course," the man consented. "Will you be all right here alone until I return?"

The woman laughed. "Oh, Samuel, don't be silly. These are all John's friends. I'm in no danger."

"I know, dear." He sighed. "But I didn't like the way that man stared at you."

"He hasn't been the first, my sweet, and I certainly hope he won't be the last. Now run along. All this dancing has left me quite thirsty."

"Yes, dear." Relenting, he turned to leave. "But you stay right here so I can find you."

"Will you just go?" she scolded playfully and smiled as she watched his stout figure disappear into the crowd. She waited until even his bald head was obscured from view by the crowd inside; then she turned her attention to the real reason she had come onto the terrace. She headed into the garden, but before she had taken a step, someone called out to her.

"Mrs. Rutherford"—the man smiled—"how nice to see you again."

"Why, hello Colonel Winslow."

Dara's eyes flew open immediately. She instantly recognized the man standing only a few yards away, even with the mask he wore. Afraid to move lest she draw his attention her way, she sat perfectly still, listening and waiting for the chance to lose herself in the group of people standing on the patio.

"Where's your husband?" Winslow asked.

"Oh, I sent him after a glass of wine, but he's been gone so long I fear he's stopped to chat with some of his friends."

The low-hanging willow branches of the nearby tree

veiled the woman's figure from the muted light of the torches placed about the area, but Dara thought she saw her flutter a handkerchief daintily beneath her chin.

"Would you be a darling and see if you can find him for me? I swear I shall swoon if he doesn't return soon."

"Of course," the colonel offered. "I wanted to speak with him anyway, and I shall do so as we return with your wine."

"Thank you," she smiled.

Taking her hand in his, Colonel Winslow placed a light kiss on her knuckles and replied, "My pleasure. We will be right back." With that, he stepped through the doorway and was gone.

Dara hadn't realized that she had been holding her breath until she collapsed back onto the settee with a sigh. Every muscle in her body ached from the tension caused by holding herself motionless for fear that at any moment the colonel would turn and see her. Justin had told her that Colonel Winslow might be in attendance, but until she saw him, she hadn't truly given his presence much thought. Now all she wanted to do was find Senator Manning and return to Justin's ship where she would be safe. She sat upright suddenly, wondering if Justin had seen the man too, and she was starting to rise when the woman with whom Winslow had spoken moved out of the protective cover of the tree branches and started toward her. The moment Dara saw the color of the woman's hair and the diamonds that trimmed her neck, Dara's throat constricted with unshed tears, for she knew from the direction of Monica's steps that this woman intended to talk with Justin. Twisting on the settee to hide her face from Monica and to make it seem that she paid her no heed, Dara watched from the corner of her eye as the shapely blonde approached her husband.

"Hello, Justin," Monica whispered when she was certain no one was near enough to hear. "Are you looking for me?"

A chill raced down Justin's spine as he instantly recognized the sweet sound of Monica's voice and her soft, familiar fragrance. Using every ounce of self-control, he could muster, he pretended not to hear her or for appearance's sake that she had mistaken him for someone else. Too many years had passed, and he had traveled too many miles to suddenly trust her. She was married to a senator and that made her the enemy. It was quite possible that she was a decoy set to trap him, and spending a moment with her in trade for being hanged was no longer worthwhile. It might have been ten years ago, but the day she walked out on him his love for her had died. Or had it?

"If you're afraid I'll tell someone who you really are," she continued, moving to stand before him, "I assure you, I won't. I'm not out for revenge. I'm the one who left." She smiled sweetly up at him, then moved away from the doorway toward one of the paths. "And I'll prove it by suggesting we go somewhere where no one will hear or see us." She walked at a leisurely pace not once turning back to see if he followed, for in her heart she felt certain he would.

Justin closed his eyes, fighting the desire to do as she suggested, for although he'd vowed his hatred of her, being with her again churned up all his good memories: the kisses they'd shared, the times they'd lain in each other's arms after they'd made love. But she was married now, and there would never be a future for them, not the kind that he'd wanted. She had hurt him more deeply than anyone else in his life, and he had the right to shun her, to pretend that her offer had little effect on him. But before he knew what he was doing, he turned and slowly followed her down the narrow walkway lined with tall hedges, unaware of the green eyes that sadly watched.

Dara couldn't explain the ache she felt in her heart as she tearfully witnessed her husband walk away with another woman. She truly cared that he preferred someone else, and if she cared then she must love Justin. She blinked and the moisture that rimmed her lashes spilled over and raced down her cheeks, beneath the mask she wore. She couldn't love him. She hadn't known him long enough. Maybe she only longed to have someone care that much for her, enough to risk his life to be with her. Yes, that had to be it. She was only jealous of the attention Monica received. Her lower lip quivered, and she knew that she lied to herself. It wasn't jealousy that caused her tears; it was pain. She loved Justin, but she now knew that he would never love her . . . not as long as thoughts of Monica haunted him. Coming to her feet, she absently pulled the mask from her face to dry her tears with the back of her hand. Maybe a glass of wine would help. Maybe if she concentrated on the couples inside, who enjoyed the dancing and the companionship of others, she could forget where Justin was at the moment. Moving in the direction from which the music came, she stopped suddenly when she heard a woman's laughter and decided she would prefer being alone. Then a thought struck her, and she glanced back over her shoulder. Maybe Justin didn't love his wife, but did that mean he still loved Monica? Knowing that if he caught her he would probably ring her neck, Dara ignored that possibility and turned down the path the couple had taken. She would listen to what he had to say and then judge for herself.

The tall, thick shrubbery growing on either side of the footpath made it impossible for her to see Justin or the woman he was with as the lane twisted and turned in the shadowy darkness, and Dara was forced to judge the distance between them and herself by the sounds Monica's heels made as they clicked against the flagstones. She walked for several minutes before all was quiet except for the rhythmical song of crickets; then Dara slowed her step. Carefully peering around the last bend in the trail to see where they had gone, she jerked back instantly when she spotted them standing in the ornately decorated gazebo. Sighing disgustedly when she realized there was no way for her to get closer without them seeing her and realizing she could not hear their conversation, she decided instead to watch. His actions would tell her what she wanted to know. Staying in the shadows, she leaned forward to get a clear view.

"How did you know it was me, Monica?" Justin asked, watching her sit down on the wooden bench built around the edge of the interior of the gazebo.

Taking off the mask that matched the shade of her gown, she leaned back and smiled over at him. "Oh, I don't know. Maybe it was the way a total stranger kept staring at me with a hungry look in his eyes."

Justin gave a short laugh. "Do you expect me to believe that I'm the only man who's ever stared at you? It had to have been something else," he said, his tone flat.

"Well, of course it was, silly." She laughed coquettishly. "I knew the minute I saw you . . . even with your clothes on."

Memories of the last time they had made love flashed into Justin's mind. It had been on the wind-swept shore of a deserted stretch of beach near his home . . . the day he had told her of his decision to join the Navy . . . the day before she had left him for good. Forcing away the vision of their naked bodies entwined, he looked toward the partially obscured lights of the city. "That was a long time ago, Monica," he said quietly. "A lot has happened since then."

"Yes, so it has." She sighed then fell quiet for a moment, wondering how to broach the reason she had lured him here. "I heard about your trouble. I must say I was relieved when I learned of your escape."

"Were you?" he asked a bit sarcastically and smiled over at her. "Somehow I didn't think you capable of feeling anything . . . especially for me."

"Now, Justin," Monica scolded, "I didn't ask you out here so we could insult one another."

"Why did you ask me to come?"

"Because you're the only man I can trust." Leaving her place on the bench, she came to stand before him. "I need your help."

A vague smile touched the corners of his mouth as he raised a doubtful brow. "To do what, Monica? Find you a wealthier husband when this one dies?"

"Justin, that's cruel," she gasped. "I love Samuel . . . in my own way and that's why I need your help. I had decided to do something but I didn't know how until I saw you."

"Do something? About what?"

"Well, it's not a secret that many merchants in the northern states are against the Embargo Act. And they, in turn, are putting pressure on their senators to have President Jefferson lift it. It doesn't matter to me one way or another, but it does to Samuel. I overheard him talking with some of his colleagues about a plot to assassinate the president. If that happens, Samuel very well could be implicated. It would ruin us."

"And you'd be left penniless," Justin grinned.

"And shamed," she snapped; then she quickly brought her ire under control. She smiled sweetly. "I need you to stop it."

"How, Monica? Kill the president first and take all

responsibility for it? After all, my life isn't worth much. I'm a traitor and everyone would expect it of me. That way your husband would have what he wanted and so would you. Very ingenious, my dear. There's only one problem."

"And what's that?" she frowned.

Justin studied Monica's beautiful face and the warm brown eyes staring back at him, remembering the times when he'd thought no one else mattered to her. What a fool he had been. Smiling sardonically, he replied, "What would I get out of it?"

A sliver of white teeth showed as Monica smiled coyly. "Why anything you want, Justin, anything at all." Lifting her arms, she encircled his neck and drew him down to meet her parted lips.

Justin did not hesitate to take what she offered. Slipping his own arms around her slender form to pull her body close to his, he longed to feel the warmth and passion that only Monica could arouse. But when their lips touched, a vision of auburn hair and green eyes exploded in his head. Confused, he broke the embrace and moved away from her.

"It isn't enough," he said sharply before she could question his abruptness. "A simple kiss is not worth the risk."

"That wasn't all I was offering, Justin," she said quietly, coming to stand beside him. "After it's over, we'll meet somewhere. We can do the things we used to like to do . . . for as long as you want. I'd like that. It's been a long time since a real man made love to me."

His blue eyes darkened as he glanced over at her. "Another promise, Monica? Promises are easily broken, and I think you'll understand when I say I don't trust you anymore."

"What then? Money?"

Sighing, he looked up at the moonlight struggling to

shine through the branches of the trees. "No. You can help me accomplish what I came here to do."

"Which is?"

"Find George Manning for me and send him here. But you're not to tell him who's waiting. If he knew, I'd never be allowed to leave and your request would go unfulfilled." He looked at her again. "Is it a bargain?"

"Yes . . . with one exception."

Justin raised his brows questioningly.

"That you and I will still meet somewhere." She turned to face him and slid her arms around his waist. "I've missed you, Justin," she whispered alluringly. "Say you will."

His heart ached at her confession, for he, too, had missed the times they'd spent together. A long while passed as he fought with himself, knowing the consequences such a meeting might bring. Finally, he relented and nodded his head. After all, what did he have to lose? There was nothing left to sacrifice.

"Good." She smiled, letting go of him. "Now you stay right here and I'll send George to you."

But as she turned to leave, Justin caught her wrist and pulled her back into his arms, crushing his mouth to hers in a hungry kiss.

Tears filled Dara's eyes as she watched the couple embrace. She felt that her heart had been torn from her. Turning away from the scene before her, she fought the sobs that threatened to overcome her. He still loved Monica. She knew that now, and there was nothing she could do to change it. Angrily, she wiped the tears from her face. Well, if he wanted her, he could have her, but Dara wasn't going to stick around and be a witness. She would go home where someone loved her. Squaring her shoulders, she started back down the path but suddenly she heard the sound of footsteps on the flagstones behind her. Fearing Justin would find her, she began to run, and frantically glancing over her shoulder to see how close he might be, she tripped over her own feet. In trying to catch herself, she let go of the mask she held in her hand, and it went scooting across the smooth stones of the walk. Scrambling to her feet, she quickly retrieved the wayward item, ready to run again, but to her horror, she sensed a presence behind her and stood frozen to her spot, a million excuses for being there running through her head. Unable to choose a valid one, she forced a smile to her lips and turned around, surprised to find that only Monica had returned from the gazebo. Both women nodded politely, and as the older one passed by, Dara's smile faded into a curious frown. Had she gone to tell her husband some lie that would excuse her from the ball so she and Justin could leave together? Chin quivering, Dara forced herself not to cry as she absently traveled the remainder of pathway, pausing in the shadows near the terrace to watch Monica go inside the house. A few moments later she returned with a tall, dark-haired man at her side. They talked for several minutes before Monica pointed in Dara's direction. Fearing the woman had recognized her and that the man was one of Colonel Winslow's companions, Dara quickly spun around and raced back down the pathway.

"George," Monica objected sweetly, "how long have we known each other? You can trust me. He's a friend who hasn't seen you for a long while and he wants it to be a surprise. You'll be perfectly safe. Now go on," she added, giving him a gentle nudge.

"Then why doesn't he meet me here in the light?" George Manning argued.

"And spoil the fun? Go!"

"Well, it's against my better judgment, but since it's

you who's doing the asking . . ." He smiled back at her, shook his head, and pulled his pipe from his pocket. "However, if this is a trick designed to make me look foolish and no one's out there, you're going to pay, Mrs. Rutherford." Stuffing the bowl of the pipe with tobacco, he struck flint and steel, and sparked a flame to it as he started toward the spot where Monica wanted him to go.

He had followed the winding path nearly to its end when he heard bushes rustling ahead, so he stopped, waiting for someone to jump out at him. No other sounds greeted him, and he shook his head, blaming the last glass of wine he'd drunk for fogging his mind. Then he continued on his way. But when he moved into the clearing where the gazebo stood and where his so-called long-lost friend was supposed to be, George pulled up short, for the place was empty. Chuckling at the way Monica had so easily duped him, he turned back toward the mansion, intending to playfully give her a piece of his mind, when he suddenly felt something prod his back.

"Don't make a sound," the deep voice behind him warned. "Otherwise, I might be forced to use this."

"Justin?" George frowned, half turning. "Is that you?"

"Yes."

"But why the gun? I never carry a weapon at social functions and you know it. Besides . . . I thought we were friends."

"We are, but through an odd turn of fate, we're on opposite sides of the law now."

"I don't believe that, Justin. I never did. I just couldn't prove it. And to be very honest, I'm glad you escaped."

"If that's true, then maybe you'll prove my innocence by helping me."

"To do what?" Manning asked. "And will you take that thing out of my ribs?"

"You don't have to worry, George," Justin grinned. "My finger isn't loaded."

"Your—" Spinning open-mouthed to discover that it was indeed Justin's finger that held him at bay, George burst into laughter. "Promise me you'll never tell anyone; I'd never live it down." His laughter died suddenly when he noticed Justin's blond hair. "I guess it has been awhile since I've seen you. As I remember, you were a brunette."

"I still am," Justin assured him. "It's just a disguise."

"Well, no one can say you ever lacked imagination . . . or courage. You're taking a big risk coming here."

"I know. But it was important that I talk with you and I didn't know any other way to accomplish it."

"So . . ."

"There's a plot to kill President Jefferson and I need your help in stopping it."

"Need you ask? What is it?"

"I was approached by someone to be the assassin. I agreed only because I knew if I didn't, they'd find someone else. The attempt is to take place in Norfolk next week at the christening ceremony of Jefferson's new warship. There will be some men there to create a diversion while I supposedly shoot Mr. Jefferson. I want someone you trust to arrest them. With a little persuasion, they'll admit who hired them and you can then arrest Colonel Emerson Winslow for being behind it all."

"You're not serious?" Manning replied in surprise.

"I'm afraid I am, George. He's the one who hired me."

"Why that two-faced hypocrite. He just told me how he thought the president's—"

"You've talked to him? Here?" Justin interrupted, panic in his voice.

"Ah . . . yes. The last time I saw him he was with Monica's husband. Why—"

"Oh, my God . . . Dara," Justin moaned, glancing toward the house then back at his friend as he started to hurriedly move away. "I can't explain now, George; just promise you'll have someone in Norfolk next week."

"Consider it done," George called, a perplexed look on his face as he watched his tall, muscular companion race off. With a sigh, he looked at the pipe in his hand and shook his head, wondering how justice could have been so blind as to find a man like Justin Whitelaw guilty of treason.

Dara had panicked when she'd heard the stranger's footsteps behind her. Maybe he had been sent to kill her, and maybe at Justin's suggestion. Confused and very frightened, she eluded both men by wriggling through a sparse patch in the thick growth of hedge. She came out on a grassy clearing on the other side and paused to wipe away her tears and to collect her wits. Maybe Justin wanted to be with Monica, but Dara knew he wouldn't kill his wife to do it. They had already agreed that she would simply go home once they'd found Lane.

Suddenly the excitement of the ball had lost its glitter; she no longer wanted to be a part of it. She would go back through the house, out the front door, and find Mark. He would take her back to the ship. Of course she would have to make him promise not to tell Justin how upset she was, for Justin would probably laugh at her and then remind her that she had no right to object to anything he did. And maybe she didn't . . . not verbally . . . but he could never stop the feeling in her heart.

Aimlessly, she walked across the opening to the hedge on the other side and found a spot where the branches of the shrubs weren't as dense. Certain she would find another pathway on the other side that would lead back to the mansion, she pushed through the narrow hole, her arms crossed over her face to protect her. Once again she stood on a flagstone walk, and unmindful of the way she looked or that she had not donned the mask again, she started forward, head down. Failing to watch where she was going, she rounded a bend in the walk and collided head-on with one of the two gentlemen coming down the path.

"Oh, excuse me," she apologized without looking at him as she bent to retrieve the mask that had been knocked from her fingers. "I'm afraid I wasn't watch—" The rest of her words lodged in her throat, for when Dara arose to finish her explanation she came face to face with Colonel Emerson Winslow.

"Good evening, Miss Brandon," he snarled, quickly catching her elbow when she started to back away, his other hand covering her mouth. "I've been looking for you."

"Do you know this young woman, Emerson?" Rutherford frowned.

"Yes, Samuel, I do. She's the lady I told you about"—he smiled evilly—"the one who knows too much."

"Oh, my God," the senator breathed, hurriedly glancing around to make sure they were alone on the walkway. "What do you plan to do with her?"

"What I planned to do all along once I found her."

Rutherford's face paled. "But surely you don't intend to kill her here? There are too many people."

"And why not? With so many guests milling about

who can say which one strangled the life from this pretty little wench?" He gazed dispassionately at the horror shining in Dara's eyes, and tightened his grip when she tried to pull away. "Now, Samuel, go find your wife while I take care of some unfinished business." Slipping his arm around Dara's waist, he nearly lifted her from her feet as he started down the narrow path.

"I know just the place, Miss Brandon," he whispered as he dragged her along. "It's a beautiful spot, but its beauty is not equal to your own." He laughed at the muffled sounds she made, knowing she was not complimenting his heritage. "It's just on the other side of the gazebo where the trees surround a stream. Whoever finds your body will think you slipped and fell in."

Knowing this man held her life in his hands, fear bolted through every fiber of Dara's being, and she struggled with all her strength. She prayed that Justin still lingered in the summerhouse, for she was no match for the colonel and unless he took his hand away, her screams would go unheard.

Winslow half dragged, half carried her down the path, not pausing when they came upon the white latticework of the gazebo for the delicately framed structure was empty. Tears filled Dara's eyes when she saw it, for she was certain that while her life was being brutally taken from her, Justin was spending those moments in another woman's arms. Her will to fight fled. But as they traveled through the dense growth of trees that led to the stream, Dara suddenly realized she didn't want to die, whether Justin loved her or not, and she vowed Colonel Winslow's task would not be an easy one. As soon as he let go of her, she would scream. Maybe . . . just maybe . . . someone would be close enough to hear her.

Suddenly, without warning, the colonel took his hand away. But before she could fulfill her pledge, he twirled her around and viciously struck her cheek with the back of his hand, knocking her, dazed, to the ground. Through a blur, she saw him kneel over her, his huge hands open wide as they sought her throat.

From the shadows, a dark figure suddenly emerged, his clasped hands raised over his head. He rushed forward and brought his fists down against the back of the colonel's neck, plunging the man into unconsciousness. Winslow fell forward, nearly crushing Dara beneath him before the stranger lashed out with his booted foot and kicked the body to the side.

"Dara? Dara, are you all right?" he asked, his voice tight with worry.

Pushing herself up, her eyes trained on the unmoving shape lying beside her, she nodded. "I . . . I think so. He . . . he was going to kill me." Stifling a sob by pressing her fingertips to her mouth, she lifted tear-filled eyes to her rescuer as he knelt beside her, and her breath caught in her throat when she saw the moonlight glistening in his blond hair. "Lane? Oh, God, Lane?" Scrambling to her knees, she threw her arms around him and sobbed uncontrollably.

"Yes, Dara, it's me," he whispered, smoothing the long strands of auburn hair that had tumbled loose from their pins. "I saw you in a carriage and followed you here. I wasn't truly certain it was you, so I came out here to wait for a while on the chance I might get a better look. I thank God I did."

"Oh, Lane," she cried, pushing back to look at him. "Where have you been? I've been so worried about you."

"It's a long story, Dara, but I'm in trouble. It's not safe here for me and from the look of things, I'd say it's not safe for you either." Taking her by the elbows, he helped her to her feet, then frowned suddenly. "Why did this man want to kill you? And what are you doing here anyway?"

Brushing the tears from her face, she laughed. "It's a long story too." She sobered instantly at a thought. "Have you been home yet? Father is ill and he needs to see you."

"No, I—"

The sounds of running footsteps cut short his response, and he jerked his head around to find the tall, blond-haired stranger with whom he had seen his sister arrive racing toward them. Leery of everyone and lacking the time to ask Dara if the man could be trusted, he roughly kissed her cheek, spun around, and dashed off into the darkness.

"No!" Dara screamed. "Don't go! Please come back!" Tears flooded her eyes, for she was certain that if she didn't go after him she would never see him again. In a panic, she lifted the hem of her skirt and blindly stumbled in the direction he had gone. But before she had traveled two steps, Justin's hand caught her wrist and yanked her back into his arms.

"Dara. Dara!" he shouted, giving her a jolting shake when she began to sob hysterically.

"Make . . . make him come back," she cried, her face twisted pleadingly. "Don't . . . let him go away again."

"Who? Who was he?" Justin demanded.

"He . . . he needs me . . . he saved me. . . ."

Reminded of the reason he had frantically searched the woods for her, Justin glanced down at the man lying on the ground and heard the colonel moan.

"Come on," he urged. "We've got to get you out of here before Winslow comes around."

"No," Dara objected weakly, trying to pull away from him, but Justin's grip tightened. "I want my brother. I want Lane."

334

"And so do I," Justin frowned, stooping to sweep her tiny frame up in his arms.

Too exhausted to fight or even complain, Dara wrapped her arms around her husband's neck and hugged him to her, sobbing softly as he carried her through a leafy archway in the trees, leaving behind the events that would live in their memories for a long time to come.

Chapter Twelve

A dark carriage careened through the narrow streets at the edge of town as if Satan himself were chasing it, the driver hurling oaths as he laid the whip to the team of dapple grays. Behind it raced a half dozen or more horses and riders, each man darkly clothed, each checking to make certain no one followed them. All the men were silent, more concerned for the welfare of the couple in the open-topped carriage than for their own safety. The caravan never slowed its pace until the last lights of the city had faded behind them; only then did they relax.

Mark Wallis edged his horse alongside the rig heading toward Harold Miller's farm. Skillfully, he swung down from the saddle onto the seat opposite his captain and the man's silent companion, tossing his steed's reins to one of the mounted men.

"So tell me what happened, Cap'n." Mark spoke softly, leaning forward as he braced his arms against his knees. "Was your wife hurt?"

Justin shifted his weight and tucked Dara possessively within the circle of his arm. Lifting the mask from his face, he raised it over his head and pulled the blond wig off with it. Somewhat angrily, he tossed the disguise on the seat next to him and ran his fingers through his dark hair, venting a long sigh.

"She was nearly killed, thanks to me," he grumbled.

"Killed?" Mark exclaimed. "By whom?"

"Winslow. I didn't know he was there and I foolishly left her alone long enough for him to find her."

"Well, obviously you got to her in time," Mark pointed out, looking at the sleeping face nestled safely in her husband's embrace.

"Quite the contrary, Mark. Someone else did what I should have done."

"Someone else? Who?"

"I don't know," Justin said. "He ran off before I could get to them. But apparently whomever it was knocked the colonel out before he could finish what he started. I found him lying on the ground unconscious and Dara and the stranger standing near him."

"Did Mrs. Whitelaw know him?"

Justin shrugged. "She was too distraught to make any sense and I didn't want to stay there any longer than I had to. You know the rest."

"Did you find Senator Manning?"

"Yes, and everything's set for next week . . . or it will be as soon as he arranges it. At least then Winslow will be out of the way and we won't have to worry about him anymore."

"If I had been you, Cap'n, I'd have finished him off right there. You had the perfect opportunity . . . and the right."

"Don't think I wasn't tempted, Mark," Justin said, "but I'm after bigger game. He has to be working with someone, and if I'm going to all this effort, I want every one of them."

"So what do we do now?"

"I think we should weigh anchor and sail farther down the bay. We've stayed here too long as it is."

Leaning back in the seat, Mark studied his captain for a moment. "Did something else happen that you're not telling me? You seem a little anxious." When Justin merely looked up at him and then quickly glanced away, Mark frowned. "Did someone recognize you?"

A long while passed before Justin sighed heavily. "Monica Dearborn . . . or should I say Rutherford?"

"She was there?"

"Yes."

"Did you talk to her? I mean, are you sure she knew who you were?"

"Oh, she knew all right. Dara and I had gone out on the terrace for some fresh air, and before I knew it someone came up from behind me and called me by name."

"God, Justin, what did you do?"

Chuckling, he smiled over at Mark. "I just stood there pretending I didn't hear her. I was hoping she'd think she'd made a mistake. But Monica's smarter than that. She guaranteed that she wouldn't tell anyone who I was, and to prove it, she offered to walk out into the gardens where no one would see or hear us."

"And did you?" Mark questioned.

"Yes. I can't really tell you why I did . . . curiosity, I guess. But now I'm glad I did. She told me something very interesting."

"What?"

"It seems her husband knows all about the assassination plot but not that Winslow hired me to do it. She asked me to help . . . because her husband knows about the plan and could be implicated if it's carried through." He laughed. "She wants me to stop it."

"And you told her you would," Mark concluded with a grin and saw Justin smile in return. "I don't suppose she told you how he found out in the first place?"

Justin shook his head. "She said she overheard him talking with some of his colleagues, and I'll wager

Winslow was one of them. I sure hope this scheme works," he sighed. "Maybe one of them will know something about my trial, or at least have an idea where to find Lane."

Mark raised his brows. "It sure would be nice not to be looking over our shoulders, but I have to admit I've enjoyed the adventure."

"Me too, Mark. But you know, I'm looking forward to the day I can settle down in one place." He chuckled. "I never thought I'd hear myself say that, but it's true."

"Where would that be, Cap'n?"

"Back home, I suppose. You know my father left the shipping line to me even though I told him I didn't want it, don't you?"

"No, I didn't. I thought your brother owned it now."

"He's just managing it for me." One corner of his mouth turned up. "I don't imagine he sees it that way, but that's the way it is. Of course, I had always planned on making him a partner once I did take over. Maybe that would appease him."

"Have you told your wife?"

Justin stiffened suddenly when Mark inadvertently reminded him of the fact that he was married now. "Told her what?" he said, more sharply than he'd intended.

"About settling in Massachusetts."

"No," Justin growled; then he looked off to his left to study the shadowy scenery.

Mark laughed. "Well, it would be nice of you if you did, don't you think?"

"Mind your own business," Justin snapped, shifting his weight as if the seat radiated a burning warmth, and in doing so, jostled Dara awake. Moaning, she sat up, rubbing her eyes.

All Dara could remember after Lane ran away from her in the gardens was the strong pair of arms that had

340

lifted her and carried her away. She had felt safe in the embrace yet lost, as if something had been taken from her, something very dear. Those same arms had placed her in a carriage then wrapped themselves around her and she had drifted into a fitful slumber. Now they seemed stiff, uncaring, and the happenings of a short while ago exploded in her mind. Her eyes flew open as she sat straight up in the seat.

"Lane!" she screamed, and rose as if to hurl herself from the carriage, but a strong hand caught her wrist and pulled her down again. "No," she wailed, clawing at the fingers that held her. "Let me go. I must find him. Lane!"

"Dara!" Justin shouted, his brow furrowed for fear the evening had proved too much for her and her mind had snapped. "Dara, stop!"

"No-o-o," she sobbed, her tiny fists beating against his chest. "You've got to go after him. Don't let him leave. He's in danger."

"Dara, listen to me." Justin tried again. "Lane isn't here. You were dreaming."

Suddenly she ceased her struggles and stared back at him through tear-filled eyes. "No, I wasn't," she wept. "He was there . . . in the gardens . . . before you came. He's the one who saved me, Justin."

Feeling as if something heavy lay upon his chest, Justin fought to draw a breath. "What?"

Brushing the moisture from her face, she nodded. "He ran when he heard you coming. He didn't know who you were and I didn't have the chance to tell him. We must go back, Justin. He told me that he's in trouble. It wasn't safe there for him." Her tears started again. "Please, Justin?"

"Hush," he soothed, pulling her to him as he turned to look at Wallis. "Take the men and go back. When you get there I want you to split up. You can cover

341

twice as much ground that way. And remember, Mark, he doesn't trust anyone. If he spots you first, he'll run again. So if you get the chance, tell him his sister is safe with us on board my ship and that you'll take him to her. Tell him I know what happened and that I'm not out for revenge, that I want to help us both. You got that?"

"Aye, Cap'n. You can count on me."

"And for God's sake don't hurt him. He's been through enough already."

"Aye, Cap'n," Mark nodded, motioning for his horse. "If he's still in Washington, we'll find him." Sliding to the edge of the seat, he reached out and patted Dara's hand. "Don't worry, Dara. I'll bring him back to you safe and sound."

He waited until she smiled weakly up at him; then he stood upon the seat, balanced one foot on the edge, and skillfully swung himself back into the saddle of his horse which was trotting alongside. Calling out to the men, he reined his steed around and galloped off toward Washington, the others close behind.

"Miller," Justin called to the driver, "I'd be most grateful if you'd get us back to the ship as quickly as possible."

"Aye, Cap'n." The man nodded and cracked the reins to hurry the rig. "I'll have you there in half an hour."

Justin and his wife rode the rest of the way in silence, each thinking troubled thoughts. Justin was blaming himself. If he hadn't let his feelings for Monica interfere with his purpose for being at the ball, Dara wouldn't have been dragged off into the gardens and nearly killed, and Lane might be sitting across from him in the carriage right now. As it was, Mark and his men would scour the streets and backalleys of Washington looking for a man Justin was sure they wouldn't find. If Lane

342

was, indeed, in trouble as Justin was sure he was, the young man had learned how to protect himself for the past three months. If he were Lane, he would have left the city by now and found a place to hide for a while. But where? Where would *Lane* go? And where had he been all this time? Was it possible Lane had found someone he could trust, one among all the others, and taken refuge with that person? Justin's dark eyebrows came together angrily. Damn. Why couldn't he have stayed with Dara? Why had he let the memories and yearnings of long ago rule him?

Thinking of his wife, he glanced down at the beautiful young woman cradled in his arms. In the short time he had known her, Dara had proved to be more faithful to him than Monica had ever dreamed of being. She had believed that he was innocent of the charges brought against him, and had even put her own life in danger to help prove it. Would Monica have done as much?

Gritting his teeth, he lifted his face toward the starfilled sky, his nostrils flaring as he exhaled a long, irritable sigh. Of course, she wouldn't. She cared too much about herself ever to put her life in danger . . . especially for someone else. She was self-centered, a snob, a fortune seeker, and a prude. So what had drawn him to her in the first place? He snorted derisively and set his gaze on the shoreline of the bay a few hundred yards ahead and on the dark mast of his ship spiraling skyward. Monica had bewitched him with her charm and beauty. He had fallen victim to her ways as had many a man before and after him. Even his brother had fancied himself in love with her.

Justin's eyes clouded as he thought of Stewart. Although they were only two years apart in age, they had never been close as youngsters, and Justin couldn't honestly blame the boy. Sinclair Whitelaw had

343

constantly reminded the younger son of his disability, always comparing him with his stronger, older brother, and telling Stewart that he would never amount to anything. That had been the root of many arguments between Justin and his father, and it was probably the reason Justin had left home. He had somehow hoped that in his absence the eldest Whitelaw would come to know Stewart for the bright, capable man he was. But death had claimed their father before that understanding had had a chance to bloom and grow. And with their father's blessing, the hatred Justin's brother had harbored all those years flourished anew.

"We're here now, Cap'n."

Justin blinked and looked up to find Miller standing next to the carriage, the door open as he waited to assist the occupants to alight, and he realized he had been so caught up in his thoughts that he'd failed to notice that their journey had come to an end. Nodding his thanks, he quickly descended from the rig and turned to lift Dara to the ground.

"Do you want me to stay until the others return?" Miller asked.

"That won't be necessary," Justin replied, gently resting his hand on his wife's narrow waist as they started for the longboat tied nearby. "But you can do something for me."

"Sure, Cap'n. Anything," Miller agreed.

"Tomorrow . . . in the daylight . . . I want you to go back to Washington if Mark was unsuccessful in finding Lane. He'll be easier to spot in the full light of day."

"Aye, Cap'n," the mate nodded then hurried ahead to ready the boat for the captain and his lovely wife.

The man in the crow's nest had spotted Justin and Dara's arrival the moment the carriage rolled to a stop near the trees at the edge of the water, and by the time

344

the couple boarded the *Lady Elizabeth,* the entire crew along with Douglas Callahan awaited them. All aboard hoped that their captain had been successful in finding Senator Manning and that their next adventure would go off without a hitch. But the moment they saw the distraught look on Captain Whitelaw's face, the grass-stained clothing of his wife, and her long hair tumbling wildly about her shoulders, they knew something had gone wrong.

"Are you two all right, Cap'n?" Callahan asked worriedly, watching Justin wrap his arms around his wife and guide her toward their cabin.

"I'm fine, but Dara's been shaken up a bit. See if you can have the cook make her some hot tea and bring it to my cabin. I'll explain everything once you have," he stated, pausing when they reached the ladder that led to the bridge. "Have the crew prepare to weigh anchor and drop the sails as soon as Mark and the rest of the men return. And have everyone stay on alert for any unwelcome visitors. Winslow knows Dara was at Prescott's and he may have sent someone after us."

"Aye, aye, Cap'n," Callahan nodded, then turned and hurried across the quarter-deck toward the galley.

"Justin," Dara said as he guided her through the door and into their cabin, "do you really think Mark won't find Lane?"

Before he answered, he took her to the bunk and gently forced her to sit down. Lowering himself on one knee, he cupped her hands in his. "I pray to God I'm wrong, Dara. But if I were Lane and in the kind of trouble he's in—if I'd clubbed a man at one of the most prestigious affairs in Washington, even though that man had tried to kill my sister—I wouldn't waste any time in getting as far away from there as I could. He probably figured no one would believe him if he tried to explain why he had attacked the colonel, and we both

345

know Winslow wouldn't admit what he was doing even if the two of you accused him. He carries a lot of weight in Washington, I'm afraid." Sighing, Justin glanced down at the floor. "And then I had to make an untimely entrance and scare him off. I never should have left you alone," he added, looking back up at her, his guilt registered in his eyes.

The smooth line of Dara's brow wrinkled into a confused frown. She hadn't expected him to say such a thing, to sound as if he truly regretted his actions. A small glimmer of hope came alive within her. She smiled softly.

"And if you hadn't, Lane wouldn't have come out of hiding. There would have been no reason. At least now we're certain he's still alive and we know where to look for him."

Justin's own brow crimped. "You mean . . . you don't . . ."

"What?" she laughed. "Blame you for what the colonel tried to do? For not being there to protect me? I knew the risks before I ever left this ship, and I'd go again if it meant finding my brother"—she looked past him suddenly, not wanting to meet his eyes—"and clearing your name."

Justin gave a short laugh and shook his head as he came to his feet. "You're one remarkable lady, Dara Brandon." His smile faded and he glanced away. "Whitelaw," he corrected quietly.

"Why?" she queried somewhat irritably. "Because I want to protect my men? It's what a wife and sister is supposed to do."

"But you knew where I was when I should have been with you," he rallied, his voice raised a notch.

She lifted one shoulder slightly and idly brushed at the dirt on her satin gown. "It was what you had to do."

"No, it wasn't," he stormed. "It was foolish and

346

damn stupid of me and you know it. How can you sit there and make excuses for me? I nearly got you killed! And to top it all off, I let down my guard and allowed Lane to slip right through my fingers. If he gets killed before all of this is over, there will be only one person to blame, and that's me!"

Whirling away from her, he angrily yanked off his jacket, slid from his waistcoat, and threw both garments at the bench as he marched to his desk and the bottle of whiskey sitting on top. Not bothering with a glass, he pulled the cork free and raised the clear cylinder high in the air, pouring a liberal amount into his mouth. It burned going down and brought tears to his eyes, yet its dulling effect eased his distress a bit. Slamming the bottle back down on the deck, he reached for a cheroot and glared at the door when someone had the unfortunate timing to intrude with a knock.

"What is it?" he bellowed then proceeded to light the cigar.

"Mrs. Whitelaw's tea, Cap'n," the muffled voice on the other side replied. "It's what you asked me to get."

"Well don't just stand there," he shouted. "Bring the damn stuff in."

The door opened immediately upon the confused first mate. Balancing a tray in one hand, Callahan glanced briefly at his captain, then stepped inside and insured their privacy by closing the wooden barrier behind him. Crossing the cabin he lifted the chair by the desk and carried it toward the bunk and the woman waiting there.

"I brought some honey to sweeten it with," Callahan said with a soft smile, positioning the chair next to her then setting the tray on the seat. "Sometimes it can be a little bitter." He glanced over at Justin and then back again. "Sort of like the captain."

Dara bit her lower lip to keep from smiling at Callahan's dry wit, but she quickly cleared her throat when she saw Justin scowl. "You'll have to forgive him right now, Mr. Callahan. He's upset," she explained, pouring a cupful of tea and adding just a little honey.

"So I noticed," he mocked, folding his arms over his chest and leaning a shoulder against the wall near the bunk. Although he spoke to Dara, he settled his gaze on the third member of their group. "I'd ask him why, but I'm afraid I'd get my head torn off."

Dark blue eyes glared at Callahan, but the only other response he received for his comment was a curl of Justin's upper lip.

"Then maybe I should tell you," Dara offered after taking a sip of her tea and kicking off her shoes. Cradling the cup in both hands and resting it on her lap, she took a deep breath and pondered over the best place to start. "Well, the disguise worked perfectly in getting us into Mr. Prescott's home, but there were so many people there, Justin couldn't find Senator Manning right away. We mingled with the crowd, even danced a waltz, then went to the terrace for some fresh air and to find a place where Justin could have a full view of the ballroom."

"That doesn't explain the grass stains on your skirts," Callahan observed.

"Well," she began again, peeking over at Justin from the corner of her eye and wondering how he would react to the way she worded the next events, "we became separated, and I, unfortunately, ran into Colonel Winslow and his companion."

"By yourself?" Douglas exclaimed setting a disapproving frown on his captain only to find that Justin had turned his back on him to perch one hip on the edge of his desk.

"Of course, he knew who I was right off." Dara

348

rushed on, hoping to distract the first mate's attention away from Justin.

Callahan's head jerked around. "Even with the mask?"

"Oh, I didn't have it on at the time," she blurted out.

"And why not?" he demanded.

Dara could feel the heat rising in her cheeks. There was no way to get around the truth. Nervous, she reached up to pull long strands of auburn hair from her brow, frantically trying to come up with an answer. She didn't want to admit to anyone that she had spied on Justin and Monica, or that the results had made her cry.

"I think I can answer that," Justin threw back over his shoulder without turning around to look at either of them. "She had probably been crying and had taken the mask off to wipe her face."

"Crying?" Callahan and Dara echoed in unison, though for two very different reasons.

"Why . . . you . . . pompous ass," Dara ranted, hurling the first epithet that came to mind before Callahan had a chance to say another word. "What makes you think I might have been crying?"

Clamping the cheroot between his teeth, Justin twisted around on the edge of the desk to look at her. "Because I left you to be with Monica."

Callahan's mouth dropped open and before he could catch his breath again to ask about Monica's presence and how Justin came to be with her, the loud bang of a teacup against the metal tray startled the thought from his head.

"And why would that matter to me?" Dara shouted, coming to her feet, her hands knotted in tiny fists at her sides. "I wouldn't care if you were with the president's wife! In fact," she continued irately, "if it hadn't been for me, you still wouldn't have any idea where to look for Lane."

"Lane?" Douglas interjected with a puzzled frown, but neither Justin nor Dara paid him any heed.

"Oh, really?" Justin challenged, grabbing the cheroot from his mouth and standing up. "Do you know something I don't?"

"Yes," she proclaimed with a lift of her pretty nose in the air.

"Like what?"

"Like for instance, he could very well be on his way home."

Justin's shoulders drooped as he tilted his head to one side. "He hasn't been home in three months. Why would he change his mind all of a sudden?"

"Because I told him that father was ill and needed to see him, that's why," she sneered.

Justin straightened immediately. "Dammit, Dara. Why didn't you tell me that before?" he scowled then abruptly turned his attention on the man who had listened to it all, his head pivoting left then right with each round of words. "Callahan, ask for a volunteer to go ashore and wait for Wallis and the others. Then weigh anchor. We've got to get across the bay and position some of the crew around Brandon's farm before Lane gets there ahead of us. It may very well be the last chance we have to find him."

"Aye, aye, Cap'n," the mate quickly agreed and made a hasty exit.

At the sound of the door closing, Justin looked back at his wife with a disgusted snarl. "Honestly, Dara. Sometimes you act as if you haven't an ounce of sense."

"Me?" she shrieked. "You're the one who went running off with Monica."

Dark eyebrows lifted in surprise. "I thought you said you didn't care who I was with."

"I don't!" she snapped. "If you like kissing someone

350

like that, you can do it all day long, and it won't bother me in the least."

Justin's chin dropped. "Kissing? How do you know I kissed her?"

Dara's face flushed instantly. Turning, she settled herself on the bunk again and picked up her teacup. "I don't. I just assumed you did," she said quietly, eyes averted.

"You spied on me," he continued.

Dara's head shot up. "No, I didn't."

"Oh yes, you did. You followed us. Where were you standing? Right behind the tree close enough to hear everything?" With each question he hurled, he moved closer to the bunk.

"I could have been standing right beside you. I could have tapped you on the shoulder and you'd have flicked a hand at me thinking I was a pesty fly. I could have screamed in your ear and you still wouldn't have known I was there. Men," she hissed, leaning over to refill her cup. "You all act like dull-witted buffoons whenever a pretty face catches your attention and looks up at you with big, round eyes and a flutter of lashes. She's a brainless twit, Justin, and you're as big a simpleton as she if you think for one second anything she said had an ounce of truth in it."

A bright smile appeared on his face as he stood before her, his hands resting on his hips. "Listen to you. Not two minutes ago you said you understood why I had left with Monica. Now you're attacking her. I do believe you're jealous."

"Jealous?" she raged, thumping down the teacup on the tray again. Angrily she came to her feet to confront him. "You conceited lout. Why should it matter to me if you want to make a fool of yourself with her? Why should I care if you prefer her over me? Who do you think you are . . . a gift from heaven for every woman

351

to swoon over? Well, as soon as we find my brother and he settles this mess you're in, *I'm* going back home and you can be with *Miss Monica* all you want!"

She started to brush past, intending to go topside for a breath of fresh air and a chance to be alone, certain that at any moment tears would flood her eyes and shatter the bravado she had worked so hard to achieve. But he suddenly reached out and trapped her elbow in an unyielding grasp. She tried to jerk free, but he held her more tightly. Glaring up at him, a tremor of excitement bolted through her, for his smile had faded and his pale blue eyes had softened.

"Maybe," he whispered, and in the next instant his lips were on hers.

The kiss took her breath away and set her mind racing. Did he mean to prove that she was as helpless when he caressed her as she had claimed all others were? If so, he had succeeded, for when his arm slipped around her waist and pulled her to his hardened frame, she surrendered to the moment and the bliss his touch aroused, kissing him back with equal yearning.

His mouth moved hungrily against hers, parting her lips with his tongue to probe inside while his fingers undid the fastenings of her gown and petticoats, letting them glide effortlessly to the floor, and Dara did naught to stop him. Her own fingers moved to the buttons of his shirt then pulled the garment free of his breeches, her hands sliding across his iron-thewed chest to his shoulders, taking the silk fabric with her.

His kisses moved to taste the satiny smoothness of her neck, and Dara instinctively tilted her head back and released a sigh of pleasure, reveling in the splendor of his caress as his lips trailed a fiery path across her throat. She experienced no shame when he untied the strings of her camisole and freed her breasts for him to sample or when he stripped the garment from her and lifted her in his arms. Their lips met again as he carried her to the bunk, and for a fleeting moment she wondered what thoughts filled his head. Was it his wife he held in his arms or the vision of another? As he laid her gently on the soft cushion of his bed, she stubbornly refused to believe that Monica or any other woman could intrude upon this moment. He was hers, and given a little time, he would soon come to realize it as well.

Justin's eyes never left her as he stripped himself of the rest of his clothes, the flame of his passion spiraling higher as he studied the beauty of her hair fanned out against the pillow, the finely boned features of her face, and the womanly curves that were his for the taking. She smiled temptingly up at him, her red lips slightly parted, and his heart raced wildly. His eyes darkened with desire as they traced the creamy whiteness of her shoulders, her delicately hued breasts, and her long, sleek limbs cushioned on a bed of red velvet. His blood raged through his veins and his breath lodged in his throat when he saw her eyes, in turn, slowly travel the muscular length of him, boldly appraising his manhood without the slightest blush or blink of shyness. And when he lowered a knee to the edge of the mattress, she opened her arms in breathless anticipation, urging him to take her, to sate the hunger that consumed them both.

Their lips met again as Justin pressed against her, bearing the brunt of his weight on his elbows as he covered the length of her with his body, their warmth searing each other in a burning ecstasy. Breathing in the scent of her, his passion soared, and Justin realized in that moment that if this would be the last time for them, their parting would leave an emptiness in him,

353

for though he'd doubted he could ever love again, this woman, his wife, had touched his heart.

"I don't care what you want, Dara," Justin frowned, "you're not going with me."

Dara gave a stubborn toss of her head, sending silky auburn hair flowing all around her. Then, her cheeks still warm from their lovemaking, she defiantly crossed the room to where he sat behind his desk. "You have to take me along," she argued. "If he's there and sees you or your men, he'll run again. But with me beside you, Lane will wait long enough for me to explain. Besides," she added, bracing forward, her hands pressed against the desk top, "I want to see my parents and make sure they're all right."

She had donned the yellow cotton dress again, and as Justin studied the determined face staring back at him, he silently observed how that soft shade brought out the rich brilliant color of her auburn hair with its entwined golds and reds. High cheekbones and softly arched brows added a delicate line to her features, almost a fragile quality. Justin smiled to himself, thinking her anything but that.

"No," he answered calmly and pulled open a desk drawer.

"Why not?" Dara's voice revealed her annoyance.

Continuing his search through the drawer without looking at her, he said flatly, "Because you'll slow us up."

Her temper soaring, for she had never fallen far behind Lane in any foot race they had had, she brought the palm of her hand down against the desk top. "If that's what you think, then I'll slow you even more, Justin Whitelaw." Standing erect, she crossed her arms in front of her, her nose lifted to a lofty elevation, and

354

waited for him to look up. "I'm not going to tell you how to find our farm."

A lazy smile drifted across his face as he considered her, thinking how easily she could change from tempting seductress to impish brat. "I've known where you live for the past three months, Dara. It was the first place I looked for your brother." His grin broadened when he saw her lovely chin drop, and he chuckled at the way Dara grabbed a fistful of skirt and yanked the garment around so she could move more freely back toward the bunk. There, she plopped down in muted frustration. With a shake of his head, he returned his attention to the drawer and withdrew the pistol from inside.

"What's that for?" Dara gasped when she heard the dull thud of the weapon as it was laid on top of the desk.

Justin gave a short laugh. "Well, I'm not going to shoot your brother if that's what you're thinking. I'm taking it along for protection."

"Against what?"

"Dara, just because you believe I'm innocent doesn't mean everyone else does. It's more than ten miles to your farm and there's no telling who I might meet along the way." Rising, he stuffed the pistol into his waistband.

"You're not going alone, are you?" she asked worriedly, watching him shrug into the dark coat he retrieved from the back of his chair. "Why not wear a disguise?"

"I haven't the time to put one on now," he smiled crookedly. "I was preoccupied when I should have been picking one out, so I must pay the price for doing something more to my liking."

Dara's face flamed instantly at this bold reminder of the intimate moments they had shared, and he grinned all the more.

"But don't worry. I'm taking several of the crew with me. You haven't left me so bewitched that I've taken leave of all my senses." He smiled suggestively at her. "Only a few," he teased, and started for the door. "I've asked Callahan to stay behind, so if you need anything before I get back, just tell him."

"Justin," she called, stopping him as he reached for the latch. He turned a questioning look on her and she slowly came to her feet. "Be careful. I don't know what Lane is running from, but if you're caught . . . well, just don't take any chances. I don't find black becoming."

A flash of white teeth showed against his bronze complexion. "Madam, making you a widow is the furthest thing from my mind." He nodded toward the bunk. "Keep a spot warm for me."

The click of the latch shattered the quiet of the cabin and brought a lump to Dara's throat. She had wanted to say more, to tell him how she truly felt and why. But she couldn't. Not now. He wasn't ready to hear it.

They had spent the short time it took the ship to cross the bay making love, sating a hunger not only of their bodies but of their souls. And when a shout from above had told them that the sails had been hoisted and the clanking of the anchor chain confirmed it, they had lain silently in each other's arms wanting the moment to last forever, yet knowing it wouldn't.

Justin had been the first to rise while Dara snuggled deeply into the covers of the bunk, content to watch him dress. Her eyes had warmly caressed his broad back, sinewy arms, narrow hips, and firm buttocks before he'd hidden them from her view; and a playful pout had curled her lips when he'd turned back to look at her. His response had been an amused chuckle. He had returned to the side of the bed, stooped, and kissed her lips as if thanking her for her approval; then he'd gone to his desk and sat down behind it. At that moment Dara had realized he was planning to leave without her, and that comprehension had brought about their argument. His implication that she would be a burden hadn't really upset her, nor had the fact that she wouldn't be able to talk to her brother because he refused to take her along. No. It had been the thought of being separated from him, no matter how long or short the period of time. Of course she wouldn't tell him as much. She was certain he would laugh at her or, worse yet, feel suffocated by her desire to be with him. No, that was something she couldn't risk. He would have to be the one to decide whether or not they would live as man and wife or go their separate ways, for Dara already knew what she wanted.

Crossing to the portholes in the cabin, she sat down on the bench beneath them and gazed out at the waters of the bay sparkling in the moonlight, feeling empty and afraid. He had tenderly held her in his arms and had made love to her, but he'd promised nothing for the future. Dara knew the challenge there, for her foe was not his unwillingness to surrender his heart, but the woman in his past who was still very much alive in his thoughts.

Darkness shadowed the moves of the men stealing through the leafy foliage of the woods. Crouched low, he darted from bush to tree, constantly glancing back over his shoulder as he edged closer to his destination. Ahead he could see the tall, blackened shape of the deserted mill, its huge paddle wheel now silent and still. Crickets chirped their night song and occasionally the hoot of a barn owl joined the melody. The gentle, seaborne breeze wafted across the land, rustling treetops and bringing a quiet peace to the midnight hour. All seemed as it should, yet the man was ever alert for any movement that bespoke the contrary, his steps slowing from exhaustion that resulted from the grueling journey he had just taken.

When acrid smoke suddenly filled the air, Lane stumbled toward a fallen tree stump and lowered himself upon it to rest awhile, knowing that his father's home lay only a few hundred feet farther on. But he also knew that he mustn't dally too long, for the protective shadows of night would not last. Within a few short hours he would face his enemy once more, the bright streams of morning light.

He hadn't wanted to leave his sister behind, but taking her with him would surely have put her in even more danger. He had sensed that the tall, blond-haired man who had accompanied her to the ball, the one who had come racing toward them as they'd stood near the stream, would see her safely home. Although, in his opinion, Dara could behave in such a way that she didn't seem to have a brain in her pretty head, he knew she did not trust strangers. Furthermore, from behind the cover of thick underbrush, he had watched long enough to see the man gently lift Dara in his arms and carry her off. Lane had started to follow, his curiosity about the finely dressed gentleman tempting him to overrule his cautiousness, but he'd fallen back suddenly when the man he had knocked to the ground had moaned and sat up. Deciding he would have to wait until later to learn more about Dara's companion, Lane had spun around and raced off, certain he would find her waiting for him at their father's farm.

Glancing up at the stars peeking through the densely foliated canopy of trees, Lane heard his stomach rumble. He hadn't eaten since breakfast, not only because time hadn't allowed him a moment to indulge, but because he had run out of money the day before.

Grace Mitchell had been kind enough to pack him a good quantity of food the morning he'd left the Mitchell farm but that had been nearly four days ago and he had eaten the last crust of bread on his way to Washington.

Before Lane had started out, he and Edwin Mitchell had talked at great length on how Lane should go about finding Captain Whitelaw, and they had decided it would be wise to go to the capital first. Rumors of the man's whereabouts were sure to be the center of gossip in every local pub. Lane would have to check out the rumors to see if one of them was true. But much to his dismay, no news more recent than that of Captain Whitelaw's escape had been circulating in the places he visited. Exhausted by a day spent walking the streets, he had been heading toward the livery stable, hoping its owner would allow him to bed down in the loft, when he'd spotted the elegant carriage traveling along the main thoroughfare. He had paused to watch it out of envy, wondering what it must feel like to ride in such a magnificent rig, let alone own one. Then the beautiful auburn-haired woman inside had caught his attention, and for some strange reason she'd reminded him of Dara. Mentally laughing at the probability, he had, nonetheless, followed the conveyance. His curiosity had demanded it. Something all too familiar about the woman had drawn him on. As he thought about it now, he decided maybe God had had a hand in putting him on that specific street corner at that moment. Maybe He had given him a gentle nudge to follow the carriage, for if he hadn't, his sister would be dead.

"And if you don't get something to eat soon, you're not going to be around much longer either," he said aloud, pushing himself to his feet.

As the way ahead opened up to reveal a small house and a stable nestled at the edge of the clearing, memories of the times Lane had spent plowing the acre of land Taylor Brandon called his farm rushed into his mind. It had been hard work for the two Brandon men, but Lane had loved every minute of it, nearly as much as he loved his father. A frown settled on his brow as he started toward the house. He prayed he wasn't too late.

The low fire in the hearth softly illuminated the room, and when Lane quietly crossed the porch to peer in through the window, he could easily see the figure of a man staring into the dying flames, the rocker in which he sat gently swaying to and fro. Tears burned Lane's eyes when he recognized the slouched figure of his father, and he silently thanked God that he had found the man alive. Letting out a deep breath, he moved to the front door of the house and lifted the latch.

"Papa," he said quietly, pausing at the threshold. "Papa, it's me, Lane. I've come home."

Blue eyes, very much like his, turned slowly to look at him, reflecting a mixture of surprise, doubt, and then relief clouded by the tears that instantly filled them. The old man swallowed hard, his chin quivering as he stared at his son, and in the next moment he had left his place, crossed the room, and desperately taken the young man in his arms. A long while passed before Taylor Brandon could speak, and when he did, his words were choked and filled with love.

"I thought they had killed you, Lane," he said. "I thought they took my boy from me."

Wrapping his father's frail form in one arm, Lane guided him back to the rocker and, gently pushing the old man into it, knelt down beside him. "I'm too much like you, Papa, to ever let anyone get the better of me."

"Stubborn too," Taylor added gruffly though his eyes belied the disapproval he fought to convey.

"Yeah, stubborn too." Lane smiled tenderly. Glancing up at the archway leading to his parents' bedroom,

360

he asked, "Is Mama all right?"

"Yes," Taylor said. "She's asleep. She's a strong old lady, son. She never doubted for a minute that you'd come home to us."

"But you did," Lane finished, noticing how tired and drawn his father looked.

Taylor quickly rubbed the back of his hand against his nose. "Only 'cause I figured God would punish me for sayin' the things I did to you before you left."

"You said what you felt, Papa. I understood that. I think God did too." He smiled reassuringly when his father finally found the courage to look at him. "Is Dara home yet?"

"Dara?" Taylor frowned. "No. Was she supposed to be? Did you talk to her?"

"Yes. I saw her in Washington and I assumed she'd get home before I did. Have you heard from her?"

"Only the letter that came a few days ago," his father replied. "We weren't expectin' her for some time from the sound of it."

"Why?" Lane frowned, settling himself on the floor beside Taylor. "And come to think of it, what was she doing in Washington?"

"She went there to ask for help in freein' you from the British."

"What? Who told you I'd been taken prisoner?"

"Why . . . ah . . . we got a letter several weeks ago sayin' that you had." The old man's brow furrowed. "You mean you weren't?"

"No," Lane said, shaking his head. With a sigh, he pushed himself up from his place on the floor beside his father and rubbed his hand over his stomach. "It's a very long story and I'm hungry. If you don't mind, I'd like to get something to eat while I tell you about it. I'm in a lot of trouble and maybe between the two of us, we can figure out what I should do."

The eldest Brandon sat by quietly listening to every word his son spoke, and although he never opened his mouth to reply or ask a question, Lane could tell that some of his father's spirit had returned by the youthful gleam in his eyes. When Lane had finished, Taylor left his rocking chair and went to the stack of wood piled beside the fireplace. Hidden behind it was a bottle of whiskey that the old man quickly retrieved. Turning to look at his son, he smiled devilishly, then went to the cupboard and took down two glasses, filling both and giving one to Lane.

"I've been keepin' it for a special occasion," he whispered, glancing over his shoulder toward the bedroom. "Sarah doesn't know I have it." Pulling out a chair next to his son, he sat down at the table and cradled the glass in both hands as he contemplated his advice. "Well," he said after a long while, "I'll tell you what I would do and you can decide if you think it's best."

"You've never been wrong so far, Papa." Lane grinned, lifting his glass in a silent salute to the man's wisdom.

"Hah!" Brandon snorted. "If that was true, *I'd* be the one givin' that fancy party in Washington instead of livin' out here on this worthless piece of land."

"Money doesn't make the man," Lane argued. "It's what's inside that really matters—and that makes you the richest man in all of America."

Warm, blue eyes stared back at the young man before a half-smile settled on Taylor's face. "Not really," he replied. "What makes me rich is havin' two children like you and your sister." His grin widened, then disappeared behind the glass he raised to his lips. Downing the entire drink, he let out a long sigh of pleasure before he leaned forward against his elbows. "But enough of this sentimental dribble. We've got

362

more important things to discuss. I think it's rather obvious how difficult it's goin' to be for you to find this Captain Whitelaw. If he's wanted by the authorities, he won't leave a trail for just anybody to follow, and since you don't know who set you up, you can't trust anybody either . . . except for one man . . . the President of the United States."

Lane gave a short laugh. "I agree, Papa. But it would be easier for me to find Captain Whitelaw than it would for me to get within twenty feet of Jefferson. No one is allowed near his home, and with all the unrest about the Embargo Act, I'm sure he's well protected."

"Well, isn't there one man close to the president that you can trust?"

Lane studied the whiskey he swirled in his glass. "I suppose there's one man," he said after a while. "Captain Whitelaw always told me that of all the men in Washington, George Manning was the best." He sighed heavily. "But I'm not too sure about that now."

"Why do you say that?"

"Because after I testified, no one came forward in Captain Whitelaw's behalf. They just hauled him off to prison to hang."

"Maybe Manning didn't know about the trial until it was too late and couldn't do anything about it. After all, the only witness to the crimes had disappeared. Right?"

Lane shrugged one shoulder. "Yea, I suppose."

"Then go back to Washington and find this George Manning. If Captain Whitelaw trusted him then so should you. You might not be able to tell your captain face to face what happened, but he'll soon find out who was responsible for clearing him. When he comes out of hiding then you can tell him everything, and if he's half the man you say he is, he'll forgive you before you say a word."

"Just like you, Papa?"

Taylor smiled. "Yes, son, just like me."

Brandon reached out to touch Lane's hand and froze when both men heard the distant whinnying of a horse. Neither of them spoke, for each knew the danger that threatened to invade the tiny house hidden among the trees. Nor did either need to express the love felt for the other. It shone clearly in their eyes. Hurriedly coming to their feet, Taylor grabbed his son in a brief, desperate embrace.

"God speed, Lane," he whispered; then he stepped aside to watch the young man rush for the door. A moment later the dark shadows of the night swallowed up Lane's slender form, and Taylor Brandon wiped a tear from his eye.

Chapter Thirteen

"I had him . . . right there!" Justin howled, looking at the palm of his hand. "Twice! And he still managed to get away!"

"Take it easy, Cap'n," Mark soothed. "We don't know for certain it was Lane. It was awfully dark, remember?"

"I couldn't be more certain if it had been broad daylight, and I'd stood right in front of him," Justin continued in a rage, whirling away from his friend as he angrily yanked the coat from his shoulders and threw it on the bench. "Who else on God's green earth would have sneaked around the Brandon farm and then run off like a scared rabbit?" In a fit of temper, he slammed a fist down on the top of the desk, rattling the hurricane lamp sitting there. "Dammit, why couldn't we have been two minutes earlier?"

Mark shrugged, knowing the question had no answer, and glanced over at Dara standing near the door, her back to his captain. "We'll find him, sir."

"Hah!" Justin exploded. "His own father didn't know where Lane was going or that he had even come to the house. He was asleep, remember? He was more surprised to learn his son had been there than he was to see you stand outside his door."

"But he assured me that he'd send word to us if Lane

should come back. And he promised to have Lane wait there for us."

Justin scowled disbelievingly and Dara was quick to notice his reaction.

"Papa wouldn't lie, Justin," she stated quietly. "And I'm sure that if Lane knew you were looking for him he'd try to contact you."

"Oh?" Justin scoffed. "And what if our theory about Lane is wrong? Do you think he'd try to find me if he'd accepted a lot of money to lie about me? In his shoes, I wouldn't. I'd be too afraid of getting my head blown off."

"He didn't do that," Dara snapped, her anger apparent in her voice. "He told me he was in trouble and that he couldn't trust anyone. If he was working for someone, they would protect him."

"And what if the people who hired him changed their minds?" he retaliated. "Suppose they decided not to pay him after all and he threatened to turn them in. They'd be looking for him too, only for a very different reason than I. They want to kill him. I don't."

"Cap'n, you won't know that until you talk to Lane," Mark cut in. "We've all agreed Lane wasn't that kind of man. You're just upset because he got away from us."

"You're damn right I'm upset," he growled, rounding the desk to throw himself in the chair behind it. "And the worst of it is that I can't afford to stick around looking for him. We've got to be in Norfolk in a few days."

"If it's any comfort, Cap'n," Mark smiled reassuringly. "I rather doubt we would have found Lane anyway. He grew up on that land and knows every inch of it. He could hide out there for weeks and we'd never know where to look. Besides, Mr. Brandon promised to send word—"

"I know, I know," Justin interrupted, resting his chin

on his fist as he leaned against the arm of the chair.

Glancing over at Dara again, Mark sadly shook his head, then sighed resignedly. "Well, if you'll excuse me, Cap'n, I'm going to get some sleep. It's been a long day and tomorrow doesn't look as if it'll be any better." He nodded toward Dara. "Good evening, Mrs. Whitelaw," he said quietly then left the cabin.

Dara could understand her husband's distress at not finding Lane, and she knew he really hadn't meant what he'd said about her brother turning against him for the sake of money. So much had happened that night that no one was able to think clearly. After studying Justin's dark profile for a moment, she crossed to the bench and sat down where she could see his face.

"Mark was right, you know," she said after a while, "about Lane being able to hide from you for days. When we were children he used to hide from me whenever he didn't want his bothersome little sister around, and I'd finally give up and go home. Even Papa couldn't find him the time Lane and he had an argument and Lane ran away. If Lane didn't want to be found, there was nothing anyone could do to change it. So don't feel badly."

"This isn't a game I'm playing, Dara," Justin replied, his voice low. "My life is at stake."

"I know," she said quietly. "Right now so is President Jefferson's, and you're the only one who can save him."

"Isn't that ironic?" he answered bitterly. "Captain Whitelaw, traitor to his country, is out to spare his president's life while no one gives a damn about his." Closing his eyes, he let his head fall back. "I'm tired, Dara. I want it to end. I want to live a normal life. I want to sail the coastline a free man, a captain in the United States Navy, not labeled as something I'm not."

Leaning forward, he reached for the bottle of whiskey sitting on the desk and took a long drink, letting it burn his throat and bring tears to his eyes before he sighed heavily and looked at her with a vague smile. "I'm not the man you and everybody else think I am, Dara. Captain Whitelaw . . . hardened criminal . . . traitor to his country . . . murderer . . ." He choked back tears that refused to dry. "I'm just a man," he whispered. "Like Lane. And the only thing both of us want to do is just go home."

"You will, Justin," Dara assured him, her own eyes glistening with moisture. "Maybe not right away, but you will. And you're wrong about no one caring about your life. I care. I care a great deal."

"Sure," he jeered, concentrating on the bottle he held in both hands, his elbows resting on the edge of the desk. "Only until I find your brother and make certain he's safe again. Then I won't matter to you either."

"That's not true," she objected, coming to her feet.

"Oh?" He laughed sarcastically. "Why should you or any woman care about me? What do I have to offer?"

"Yourself," she stated firmly, her brow crinkling in a frown.

Dark blue eyes stared doubtfully up at her and Dara's temper surfaced. Lifting her chin, she returned the look he gave her with an angry glare.

"Maybe I was wrong about you, Justin Whitelaw. You're not as smart as I thought you were or you'd realize not every woman in the world is as selfish, conceited, narrow-minded, and conniving as Monica Dearborn Rutherford. I take great offense at being likened to her. When I met you, you were running from the authorities and had to steal just to feed yourself. You didn't buy me lavish gifts or take me to fancy places to eat, and our first and only ball was a disaster. Yet I still managed to see the good in you. I fell in love with a man whose only goal in life was to help others, a man who never expected anything in return for what he did, a man who still fights for his country even though she has turned her back on him. What woman in her right mind wouldn't want a man like that?"

Standing, arms akimbo, she waited for his answer. But when she noticed the shade of his eyes soften and one corner of his mouth lift upward, she mentally retreated a step to recall the words she had spoken. Failing to understand what had elicited his smile, she cocked her head to one side, silently questioning him.

"Love, Dara?" he challenged, pushing himself away from the desk.

Her heart started to beat a little faster. "What?" she asked, watching him rise from the chair and turn toward her.

"You said you fell in love with that man. Are you sure?"

Suddenly each syllable she had spoken echoed in her brain. She gave a nervous laugh and moved away, halting her trek when she saw the direction in which she had started, the bunk only a few steps from her. Changing course, she went back to the bench and sat down. "I didn't mean I had"—she smiled lamely as she toyed with the ring on her finger, glancing up at him and then back to her lap when he continued to advance—"only that it was possible. What I meant was that I could see all your good points and that you'd make a fine husband even without money." She laughed again. "I didn't mean I was in love with you, Justin. It simply wouldn't work between us. We're much too different for us to ever get along."

"Yes, Dara, that's true," he said softly. "You're different from me and every other woman I have ever known." He paused beside her. "Maybe we could never love each other as a man and woman should, but I know I'll always consider you a friend."

Tears gathered in her eyes and she blinked them away.

"I don't know many ... men or women ... who would risk their lives to help me. But you did, and I'm honored." He reached down and took her hand. "May I give a friend a kiss?"

Dara longed to fly into his arms, but to do so she felt would give Justin the power to mock her. He thought of her as nothing more than a friend, and until he claimed otherwise, she would pretend his touch meant nothing. Smiling bravely up at him, she stood, silently consenting to his wishes. But when he slipped his arms around her and drew her close, a tiny seed of longing burst into full-grown passion. And when their lips met, his parted and moving against hers, her head began to spin, and she unknowingly slid her arms around his neck. He kissed her gently, almost as a friend might, and Dara felt the ache in her heart grow as tears burned her lowered lids. Then he broke the embrace and smiled down at her.

"Somehow, Dara Brandon Whitelaw," he whispered, "I truly think friendship will never be enough for us."

Stooping, he swept her into his arms and carried her to the bunk, their lips touching again, but with an urgency both experienced. Slipping his arm from beneath her knees, he let her feet glide slowly to the floor and, with both hands, began to unfasten the buttons of her gown. When he had stripped away the last of her garments, he stepped back to shed his own, but Dara quickly pushed his hands aside to complete the task herself, smiling wantonly up at him.

Justin's heart pounded in his chest, his blood pulsing wildly through his veins as he studied the beautiful face staring back at him. The soft light of the lamp caressed her lovely features as this vision took his hand and pulled him to the bed. Their naked bodies touched and he kissed her—her mouth, the tip of her nose, each closed eyelid, her long, slender neck, and the rose-hued peaks of her breasts. She moaned as his tongue played lightly upon them. Meanwhile his hands traced the smooth curves of her narrow waist, slim hips, and silken thighs. Finally he rose to gaze upon the darkened depths of those splendid green eyes, unaware that the woman from his past no longer haunted him.

Bracing himself, one hand on each side of her, he started to lower himself upon her, but Dara shook her head, her tiny hands pushing against his chest as she guided him onto his back. Magnificent locks of auburn hair fell about her shoulders as she raised up on one elbow to boldly appraise the hardened muscles of his chest and lean belly, one long, willowy leg resting intimately across his. He involuntarily sucked in his breath when her fingertips trailed the dark path of curls downward, the feathery caress sending shivers of pure delight coursing through him. The fire of his desire was ignited to a branding heat when she touched his manhood. Lust raged within him and he sought to fulfill the craving, only to have Dara gently push him back upon the softness of the mattress and press her body over his. His arms went around her as he accepted her kiss, but when their lips met, her tongue darted inside his mouth while she moved her hips against him, guiding his manly hardness deep within her. Wild rapture careened through him. His heart thudded in his chest, and he vowed if he died at this moment, it would be willingly. Yet the blissful torment did not end there, for suddenly Dara pushed herself up, the gentle thrust of her hips stoking the fires of his passion beyond restraint. Rising, his hands in the thick mass of her silken tresses, he pulled her to him and kissed her

371

hungrily, rolling her beneath him to sate his frenzied need for fulfillment.

They soared ever higher on love's wings, transcending their earthly forms, and time seemed eternal until, at last, their spiraling galaxy exploded in tiny shards of sparkling ecstasy. They descended from the heights of passion ever so slowly, breathless, deliciously exhausted. Nestled in each other's arms, they lay quietly watching the pinks and yellows of the morning sun steal across the sky outside the portholes, and a long while passed before Dara heard the steady breathing of her husband as he drifted off to sleep. A smile played upon her lips and she moved slightly to look at him. What they shared was far more than friendship. He had realized that, and in time he would accept it. Sighing contentedly, she snuggled closer to him and quickly fell asleep.

A soft fragrance assailed Justin's sleep-sodden mind just before something tickled the tip of his nose, and without opening his eyes, he flicked it away with the back of his hand. Yawning, he settled back comfortably into the thick cushion of his pillow, ready to drift off again. But he was disturbed a second time, so he waved blindly at the intruder, and scowled disapprovingly, annoyed at the interruption of his much-needed and satisfying slumber. When the intruder's identity dawned on him, he no longer desired to rest. Feigning sleep, he waited until the precise moment when Dara bent to brush an auburn lock of hair against his cheek, and with lightning speed, he shot out a hand, trapping the slender wrist of his wife in an unyielding grip as he brought her, squealing, onto the bunk, his strong arms clamped around her.

"Expect to get burned, little minx, if you play with

fire," he murmured, rolling her beneath him.

Bright, sparkling eyes smiled up at him. "I only meant to wake you before your breakfast got cold." Dara giggled as his fingers found a ticklish spot in her ribs.

"Breakfast?" he echoed, glancing briefly over his shoulder at the desk and the tray sitting there. "To be quite honest, I don't hunger for food." Burying his face in her neck, he nibbled deliciously on her earlobe and Dara began to squirm frantically.

"Justin, stop!" she begged. "Callahan and Mr. Wallis are waiting to speak with you."

"Let them wait," he murmured, tugging at the neckline of her gown so his lips could press against the hollow in her throat.

"But it's important," she said quickly and slid from beneath him when he reluctantly relinquished his pursuit.

"What could be so important that they'd deny me the pleasure of the morning?" He sighed, propping himself up on a pillow as he lay on his stomach, his chin resting on his folded arms.

Seeing his buttocks bare where the covers had fallen away, Dara gave him a stinging slap as she scooted off the bed and out of reach. She laughed gaily at his startled response, then she answered his question. "Because we'll be docking in Norfolk early tomorrow and they want to discuss your plans."

Warm, blue eyes devoured the lovely sight standing before him, and he smiled suggestively. "Will you promise that they'll leave us alone after the discussion?"

Feeling the warmth of a blush in her cheeks, Dara turned away and gave a tiny shrug. "'Tis your ship and crew to command, Captain. Only you have the right to demand privacy in your cabin. If you wish them to

373

leave, it must be at your command."

A flash of white revealed his amusement. "Then tell them I do not wish to see them now. I have more important things to do at the moment."

"I will not." She gasped and turned back to stare open-mouthed at him. "They would know in an instant what it is you prefer to do, and I would never be able to look either of them in the eye again."

"And why should that upset you? We're married. And I guarantee you that Callahan and Mark are well aware of what married couples do in their spare time. But"—tugging the covers free, he came to his feet and draped the spread around his long, lean frame—"if the thought disturbs you, I will force myself to wait until later. Send them in." He started for the desk.

"Not dressed like that," she cried, her chin sagging as she worriedly appraised his attire.

Justin stopped midway across the room and glanced down at himself. "They've seen me like this before," he told her. "I can't see putting on my clothes just so I can take them off again once they're gone." He moved toward the desk again.

"Justin!" she wailed.

He stopped and glanced over at her from the corner of his eye, his brow raised innocently.

"Please?"

Fighting with the smile that tugged at the edges of his mouth, he shrugged as if giving in to her whims. "All right, I'll compromise. I'll put on my breeches. Will that do?"

Afraid he would strip himself completely if she argued the point, Dara nodded resignedly, and turned her head while he donned his trousers. Although she had seen him naked before there was something about blatantly watching him dress that plucked at the strings of her modesty. There was no doubt in her mind that he was a fine example of masculinity and she felt an odd prickling of pride that she could claim him as her husband; at the same time she didn't think she had the right to invade his privacy. Or could it possibly be that she feared the pleasure of studying his wide shoulders, narrow hips, and taut belly would kindle her own desires anew, and she would be the one to tell Callahan and Mark Wallis to wait? Shaking off the thought, she waited until she heard Justin sit down behind the desk before she went to the door and bade the men to enter.

"Good morning, Cap'n," they parroted as they walked into the cabin.

Justin nodded in return as he smeared cherry preserves over one of the biscuits Dara had brought him. "How long before we drop anchor?" he asked, then took a bite.

Grabbing the chair alongside the desk, Callahan turned it around and straddled the seat. "Hopefully just before daybreak tomorrow. If we're lucky there'll be enough other ships moored there for us to go unnoticed."

"So what's the plan?" Mark asked, moving to the bench to sit down.

"Well, it seems simple enough, but knowing the way Winslow's mind works, I wouldn't guarantee it," Justin replied, cutting into the piece of ham on his plate. "I told him that I wouldn't try anything until some of his men caused a disturbance that would draw attention away from me. Then I'm supposed to shoot Jefferson."

"Then what?" Mark asked, frowning.

"Then George Manning will see that Winslow's men are arrested, and with any luck, they'll tell Manning everything he wants to know."

"Sounds too easy to me," Mark added with a shake of his head. "I wouldn't think Winslow would go for something like that."

375

"He might if he trusted me," Justin replied; then he grinned at Mark. "Which he doesn't."

"So what are you expecting him to do?"

"Just what I would do if I were in his place."

"Which is?"

"He'll see that I never get away from there alive . . . nor will the men he sent to create the diversion. You see, Mark, part of the deal was that after I'd succeeded in assassinating the president, Winslow was to have my name cleared. But he knows if he does that I'll be right back out there arresting smugglers again. And that's what this whole thing is about. Winslow's losing money because of the Embargo Act. He'd be defeating his own purpose if he frees me."

"But all he'd have to do is turn you in for the murder of President Jefferson," Mark objected.

"And all I'd have to do to get even is tell them who hired me."

"Ohhh." Mark smiled and nodded his head. "I get it. So in other words, you're as good as dead the minute you pull the trigger."

"As far as he's concerned, yes." Justin smiled. "However, I don't intend to accommodate him."

"I don't think a disguise will be enough this time, Cap'n, if that's what you're planning," Callahan broke in. "His men will have orders to shoot the man who pulls a pistol on Jefferson no matter what he looks like."

"I agree. But in order to spot me in the crowd, they'll have to have a good vantage point."

"Like a roof?" Wallis speculated.

"Uh-huh," Justin nodded, popping the ham in his mouth.

"So you want us stationed all around watching the rooftops."

Having swallowed a mouthful of food, Justin said, "Yes. And if it's at all possible don't kill the man you

376

spot. We could use him too. Now, as I understand it this christening ceremony is in three days. The day before, I want us to scout around the docks where it's going to be held. If we're lucky, we can position ourselves in the least vulnerable place. I'd like to catch Winslow but I don't intend to lose my own hide."

"How many of us do you want to go along?" Callahan inquired.

"As many as possible. Leave only a skeleton crew, but have them ready to weigh anchor on a moment's notice. There's no telling what might happen, so they should be prepared."

"All right," Callahan nodded. "Is there anything else?"

"Yes." Justin turned to Mark. "I want you to go into Norfolk the minute we dock tomorrow and visit a few of the pubs. Keep your ears open for anything that might help us out."

"Aye, Cap'n."

"Unless either of you have any more questions, I think that's about all for now." As both men shook their heads, Justin smiled. "Good. And I suggest you get some rest. Once we're in Norfolk you might not have the chance for some time."

"Aye, Cap'n," the men chorused as they rose to their feet and headed for the door.

"And don't worry, Cap'n," Mark added before they made their exit, "between Callahan and I, we'll see nothing happens to you." After presenting Justin with a wide grin, he lifted the latch and followed his companion from the cabin.

Justin stared at the sealed entryway for a long while, his dark eyebrows drawn together. Although it appeared that every detail of their venture had been taken care of and undoubtedly Mark Wallis, Callahan, and the others were trustworthy, he worried about the plan going off without a hitch. It wasn't that he would be putting his life on the line—hardly a day went by that he didn't—but there was something eating away at his subconscious, a premonition that everything wasn't as it should be. Not one to let fear of the unknown get the better of him, he shrugged off the thought and leaned back in his chair, his gaze falling on the auburn-haired beauty staring at him from across the room. His face lit up the moment he saw her, but his smile quickly faded when he noticed the troubled look she gave him.

"Something wrong?" he asked.

Dara had moved to the bunk after Callahan and Mark had entered the cabin, and she'd forced herself to remain quiet during the entire discussion. But now that she and Justin were alone, a million thoughts ran through her head . . . the most pressing being that in a few days she might never see Justin again. Swallowing the knot that had suddenly formed in her throat, she slowly came to stand beside the desk.

"Is it true?" she asked in a whisper.

"Is what true?"

"What you said about Winslow . . . about his wanting you dead."

Justin gave a short laugh and turned his concentration back to his half-eaten breakfast. "There are a lot of people who would like to see me dead, Dara," he pointed out, cutting another piece of the ham and popping it in his mouth, "he isn't the first and probably won't be the last, unfortunately. But he has to be dealt with and I know of no other way to do it. Besides"—he smiled up at her—"once this is over you won't have to be afraid of him anymore. He'll be in prison where he belongs."

"And you could very well be dead." She frowned.

A look of surprise replaced the smile on Justin's face. "Is that what's worrying you?"

"It's worrying Callahan too," she rallied. "You heard him. He said a disguise wouldn't be enough."

"And he was right. That's why I'm taking most of the crew with me. We'll be checking out the docks before we go through with the plan. It'll be risky, I don't deny that, but it's something that has to be done."

"No, it doesn't," she argued.

"Oh?" he grinned, setting aside his cup to lean back in the chair. "You have a better idea?"

Dara nodded firmly, making her bright coppery locks sway. Then she edged the chair Callahan had vacated closer to Justin, and sat down to discuss her plan. "It's something we should have done in the first place."

"Which is?" he asked through lowered brows.

"You can take me to see Senator Manning."

"What?" he exploded.

"Justin, I'm a witness to the fact that Colonel Winslow wanted to hire you to assassinate President Jefferson. That's why he wants to kill me. Remember? All of this can be avoided if I tell Senator Manning what I heard and he arrests the colonel. That way you and your men won't put themselves in danger and—"

"No," Justin interrupted sharply.

Startled by his angry reply, she straightened in the chair. "Why not?"

"Because it wouldn't end there. You'd have to testify at his trial and that could take weeks. If you're the only witness, I can guarantee you that you'd never live long enough to see the inside of the courtroom." Lifting his cup, he took a sip of tea and added, "Forget about it, Dara. It was a stupid idea."

"Why? Because I thought of it?" she snapped. "What makes you think your idea is any better? We're both after the same end . . . to see that President Jefferson is spared. Why should you get all the glory?"

"Glory?" he shouted. "Is that why you think I'm doing this? For the glory?"

"Well, if you're not, you're sure doing a good job of making it look like it. Besides, how could Winslow kill me if he's in prison awaiting trial?" she jeered, coming to her feet. With a flip of her silky mane, she whirled away from him.

"Oh, use your head, Dara. Winslow isn't the only one behind this. When the others learn what you've done, they'll simply come after you. If there's no one to testify, the authorities will have to let him go."

"Senator Manning would protect me," she insisted stubbornly.

"Night and day?" Justin's temper was rising. "Do you think he'd take you home and share his bedroom with you to protect you as I have? I'm not too sure, but I think his wife would object."

"There are other ways to protect me." Dara tried to remain calm. "He could have one of his men stay with me or he could hide me until the trial was over."

"One of his men," Justin replied. "Sweetheart, are you willing to take the chance that the man he chooses has the same loyalty you do? Perhaps he would agree with Colonel Winslow's views and decide to eliminate you himself?" One corner of Justin's mouth lifted sarcastically when Dara turned a surprised look on him. "Didn't think of that, did you? Now maybe you'll forget this nonsense and let me take care of Winslow."

Frowning angrily, Dara opened her mouth to retaliate, then snapped it shut when Justin glared warningly at her. There was no use in arguing with him. He was determined that things would be done his way. Let him think so. Tomorrow morning he would see for himself that she wasn't the type to be told what to do.

* * *

The harsh glow of sunlight poured into the cabin, rudely penetrating Justin's sleep-filled mind. Moaning his disapproval at the brusque intrusion, he rolled onto his stomach and clamped the pillow over his head. But even that failed to shield the glaring light that seeped through his closed eyelids, and awakening became almost painful.

He had spent the preceding day alone in the cabin with Dara, though he'd frequently looked up from his work at the desk to make certain she hadn't slipped out. Their daylight hours had passed in silence. He knew she was still very angry with him, but then again he wasn't too pleased with her either. Her idea to simply walk up to George Manning and state that she had overheard Colonel Winslow's plans to assassinate President Jefferson would merely have succeeded in getting her killed while Winslow walked away a free man. Yet he had to admire her courage. Not every woman would be willing put herself in such a situation . . . and he had wanted to tell her so. But each time he caught her eye, she had stiffened, raised her delicate nose, and turned away.

He had all but given up the thought of explaining his position on the matter until later that evening when he'd shed his clothes and slid beneath the covers of the bunk, certain he would soon find her wrapped in his embrace. He'd expected that after a blissful interlude, when he had kissed away her anger, they could lie in each other's arms until the pale light of the morning stained the eastern sky. But Dara had felt differently and had refused to share his bunk. Justin had lost his temper. He had ordered her to come to bed, and when she'd defiantly ignored him, yanking a blanket from his sea chest and fanning it out over her as she settled down on the bench, he had flown from the bunk, swooped her into his arms, and carried her back across the cabin,

381

kicking and screaming. Falling together onto the soft cushion of the mattress, he'd smothered her stormy protests with kisses, and within moments she had given in to the wanton desires he'd aroused. Apologies were never spoken as they were swept away on waves of passion to sate the all-consuming desire that engulfed them.

He had fallen asleep with her tucked possessively within the circle of his arm, and now as he lay fondly remembering the gentle thrusts of her hips in response to his, his passion stirred once more. Jutting out a hand to her soft curves, he bolted upright at finding the bed empty. A worried frown crimped his brow as he surveyed the room and found it empty, and he wondered if by chance, with the coming of dawn, her anger had returned. Flipping off the covers, he leaped from the bed and hurriedly dressed, intending to visit the galley in the hope of finding her there.

"Good morning, Cap'n," Callahan called when he spotted Justin marching determinedly across the quarter-deck. "If you're looking for Mark, he's already gone ashore."

Stopping midway toward his destination, Justin turned back to wait for his first mate to catch up to him. "No. I was looking for Dara. Have you seen her?"

Callahan shook his head. "Should I have?"

Justin started off toward the galley again, calling back over his shoulder. "She was already gone from the cabin when I woke up a few minutes ago. We had an argument yesterday and it's very possible she's still angry with me. I hope I'm wrong and I'll find her with the cook."

"Don't waste your effort, Cap'n," Callahan replied, shrugging when Justin turned back to look at him with a questioning frown. "I just came from the galley. She isn't there."

"Damn!" Justin exploded, smashing a fist against his open palm as he quickly surveyed the deck. "You can bet she isn't anywhere on this ship."

"You mean she's gone ashore? Why would she do that?"

"To find George Manning. The little fool thinks that if she tells him she heard Winslow's plan to assassinate the president we won't have to go through with our scheme. She's afraid I'll be killed." Perplexed, he combed his fingers through his dark hair. "How could she be so stuipd? She'll only succeed in getting herself killed instead." Slapping a hand against his thigh, he sighed angrily then pointed toward the longboat. "Launch it. I'm going to change. Then you and I are going into Norfolk to find her . . . and when I do, I'm going to beat her senseless." Whirling, he stalked away, leaving Callahan to do as instructed.

Platinum streams of moonlight emphasized the dark figure of the man standing near the window of the cabin. One of his hands rested on the wooden structure, the other clutched a glass of strong brew. His mouth was set in a hard line, his brow was furrowed, and his eyes bespoke the worry and anxiety raging within him. Hours had passed since he'd taken up his vigil, staring out into the night like a granite sculpture erected to protect all within its keep.

Justin had searched the streets of Norfolk diligently, praying he would find his impudent wife before it was too late. He'd returned to his ship only when the danger of discovery became too great. Reluctantly, he had allowed Callahan and several of his crew to continue the quest, instructing them not to leave the smallest, most unimportant spot unchecked. Once he'd learned that George Manning had yet to arrive in the coastal town, he'd decided that Dara Whitelaw had gone into hiding to await Manning's appearance and that their mission would be futile. Callahan had ordered two of his men to remain at the inn where Senator Manning and his party were to stay while in Norfolk. They'd been told to watch for the auburn-haired woman who would try to contact Manning. Meanwhile, the first mate returned to the ship to tell his captain the disappointing news of their failure. Justin received Callahan's report in silence, for he had expected as much. Norfolk was a big place and even the most unskilled adventurer could easily become lost in its vastness. He had dismissed his friend saying that he preferred to be alone for a while, and once Callahan had gone, he'd filled a glass with whiskey and ventured to a porthole where he'd stood unmoving, blaming himself for Dara's disappearance.

"Dara," he whispered, his throat tight, "if anything happens to you, I'll never forgive myself." One hand dropping to his side as he straightened, he studied the glass he held, then raised it to his lips and swallowed the remaining liquid, cursing his stupidity, the fair-haired boy who'd testified against him, the war, and finally life itself.

Darkness veiled the cabin and its contents as Justin instinctively moved back to the desk and the bottle he'd left there. As he reached out for it, a knock sounded, and he directed a troubled frown in the direction of the door.

"Who is it?" he called out.

"Wallis, Cap'n," came the reply. "I've brought you something. May I come in?"

Continuing the task of refilling his glass, Justin bade the man to enter, squinting when the light from the passageway spilled in around Wallis' tall figure. "If you don't mind," Justin said, a hand raised to shield his eyes, "I'd appreciate it if you'd close the door. I'm enjoying the darkness."

"Aye, Cap'n," Mark replied sympathetically. "I can understand your desire, but you'll need the light to see what I brought with me."

"Look, Mark, I'm grateful to you . . . and Callahan, and all the others for trying to make this whole thing easier on me, but if this isn't important, I'd rather be alone right now," he said, turning back to the porthole, the glass dangling from his fingertips.

"Aye, Cap'n," Mark nodded with a sly smile. "I'll just put it in here and let you decide what you want to do with it."

Even though his mind was centered on his wife and the danger she had put herself in, Justin's curiosity sparked his interest, and he absently glanced over at the doorway to watch his friend retreat a step, lean to one side, and jerk someone toward him. Although the shadows of the cabin made it difficult for Justin to distinguish exactly who it was, he instantly made out the small shape of the young boy Mark shoved into the room.

"I found this scalawag wandering near the docks, and I thought you'd take an interest in what he was doing there," Mark stated, reaching for the oversized hat the child wore. "Show a little respect for the cap'n, son"—he stressed the title and yanked the cap from the boy's head—"and he might go easy on you."

Justin's heart lurched in his chest when he saw long strands of hair cascade earthward as they were freed from their restraint. In that instant he knew this child was no boy but the rebellious woman he had married.

"Dara?" he breathed, rushing to his desk to set down his glass and quickly light the lamp. The bright glow of its flame flooded the space, illuminating emerald eyes that glared at him and the red bandana tied over her mouth. A quick examination revealed no harm had befallen her, but Justin lifted questioning eyes to his friend when he discovered that Mark had bound Dara's hands behind her.

"I had to bind and gag her, Cap'n," Mark explained. "Otherwise I never would have gotten her back here."

Justin opened his mouth to tell him that he understood, but finding it impossible to speak, he resignedly nodded his approval.

"Well, I'll leave you two alone." Mark grinned and reached for the doorlatch. "I'm sure you have a lot to talk over." With a chuckle and a shake of his head, Mark made a quiet exit.

Justin's gaze slowly traveled the length of the tiny form standing before him, his eyes roving from tattered shirt to baggy pants to bare feet. God, she looked good even in those ridiculous clothes, and he smiled for the first time that day. Then his thoughts hit upon the reason he had spent the last few hours alone in his cabin staring out the porthole, and his relief at knowing she was all right turned to anger. Reaching out, he took a handful of the faded blue cotton shirtfront in his fist and slowly pulled her toward him.

"I promised myself that when I found you I'd beat you within an inch of your life, Dara Brandon Whitelaw." He moved closer to the bunk, dragging her with him. "And if fear of me is the only way I can guarantee you'll do as you're told, then by God, that's the way it will be."

Her bright green eyes grew wide, but her gallant protests were muffled by the bandana. Her wrists burned where the ropes held them together as Justin dragged her along, and Dara silently decided this was the perfect ending to a miserable day. Early that morning before the sun had come up, she had silently stolen from Justin's bunk while he'd slept. Rummaging

386

through his sea chest, she'd taken a shirt, a floppy, brimmed hat, and a pair of pants, knowing that if she didn't disguise herself the men he sent looking for her would find her in a second. Dressed as a boy, she figured that they wouldn't give her a second glance. And it had worked . . . up to a point.

She had gone to the docks, thinking that Senator Manning might be there to supervise the construction of the platform where President Jefferson would give his speech and she would be able to talk privately with him. But when she'd arrived, she'd found only sailors working there. She had decided to wait awhile in the hope that later the senator would arrive, but then the distant church bell had pealed the noon hour, she'd lost hope and started for the center of town. Then she had seen Callahan. Spinning on her heels, she'd run back to the docks and hidden among the crates stacked at the end of the pier.

Darkness had descended before she had found the courage to leave her hideout, and that had been her downfall. A group of drunken sailors had spotted the youthful figure they'd mistaken for a lad, and being the sort that enjoyed tormenting children, they'd pushed her around and called her names, threatening to dump her in the bay. They probably would have if the sound of a pistol's hammer being cocked hadn't stopped them. Deciding their sport wasn't worth being shot, they had all run off, leaving Dara with the man who had rescued her. Once she had regained her composure and had glanced up at the man to thank him, the only sound that escaped her was a panicked whine, for smiling down at her was Mark Wallis. Suddenly, being thrown in the bay was more appealing than what she faced at the hands of her husband.

"Leave me alone," she wanted to scream at him, but her demand came out as a garbled, cacophonous noise which only brought a smile to Justin's lips.

"You know," Justin grinned mischievously, "I think I like you better this way. I can do all the talking, and for once you have to listen." Whirling her around, he roughly shoved her down on the bunk to sprawl on her back.

Again a muffled curse was hurled at him as Dara tried to rise, but with her hands tied behind her, she could only squirm about unsuccessfully. When she started to roll to her side so she could curl her feet beneath her and come up on her knees, Justin shouted an angry command, ordering her to stay where she was. She froze instantly, for the tone of his voice told her that this time she had gone too far.

"You may be pampering an injured pride, Dara, but when I'm through with you, you'll have other tender places to sulk over." His towering frame blocked the lamplight, placing his face in a shadow, and Dara felt her whole body tremble with fear. "First of all, I want you to realize who runs this ship. *I* give the orders around here, and *everyone* obeys them. *Including you!* If one of the crew had defied me as blatantly as you have done, I'd have had him flogged and thrown overboard at sea for the sharks to eat. And, by God, I'm sorely tempted to tie a rock around your ankles and see how long you'd float in the bay!"

With a quickness that hardly registered in her mind, Justin shot out a huge hand and grasped the fabric of her shirtfront once more, yanking her to her knees.

"If you're going to act like a foolish child, I'll treat you like one."

Turning, he sat down on the bunk and hauled his shaking captive over his knee. Dara's indistinct oaths gave way to outraged screams as Justin's hand connected with the seat of her breeches. Four more rounds of chastisement were administered before

Dara's painful humiliation ended, and in the next instant, the bandana was torn from her mouth. Then the ropes were removed from around her wrists, and strong arms suddenly lifted her up as Justin's kisses quickly melted away her tears and ignited the ever-present flame of passion within her. Responding to the urgency of the moment, she frantically clutched him to her as they yielded to the burning desire they wanted so desperately to sate, sampling again the sweet nectar of love. Their world, at this moment, revolved around each other, and neither heard or sensed the presence of the man who stood just outside the cabin.

"Mark"—Callahan frowned when he spotted the man near the captain's quarters—"what are you doing?"

Quickly stepping away from the door with a finger raised to his lips, Mark grinned back at his friend. "Just making sure, Cally, just making sure." Locking an arm around Douglas's neck, he led him across the bridge, his merry laughter bringing a confused look from the other. "Now all we have to do is get him to admit it."

"Who?" Callahan asked. "Admit what?"

"Cap'n Whitelaw, Douglas my friend. The poor fool loves his wife and doesn't even know it."

Glancing back over his shoulder toward the cabin, Callahan was quiet for a moment before a smile slowly spread across his face; then he turned back to stare at Mark. In the next instant they both burst into laughter as they headed for the longboat and the pub where they would celebrate their newfound knowledge.

Chapter Fourteen

In the earliest light of morning, the city of Norfolk had come alive with a fervor of excitement, for before night settled on the bustling town once more, its humble streets would be honored by the presence of Thomas Jefferson, their commander in chief. A crowd had already begun to gather near the place where the president would stand to christen the newest of his warships, and the docks had taken on a different air as sailors and wealthy merchants stood side by side. The section of the wharf near the platform where Jefferson would appear had been set off by long strands of red ribbon, and it was toward this vantage point that two men moved. Dressed in fine silk and black coats, they blended perfectly with the other businessmen who had come to be a part of the festivities. Only they were aware of their true reason for being there.

"When all of this is over, Cap'n," Mark whispered, his gaze covertly surveying the rooftops of the buildings surrounding the area, "you should consider giving up a sailor's life. You're quite impressive in that getup. You look as though you could own half of Norfolk."

"With or without the gray wig?" Justin murmured, smiling as he scanned the throng for Senator Manning's tall shape.

Mark momentarily relaxed his vigilence to lean back and appraise his captain. Noting the thick sideburns that ended at Justin's jawline, he shrugged. "With, I suppose. You don't look like such a rogue in it . . . more settled . . . like a married man."

Justin chuckled. "If I stay with Dara much longer, I won't need the wig. My hair is already turning gray."

"Yes, I suppose she is a handful," Mark observed, his gaze returning to the crowd of people moving closer. He nodded back at Callahan when he spotted his friend in the group.

"That, Mr. Wallis, is an understatement," Justin sighed.

Mark's eyes twinkled with his amusement. "How did you convince her to wait at the ship?"

"I didn't," Justin answered. "I had to lock her in the cabin. I couldn't get her to understand that she'd be more trouble to me if she came along than if she stayed aboard where I knew she'd be safe." He sighed resignedly. "We've been arguing ever since you brought her back."

Mark's mouth twitched into a smile. "Not all the time, I hope."

Knowing full well what his companion implied, Justin glanced over at him and shook his head. "We didn't argue when we were sleeping." He grinned, silently daring Mark to press the issue.

"Oh." Mark nodded and studied the crowd again. "I hope this doesn't mean you're losing your charm."

"If it does," Justin warned playfully, "that's my problem. So you can just forget about it. All right?"

"Sure, Cap'n," Mark agreed, fighting to contain his laughter. But the smile quickly faded from his mouth when a loud cheer rose from the audience that awaited the arrival of their president. "I think it's just about time, Cap'n," Mark pointed out, his brows coming

392

together as he concentrated on the sea of nameless faces all around them.

"Good," Justin replied. He then spied George Manning several hundred feet away. The senator was heading the presidential party toward the platform. "I've always hated the waiting. Look."

A hearty round of applause drowned out any reply Mark might have made, yet that didn't matter to Justin, for his attention was centered on the statesman he called a friend as Manning climbed the few steps leading to the platform and made his way to the four chairs sitting in the center. It was too late for regrets, but as Justin stood there watching, he longed to have done things differently at the Prescott ball. He and George should have planned things more carefully so each could be sure of what the other was going to do. That would have guaranteed everything would go smoothly, and that Colonel Winslow would no longer be a threat to anyone. Still, George had agreed to help in any way he could. Justin took comfort from that, but as the time drew near to execute his plan, the strange feeling Justin had experienced a few days earlier nibbled at his confidence. And it intensified when he witnessed the stream of armed soldiers parading behind the president and his men to surround the stage as if they expected an attempt on Jefferson's life.

"Cap'n," Mark whispered through clenched teeth. "I don't like the looks of this."

Justin was about to agree, to suggest they quietly disappear into the crowd and return to the ship, when Manning's gaze suddenly found him. Without blinking, the man stared back at Justin, his face expressionless, and Justin wondered if he had been wrong about George Manning. Then he caught sight of the man who sat beside the president's secretary, and the muscles of Justin's chest tightened instantly, for there, nervously wiping the moisture from his brow, was Samuel Rutherford.

"Cap'n," Mark warned once he, too, saw Rutherford, "I think we'd better abandon this idea and get the hell out of here."

"No," Justin said, looking back at Manning to find that he still watched him. "If this is a trap, we'll only draw attention to ourselves. We'll wait until after the ceremony is finished." He started to reach for the pistol he had hidden at the back of his waistband under his coat; then he froze. It was of no use to him. It wasn't loaded and George Manning knew it wouldn't be. Suddenly the burning hurt of betrayal he'd felt when Lane had testified against him raged up to choke the breath from him, and Justin could almost see the smile in Manning's eyes.

"Cap'n, look!" Mark exclaimed, giving Justin a nudge as he jerked his head in the direction of one of the rooftops.

There silhouetted against the bright blue sky was the figure of a man crouched low, the muzzle of his musket catching the sunlight, and Justin's brow furrowed with confusion. So he was right about Manning double-crossing him. But if George Manning and Winslow were in this together, why would the colonel go ahead and have one of his men try to kill Justin? All they had to do was wait for Justin to pull his pistol and aim it at the president; then Justin would be arrested. George would see to it that he never got the chance to tell anyone who had hired him for the assassination. Glancing back at Manning, Justin prayed that what he was about to do was right, and he readied himself to reach for his pistol once the disturbance was created to pull all eyes away from him.

"What are you doing?" Mark demanded when his captain moved a step closer toward the platform for a clearer view.

"I'm going through with it," Justin replied.

"No," Mark loudly objected, and he grabbed for Justin's arm when a woman's scream suddenly permeated the din of the onlookers and drew both men's attention.

A fight had broken out not twenty feet from where they stood. Justin knew this was the diversion on which he and Manning had agreed. If he intended to carry out his plan, now was the time for him to pull his gun and aim it at Jefferson. Pushing his way through the startled mass surrounding the struggling men, Justin quickly retrieved the firearm from his waistband, only to have it suddenly taken from him. His eyes barely focused on the thief before Mark's fist connected with his jaw. He reeled backward, stumbled, and fell to his knees. Through a haze, he watched Mark raise the pistol, aim it toward the president and pull the trigger, the explosion of powder inducing chaos among the hysterical crowd as they scrambled away from the man who held the gun. Then another shot echoed above the chaos, and in the next instant, Justin saw his friend hurled around and thrown to the ground by the lead ball that tore into his flesh. A volley of gunfire ensued almost immediately, and Justin knew Callahan and the others had spotted the man on the roof, but as he concentrated on the fallen man before him, he also knew their action had come too late.

Instinct warned him to run, to turn on his heels and race back to his ship, but Mark had sensed the failure of their scheme and had put himself in Justin's place. If Mark could speak, he would tell his captain to go, to leave him behind in exchange for Justin's freedom . . . but he couldn't. Nor could Justin leave his dying friend. Staggering to his feet, Justin closed the distance between them and dropped to Mark's side, lifting his friend's head in his arms.

"You damn fool," Justin moaned. "Why? Why did you do it? It wasn't a trap. You had the loaded gun. You were supposed to get the man on the roof." Gritting his teeth against the bellow of rage that twisted his insides, Justin looked down at the dark red bloodstain covering Mark's chest and felt the young man go limp in his arms. "Damn you, Mark Wallis. Damn you!" he screamed, unconscious of the hands that took him by the arms and hauled him to his feet.

The jail had a damp, musty smell to it. Due to the absence of windows no light could filter in to ease the darkness or chase away the chill. Small creatures scurried out of harm's way as the inmate relentlessly trekked across the narrow cubicle. Only the flickering flame of the torch burning in the passageway spilled light into the dark cavity through the small barred opening in the cell door, and the clicking of heels against cobblestones and the eerie clanking of chains were the only evidence of the man's aimless prowling. The last hour had dragged by in the same manner as the one before it; when the weighty shackles took their toll, the prisoner, exhausted, sought the meager comfort of the straw-covered cot, only to rise again when his tormented mind drove him from it. Back and forth he paced, first in rage then in sorrow. Justin Whitelaw had taken on the appearance of a madman. Even the hardened jailer, Luther Hadin, found other tasks that would take him from the bowels of the prison where the notorious traitor was held, remembering all too clearly the frightening look in the man's eyes when the deputies had hauled him in and the fact that it had taken four of them to do it. But what puzzled Hadin more than the instructions he'd been given to arrest anyone who caused a disturbance at the ceremonies was the order not to kill the man who raised a weapon at the president. He was to be taken into custody, held in one of the cells; and no harm was to come to him.

A troubled frown settled on Hadin's face as he walked the narrow corridor toward the place where Justin Whitelaw was held. He had tried to explain to Senator Manning that shackles had been necessary to subdue the captain, for his own good as well as that of Hadin's men. Whitelaw was like a man possessed, and if he didn't succeed in killing one of the deputies, Hadin was sure the man would do himself injury because of his desire to avenge his mate's death. Now the senator wanted the man brought to him. It would have made more sense to Luther Hadin if Manning spoke to the captain through the bars of the cell rather than face to face in Hadin's office, for among those Justin Whitelaw had vowed would pay for his companion's death, George Manning had been the first named.

"Unlock it," Hadin now said, nodding toward the door of Justin's cell. He stood aside as the guard twisted the key, then swung the portal wide. Rusty hinges creaked and moaned, sending a chill up Hadin's spine. He knew what awaited him inside and thoughts of a hangman's noose seemed more appealing. "Bring a torch," he ordered and waited until the yellow shaft of light spilled through the opening and flooded the darkened chamber with a golden glow. Again he was besieged by a prickling of fear as he watched the prisoner's long, lean frame unfold as Justin slowly rose from the cot to face his intruders. Iron bands secured his wrists and these were bound by a length of chain to the shackle around his neck. He was allowed a minimum of movement lest the halter rub his flesh bare. Such restraints on any other man would guarantee Hadin's safety, but with Justin Whitelaw, the jailer

397

doubted they would stop the prisoner if he intended to kill one of them. So Hadin raised his cocked pistol higher and motioned Justin out of the cell.

"I don't know why, Whitelaw," Hadin growled as he followed him into the corridor, "but the senator wants to talk with you. That's the only reason you're not on your way to the gallows right now. And if you don't want to limp to my office, I suggest you walk nice and slow. Otherwise I'm likely to shoot ya even though the senator told me not to harm ya. Understand?"

The figure before Hadin paused and half turned to glare back at him, and the jailer's hand trembled slightly. Forcing himself to appear in control, Hadin waved the prisoner on with a jerk of the muzzle pointed at the man's midsection, and mentally he sighed with relief when Justin merely looked him up and down before continuing on. The day Luther Hadin had heard of the traitor's escape, he had dreamed of being the man to single-handedly capture Justin Whitelaw, but now that he had that very man in his prison, Luther longed for the moment when he could turn him over to someone else. The savage look in Whitelaw's eyes unnerved him. It seemed that his prisoner wanted him to make some foolish mistake so he could hurl himself at his jailer and choke the very life from him. Absently, Hadin's fingertips moved to his throat as the trio of men ventured down the passageway. Then he paused outside the door to his office while one of the guards lifted the latch and motioned the prisoner inside.

The interior of the place Hadin called his office bore little resemblance to anything more than a small chamber where he could steal a short nap when others were not around, for the space contained only a cot, a desk, and a chair—nothing else. Justin scanned the room briefly before his gaze settled darkly on the tall figure standing near the single window. Manning was staring outside as if something there held more interest than the man who had quietly joined him.

"I brought him to ya, Senator Manning, like ya asked," Hadin said, shoving Justin farther into the room by burying the point of his weapon deeply in Justin's back. "But I think I should warn ya. He's a mean one."

"No more so than you or I would be if we were in his place, Mr. Hadin." George sighed, then turned to look at Justin, his brows coming together in an angry frown when he spied the shackles. "Dammit, man, I told you Captain Whitelaw was not to be harmed. Remove those at once."

"But sir," Hadin objected, "he's been convicted of treason and is bound for the gallows."

"Not anymore, he isn't," Manning barked. "Take those things off him immediately or you'll be the one wearing them!"

"Yes, sir," Hadin mumbled, motioning for one of the guards to fulfill the senator's demands.

The flesh on Justin's wrists and around his neck was chafed raw, and although the task of removing the iron bands was simple, it caused him a great deal of agony. Even so, his hatred for the man who had ordered it done overruled his distress. Justin remained motionless long after his hands were freed and the others had left him alone in the room with George Manning. Every muscle in his body ached from the abuse he had sustained at the hands of Hadin's men. His clothes were torn and he no longer wore the gray wig or sideburns. Yet he hardly resembled the Navy captain who had often spoken with the man he now faced about matters of great importance to his country. In fact, Justin actually wished Winslow and his cohorts would remain undiscovered, for at this moment he had little love for the nation that had put him where he was now.

"May I get you something to drink, Justin?" Manning asked. "You look as though you could use it."

"The only thing I want from you is an explanation," Justin ground out in return. "Or have I already guessed it?"

"I . . . I don't understand." Manning frowned. "Guessed what?"

"Why a good friend of mine is dead, and I'm in prison again."

Moving toward his companion, George extended a directive hand toward the cot. "Sit down, Justin, while I—"

"While you what? Lie to me?" Justin raged, his entire body tensed and ready to spring.

"Lie to you?" George repeated, stepping back. "I never lied to you. You asked me to have the men arrested who created a disturbance, and I did. And you're here because Hadin and his deputies didn't know of our agreement; I couldn't trust him. Had I known you wouldn't run once the plan was carried through, I would have chanced doing so. As it was I would have seen to it that you had gotten away when the time was right. Now I don't have to." When Justin did not respond except for his eyes which darkened even more, George turned away and ran his fingers through his hair. "Justin, I don't know what happened out there . . . why Mark Wallis knocked you aside and took your pistol . . . why Winslow's man on the roof was allowed to kill your friend, but there was nothing I could do to stop it, not without giving away my hand. I told you before I didn't know who I could trust and I had to act just as surprised about what happened as everyone else in the crowd." Spinning back to look at Justin, George's face reflected his remorse for what the day had brought. "If I could change it around—bring Mark back—I would. But I can't. And maybe you'll take comfort in knowing his death wasn't in vain. You might think I betrayed you, Justin, but I haven't and what I'm about to tell you will prove it. Before the man who shot Mark died, he confessed that Winslow had hired him to kill you, and that you had been hired by the colonel. When Rutherford heard that, he broke down and told us everything. We've got him, Justin, and all because of you and Mark Wallis."

Although that was the news he'd wanted to hear, Justin felt little satisfaction now. Mark's life in exchange for Winslow's wasn't enough. Turning away, he crossed to the window and stared out at the busy street in front of the jail. "You said there was no need to see that I escaped from here. What did you mean?" he asked quietly.

Manning's face lit up with a smile. "Sheer stroke of luck, my friend, and I doubt you'll believe me until you see for yourself. President Jefferson has dropped all charges against you."

Justin's head jerked around to stare in silent confusion.

"That's right, Justin." George grinned. "You know the two men who started a brawl near you?" He waited for Justin to nod. "Well, one of them was Lane Brandon. *He's* the reason Mr. Jefferson has cleared you."

Justin's head began to spin. It was all happening too fast. Clasping the bottom edge of the window frame, he leaned his weight on his hands, letting his head drop forward. Mark was dead, Winslow would soon be arrested, he had been cleared, and Lane had been found . . . all within the matter of a few hours. Was it possible? Or was this a cruel dream?

"He wants to see you, Justin," George said after a while. "He wants to tell you why. Will you see him?"

Standing erect, Justin covered his face with his

hands and took a deep breath. Letting it out in a rush, he wiped the moisture from his eyes then rubbed the back of his neck. He felt as if he had lived a hundred years in the last few minutes. "Of course, I'll see him." He turned to look at Manning. "And I'd like that drink now."

George's handsome face smiled back at him and he nodded. "Right there on the desk. Help yourself to all you want. You deserve it." He lingered a moment, watching his companion pour a liberal amount into a glass and then raise the liquid to his lips before he asked, "Will you believe me when I say I didn't betray you? I know it sounds shallow, after the fact, but I always knew you were innocent. I just couldn't prove it. I don't want you to leave thinking every man you put your faith in turned against you."

A tired smile lifted one corner of Justin's mouth. "I know, George. I just went a little mad, that's all." Twisting, he sat on the edge of the desk. "I've been on the run for over three months, never knowing who to trust, only wanting to find Lane and clear myself. I guess now that it's over, it just wasn't worth Mark's life. He was a good shipmate and friend, and I probably would have done the same for him. I just wish things could have turned out differently."

"We all do, Justin," George added. "Samuel Rutherford was my friend. I can never explain or forget the feeling I had as I sat there listening to a United States Senator admit that he and several others conspired to assassinate the president. Maybe you were betrayed, Justin, but so was I. And now that it's all behind us, we must move on, grow from this, and strive for a better way of life. Our ancestors fought for this country and its freedoms; now it's our turn. Sacrifice has always been necessary to insure those freedoms, and that's the way I'll remember Mark Wallis. He was a man who gave his life for his country." He waited for Justin to look up at him, smiled, then turned and left the room.

For the hundredth time Dara ceased her random pacing to stare out a porthole at the monstrous shapes of the frigates anchored near the *Lady Elizabeth* and at the shoreline cluttered with fishing boats. Among the small crafts was the longboat Justin, Mark, Callahan, and the others had taken that morning. Somewhere farther on, hidden behind the row of buildings on the waterfront, they had positioned themselves among the crowd to execute their plan to trap Colonel Emerson Winslow. And with each hour that elapsed, Dara sensed something had gone wrong.

Pressing a knee on the bench, she slowly lowered herself to sit before the porthole, a troubled frown marring her lovely brow. It was too late to change things, but she longed to have Justin with her, smiling as he had just before he'd left that morning. They had argued again. She wanted to go with him and he had been firm in telling her she couldn't, that it wasn't safe for her, and that he needed to concentrate on the scheme they had devised rather than worry about her welfare. Tears came to her eyes as she recalled the bitter words she'd flung at him when he'd closed the door and turned the key in the lock. She hadn't really meant what she'd said. She didn't want him to be hurt or captured. She just hadn't wanted him to go. She was certain there was some other way to trap the colonel, one that wouldn't risk Justin's life.

A sob shook her. The sunlight blinded her. The fresh smell of salt air sickened her. The cabin was too small. Everything in it reminded her of Justin. The gold band on her finger was too tight and she couldn't get it off. The safe, little world in which she had lived suddenly

403

had turned dark and ugly, and life itself didn't seem worth the effort anymore. Struggling to her feet, she blindly made her way to the bunk and threw herself upon it, burying her face in the pillow, sobs racking her body as she cried for the injustice brought upon them all.

A long while passed before exhaustion claimed her and Dara fell into a fitful slumber, visions of a man dangling at the end of a hangman's noose flashing up to haunt her.

"Dara, it's Justin," she heard someone tell her. A hand touched her arm, and in her dreams she knocked it away, refusing to accept the dead man as her husband.

"No," she murmured, her head rolling from side to side.

Then the voice came again, stronger than before, and the same hand shook her.

"Dara. Wake up. It's me, Justin."

What sort of game did this man play, so cruelly claiming to be her husband? Justin was dead and no other could ever take his place.

"Dara?"

Suddenly her world reeled about her. No corpse hung from the tree. Bright sunlight penetrated her brain and someone was brushing the long strands of hair from her brow. Her eyes flew open, instantly focusing on the man who hovered over her.

"Justin!" she screamed, throwing her arms around his neck. "Oh, Justin, I dreamed they had hanged you."

"Not this time." He laughed, enjoying the feel of her slender form pressed against him. "In fact, no one now has a need to do so."

"What?" She frowned, pushing back to look at him.

Cradling her face in his huge hands, he wiped the tears from her cheek with a thumb. "That's right. All charges against me have been dropped. I've been completely exonerated, even given back the command of my ship, and my original crew may again serve under me."

"Justin, that's wonderful. But how? . . ."

He smiled. "Oh, it's quite simple. You see, someone testified in my behalf."

"Who? Who could do that for you?"

"Him," he said, jerking a thumb over his left shoulder toward the cabin door.

Dara's gaze followed his gesture immediately, and her chin sagged as she spotted her brother standing beside Douglas Callahan.

"Lane!" she shrieked, scurrying off the bed to race across the room and fly into his outstretched arms. "Oh, Lane. Thank God you're all right," she cried, hugging him to her. Then she straightened suddenly and put him at arm's length. "How did you find us? What made you think to look here in Norfolk of all places? The last we knew you were still in Maryland."

Lane had fought to keep his balance while his sister dangled in his arms, his own relief at seeing her safe choking off any reply he wanted to make. But now as a flood of questions poured over him, he could do naught but laugh at her sudden change in mood.

"I'm fine, Dara," he chuckled. "It's good to see your little adventure hasn't dulled your spirit any . . . or your never-ending chatter. I'll explain everything if you'll be kind enough to allow me a chance to sit down and have that drink Captain Whitelaw offered on the way here. It's been a rather trying day to say the least."

Unaffected by his playful chastising, Dara quickly guided her brother to the bench, gently pushed him down on it, and went to the desk to fill a glass with whiskey. After handing the drink to him, she sat down beside him, hands folded in her lap, and politely waited for him to drain the glass and begin his story, only slightly aware of the two men who watched her. A frown flitted across her brow and disappeared as she observed him drinking the whiskey. Drink had never been one of Lane's weaknesses before he'd joined the Navy. But then again, a lot had happened since that day.

Lane felt the effects of the drink almost immediately, and he let out a long sigh as he studied the empty glass. The past several months now seemed like an awful nightmare, one that had ended very differently from the way he had intended. Glancing up at Justin, he smiled softly back at him, silently thanking the Lord for making his captain the kind of man who had never doubted his friendship. Had he testified against any other, Lane probably wouldn't be sitting where he was now sharing the man's whiskey.

His gaze moved from where Justin sat on the bunk to the second man who shared the cabin with them— Douglas Callahan, the captain's first mate. He was sure Justin's faith in his wayward crewman had been bolstered by this man. He was very fortunate to have found two men like Justin Whitelaw and Douglas Callahan.

"Well," he began, looking back at Dara, "the reason I'm in Norfolk is because I was trying to get to Senator Manning."

"And obviously you found him." She smiled.

Lane's brows lifted. "But not the way I meant to find him."

"What do you mean?"

"I had gone back to Washington after I talked with Papa—"

"You saw him?" Dara frowned, glancing over at Justin and back.

Lane chuckled. "Yes. I went home after talking with

406

you that night. Captain Whitelaw told me that he was the one I ran from." He leaned back and sighed. "I could have saved everyone a lot of trouble if I had known who had ridden in that night." He shrugged. "Well, anyway, Papa suggested I find someone Captain Whitelaw trusted so I thought of Senator Manning right off. I went back to Washington, but when I got there, I found out he and President Jefferson had already gone to Norfolk. So I came here. I had decided to wait until after the ceremonies were over and then try to talk with the senator. But things didn't quite work out that way."

"Why?" Dara asked. "What happened?"

"I was standing in the crowd, watching, minding my own business—in fact, I was trying to be inconspicuous—when a total stranger turned around and hit me."

"Hit you? What for?"

"The diversion, Dara," Justin broke in as he left the bunk and crossed to his desk. "As Manning said to me, it was a sheer stroke of luck that man picked your brother out of all the men there. Otherwise Lane probably would have run off again, if he hadn't been arrested." Reaching over, he took Lane's glass and refilled it along with two others.

"Then the man who started the fight was the one hired by Winslow."

"Sort of," Justin replied, handing Lane then Callahan a glass. "The man said a stranger approached him just before the president and his party took the platform. He gave him some money and told him to start a fight. That was all he knew."

"You mean the plan didn't work? Is Winslow still free?"

"No. You don't have to worry about him anymore. You see, there was a second man, one who worked for

407

the colonel, stationed on one of the rooftops. He's the one who confessed."

"Then it was a trap. Thank God no one was hurt," Dara sighed. She smiled up at Callahan only to see the pain expressed in his eyes. Frowning, she looked from Justin to her brother. "What's wrong?" Suddenly she missed Mark Wallis' presence. "Where's Mark?" she asked, dread knotting her stomach. "Is he all right? Justin, what happened? Where's Mark?"

Rounding the desk, Justin slowly sat down in the chair behind it and rested his arms along the edge, a glass cupped in his hands. "Mark thought Senator Manning had double-crossed us, that if I pretended to shoot the president, I would be arrested and sent back to prison to hang. At first I thought so too . . . until I saw the man on the roof. If that was what he had planned, he wouldn't have had someone shoot me. But Mark didn't see it that way, and when I pulled the pistol and started toward the president, Mark took it away from me, knocked me to the ground, and did it himself. Mark was supposed to have covered me. Once he spied anyone who raised a gun at me, he was to shoot. Between the two of us, Mark had the only loaded pistol, so all I could do was stand by and watch him take the shot that was meant for me. He's dead, Dara. He died trying to protect me."

Tears had filled Dara's eyes while she'd listened to Justin, and although she wanted to throw herself on the bunk and cry away the grief she felt at losing a friend, she sensed Justin's sorrow was much deeper than her own. Without a word, she left her place beside Lane and knelt down at Justin's side, gently touching his arm. "You mustn't blame yourself, Justin," she said softly. "Mark cared very much for you, and I think if he had to make the choice again, he'd do exactly the same thing. Not many can say they've ever had a friendship as strong and deep as the one you and Mark had. You should take great pride and honor in the fact that he willingly gave his life for you."

One corner of Justin's mouth lifted in a feeble smile. "I know, Dara. And I do. But it doesn't erase the hurt I feel."

"It shouldn't," she told him, wiping a tear from her face. "He wouldn't be a real friend if his death meant nothing to you, and to prove what it did mean, you have a job to finish."

Blue eyes glistening with unshed tears looked down at her.

"You and Lane must bring the man who framed you to justice."

"I wish I could, Dara," Lane interrupted. "But I'm afraid I won't be of much help."

Turning to look at her brother, she asked, "Why?"

"Because I don't know who was behind it. The day before Captain Whitelaw was arrested, I received a letter, unsigned, stating that you and our parents would be murdered if I didn't testify against the captain. There was no way I could find out for sure if you were being held, and I couldn't take the chance that the message lied. So I did as I was told, only because I had planned to go to the authorities with the truth once I knew my family was safe."

"But you didn't. Why not?"

"After I testified and started out of the courthouse, two men grabbed me. I was taken north into Pennsylvania and held there until about two weeks ago when I managed to escape."

Dara's startled gaze moved from Lane to Justin and back. "Who were they?"

"John and Willy Thornton."

"Thornton," she repeated. "I've never heard of them. Have you, Justin?"

"They're not the ones behind this, if that's what you're thinking," he replied. "Lane and I talked this all out on the way back to the ship. The Thornton brothers were simply a pawn. We're after bigger game."

"And the trouble is I don't know where to look," Lane pointed out. "The Thornton brothers are dead."

"That's right, but the men who killed them more than likely are the ones who can lead us to the one who ordered it done," Justin added.

"So where can we find them?" Dara asked.

"That could be a problem," Lane said. "I don't know who they were, and by now they've probably given up looking for me. I would imagine they've gone back to report their failure."

With a sigh, Justin leaned back in his chair, staring up at the ceiling as he stroked his chin with the back of his knuckles. "Then I guess we'll have to try to pick up their trail," he said after a while.

"You mean go back to Mitchell's farm?"

"Unless you have a better idea."

Lane shook his head slowly and studied the glass he held. A moment later a smile touched his mouth.

"From the look on your face, Cap'n," Callahan put in, "I'd say he hasn't told us everything."

A light blush rose in the young man's cheeks as he glanced up, first at Callahan, then Justin, and finally his sister, all of whom watched and waited for his explanation. He had been thinking of Prudence and the chance to see her again. Although he had told Justin that he'd spent time in the care of the Mitchell family, he hadn't admitted that he'd grown fond of Edwin's daughter. In fact, he couldn't remember if he had even mentioned her name to Justin or Callahan. But before he could open his mouth to assure them that he had recited every important detail, Callahan stepped forward, settled one hip on the corner of

Justin's desk, and spoke as if Lane wasn't even in the same room with him.

"Cap'n," he began, "I've been around a long time, and I can usually tell when a man is trying to hide something. Maybe I'm wrong this time, but I think young Brandon here is rather looking forward to going back to the Mitchell place. My guess would be that Mr. Mitchell has a daughter who caught this young man's fancy." Sparkling gray eyes moved to look at Lane, a devilish smile tugging at Callahan's mouth. "Am I wrong, Lane?"

Opening his mouth to object, Lane suddenly found that he didn't want to, and he surrendered to the man's astute observation with a laugh. "I really wasn't trying to hide it," he admitted. "It just wasn't something that would help Captain Whitelaw in finding out who framed him, but, yes, I do care a great deal for Prudence Mitchell and I'm looking forward to seeing her again."

"Wait a minute," Dara cut in when all three men laughed, Justin and his first mate raising their glasses in a silent toast to Lane's happiness. "I think I missed something. Who's Prudence Mitchell? Where did you meet her? And how did you have time to decide that you cared about anyone . . . especially a girl?"

Lane's tawny brows lifted in surprise at the jealousy he heard in his sister's tone. Casting his friends a vague smile, he settled his attention on Dara once more. "Prudence isn't a girl, little sister, she's a woman. And in case you've forgotten, I'm not the boy who used to go barefoot in the woods or play hide-and-seek with you. I've grown up. In fact, if Prudence is interested, I'm going to ask her to marry me once this thing is settled."

"Marry?" Dara echoed, coming to her feet. "You're too young to get married."

"I'm older than you," he said with a chuckle. "And to

be quite honest, I think it's time you thought of settling down as well." He missed the slight squaring of her shoulders when he glanced up at Callahan and winked, and he thought nothing of the odd way his captain suddenly elected to refill his glass with whiskey. "The sooner the better," he continued light-heartedly. "When word gets around that you've spent the last week or so aboard a ship with no other women as companions—" His smile disappeared when he noticed that Dara had quickly put her hands behind her as if she wanted to hide something. Frowning, he looked first at Callahan then Justin, sensing from the way they avoided meeting his eyes that something was amiss. He looked back at his sister. "Dara. Give me your hands," he ordered, setting aside his glass.

Dara's face paled instantly. "What?" She laughed nervously. "Have you had too much to drink?" she asked. She tugged harder at the ring on her finger, but it wouldn't budge and she grew panicky. How would she explain her marriage to Lane? She tried to distract him. "So . . . tell me about Prudence. What does she look like? How old is—"

"Dara," Lane repeated a bit more firmly, "I want to see your hands."

Maybe if she obliged quickly and then retreated toward the bunk, he wouldn't notice the band she wore. Bringing her hands out, palms up, she said, "There . . . are you satisfied?" But as she turned, Lane caught the wrist of her left hand, pulling it toward him.

His brow furrowed the instant he saw the gold ring on her finger. The only explanation for its presence was the fact that she had wed sometime during his absence, so he raised questioning blue eyes to hers.

It had been a long time since Dara had felt as she did at that moment, not since the time she'd sneaked out to go fishing with her brother instead of doing her chores as her mother had told her to do. She had lied when she'd explained the reason for her disobedience, but her mother had seen right through her. Dara had never been a good liar. Now if she told Lane that she and Justin had married, he would certainly question the suddenness of such a decision and she couldn't tell him the truth.

"The ring belonged to my father's mother," Justin's deep voice began, and Dara held her breath, wondering what he planned to tell Lane, how he would spare them both embarrassment. "When my father married my mother, he gave it to her, and I gave it to Dara a few days ago. When I met your sister, Lane, she was on her way to find you, and I knew just from looking at her that she wouldn't get very far on her own, so I brought her aboard my ship. I explained that to you already. However, I soon realized that she wasn't much safer here with my crew wandering about, so we agreed on this way to insure her well being. A ring on a woman's finger, especially a captain's woman, can change a man's thinking very quickly."

Lane was quiet for a moment, glancing first at Justin and then at Dara and finally at the gold band. "Then you're not really married," he said, more to himself, and let go of his sister's hands. "A shame. Not only would it have been an honor to have Justin as a brother-in-law, but he's one man who could control you and do so without abusing you." He smiled up at Dara when he heard her gasp. "Now don't pretend you've been misjudged, little sister." He grinned. "I've known you all of your life and you've always been a handful. Just consider yourself very fortunate that the captain took you under wing. Any other man would have taken advantage of you."

Dara's rage nearly strangled her, and without thinking, she blurted out, "And what makes you think he hasn't? No man is that honorable!"

Still seated in the chair behind his desk, Justin closed his eyes and rested his forehead in one hand. Would she ever learn?

"Because I know Captain Whitelaw"—he heard Lane argue—"and I know you. He might have been tempted . . . what man wouldn't be? You're a very beautiful woman, but if he had, I'm sure you threatened to do him great harm or worse yet talk him to death. Any sane man would have given thought to tossing you overboard." He looked over at Justin when he heard the man clear his throat and saw the way he tried to hide his smile behind the fist raised to his mouth. "Seems to me," he observed, "that it has crossed his mind."

"And I suppose you would shake his hand if you learned that's exactly what he did? I'm your sister, Lane Brandon," she raged. "You're supposed to care about me. He's just a . . . a . . ."

"Friend," Lane finished with a smile. "One I trust. Whatever treatment you received while in his company, I'm sure you deserved it. Now," he added, coming to his feet to take her by the arm and guide her toward the bunk, "I want you to sit down here and be quiet while the captain and Callahan and I decide what we're going to do next." He gave her a stern look when she opened her mouth to argue. "Otherwise, Dara, I'll ask Captain Whitelaw to have one of his men take you home right now. Understand?"

Jerking free of Lane, Dara plopped down on the bed, arms folded over her chest, and raising her pretty, little nose in the air, she silently schemed to get even with both her brother and Justin. She couldn't let Lane go on thinking that Captain Whitelaw was the perfect gentleman.

"She may look like a woman," Lane whispered when

he returned to the men at the desk, "but I swear most of the time she acts like a little girl." He glanced briefly over at Dara, then back at Justin. "I can only imagine what it's been like for you to have to put up with her antics." He missed Justin's pleased smile as he pulled a chair closer to the desk and sat down.

"Oh, it was rough at times," Justin replied, amused by the arrogant way Dara held her chin in the air, "but I managed."

Lane chuckled at his captain's reply. He was about to offer an apology for the trouble his sister had caused, but the words never came because he'd noticed the way Justin was staring at Dara. He now realized that there was more to what had been said than the simple explanation the man had given him.

Tears filled Samuel Rutherford's eyes as he signed his name at the bottom of the letter he had labored over for the past quarter of an hour. After returning the quill to its well, he tenderly folded the parchment over twice, then lifted the single taper from its holder and carefully dotted the edge with a drop of wax. His throat tightened as he propped the letter up against the brass candlestick where it was sure to be seen. The allotted time Senator Manning had given him to pack his things before he was to board the ship bound for Washington had nearly run out, and he knew the men who waited outside the door for him would be coming soon.

Rising, he crossed to the bed and the satchel that sat upon it, pulling it open to search inside. His hand trembled as he withdrew the pistol he had hidden there. He had always detested violence and ordinarily wouldn't have carried a weapon with him, but he was glad he had brought one this time. His knees weakened, and before he fell to the floor, he twisted around and sat down on the bed, the gun hanging limply in his hand. He didn't want his life to end this way. He would have preferred telling his wife face to face rather than letting her read his reasons in the letter. He loved Monica very much, although he'd known from the first that she had only married him for his money. It hadn't mattered to him. He was happy merely to see her happy with the things he could buy for her. Now even that would be taken from her, for unbeknownst to her, Samuel Rutherford was near ruin.

A knock sounded on the door, startling him, and he nervously called out to the man, requesting one more moment alone. The voice that consented was sympathetic, but Samuel knew that he must go through with his plan now or he would never have another opportunity. Unable to bear the thought of living a moment longer in shame, he lifted the pistol and pointed its black muzzle at his temple.

"I love you, Monica," he whispered, and pulled the trigger.

Chapter Fifteen

The lone figure of a man stood at the helm of the ship that sailed northward up the Chesapeake Bay, peacefully watching the eastern sky brighten with the first rays of morning sunlight. There had been a time when Justin had wondered if he would ever be allowed to command his ship as a free man, to spend his days traveling the coast without fear, and now that he could, he discovered that doing so wasn't so exciting anymore. Maybe Mark's death had made him realize there were other important things in life besides chasing smugglers or upholding the laws governing the waterways—less dangerous things. He had meant it when he'd told Mark that he was tired of never having a place to call home. Yet he also knew he could never give up life at sea completely. Maybe that was why the idea of returning to Provincetown and his father's shipping line suddenly seemed so appealing.

A sea gull squawked overhead, and Justin lifted his gaze to watch its graceful descent. They were on their way to Baltimore where they would dock. Then they would travel on foot to Emmitsburg and the Mitchell farm. They hoped to learn what they could about the men who had tried to kill Lane, possibly discover who was behind the whole affair, but before they did, Justin intended to drop anchor near Cambridge. Dara would be going home to her parents.

A strange sadness clouded his blue eyes as he thought about leaving her behind for good, for once they had checked out all the possibilities in Emmitsburg whether they were successful or not, he would set sail for Massachusetts and never return. He had always loved the bay, but now it held too many bad memories and to return there would only stir them up again. He wanted to start a new life, and managing the Whitelaw Shipping Lines would be the way to do it. His only regret was that he had married Dara because, thereby, he had sentenced her to a life of loneliness. Sucking in a breath of salt air, he let it out slowly. Well, maybe he could fix that. Once he had his life in order, he would seek out a lawyer and free Dara of the vows they had spoken.

Dara. A soft smile touched his lips as he thought of her. He had misled Lane into thinking they weren't really married to spare her the embarrassment of explaining how she could marry someone she had only known a few days. And he had done it for Lane. Even though the young man had said he'd be honored to have Justin as his brother-in-law, Justin was sure he'd have different thoughts if he knew his captain had forced himself on an innocent young girl, especially if that girl had been his sister. Chuckling to himself, Justin thought of the consequences he had suffered by not telling the truth. In order to carry out the charade, he had offered his cabin to Lane and Dara, telling Lane that he would share Callahan's. He had only said that because he was sure Lane would not want the crew to become suspicious for then Lane might have insisted that Dara and he continue to share the cabin. At any rate, Justin had spent a restless night, longing for the comfort of Dara's soft, supple curves. He also rued his careless words because last night might have been their

418

last time together and he had ruined it.

The slamming of a door echoed in the early morning stillness, and Justin frowned, wondering who might be up this early. A moment later his question was answered when he spotted Dara's coppery curls bouncing with each step she took up the ladder toward him.

"Justin," she snapped irately as she crossed the deck, "we have to talk."

A lazy smile parted his lips. "You seem irritable this morning, Dara. Didn't you sleep well?"

His question stopped her cold until she realized he only mocked her. Curling her upper lip, she sneered back at him. "Very," she told him. "It's the first comfortable night's sleep I've had since I met you."

"Me too," he replied casually, nodding his dark head and then looking out over the bow of the ship. "It was quiet for a change."

Dara stiffened. "I don't have to remind you, Captain, that if you had discovered that earlier, we wouldn't be in this situation."

"And what situation is that, Dara?" he grinned back at her, noticing how her long, coppery strands of hair glistened in the pale morning sunshine.

"Lying to Lane." She frowned. "He's bound to find out the truth sooner or later."

"He won't learn it from me. So unless you tell him, which you already tried very hard to do, I don't see that it will be a problem. You'll be home soon and we won't have to pretend anything."

"So it's true," she stated, resting her tiny fists on her hips.

"What's true?"

"What Lane told me. He said we'll be dropping anchor near Cambridge so that I can be put ashore."

"That's right," Justin told her, then concentrated on

419

the course the frigate took.

"Well, I have a surprise for you, Justin Whitelaw," she replied, her chin held defiantly in the air, "I'm not going home. I'm going to Emmitsburg with you and Lane."

"Oh, no you're not." He scowled over at her. "We have no idea what to expect once we're there and it could be dangerous. You're going home whether you like it or not."

A devious smile parted her lips. "What do you suppose Lane would say if he knew the conditions of our rather hurried marriage?"

Justin flashed her a black glower.

"Or should I rephrase that? What will he think of *you?*" When she saw the muscle in his cheek flex, she knew she'd driven her point home. She smiled triumphantly. "Besides, Justin, you never know when it might come in handy to have a woman with you . . . like at the ball?"

He snorted and looked away. "Yes. And we all know the outcome of that little escapade." He was quiet a moment longer; then he asked, "Why, Dara? Why do you want to go with us?"

"Because I want to help," she said. "Maybe our marriage is a little unusual, but you are my husband. I feel I owe it to you."

Justin gave a short laugh. "Owe it to me?"

"Yes. You never lost faith in my brother. You were sure he had been forced to testify against you, and you continually risked your life trying to find him. Maybe to others it would appear you only did it to save yourself, but I know better. That was only part of the reason. You like Lane and you wanted to help him out of the trouble he was in." She studied Justin a moment, then moved to stand near the railing and gaze out across the bay. "I missed you," she whispered.

420

Justin turned a questioning look her way. "Missed me?"

"Last night. I guess I've grown used to having you lie beside me," she admitted, refusing to look at him.

"Careful, Dara," he warned with a smile. "That sounds awfully close to a confession of the heart."

Tears suddenly filled her eyes and she bit her lip to stop them from spilling over. "And what would you say if I told you it was?"

Suddenly Justin realized she was no longer playing with him. He had suspected some time ago that she really cared for him, but he had foolishly told himself that as long as she never conceded her feeling he could disappear from her life as quickly as he had ventured into it. He would leave behind only memories, and they would fade in time. Dara was a beautiful woman. She deserved a man who would love her, care for her, devote his life to her. Justin doubted he ever could. He braced himself for what he was about to say.

"It's only infatuation, Dara," he said quietly, forcing his attention away from her. "It will pass in time. I'm the first man who ever held you in his arms, so it's only natural for you to mistake your feelings for love. I'm sure you'll come to realize that once you've found the man you were meant to be with for the rest of your life."

Dara felt as if he had thrust a knife into her heart, and she reached out to catch the railing for support. Maybe he thought of it as infatuation, but it was real to her. She had suspected the depth of her feeling when she'd seen him with Monica, but the day before as she'd paced the floor of his cabin, not knowing if he would come back to her or not, she was certain of it. If she lived another two score of years, no other man would ever take his place. Bravely pulling herself up, she briskly wiped the tears from her eyes and turned toward the ladder.

"I'm sorry to have confused matters for you, Justin," she said, brushing past him. "It won't happen again." She paused near the steps and added, "And unless you want Lane to find out everything that has happened between us, I *will* be going with you to Emmitsburg." Chewing on her lower lip, she quickly descended the stairs, disappearing from view.

His hands clasped the wheel in a white-knuckled grip as he stared at the place where she had stood. He had hurt her. He knew he had. Yet he had done it to spare her added grief later on, when she learned he couldn't return her love. A troubled frown marred his brow. If that was really true, why did he feel such pain?

Opaque clouds of dust languidly drifted skyward behind the group of riders traveling down the barren country road. Ahead lay their destination, a small farm just over the Pennsylvania border, and a man who might be able to tell them what they needed to know. It had taken the *Lady Elizabeth* and her passengers nearly two days to reach the shoreline of northern Baltimore, and by noon of the third day they had secured the horses needed for the journey. They had stopped that night at an inn along the way and had risen early the next morning, hoping to reach Mitchell's farm by midday. Few words had been spoken during their travels or at the table where they had eaten both the evening meal and breakfast. No one had dared to speak for Captain Whitelaw's mood had been the blackest any of them had ever had the misfortune to experience. Lane and Callahan could only guess at the reason, but they were sure it had something to do with Dara. While Justin's anger seemed aimed at her, she acted as if she didn't notice, possibly as if she even enjoyed being the cause. Neither man could understand why their captain had changed his mind about allowing Dara to come along, but when she hadn't appeared to be surprised that he'd done so, they were certain she had had something to do with his decision. Both men had tried to talk Justin out of letting her come with them, but they had only succeeded in arousing his temper and receiving a stern reminder that *he* was the captain of the ship and that his orders were not to be questioned. And talking with Dara was impossible. She listened to everything they had to say, a soft smile gracing her lovely face, then she politely reminded them that the captain had said that she was allowed to accompany them. If they wished him to alter his decision, she suggested they speak to him.

Justin and Callahan led the way while Lane rode beside his sister. Behind them Maddock, Peters, and Phillips followed, and Lane wondered which of the men was most uncomfortable astride a horse, Callahan or one of the other crew members. He felt safe in guessing that it was Callahan, for it was quite obvious from the way the first mate bounced in the saddle that he had very seldom ridden a mount. But the man had yet to complain, and Lane was reasonably sure he wouldn't. It had become quite apparent to Lane on the first day he'd served under Captain Whitelaw that Douglas Callahan's feeling for Justin was different from the usual captain-first mate relationship, and he was certain of it after talking with Callahan a few times. The man thought of Justin Whitelaw as a son and would probably go to any length to insure his happiness and safety. Lane cringed inwardly, thinking of the punishment Douglas Callahan would have bestowed on him if he had lied about their captain strictly out of malice and not because he had been forced into it. Fortunately, that hadn't been the case, but Lane found himself pitying the man who was responsible for the whole affair.

The road ahead wound off to the left and Lane knew that just beyond the stand of trees lay Mitchell's farm. Nudging his horse, he moved alongside Justin.

"It's over there," he stated, gesturing toward the farm.

Justin studied the area a moment, then he reined his horse in and rose in the stirrups to look around. "I doubt the men who were sent after you have stayed this long, but I think we should play it safe. Callahan and I will go on ahead and check out Mitchell's farm. If it's clear, I'll have Callahan come back for the rest of you." He nodded toward a stand of oaks twenty feet off the road. "Wait in the cover."

"Aye, Cap'n," Lane agreed, motioning for the rest of the party to follow him.

"I don't want to ride in with pistols raised," he said to Callahan, "but be ready to draw them if something looks suspicious."

"Right, Cap'n," Callahan nodded, kicking his horse into a canter.

The sun was now high overhead, and when the farm came into view and the yard around the house and barn was empty, Justin assumed the family was inside eating their noon meal. Slowing their horses to a leisurely pace, they covertly surveyed the grounds, listening for any unusual noises that might hint of trouble. All seemed peaceful, but Justin had learned long ago to be leery of such a situation. Many times it was a façade.

They had nearly reached the front porch of the house when the door opened and a man stepped outside. Justin knew from Lane's description of Edwin Mitchell that he was facing the man, but he also realized he would have to be careful about explaining who he was. When Lane had left the farm, Mitchell had advised him to be guarded where Justin himself was concerned.

"Edwin Mitchell?" Justin asked, appearing casual though his senses were alert for any possible danger.

Edwin nodded, eying both visitors warily.

"A mutual friend of ours sent me here."

"Friend?" Edwin repeated. "Who?"

"Lane Brandon." Justin could see Edwin stiffen. Quickly he added, "Please allow me to explain."

Mitchell's gaze moved from Justin to Callahan and back again. "All right. But I should tell thee first that I do not know a Lane Brandon."

Justin smiled. "Maybe you will once I've told you how I found your place. Two or three weeks ago, you found a young man along the road near here. He had been shot and was dying. You took him in and tended his wounds. Later he told you that he had been held captive for three months and that he'd been shot by two strangers when he'd tried to escape. He also told you that he was part of a plot to frame his captain, that he had been forced to lie, and that, when he was well enough, he wanted to return to Washington to clear up the matter. I'm here to tell you that he succeeded."

Edwin remained motionless. These men could very well have been sent by the two strangers who had tried to kill Lane. They could have learned the whole story simply by snooping around. But Lane wasn't here anymore. So what did they want with him?

Justin shifted in the saddle, knowing Edwin Mitchell was far from convinced that he was with friends. "Lane told me that you hid him in the attic while he was healing, your wife's name is Grace, he cares a great deal for your daughter, Prudence, and he promised to come back as soon as he could."

Edwin raised one eyebrow. "Did he show thee the ring my daughter gave him? He wore it on a chain around his neck."

Justin frowned over at Callahan who shrugged. "No,

Mr. Mitchell, he didn't, nor did he tell me about it."

One corner of Edwin's mouth twitched. "Would have been rather difficult. She didn't give him one." He grinned. "Thee were wise to tell the truth. I hope thee will continue to do so when I ask thy name."

"And I hope you will understand when I ask if no one other than your family is here. I fear those who tried to kill Lane may still be lingering somewhere nearby and they may not know that he has cleared my name. His death would therefore be for nothing."

"Captain Justin Whitelaw," Edwin concluded with a smile. "I should have known." He turned to Callahan. "And thee must be the first mate, Douglas Callahan."

"Aye," Callahan nodded.

"Rest thy worries, Captain Whitelaw. Since Lane left, no one has come here looking for him. If they had, I would have sent them north. Please," he said, extending a hand, "come inside and share our food. Thee must be tired from thy journey."

"Yes, Mr. Mitchell, we are, but Callahan and I have not come alone." At Edwin's questioning look, Justin continued, "Lane, his sister, and three of my crew are waiting back down the road a ways."

Edwin's face lit up immediately. "Then go and fetch them while I tell Grace to set more places at the table."

"I'll get 'em, Cap'n," Callahan said, swinging his horse around and bolting off down the road.

"And while we wait, thou will have a glass of wine." Edwin smiled as he watched Justin dismount and start toward the porch. Then his dark brows came together briefly as he sought to explain. "'Twas a bottle given to me by a friend who did not know I would not drink it. I kept it out of loyalty to him and for occasions such as this. It will be an honor, Captain Whitelaw, for thee to be the first to open it."

"It is an honor for me to know you think me

worthy." Justin smiled in return and followed Edwin into the house.

The moment Justin saw the youngest Mitchell woman he knew why Lane cared so much for her. The dark-eyed Prudence was quite lovely, and she radiated a shyness that could only be matched by that of the young man who had fallen in love with her. He smiled, then nodded as Edwin introduced him to his wife and daughter. Mrs. Mitchell urged Justin to sit down and he did so, taking a place beside Edwin at the table after the man had secured the wine and a glass from the cupboard.

"So tell me, Captain Whitelaw," Edwin asked, leaning forward against the edge of the table while Justin took a sip of the wine, "how did Lane find thee?"

Sitting sideways to the table, Justin relaxed in the chair and crossed his legs, resting one elbow on the edge. "Quite by accident, Mr. Mitchell. He was arrested for fighting—"

"Fighting?" Edwin parroted.

"Was he hurt?" a soft voice behind Justin gasped, and he turned toward the worried face of Edwin's daughter.

"No, Miss Prudence, he wasn't hurt," Justin assured her, then he turned back to her father. "The other man was hired to start the fight and I'm very fortunate he picked Lane. Both men were taken into custody and luckily Lane was turned over to a mutual friend of ours. Lane told the man everything that had happened to him, and as a result, I was cleared."

"But there's more. 'Tis why thee are here," Edwin observed.

"Yes, there is. Lane probably told you that he has no idea who blackmailed him into testifying against me. The only lead we have is the attempt to kill him. We're seeking the two men responsible for it."

427

Edwin frowned. "I doubt they're still around here. They probably figured Lane was dead by now and went back to report to the blackguard who's behind all this."

Justin nodded. "I imagine they have. But I'm hoping that someone in this area talked with these men and might be able to give me some idea about where they've gone. If we can pick up their trail, they're sure to lead us right where I want to go."

"How can I help thee?" Edwin asked, his face serious.

"Allow us the privilege of using your barn as a meeting place."

"Certainly," Edwin quickly consented.

"I've brought three other men with me besides Callahan. We will split up and cover much more ground. Then if any one of us learns anything, we can meet here and decide what to do."

"I'd like to come along," Mitchell offered.

"Edwin, no," his wife gasped; then she covered her mouth when she realized she'd attracted both men's attention. "I'm sorry, Captain Whitelaw. It isn't that I don't want Edwin to help thee, but—"

"I understand, Mrs. Mitchell." Justin smiled reassuringly. "And your husband can be of much greater help staying here."

"How?" Edwin cut in.

"I don't want Lane being seen, just in case these men are still around. I want him to stay here with you, his sister too."

"Dara, isn't it?"

Justin nodded.

"Then apparently Lane's family was not harmed as he was told they would be."

"No," Justin said. "The threat was simply intended to get him to do what they wanted. Now, Lane told me what one of the men looked like, and that they came

428

here one morning and you talked with them. Is that right?"

Edwin nodded. "They wouldn't tell me their names, but they shouldn't be too hard for anyone to remember. They were the same height, but one was very heavy and the other very thin. One was blond, the other had dark hair, the skinny one. I remember thinking how close-set his eyes were, and his nose was very long and thin. The heavy one did all the talking and he had a strange accent." He shrugged. "I can't tell thee what kind, only that I'd never heard it before."

"And they never came back?"

"No," Edwin said, raising a finger in the air, "but they did go into Emmitsburg. A friend of mine who owns the general store told me about them. He said they claimed to be looking for an acquaintance of theirs who'd moved to the area but they didn't know exactly where. They described Lane perfectly. Of course, Connelly couldn't help them. He didn't know about my house guest." An impish grin spread across Edwin's face, but it disappeared when he heard the rumble of horses' hooves coming toward the house. "We will speak more of it after all of thee have eaten. But first I will welcome a friend into my house."

Justin nodded, stood, and followed Edwin and his wife and daughter out onto the porch.

Lane was the first to reach the front yard and dismount. Dropping his horse's reins without a care as to where the animal might wander, he hurried up the steps to the outstretched hand of Edwin Mitchell.

"I prayed thee would come back," Edwin smiled warmly, clasping the young man's hand in one of his and planting the other firmly on the back of Lane's elbow. "And even more so to come as thee have, with thy friend."

"Thank you, Edwin," Lane replied, but his eyes had

already sought and found the one he truly wished to touch. Prudence blushed and studied her hands, and Lane, too, forced himself to greet the other woman who smiled back at him, tears brimming in her eyes. "Hello, Mrs. Mitchell."

"Oh, Lane," Grace sniffed. "Thank God thee have come back to us." Then much to the surprise of her family, she threw her arms around him and hugged him tightly to her. "Promise thee will stay awhile."

"As long as I can," he replied, patting her hand once she broke the embrace. Then he turned to her daughter. "Hello, Prudence," he said in hardly more than a whisper, his eyes warmly caressing her face. Only out of respect did he manage not to crush her in his arms, to kiss her lips, to tell her how much he had missed her. Finally someone nudged his shoulder.

"Oh, go on, son," he heard Edwin urge, and he looked up to see him nod approvingly. "If thee doesn't kiss her, she will think thee don't care."

It was all the prompting Lane needed. In a rush he swept her into his arms and kissed her hungrily, oblivious to those who watched and not caring if they did.

"These young men." Edwin chuckled as he wrapped his arm around his wife and pulled her with him to the top of the stairs and toward the strangers that had come with Lane. "What would they do without their older counterparts?" He grinned devilishly; then he spied the beautiful young woman standing before him. "And thee must be Dara. Lane told us all about thee. Welcome to our home, Dara."

"Thank you," she replied. "It is good of you to allow us to come."

"Allow?" he repeated. "I prayed for it. Now come inside out of the hot sun and have something to eat." He held out his arm and waited for her to ascend the stairs before he turned to Justin. "Have thy men take the horses to the barn. There is feed there and water in the trough. Then all of thee are welcome at our table." At Justin's nod Edwin turned, his wife on one arm and Dara on the other, to face the couple who whispered quietly to each other. He cleared his throat. "Excuse the interruption," he said, smiling once he had their attention, "but I'd like Dara to meet my daughter. Prudence, this is Lane's sister, Dara."

"I am pleased to meet thee," Prudence said with a bob of her head.

Dara studied the simplicity of the young woman's beauty as Prudence smiled shyly back at her, and she suddenly realized that if she had been allowed to choose a wife for her brother she, too, would have picked Prudence Mitchell. A warm smile spread across her face, and without a word she stepped forward and gently hugged the young woman. "Thank you for taking care of Lane," she whispered, gently squeezing Prudence's hand. "And thank you for making him so happy."

The color in Prudence's cheeks heightened and she timidly glanced over at Lane. "As he has done for me."

Slipping his arm around Prudence's narrow waist, Lane leaned forward and kissed Dara. "I knew you'd like her." He smiled, then spotted Justin moving toward the steps. "Will you excuse us for a minute? I'd like to talk with Captain Whitelaw."

"Of course," Dara nodded. "I'll help Mrs. Mitchell set the table. We can talk later." With loving eyes, she watched her brother guide Prudence away, thinking how difficult it would be to share him with another.

"Captain Whitelaw"—Lane beckoned to Justin— "I'd like you to meet Prudence."

"I already have, Lane." Justin grinned. "And I can understand why you wanted to come back here. She's a

431

very pretty young lady."

Feeling a blush scorch her cheeks, Lane cleared his throat and nodded. "And maybe you'll understand why I've decided to give up being a sailor."

Justin laughed. "I understand better than you think. In fact if everything goes well, I may do that too."

"Really?" Lane asked in surprise. "What would you do instead?"

Justin shrugged one shoulder. "I'm thinking about going home to Provincetown to run my father's shipping line."

"Provincetown? That's a long way off. We might not see each other again."

"Oh, don't worry. I'd make sure we do." Justin reached up to give the boy's arm a good-natured slap. "Now go spend your time with Prudence. I'll take care of your horse."

Justin lingered a moment longer to watch Lane and Prudence follow the Mitchell couple inside, and as he turned to descend the remainder of the steps he spotted Dara still standing on the porch, an odd look in her eyes. He raised a brow inquiringly.

Provincetown, Massachusetts! Did he truly mean it? Would he honestly go back there to live? Blinking back a rush of tears, she straightened and went into the house without a word.

Darkness was closing in on the pair of riders traveling the road to Monterey, a small town at the edge of a forest that ran ten miles east and nearly forty miles north. Justin and his men had gone to Emmitsburg to talk with Mitchell's friend, Paul Connelly, and to learn anything they could about the men they were after. Connelly was willing to tell them what he knew about the strangers, but other than verifying Edwin's

432

description of them, he was of little help. However, he suggested that Justin try the town of Monterey or possibly Fairfield to the north, for during Connelly's brief visit with the strangers, he had told them that the only property he had heard was for sale was a small parcel of land somewhere between the two towns, and if their friend was somewhere in the area, someone in either Fairfield or Monterey could tell them. Of course Justin knew their search would be futile, for the "friend" they sought was Lane Brandon, and he was safely hidden back at the Mitchell's farm.

Once they came to where the road divided, Justin sent Maddock, Phillips, and Peters north, while he and Callahan continued on. They had agreed to scout around the towns, and if no one had seen or heard of the strangers then everyone was to meet back at Mitchell's later that night. Although Justin hadn't spoken a word since they'd left Connelly's place, Callahan was sure his captain suspected their trip would be futile.

"I'm surprised Dara didn't insist on coming with us," Callahan said as he tried unsuccessfully to find a comfortable spot in the saddle. If finding the culprit responsible for turning their lives upside down wasn't so important, Douglas Callahan vowed he would get off this worthless piece of horseflesh he rode and walk back to the ship.

"She tried," Justin said. "That's why we left without telling anyone. She's got to be one of the most mule-headed women I've ever come across."

Callahan scratched his chin. "Maybe that's why the two of you don't get along so well. You're too much alike."

Relaxing with the slow gait of his horse, Justin let his head fall back and stared up at the stars beginning to show in the gray blue sky. "Maybe you're right," he said after a while. "Maybe we are."

Both men fell quiet, listening to the gentle breeze rustling the leaves in the treetops and the soothing sounds of the crickets hidden in the tall grass. It had been a long while since they'd been able to leave the ship without worrying about someone recognizing them or fearing they'd wake up the next morning in prison. Yet neither man was at peace.

"Was that true what you told Lane . . . about going back to Provincetown?" Douglas asked, concentrating on the road ahead.

"Yes," Justin looked directly at him. "But I was planning on asking you to come with me. I could always use a good captain."

Douglas chuckled. "Thank you for the offer, but that wasn't really why I asked."

"Oh? And what was the reason?"

"Well," Callahan began hesitantly, "I get the feeling your wife won't be going with you."

Justin considered him askance. "I thought it was your practice never to interfere with my life."

"'Twas hers I was thinking of." Callahan frowned somewhat angrily. "If you didn't love her, why did you marry her?"

Justin's lean jaw dropped. "You've known her now—what?—two, maybe three weeks, and you're taking her defense? My wife can very well handle herself without someone's help, I assure you."

"Then you are planning to leave her behind," Callahan observed.

"Yes!" Justin snapped. "But I'm not simply going to abandon her. Once I'm settled in Provincetown, I'll have divorce papers drawn up and leave her free to marry whomever she wants."

"Is that what she wants?"

"I don't know! I didn't ask her!"

"Maybe you should," Callahan persisted.

"Why? So only one of us has to be miserable?"

"You'd be miserable without her."

Justin's head jerked around to glare at him. "What are you saying?"

"I'm saying," Callahan began clearly, "that if you send her back to Drawbridge to live with her parents, you'll regret it."

"Ha!" Justin exploded. He scowled darkly at the rutty road that stretched out before them.

"Justin, my friend," Douglas said softly, "I've never advised you on the way you should live without your asking for my opinion first. But this time I can't idly stand by and watch you make yourself unhappy." He quickly raised a hand when his companion sucked in his deep breath in preparation for an argument. "I can't even begin to guess why you and Dara got married. It surprised the hell out of me, and I more than anyone should know what to expect from you. But that's over and done with. What you should concern yourself with now is your future." He frowned, considering the best way to tell Justin what he suspected.

"The night Mark found Dara roaming the streets of Norfolk and brought her back to the ship bound and gagged, he and I went to a pub to share a drink. You know what he told me?" Douglas waited for Justin to shake his head, but when the man only continued to stare as if he didn't hear, Callahan glared at him through lowered brows. "He could see it, but I couldn't. I guess it's because it was right under my nose."

"See what?" Justin growled.

"That you love your wife."

Justin snorted. "Mark always was a poor judge of character."

"Then why were you so worried about her?"

Callahan barked. "If she had been any other woman, you would have considered yourself lucky to have her no longer underfoot."

"I never said I didn't like her," Justin mumbled.

"Oh, quit lying to me. And quit lying to yourself!" Douglas roared. "What's so awful about being in love?"

Justin's angry scowl warned Callahan to say no more, and he instantly wished he could retract his statement. For Justin, being in love had been very painful. The memory of it was a hurt that he continually carried. He was afraid to love again, afraid that it would only bring him pain, and Callahan suddenly realized why the man fought so desperately to hide the emotion from Dara *and* from himself. Callahan also knew that nothing he could say would ever convince his friend that this time it could be different, that Dara Brandon was not Monica Dearborn Rutherford. Gripping his steed's reins, he silently chastised himself for sticking his nose in where it didn't belong.

Night had fallen by the time Justin and Callahan reached the little town of Monterey. Most of the shops had closed their doors and the merchants had gone home. No buggies or horsemen traveled the narrow street that divided the rows of buildings, and the two men silently realized they would have to spend the night and ask their questions in the morning. At the far end of town, they saw a pale shaft of light spilling onto the street from the only place that still welcomed customers, and it was in this direction that Justin and Callahan guided their horses. As they neared the establishment and heard laughter coming from inside, they could only assume it to be the local tavern. Dismounting, they elected to go inside for a drink and possibly something to eat.

436

The interior of the pub was dimly lit and smelled of stale cigar smoke and ale. Off to one side was a roughly constructed bar made of long wooden planks resting on oak barrels, and the men who had stopped there for their customary evening tankard of grog fell quiet the moment they realized they had been joined by two strangers. Accustomed to wary eyes following their every move, Justin and his companion casually went to a table set apart from the rest and sat down.

"What will ya be havin'?" the barkeep asked as he approached the pair.

"Anything that is fit to drink," Callahan replied, wrinkling his nose at the offensive smell that seemed to engulf him. "And put it in a clean glass, if you've got one."

"We're here to ask questions," Justin said to him as the barkeep walked away, "not make enemies."

"I know, Cap'n," Callahan concurred. "It's just that I can't understand how people can live in filth." He wiped a fingertip across the top of the table. "Look at this. I'll wager this hasn't been washed in a month." Irritably, he glanced around the room. "I'll even wager one step further and say if those two we're looking for had died in here and been swept into a corner, nobody would notice."

Justin chuckled. "I agree this isn't the pleasantest of places, but it's not that bad."

"Maybe. But I know *I'm* not going to eat here." Settling back in his chair, Douglas crossed his arms over his chest and watched the barkeep return with their drinks.

"You fellows got business in Monterey?" the man asked, wiping his hands on the dirty towel he had draped around his midsection.

"Sort of," Justin answered, lifting the glass to his lips and taking a drink. "We're here to meet a couple of friends of ours."

"What's their names? Maybe I can help."

Justin shook his head. "They're not from here. I doubt you'd know them."

"Oh," the barkeep replied, half turning away. "Ain't been no strangers hereabouts, not since a couple of weeks ago."

Callahan straightened in his chair and looked hopefully at Justin.

"Well, it could have been them, I guess," Justin continued, stopping the man before he had walked very far. "We were supposed to be here ten days ago, and ran into some trouble down near Baltimore."

The barkeep shrugged. "Maybe. They didn't tell me their names, but I remember what they looked like. They were the same height 'cept one was real heavy and the other one was skinny. The skinny one kinda reminded me of a rat. Had beady little eyes, close-set, and a long nose. The fat one got drunk in here and turned real mean. Were they your friends?"

Forcing himself not to show his excitement, Justin shrugged indifferently. "It's possible," he replied casually. "Did they say where they would be?"

"Oh, they ain't here no more. Left the next morning. But I did hear the skinny one say something about not wanting to have to tell somebody that he couldn't find the boy. Are you the one he was talking about?"

Justin felt as if his world had just crashed down around him. The only hope he had of finding the man responsible for everything that had happened to him in the past four months had vanished into thin air, and he suddenly wanted to hit something. Doubling up his fist, he slammed it down hard against the table, opening a narrow slit in the top.

The barkeep instantly retreated a step, frightened of this stranger's behavior. "I-I can understand your being angry," he stammered, "coming all that way from Provincetown and all, just ta learn from me that your friends didn't—"

Justin's dark scowl shot up to glare at the man. "What?"

"I-I said I can understand—"

"Not that," Justin growled. "You said Provincetown. What did you mean?"

"That's where your friends said they were going . . . back to Provincetown."

Justin felt a cold dread stir in the pit of his stomach and spread through his every limb, its icy fingers wrapping around his heart. Only one person in Provincetown hated him enough to do something like this, and his name was Stewart Whitelaw.

Chapter Sixteen

The ride back to the Mitchell farm had been long and tiring, and they had traveled in silence all the way. Justin didn't have to say what he was thinking, Callahan knew. He wanted to offer words of comfort, encouragement; to say there was always a chance it wasn't Stewart Whitelaw who had blackmailed Lane Brandon into testifying against Justin. But he couldn't. He had only talked to Justin's brother a few times, and those occasions had been brief. However, Callahan had often seen Stewart at a distance, and from the very first he had sensed that the younger Whitelaw detested his brother. There was a hateful gleam in Stewart's eyes and a hard set to his mouth whenever he watched Justin. And Callahan had noticed it was nearly impossible for Justin to talk to Stewart. Whenever he asked a question about his health, the shipping line or even the weather, Stewart would explode in a fit of rage and suggest that *Captain* Whitelaw return to his ship and to the people who cared about him. Justin had always made excuses for the man, telling Callahan that Stewart's life as a youngster had not been very pleasant and that he had been constantly reminded of his disability. Somewhere in the pit of Callahan's belly he knew that Stewart was the one for whom they had searched these past months, yet at the same time he prayed he was wrong. Justin loved his brother very much. To discover that his affection had been one-sided and that Stewart's hatred had driven him to such lengths would be enough to test any man's sanity.

The road they took rounded a bend and entered a small clearing in the middle of which sat Mitchell's farm. The barn was dark, telling them that Maddock, Peters, and Phillips had yet to return. But the pale light coming from the house assured them that either Lane or Dara, possibly both, were waiting up for them. Deciding to bed down their animals for the night before going into the house, Justin easily slid from the saddle, lifted the bar from the double doors, and followed his first mate into the barn. A few minutes later, as they headed for the house, they spied a slender figure standing on the porch. The light from inside spilled over her and set her rich auburn hair aflame.

"Justin?" Dara asked once the pair neared the front steps. "Did you find out anything?"

"Too much, I'm afraid," he replied, his voice tired. He climbed the steps and gently took her arm to guide her back inside. "Is Lane in bed?"

"Yes," she said, "but he told me to wake him the minute anyone returned." She glanced worriedly over at Callahan, watching him close the door behind him before he turned and shrugged in response. "Would you like some tea? I can heat up the water while I go get Lane."

Justin smiled lamely as he sat down in a chair by the long, trestle table. "Yes, Dara," he said quietly and glanced up quickly when he noticed a movement to his left. He nodded at Lane as the young man entered the room.

"I heard you ride up." Lane haphazardly tucked his shirt into his pants. "Did you learn anything? Were the men gone?"

442

"Yes, they were gone, but the barkeep in Monterey told us where." Justin nodded at one of the chairs and waited for Lane and Callahan to sit down before he continued. "I can't prove anything, Lane, but I have an awful suspicion of what I'll learn if I go after them."

"What Justin?" Dara asked as she slid into a chair next to her brother.

"The barkeep said the men were upset because they couldn't find Lane and they'd have to go back to their employer and tell him that they'd failed."

"And?" Lane urged.

"They left a few days ago for Provincetown."

"Provincetown?" Lane repeated, looking over at Callahan. "Who'd be in Provincetown that—" Suddenly Lane's face paled and his breath caught in his throat. He knew. Resting an elbow on the table, he cradled his forehead in his hand, and sighed heavily. "My God, how could he?"

"Who?" Dara's lovely face revealed her concern.

Reaching over Justin squeezed Lane's arm for comfort, then he looked at his wife. "I never told you much about myself, Dara, but I have a younger brother named Stewart. From the day he was born our father rejected him because he was a cripple, inferior as our father saw it. That had nothing to do with me, but Stewart somehow blamed me for being healthy. I guess he thought that if I had been crippled too our father would love us equally. When my father was dying, he told me to give up my life as a naval officer. He wanted me to run Whitelaw Shipping. I told him I wouldn't, that Stewart was just as capable as I and that I didn't want to settle down in one place. But Father still wouldn't accept Stewart for the skilled businessman he was and he left the shipping lines to me. I think that only added to Stewart's twisted perception of me."

"Maybe all of that is true, Justin," Dara speculated,

"but you're only guessing that your brother hired those men. Perhaps someone in Provincetown wanted to ruin the shipping line and thought he could discredit the Whitelaws by framing you for treason."

"I'd like to believe that, Dara." Justin smiled crookedly, then shook his head.

"In any case you must go back to Provincetown. You must find out one way or another." She leaned forward, the soft light of the candle enhancing her green eyes. "What if Stewart is innocent? It wouldn't be fair for him to be blamed for something he didn't do, just as it wasn't fair that you were."

"She's right, Cap'n," Callahan agreed. "You were planning on going home anyway."

"And what if it is true?" Justin asked with a raised eyebrow.

"Then you'll know for certain," Dara quickly replied. "You don't strike me as the kind of man who's incapable of forgiving or understanding, simply as one who runs away to avoid facing a problem."

Justin's blue eyes darkened, but Dara was not swayed.

"Why did you leave home in the first place?"

"Dara," Lane warned, twisting around to glare at his sister in the hope of silencing her.

"No, Lane," she answered stubbornly, "this has to be said." She settled her gaze on her husband once more. "Why, Justin? What drove you away?"

A muscle in Justin's cheek flexed and he considered telling this little troublemaker that it was none of her business. His eyes moved to look at his first mate. Certain Callahan would agree, he frowned all the more when he discovered that his long-time friend was patiently waiting to hear his answer. His gaze shifted twice between his wife and Callahan before he realized that neither of them would let the question go unanswered.

444

"I left because I thought if I wasn't around my father would be forced to deal with Stewart, that in time he would see his youngest son for what he was, a shrewd entrepreneur."

"And did he?" Dara pressed.

"No," Justin replied. "He was too stubborn and he died shortly afterward."

"And you never went back?"

"There was no need," he answered emphatically.

"Did you ever tell your brother how you felt about his talents?"

"I didn't have to. He knew."

"Did he?" Dara asked softly, challengingly.

Justin sucked in a deep, angry breath, ready to tell his meddlesome wife that she didn't know what she was talking about, when he suddenly realized how very right she was. The deep lines in his brow disappeared, and he looked away with a sigh. "No. I never told him, and I doubt he could ever tell from the way I behaved."

"Then if what you suspect is true, you understand what made him do it?"

"Yes."

"And you'd forgive him?"

"Yes."

"And you will start back for Provincetown in the morning so you can tell him that?"

A soft smile touched his lips. "Yes, Dara, I will go back, and I will try to explain. But there's more to it than that. His resentment runs deeper." He saw the questioning look in her beautiful eyes. "Before I came into the picture, Stewart had asked Monica to marry him. He blamed me for taking her away from him." He chuckled softly at the irony of it. "We were both blind. I think if she could have found a way, she would have married my father." The smile faded from his eyes as he shook his head and looked away. "All she ever wanted from anyone was money. I'd like to tell him that too, but I don't think he would ever believe me."

"But you're going to try," Dara's soft voice added.

Justin's blue eyes lifted to study the delicate face staring at him: the softly arched eyebrows, the smooth skin, the emerald eyes framed in black lashes, and the always tempting curve of red lips. "Yes." He nodded. "I'll try."

Huge sun-bleached sails billowed majestically in the strong breezes of the Chesapeake Bay, gliding the *Lady Elizabeth* away from shore and into deeper waters. Her crew bustled about the ship readying her for the journey to Massachusetts, and leaving behind the beautiful young woman who stood on the pier watching the magnificent ship move away. Tears filled Dara's eyes as they beheld the tall, proud figure at the helm of the vessel, and she silently vowed not to wipe them away lest he might know she cried. They had said their goodbyes, wished each other happiness, and pledged one day to meet again and talk over the time they'd spent together. Dara had said the correct words, but in her heart she hadn't meant them. She knew her life without Justin Whitelaw would be filled with emptiness and laden with sorrow. Absently she ran her hand over the flatness of her belly. She would never tell him of the child she carried, *his* child. They could only be happy if he came back to her of his own free will, not if he was driven to do so because of the babe. She could only pray that her absence from his life would haunt him, plague his mind, torment his soul, and in time would make his heart ache from wanting her.

"Excuse me, Mrs. Whitelaw"—a voice behind her intruded on her thoughts—"but the carriage is ready."

Blinking away the moisture in her eyes, she turned to

face the man who would take her back to Drawbridge and her parents. "Thank you," she smiled weakly. "I'll be there in a moment."

"Yes'm," he nodded then retreated to wait for her by the rig.

Drawn to the frigate that slowly sailed away, Dara returned her attention to the ship, longing to be standing on its quarter-deck where she could listen to Justin's strong voice issuing orders to the crew. But it had been her decision not to go. Her presence would have interfered with—delayed—the realization of his desire . . . if indeed he cared.

"I love you, Justin Whitelaw," she whispered, tears spilling down her face. "And if it be your choice not to come back to me, then I will be content to look upon your son and remember what we once shared as man and wife."

The warm, bright sunshine of late September caressed the harbor of Provincetown, and the gentle sea breezes skimmed the surface of the water and formed tiny whitecaps that rolled and crashed against the bows of the ships anchored there. The pier teemed with sailors and dock workers unloading the cargo of giant vessels into various wagons that would take these wares to the merchants in town. Nearby fishermen prepared their boats to harvest the plentiful bounty of the sea. To any who first viewed the wharf, it was a grand sight to behold, yet its beauty was simple. What caught and held everyone's eye was the huge building at the end of the dock. It seemed to reign silently over all those worthy of its protection.

Justin viewed the large wooden structure from the safety of the crowd milling about the docks, a twinge of sadness darkening his eyes as he studied the black lettering of the sign that hung above the door: Whitelaw Shipping. Visions of a proud and powerful man with snow white hair came to mind. He had loved Sinclair Whitelaw, but many times he hadn't understood him, just as he hadn't understood the youngest of the clan. Startled out of his reverie when a tar carrying a large sack of flour accidentally bumped into him, Justin quickly readjusted the gold wire-rimmed glasses perched on the end of his nose and looked up.

"Pardon me, mate," the sailor apologized. "I didn't see ya standing there."

Justin's heart lurched in his chest. The sailor was one of the men who had worked for his father and was more than likely still employed with the shipping line. He smiled weakly, praying the blond wig and beard would be enough to mask his identity. "It's quite all right. I shouldn't have been standing in the way."

The man nodded, smiled, hiked the bag higher on his shoulder, and started off as he called back, "If you're looking for Mr. Whitelaw, you won't find him at the office today. He got married this morning and they're having a big celebration up at his mansion."

"Married?" Justin blurted out.

"Aye," the sailor replied, turning around to smile back at Justin. "We never thought we'd see the day."

"Who'd he marry?"

"An old sweetheart of his, Monica Dearborn."

Justin felt as if a bolt of lightning had pierced the sky and struck him squarely in the chest. At Cambridge where they'd docked to gather supplies and hire a rig to take Dara home, word had reached them that Samuel Rutherford had committed suicide, and Justin remembered he had thought that Monica had all she wanted now: wealth and the freedom to do whatever she wished. But he'd never dreamed she would want to marry Stewart . . . and so soon. She must have sprouted wings to get to Provincetown so quickly and trick his brother into marrying her. But why? Didn't she have enough? Justin closed his eyes and rubbed the back of his hand against his brow.

"Sir? Are you all right?"

Regaining some of his composure, Justin glanced up and gave the sailor a brief nod. "Too much sun," he answered and quickly turned away. He had to go back to the inn where he'd told Callahan and Lane to wait for him in the common room. None of this made any sense; maybe one of them could figure it out.

"I don't believe it," Callahan groaned once Justin had told the men everything he'd learned. "That conniving, greedy little bitch. Her husband's hardly cold in the ground and she's already got herself a new one. You'd think Stewart would have more brains than that. How could he be so easily taken in?"

"I don't know." Justin sighed, lifting his tankard of ale from the table.

"So now what do we do?" Lane asked. "Go through with our plan? I mean we still don't know for sure whether your brother was behind your being framed."

"I'm going to do what I should have done years ago," Justin said. "I'm going to talk to him, confront him. I'm going to tell him how I feel about him."

"Justin," Callahan warned, "if what we suspect about him is true, it won't make any difference to him."

"And if it isn't, maybe I can make things better between us."

Leaning forward on his elbows which rested on the tabletop, Callahan wrapped his hands around his mug and was quiet a moment. "I don't want to sound as if I'm trying to discourage you, Justin," he said softly, "but I hope you understand that a few words isn't going to change a man's feelings about you overnight. Stewart has hated you for a long time."

Justin smiled over at his friend. "I know that, Douglas, but I have to try. If we're wrong about Stewart, I want today to be the beginning of a new relationship for us."

"And what about Monica?"

Justin fell back in his chair with a long sigh. "I'll have to accept her as Stewart's wife. Apparently he loves her."

"And what about you?"

A vague smile lifted the edges of his mouth as he traced a fingertip along the handle of his mug. "Until my conversation with that sailor, I thought I still cared about her. Now I know for sure that I don't."

"Good." Callahan grinned. "That takes care of one problem. I'll have to work on the other."

Justin frowned back at his first mate, confused, and started to open his mouth to question him when Lane suddenly clasped his arm.

"Cap'n!"

There was something urgent in the tone of his voice and Justin sensed trouble. Very casually he turned to look at the young man, noting the worried frown on Lane's face.

"It's them," he whispered through clenched teeth, his eyes affixed to the two men who had just entered the inn. "The ones who tried to kill me."

Cautiously, Justin turned to look in the direction Lane indicated with a nod of his head, and he instantly recognized the two men the barkeep in Monterey had described to him. "Stay put, Lane. Callahan, you come with me."

"What are you going to do?" Lane asked, watching the pair take a table some distance away from them.

"We're going to invite those two to see the hold of my

ship," Justin grinned. "Then I'm going to pay the new bride and groom a visit."

Still disguised in the blond wig and beard, Justin was not recognized by the owner of the livery stable as he waited outside while Callahan rented a buggy for them. Hopefully he would have the same results when he knocked on the front door of the Whitelaw mansion and Edward, the butler, greeted him. He wanted to meet with Stewart privately, to discuss the reasons for his brother's actions in a calm, rational manner. Reynolds and Fletcher, the men Justin had ordered locked in the hold, had admitted everything, and now Justin wanted to know what Stewart had hoped to gain by seeing his brother hang for a crime he hadn't committed.

The Whitelaw estate was located just outside of town on a long stretch of white sandy beach overlooking Cape Cod Bay. Each room on the west side of the two-story, wood-frame house had a double set of French doors which opened to present a splendid view of the cove. A line of willows surrounded the house on three sides, offering privacy and shade from the afternoon sunshine; and a long, circular drive led the way to the wide veranda.

As Callahan had guided their buggy down the lane crowded with expensively built carriages, laughter and music floated out to greet them, and Justin knew that once again the Whitelaw mansion was filled with hundreds of guests as it had often been when his mother was alive. He would have preferred to find himself there for some other reason, yet somewhere deep inside, he knew he had always suspected this day would come.

"I want to come with you," Callahan said as he

451

reined the rig to a stop near the cobblestone walkway.

"I know," Justin sighed heavily, his gaze wandering to the tall white pillars of the veranda, giant sentinels guarding all who passed between them. A flood of childhood memories washed over him as he studied their quiet magnificence: hot summer nights he and his mother had sat on the porch sipping lemonade, the day he'd turned his back on his father and left Sinclair hurling oaths at the young man who'd defied him. Some good, some bad; but all were behind him. Blinking, he smiled over at his companion. "I want you to wait here, Douglas. Someone might recognize you and I want to get Stewart alone. Maybe I shouldn't allow him the courtesy of having this out in private, but he still is my brother."

"I understand, Justin, but please be careful," Callahan urged.

"I will," Justin assured him and climbed down from the buggy.

The thick oak door swung effortlessly inward only a moment after Justin had tapped the brass knocker, and as he had expected Edward suddenly stood before him garbed in his usual flawless attire, his gray hair seeming to have whitened since the last time Justin had seen him.

"Good afternoon, sir," Edward said in his most impressive voice, and Justin was forced to hide a smile. The butler had always prided himself on his pronounced manner of speaking as if one day he expected the President of the United States to be waiting on the other side of the door. "May I help you?"

"I would like to speak with Mr. Whitelaw," Justin replied, disguising his voice as he glanced past Edward into the foyer and the crowd of people milling about. "Tell him it's urgent and that I'll wait for him in the library."

452

"But sir," Edward objected. "Mr. Whitelaw is entertaining guests, and left strict instructions that he was not to be bothered with business matters today."

"I think he'll make an exception," Justin continued with a half-smile, "once you tell him it concerns his brother."

"His brother, sir?" Edward repeated, his white eyebrows drawn together as he looked Justin up and down. "And who shall I say is calling?"

"Tell him it's someone who knows the truth."

"The truth, sir?"

Justin grinned and stepped into the foyer. "He'll understand, Edward," he said, nodding and walking away to move discreetly through the crowd toward the room where he would wait for Stewart.

The library had been Justin's favorite room when he was growing up in the Whitelaw mansion. Every wall was lined with books. It contained books that dealt with every subject a man could want to learn about. The room hadn't changed since the last time Justin was there and he was glad to see that Stewart obviously felt the same way about it. Being on the east side of the house, the library had two tall windows instead of French doors and the windows gave it a secluded air. Opposite the entryway was a marble fireplace with two wing chairs sitting before it, and above the mantel hung the portrait of Elizabeth Whitelaw. Justin's gaze was immediately drawn to it, and a twinge of sadness touched his heart. He was glad she wouldn't have to know what her youngest son had done.

Stepping farther into the room, Justin quietly shut the door behind him and briefly glanced at the huge, oak desk sitting in the middle of the floor before he wandered to an open window and gazed outside. He had already decided that no matter what Stewart said to him they could never live under the same roof. Nor could he allow his brother's coldhearted scheme to go unpunished. Shoving one hand deep into the pocket of his coat, he raised the other high above his head and leaned his weight against it as he clasped the woodwork of the window frame. He also knew that it wasn't in him to turn Stewart over to the authorities to serve time in prison. No. He would simply banish Stewart from their parents' home with only the clothes on his back and an empty purse.

Uneven footfalls sounded in the hall and a moment later the library door opened, but Justin remained where he was. He dreaded the words they would have and wanted to postpone them awhile longer. Gritting his teeth, he finally let his hand fall to his side.

"Close the door, Stewart." He could almost feel his brother's eyes on him, and he sensed the cautious frown that furrowed Stewart's brow. "We have a matter to discuss that doesn't concern anyone but you and me."

"Who are you?" the voice behind him demanded. "And by what right do you come barging into my home?" The slamming of the door gave testimony to the anger in the man's tone.

Taking off the wire-rimmed glasses, Justin slowly turned to face his brother. Although Stewart was only two years younger than Justin, he looked older. His dark brown hair had patches of gray at the temples and the lines in his face were much deeper. Justin silently decided that any man would age if he carried as much hatred in him as Stewart had all these years. Nonetheless, Stewart Whitelaw was a handsome man despite his misshapen left leg and the hardened expression in his pale blue eyes. If only things between them had been different, Justin thought, they could have worked side by side and conquered any obstacle that got in their way, for Justin had never seen the black cane his brother carried, only his spirit to survive,

454

to be strong, to be the best at any cost. Now he knew the extent to which Stewart Whitelaw would go.

"I'm someone who knows what you tried to do," he said calmly, his long, lean fingers pinching the edge of the blond beard and carefully stripping it away. "I'm also someone who can't understand why."

Stewart's chin dropped as he watched the man before him pull the wig from his head, and in the same instant he recognized the features of his brother. But instead of the rage Justin had expected, an evil smile stretched across the younger Whitelaw's mouth.

"I thought you would come," Stewart hissed, leaning heavily on his cane as he limped toward the chairs before the fireplace. "Especially once you heard who I had married."

Justin waited as Stewart awkwardly sat down before he crossed to their father's desk and stood beside the chair behind it, one arm resting along its back. "Your marrying Monica had nothing to do with why I came . . . but I'm sure you already realize that."

Stewart's smile twisted into a sneer. "Yes," he admitted, "but I'm curious as to how you figured it out. Lane Brandon had no idea who was behind the whole thing. I was very careful about that part of it. What gave me away?"

Justin could feel the muscle in his cheek flex. How could the man just sit there and calmly discuss his plan to murder his own brother? "Quite simple, Stewart. I always was smarter than you."

"Oh?" Stewart grinned. "Then why is Monica my wife instead of yours?"

"Because I learned long ago that only money matters to her. I want more than that in a wife." Visions of Dara flashed into his mind and he frowned, suddenly missing her. He moved away from the desk and returned to his vigil by the window. "I have Reynolds and Fletcher on board my ship. They told me everything, how they had given your letter to Lane, hired the Thornton brothers to kill him, tracked the brothers down when they tried to blackmail you, and shot Lane in the process." He glanced over his shoulder at Stewart. "He isn't dead, you know. He's here in Provincetown with me. He told President Jefferson that his testimony was false and I've been cleared. You went to a lot of trouble to see me dead. I'd like to know why."

Justin wondered at the strange look in Stewart's eyes even while he marveled at the man's cool resolve.

"Yes," Stewart agreed, "it would have been much simpler to have Reynolds or Fletcher hunt you down and merely put a lead ball in your stomach, but that lacked imagination. If you're as smart as you claim, I would think you'd realize that upon your death, Whitelaw Shipping would be mine . . . as it should have been in the beginning." Lifting the cane in one hand, Stewart absently studied the minute carving in the ivory handle. "But having you out of the way wasn't enough." Cold blue eyes glanced up at Justin. "You see, in order to free Monica so that we could be married, her husband had to be done away with."

A chill bolted through Justin at his brother's admission, and he suddenly realized that Stewart teetered on the brink of madness. "I thought Rutherford committed suicide," he said, a bit confused.

"Oh, he did," Stewart smiled crookedly. "'Twas the plan. We knew he was weak and once it was known that he had conspired to assassinate the president, Samuel Rutherford would choose death rather than live in shame. Rather ingenious, wouldn't you say?"

"We?" Justin repeated, a tickling of suspicion stirring in the pit of his stomach.

But before Stewart could explain, Monica's voice called out from somewhere down the hall as she searched for her new husband, and a moment later the doorlatch rattled.

"Stewart, darling," she playfully scolded as she swept into the room. "I thought we agreed not to let business spoil our wedding. I should be very upset with you—" A frown knotted her brow when Stewart nodded, indicating the man who stood quietly watching her. As she looked in Justin's direction, the color drained from Monica's face. Her chin sagged as if she intended to speak, but no words came to her lips.

"Hello, Monica," Justin said in a smooth, solemn manner. "I understand congratulations are in order . . . though I fail to see what you've gained from all this."

"Close the door, my dear," Stewart instructed with a smile, "and we'll explain it to him." Struggling to rise, he awkwardly balanced himself against the black cane and moved to the desk, where he fell into the leather chair positioned behind it. "Monica, close the door," he said again, for she hadn't moved.

Brown eyes haloed in a mass of bright, blond curls worriedly looked from Justin to her husband then back before she mutely did as she was bid.

"Now, my dear," Stewart continued, "would you care to explain or shall I?" He chuckled softly at the way his wife nervously tugged at a platinum tendril of hair lying against her shoulder while she blindly made her way to the chair he had vacated a moment before. She was in no condition to tell his brother anything. "I suppose I shall," he murmured, lifting his eyes to stare hatefully at the man his father had always favored. It was a shame Sinclair Whitelaw wasn't able to hear this. He would finally have known who was the smarter of his two sons.

"I thought I was done with you the day you were sentenced to hang for treason," Stewart began, leaning back in the chair as he laid his cane on the desk. "But your first mate surprised me and broke you out of prison. Then things got a little sticky when the Thornton brothers didn't kill the Brandon boy as they were paid to do but tried to blackmail me instead. They were such fools to think they could outfox me." He paused to watch Justin leave his place by the window and take a seat next to Monica before the fireplace, a sinister smile twisting his mouth. "I've known every move you've made since the day you came here and stole the *Lady Elizabeth*."

"Oh?" Justin questioned.

The smile widened. "You remember Davy, your cabin boy?" Stewart laughed when he saw the surprised look on his brother's face. "Davy is very loyal to the Whitelaw family, especially since Father gave him and his sister a place to live after their parents died ten years ago. He was on board the *Lady Elizabeth* the day you and your crew stole her. He knew who you were and he also knew you didn't deserve the ship or my help. He begged you to let him stay on, telling you how cruel I had been to him and that helping you would be a way of paying me back for all the beatings I had given him. It was a lie, of course, but you believed him. Every time you docked, Davy sent me a note telling me where you were and what your plans were." He smiled over at his wife. "And then there was Monica."

The woman shifted uncomfortably in the chair, unable to look at either man.

"She came to me about two months ago and told me that she no longer loved her husband, that I had always been the one she really wanted to marry. Of course, I knew that wasn't true." He laughed when she couldn't bring herself to look at him, and her beautiful features knitted with worry. "But it didn't really matter to me. I had always wanted her and I would have her as my wife at any cost." He settled his gaze on Justin again. "I did

458

some checking around and found out that Samuel Rutherford was heavily in debt. It was only a matter of time before he'd lose everything. I confronted her with that knowledge and reminded her that I didn't own Whitelaw Shipping, that it belonged to you, and that I didn't have the kind of money it would take for her to live the way she wanted. That was when she told me of her plan."

The muscles across Justin's chest tightened. *"Her* plan?"

"Uh-huh." Stewart smiled. "Surprised?"

Suddenly all the pieces fell into place, and Justin, at last, saw Monica Dearborn for what she truly was: cold and calculating, a woman who would go to any extreme to get what she wanted. Angered that she had made a fool of him, he left his place beside her and crossed the room. Resting his hands on one of the bookcases, he let his head fall forward, trying desperately to control the rage that shook him.

"Shall I explain how we managed it?" Stewart jeered maliciously. "It was really rather simple. Davy told us that you would be at the Prescott ball and why, but we couldn't be sure whether you wanted Manning's help or merely intended to inform him about Winslow's plans. That was why Monica asked you to help, to make certain you'd be there in Norfolk. You were supposed to die instead of your friend. And when Rutherford was found out, he would be hanged and Monica would be free to marry me."

"And Whitelaw Shipping would belong to the both of you," Justin finished, biting off each word. "But it didn't quite work out that way, did it?" He straightened and turned to face his brother once more, only slightly surprised to see the pistol in Stewart's hand.

"You remember this, don't you, Justin?" Stewart waved the gun at him. "You gave it to Father one

459

Christmas. I've always kept it here in the desk as a reminder that one day I would use it to kill you."

Justin sighed. "Tell me something, Stewart. How do you plan to explain my death? Davy must have told you that I'm no longer wanted for treason. To kill me would be murder and you'd go to prison."

Pushing himself up with one hand, Stewart balanced his weight on his good leg while he lifted the cane from the desk. "So far only Monica and I know that you've been cleared," he replied, rounding the desk to stand with his back to the window. "I'll tell them that you broke in here and tried to kill me. Everyone knows we've hated each other since we were boys."

A movement at the window caught Justin's eye and he realized that Callahan stood just outside, his pistol drawn and pointed at Stewart. Hoping not to give away his friend's position, Justin quickly averted his eyes. "Part of that is true, Stewart. You've always hated me, but I never hated you."

Stewart gave a short, derisive laugh. "But you do now."

"No," Justin replied. "Not even after what you've done. I pity you, but I don't hate you."

"I don't want your pity!" Stewart raged. "I've had a lifetime of pity. All the people who looked at me had it written in their eyes. No one, not even our father, could see me as a man. They saw this twisted leg and assumed I had a crippled mind as well. But not anymore." He raised the pistol in the air. "You're the one they'll pity. 'Poor Justin,' they'll say, 'he died so needlessly.'"

"Guess again," said a deep voice. The sound came from behind Stewart. "And if you don't put down that pistol, you'll be the one who dies . . . not your brother."

Surprised, Stewart half turned to look at Callahan, but from the corner of his eye he saw Justin take a step toward him. Again he leveled the gun at his brother. The evil sneer returned to his lips.

"Mr. Callahan," he said, his eyes trained on Justin, "I'll be rich enough to give you all the money you could possibly want. All you have to do is turn your back and it's yours . . . but either way, he's going to die."

"And so will you," Callahan promised.

"Then so be it," Stewart hissed through clenched teeth as his thumb moved to the hammer of his pistol. But before he could squeeze the trigger, a crushing blow landed at the base of his skull, plunging him into darkness as he fell to the floor. Standing over him, a silver candlestick in one hand, Monica stared down at his unmoving form, a half-smile lifting the corners of her mouth.

It took Justin a moment to react to what had happened and to realize that Stewart was dead. He could only stare numbly at the disfigured shape of his brother lying on the floor, the pistol still clutched in his hand, his eyes half-open in a glassy stare. He knew Stewart had wanted to kill him and that Callahan would have prevented it if it had meant taking Stewart's life. Yet in that brief moment, he wondered if there might have been a chance to talk his brother out of it, to spare both their lives, to start again, to erase all that hatred. Kneeling beside his brother's body, he realized that was something he would never know.

"He lied, you know," the soft voice beside him said, and he looked up to find Monica watching him.

"About what, Monica? That you did this for money or that you didn't love him?"

Her beautiful face knotted into an angry frown. "He forced me to do it! He . . . he . . . blackmailed me!"

Coming to his feet, Justin took the candlestick from her hands and placed it back on the desk. "Don't bother, Monica," he told her. "I've heard all of this

461

before ... the lies, the schemes, to have whatever suited you. Well, this time you've succeeded. You wanted to be Stewart's wife, and now you are. But that's all you'll have. I'll see that he's properly buried and you shall have any money that is his. But when that runs out, don't come to me for more. You won't have this house, you won't have a share in the shipping line, and you won't even be welcome here at Christmas." Walking past her, he went to the door and opened it. "Now pack your things. I want you out of here tonight."

Tears flooded her dark brown eyes and she started to speak, but Justin cut her off by raising a hand to indicate the way out.

"Goodbye, Monica. It's been interesting."

Raising her chin in the air in a last gallant effort to sway him, she whispered, "I love you, Justin."

A smile crossed his lips. "Do you?" he asked, watching her nod. "Then it shall be a wasted love, for it shall not be returned." His pale blue eyes darkened as they seemed to pierce her through, a silent testimony to the pledge he had made. And when she moved past him into the hall, he smiled in earnest. She had left the room, but she had also left his life.

April 16, 1809
Provincetown, Massachusetts

Warm, early afternoon breezes floated in through the open window of the library where Justin fought to keep his concentration on the papers spread out before him. It was the first day in many that gentle rain hadn't beaten a steady rhythm on the windowpanes. The weather had been depressing enough, but now that the sun shone clearly and its effect seemed to cheer

462

everyone, Justin realized his unhappiness had nothing to do with the weather.

He had been extremely busy since his brother's funeral. There had, of course, been an investigation into Stewart's death, and although Monica had saved Justin's life, Justin knew her reasons had been totally selfish. A vague smile lifted one corner of his mouth as he leaned back in the chair, thinking how strange it was that he could go from loving her to feeling nothing at all. He had not pressed charges against her for her part in trying to have him murdered. He had simply wanted her out of Provincetown as soon as possible so that he could start living again . . . or so he'd thought. But things hadn't turned out that way.

Word of the scandal involving the Whitelaw brothers spread quickly through the coastal town, and even though Justin's name had been cleared of treason by a decree issued by the president's office, people were, at first, a little hesitant to have business dealings with Justin. After all, at one time this pirate-turned-merchant had stolen their goods from them, and they assumed he would continue his illegal activities under the guise of a respected businessman. Consequently, he had paid each and every one of the local merchants a visit and had reminded them that he had only taken the merchandise they were trying to smuggle to Canada. It had been hard for them to admit that he was no more guilty of a crime than they, but since Whitelaw Shipping had nearly complete control of the vessels sailing in and out of the Cape Cod area, they'd been forced to swallow their pride and treat him as an equal.

The first snows of winter had come early that year, and by Christmas, his business had slowed enough for Justin to have spare time on his hands, more than he knew what to do with. At first he had enjoyed the freedom, remodeling the house and buying new furniture. He had even given one of the finest balls Provincetown had seen in a long while. But as he had dressed for that occasion, he had suddenly remembered the last one he had attended, and from that time on, he'd been unable to get Dara out of his mind.

Then the first letter from Lane had arrived. He had started out by thanking Justin for allowing Callahan to take him home; and he'd said he was sure the first mate would enjoy working for Whitelaw Shipping. The young man wrote that he had married Prudence and that, deciding to live near her parents in Emmitsburg, they had bought a small farm and in the spring they would plant crops. The tone of his letter had been cheerful, and Justin was sure Lane and Prudence would live a happy life together. However, the young man didn't mention his sister and when Justin was through reading the brief correspondence, the pleasure its arrival had brought vanished.

Nearly a month passed before Justin heard from Lane again, and that letter had been long-awaited. When Callahan had sailed to Mexico with a shipload of cargo, he'd been instructed to stop by Drawbridge on his return. Since Lane wouldn't tell Justin how Dara was, Justin had intended Callahan to find out for him. But that idea had failed. When Callahan had met Justin at the dock in Provincetown, he had told his captain that Dara hadn't been in Drawbridge, that she had gone to visit her brother. A week later Justin was anxiously tearing open a letter from Lane. It said that he and Prudence had enjoyed their first Christmas together, that the winter months in Pennsylvania were hard, and almost as an afterthought that Dara had come to live with them for a while. It disturbed him that Dara hadn't sent a message to him in Lane's letter, but he reluctantly had to admit that was only to be expected since he hadn't tried to contact her. Then

Lane strukc a nerve; at the bottom of the page was a postscript telling Justin that Dara had met a young man who farmed near them, that he was single, rather handsome, and had taken a liking to his sister from the first moment he'd seen her. He even had the gall to tell Justin that he thought Dara and the young man would be a good match. Didn't he know she was already married?

Justin slammed the ledger shut as he recalled how angry that letter had made him, and he left his chair to go to the window and look outside. Of course Lane didn't know Dara was already married. They hadn't told him the truth. They had led him to believe that it had all been a hoax to protect Dara. But she knew it, and she knew he hadn't seen to the divorce papers. With a sigh, he ran his fingers through his dark hair. Why did it matter to him? Why should he care that Dara had found someone else? Wasn't that what he wanted for her . . . to be happy with someone who could love her?

When a knock sounded at the door of the library, Justin quickly returned to his desk and picked up the quill before bidding his visitor to enter. He didn't want anyone to suspect something bothered him.

"Good morning, Cap'n," Callahan greeted Justin cheerfully as he walked into the room. "The mail just arrived." He waved the parchment he held as he tossed it on the desk. "It's from Lane."

Justin didn't move. He could only stare at the letter as if he half expected it to grow teeth and bite him.

"Well, aren't you going to read it?" Callahan asked. "Maybe he says something about Dara."

That's what I'm afraid of, Justin thought as he laid aside the quill. He stared at the folded piece of paper a moment longer; then hesitantly picked it up.

Callahan knew every word that was in the letter since

he and Lane had agreed on what should be said. During their trip back to Maryland after Stewart's funeral, Callahan had confided in the young man about Justin and Dara's marriage. He had done so because he was sure that the couple truly loved each other but were too stubborn to admit it. Then, when he and Lane had discovered that Dara was carrying Justin's baby and had refused to tell Justin about it, they knew they had to do something to get these two together.

Prudence was the only person in whom Dara would confide her feelings about Justin, so the two men had had to learn through her that Dara loved her husband but would never force him into coming for her because of the child. If Justin didn't love her, she said she would be content for the rest of her life with his name and with his son. Knowing this, Callahan and Lane contrived their plot.

It had taken them awhile to figure out how to proceed, but once they had decided, they pursued their plan with passion. Jealousy often changed a person's mind, and since Justin wasn't immune to the emotion, their method relied on triggering that feeling in him. They had decided to give Justin a little time without even mentioning Dara's name. The next step would be to drop a hint or two that she was happy without him. Then would come the blow to his ego: there was someone else in Dara's life who could take the place of her husband.

As Callahan stood before Justin now, watching him read the letter Lane had sent, he knew it was working. Justin's face remained expressionless as he read of Lane's uneventful days on the farm, but a dark scowl had crimped his brow once he learned that Dara was seeing a great deal of the young man Lane had mentioned in an earlier letter. That scowl deepened

466

when Lane wrote that the couple would probably announce that they planned to get married in the near future. Of course, Callahan knew there was no such young man—Dara had spent most of her visit in a quiet, withdrawn mood—but Justin would never learn that from him.

Callahan had to bite the inside of his cheek to keep from smiling when Justin finished the letter and slowly crushed the parchment in his hand in a controlled fit of rage. "Is something wrong?" he asked, feigning innocence of the contents of the note.

Dark blue eyes glanced up at him. "Dara's planning to get married," Justin spat out through clenched teeth as he rose from the desk and angrily tossed the crumpled paper down.

"Why, that's wonderful, Justin. It's exactly what you wanted her to do . . . find someone who would make her happy," Douglas carefully and purposely pointed out. "Did Lane say when? Maybe we could take some time off and attend the wedding."

"She's already married, Douglas. To me!" he raged.

"That's no problem. You said you would draw up the divorce papers anyway. It shouldn't take that long, so it won't interfere with Dara's plans." Callahan took a step toward the door. "Shall I go get your lawyer? Maybe he can do it for you today."

"No!" Justin bellowed, whirling away to return to the window.

"But why?" Callahan continued. "You haven't changed your mind, have you?"

"No, I haven't changed my mind," Justin replied caustically.

"Then why are you so upset?" Callahan smiled openly now that Justin's back was to him.

"I'm not upset," Justin snapped. "It's just that I don't think she should consider marrying someone she's only

467

known a short while."

"Well, Lane seems to think it's all right. Why should it matter to you? After all, it was your idea to set her free. You make it sound as though you care." It took every ounce of control Callahan had not to laugh out loud, and he quickly raised his fist to his mouth and coughed when Justin turned back to glare at him.

"Well, of course I care. She's my wife."

Callahan shrugged. "You don't act like it," he stated quietly. "If you really thought of her as such, she'd be living here with us instead of hundreds of miles away on her brother's farm. And for her to be a real wife in every sense of the word, you'd have to love her." He sighed and looked away as though he was very much aware of his companion's feelings. "And we both know you couldn't possibly love her. She's too . . . immature, too much of a troublemaker. She'd always be making you angry. How could anyone be expected to live with someone like that?" He shook his head. "No, you were right to leave her behind. Let the poor fool have her." Callahan glanced back up at Justin, hoping to see him enraged, hoping that he would blurt out his true feelings in defense of Dara, but to his surprise and disappointment he found the man smiling back at him.

"Why is it, Douglas Callahan," Justin began, leaving the window to return to his desk and rest one hip on the edge, his wrists crossed over his knee, "that you've all of a sudden changed your mind about Dara? As I recall, you once told me how unhappy I would be without her. Now you're telling me I'd be better off that way."

Callahan shifted uncomfortably from one foot to the other.

"I thought you liked her." Justin pressed him further.

"Well . . . ah . . ." Callahan shrugged one shoulder, rubbed the tip of his nose with a finger, and then tugged at his earlobe, wondering what kind of a trap he had set for himself. "I . . . ah . . . well, of course I like her. I didn't say I didn't."

"You just wanted me to admit it that I don't," Justin finished, a broad smile spreading across his face. He chuckled when he saw Callahan's chin sag, and his eyes grow into wide, sad circles. "Well, I'm not going to admit it because it isn't true, you old seadog. I like Dara. In fact, I've come to a reckoning over the past few months while we've been separated. Dara is my wife, and she will remain that way. I love that hardheaded little imp, and I'm going to Pennsylvania to tell her so."

Callahan let out a yowl that nearly rattled the roof; then he dashed across the room and heartily slapped Justin on the back. "I knew you'd come to your senses sooner or later. When do we leave?"

Smiling, Justin nodded at Lane's letter that lay crushed on his desk. "From the sound of it, we'd better hurry."

"Aye, aye, Cap'n." Callahan grinned. "Pack a bag. I'll have the ship ready in one hour."

Justin's smile faded after his friend had left the room, for he was considering the possibility that loving Dara would not be enough. If she had found someone else in his absence and if she cared enough about the man to want to marry him, would Justin's admission of his feeling for her change her mind? What if she doesn't love me? he wondered. After all, seven months had passed and he had never tried to contact her. He had thought about her endlessly, but telling her so was not the proof she might need.

With a sigh, he left the desk and started for the door. If he lost the woman he loved this time, it would be by his own doing. He paused midway across the room. Of course he hadn't fought for Monica. He had simply let

469

her go. Straightening and nodding his dark head determinedly, he decided that *this* time it would be different. Whether Dara liked it or not, she was coming home to Provincetown.

May 8, 1809
The Brandon farm

Lightning raced across the sky in a brilliant flash, playing among the clouds to mark the coming of the storm. The sweet smell of rain hung heavily in the air, and thunder roared in the distance. Dara viewed this display from the window of her room, watching it but not really seeing it, for her thoughts were elsewhere. Would this same tempest shower its rage on the narrow peninsula to the north around which it seemed her whole life evolved? God, how she longed to be caught up in the turbulent winds to be lifted to lofty heights where nothing could touch her, carried over distances she had traveled in her dreams, and gently placed in the arms of her lover. A tear escaped the rim of her dark lashes and slowly trailed a moist path to her chin. Was loving meant to be so painful? Would she ever be truly happy again? Was she fated to spend the rest of her life incomplete, only half a woman?

A noise from the corner of the room drew her attention to it, and she turned, smiling, to look upon the crib her brother had made for her when she had first come to visit. He hadn't thought at the time that it would be used so soon, but Anthony Jon Whitelaw had come into the world, with a healthy cry of protest, nearly a month earlier than expected. She had been in labor for little more than eleven hours and as she thought about it now, she recalled how upset Lane had been. As if he were the father, he'd paced back and

470

forth, demanding that the doctor do something more than he had already done or could do. Only his wife had been able to calm him with her assurances that everything was as it should be.

Crossing to the tiny bed next to her own, Dara lifted the delicate bundle in her arms, cooing at the precious face that smiled back at her. Bright blue eyes framed in dark lashes stared curiously up at her, and with a look of love shining in her own, she curled the single tuft of black hair around her finger. Even at this young age Anthony Jon bore a striking resemblance to his father.

"He would have been so proud of you," she whispered, lifting Anthony's face to place a gentle kiss on his cheek. A clap of thunder echoed around the small house, and Dara laughed when she saw her son's bottom lip quiver and tears well up in his eyes. "It won't hurt you," she assured him, sitting down on the edge of her bed. "I won't let it." Placing his blanketed form on the feather mattress, she lay down beside him and wrapped his tiny hand around her finger.

He had brought joy to her meager existence, made her smile for the first time since the day she had stood at the harbor in Cambridge and had watched Justin's ship sail away. Although her husband had never told her that he loved her, Dara had been sure he did, that given time he would come to know it. But as the days had turned into weeks, the weeks into months, she had begun to lose faith.

Douglas Callahan had come to see her as often as he could. He had taken the job Justin had offered him, and as captain of the largest of the Whitelaw ships, many of his travels took him near the Chesapeake Bay. His visits had always left her a little hopeful, for he would tell her how busy Justin was and would say that many times he found Justin asleep at his desk in the library when exhaustion finally claimed him. But when the winter months settled in and Justin's business slowed, Callahan couldn't give her any logical answer as to why the man still hadn't come to see her.

After spending Christmas with her parents, Dara had given in to Lane's insistence that she spend some time with him and Prudence on their farm. The baby wasn't due until spring, and Lane had thought that a change of scenery would help get her mind off Justin. It was mid-January before Callahan again visited the Brandon farm, and the minute he saw her rounding form he exploded in a fit of anger. He hadn't known she was carrying Justin's child or, he vowed, he would have tied Justin to mainmast of the ship and forcibly brought him to his wife's side, where he belonged. He calmed down only after Dara swore that Justin didn't know of the baby, and he reluctantly agreed not to tell him since she explained how important it was to her that he remain ignorant of the fact. He could understand her reasoning, but at the same time he thought it rather foolish. As far as he was concerned there was no doubt that Justin loved her, the man simply hadn't figured it out for himself yet.

Dara's curiosity was aroused later that day because her brother and Callahan were talking quietly and their conversation invariably ceased whenever she ventured to their corner of the room. It appeared they shared a secret, but Dara never learned what it was, and after Callahan left, she forgot all about their unusual behavior.

Anthony Jon surprised everyone when he made his noisy and premature entrance on the twentieth of April. He had been a small baby, but as far as the doctor could tell, he was a healthy one that began to gain weight immediately. Dara, her brother, and Prudence, lavished attention on Anthony Jon, and love; and in his innocent way, he brought a special happiness to the people who cared for him. If only Justin had shared in that joy, Dara's life would have been everything she'd ever dreamed it might be.

The storm outside her room grew more intense. Cradling her son in the crook of her arm, Dara left the bed and returned to the window to watch the wind whip about the trees in the yard. The rain was coming down in torrents, and Dara had just reflected that it wasn't a fit night for travel when she spied two men on horseback galloping down the road toward the house. What could be so important that they would allow themselves to be drenched to the bone? A worried frown suddenly wrinkled her brow. Maybe something had happened to her father or mother and these men had come to tell her. Hurriedly tucking Anthony Jon back into his crib, she crossed to the door of her attic bedroom and headed down the steps that led to the back of the kitchen, wondering if her brother had heard the visitors ride up.

She paused at the bottom of the flight of stairs when she recognized Callahan's voice coming from the parlor, and she suddenly felt faint. Had something happened to Justin? Was that what had brought Callahan here on such a horrible night? Or had Justin sent word that he wanted to legally end their marriage? Choking back a sob, she braced herself by pressing a hand against the wall. Shutting out the voices in the other room, she wondered if she had done the right thing in keeping their son's birth a secret. Was it fair to little Anthony Jon that he should grow up without a father because of her? Pulling herself up, she drew in a long breath and let it out slowly. Well, whatever Callahan had come to tell her, she would hear him out and then send a message to her husband. Maybe Justin didn't love her, but he certainly couldn't turn his back on his own son.

"If you'll wait right here, I'll go and get her," she heard Lane say, so she quickly brushed away the tear that moistened her cheek. She would not make it difficult for Callahan by complicating his mission with tears.

"Oh, there you are." Lane smiled when he met her in the kitchen. "There's someone here to see you."

"I know," she answered softly as she walked past him toward the parlor. "I heard you talking."

She missed the bewildered look on her brother's face or she might have lingered a moment to ask him why he found her lack of enthusiasm so surprising. It wasn't every day that a woman was told her husband no longer cared, nor was there any sense in postponing the delivery of that message. Reaching the doorway that led into the parlor, Dara didn't hesitate to join those who awaited her.

She spotted Callahan's tall figure immediately as he stood before the fire in the hearth warming his hands, his back to her. But it was the figure beside him that drew her attention, and Dara's heart began to pound in her chest. She blinked, certain her mind was playing tricks on her. Was it possible after all these months that he was honestly here? Or had she so longed to see him that she was only imagining his presence?

"Justin?" The name sounded small and weak, and at first she wondered if it came from her lips until she saw the man at Callahan's side turn and face her.

Dara's gaze lovingly traveled the length of him from his dark hair glistening with raindrops to his well-fitted black boots and up again, over his narrow hips and muscular chest. He was just as she remembered, only more handsome, and she found herself fighting the urge to run to him with outstretched arms. But she had waited too long for this moment to ruin it. He must tell her first that he loved her.

474

Months ago, Justin had discovered that he missed the beautiful young woman he had crashed into that night on the dock at Cambridge. But until this very instant he hadn't realized how much. He couldn't take his eyes away from the exquisite face haloed in red-gold hair. His arms ached to hold her, his lips burned to touch hers, and the desire to make her his once more stirred in his loins.

"Hello, Justin," he heard her say, and the sound of her voice was music in his ears.

A smile flitted across his face, then vanished. They would have this out before another minute ticked away. She would hear his terms and not argue, for he had come to take her home where she belonged. Moving away from the fireplace, he faced her, hands clasped in front of him.

"We have a matter to discuss, Dara," he said sternly. "I know of the boy, and I'm here to see that you will not spend another night with him."

Dara felt as if the breath had been knocked from her. She opened her mouth to speak, found it impossible, and instead glared at Callahan. How could he have betrayed her? And how dare Justin think he could simply walk in here and take her son away from her. She stiffened her spine, lowered her chin, and gritted her teeth to block the bellow of rage erupting in her throat.

"Oh?" she hissed. "And how do you intend to do that?"

"Quite simply," he stated. "You're coming home with me."

"Oh no, I'm not," she declared, his meaning failing to register. "I'm not going anywhere without him."

Justin's face paled at her declaration; then it darkened with fury. "And would you have him share our bed?"

"No," she snapped. "He has his own. Lane gave it to him."

"What?" he shouted, dark blue eyes looking past her to the man standing in the doorway of the kitchen. Lane shifted under the penetrating glare he received and opened his mouth to correct the misunderstanding, but Justin rushed on before he had the chance. "And I suppose you're going to tell me he's in your bedroom right now?"

"Well, of course, he is," she shouted back at him. "Where do you think he'd be?"

"Out on his ear," he growled, stalking past her toward the kitchen, "that's where he's going to be."

"No!" Dara screamed, grabbing for his arm, but Justin easily eluded her, knocked Lane aside, and rushed through the adjoining room to the stairway.

He mounted the steps two at a time, Dara racing after him, and the two men responsible for the whole bizarre situation could only stare at each other openmouthed, wondering how their well-thought-out plan could have gone astray. They heard the door to Dara's room crash open when Justin kicked the heel of his boot against it, and they both snapped to, whirled toward the kitchen, and frantically dashed for the stairs.

The explosive noise startled Anthony Jon from a sound sleep, and before his father could demand to know where his wife was hiding her lover, the baby let out a terrified wail.

"Damn you, Justin Whitelaw," Dara howled, pushing him aside as she hurried to the crib opposite them. "You've frightened him with your ranting."

The rage that had darkened his eyes vanished as he watched his wife lift the tiny infant in her arms and rock him to and fro in an effort to hush his crying. But what surprised him more than finding Dara with a baby in her arms was that it seemed quite natural to her. Venting a long sigh, he closed his eyes and rubbed his forehead with his left hand, totally confused.

"Would someone care to explain what the hell is going on here?" he asked after a moment, settling his gaze on the two men crowded into the doorway. "Whose child is that? And where is the young man my wife intended to marry?"

"Marry?" Dara echoed. "What are you talking about?"

One corner of Justin's mouth crimped in a sarcastic snarl as he turned to look at her; then the truth of the matter hit him with the force of a raging bull. His shoulders drooped, his chin sagged, and the longer he thought about it, the funnier it became. With a half-smile, he faced the pair sheepishly watching him.

"Let me guess," he began. "There never was a neighbor who caught my wife's eye. There were never any plans for marriage, and the whole story was plotted by the two of you. You did it to make me jealous, to force me to realize how much I love Dara. But I don't understand why you needed a baby for this scheme." He glanced over at Dara. "Whose baby is it, anyway?"

Dara had listened to his recital with complete surprise until she, too, suspected what Callahan and her brother had done. They confirmed it when neither of them could look her in the eye, and she was suddenly filled with love and appreciation that they would go to such extremes to see her happy. But it was the fact that Justin had said the words she had waited so long to hear that brought the smile to her lips.

"He's yours, Justin," she murmured. "His name is Anthony Jon, and he was born more than two weeks ago. He's the one you wanted to throw out on his ear. Would you like to hold him instead?"

Unable to believe what she was saying, Justin looked

at Callahan for reassurance. "Mine?" he asked numbly.

"Aye, Cap'n," Callahan nodded. "'Twas the reason Lane and I tried so hard to get you to come after your wife. She wouldn't let us tell you about the baby."

"But why, Dara?" Justin frowned.

"Because I wanted to be sure you loved me, and if you had known about Anthony Jon before you were sure about your feeling for me, I would have lived the rest of my life wondering."

A soft smile parted his lips. "Then stop wondering, Dara Brandon Whitelaw," he said, closing the distance between them, "because I do love you." Gently wrapping his arms around her to include their son, he whispered, "As I've never loved another in my life."

He kissed her then, long and passionately, and Dara suddenly knew that her life was complete.